LOTUS OF THE SANDS

LOTUS OF THE SANDS

Georgeanna Marie Hanson

VANTAGE PRESS
New York

Published by Vantage Press, Inc.
516 West 34th Street, New York, New York 10001

Manufactured in the United States of America
ISBN: 0-533-11652-X

Library of Congress Catalog Card No.: 95-90594

0 9 8 7 6 5 4 3 2 1

CHAPTER I

Ameur twisted the tiny, grinning cherub's head, sliding it down the line of the chubby shoulder. A thin wire attached to a ring popped out of the exposed depression. He pulled the ring twice, then slid the head back into position. Only microscopic inspection could have detected the cleverly concealed signaling device in the ornately carved paneling.

The door swung open noiselessly, revealing a high-ceilinged, dimly lit sanctum. Ching Li smiled a welcome, stepping aside with a slight bow to admit the caller.

"So early today, Ameur?" a musically soft voice questioned, speaking from the recesses of a deeply cushioned chair at the extreme end of the rectangular room.

"I hadn't expected you until the regular time," the voice continued as Ameur advanced soundlessly across the thick carpeting.

"A party of horsemen has just been spotted passing the Dry Well. They're headed this way. There's little possibility that they'll miss us." Ameur paused, then added apologetically, "I assumed you'd want to know."

The woman sat up lazily.

"Probably just a band of stray nomads who haven't heard the native rumors," she said with an amused laugh. "You can easily frighten them off."

"It appears rather to be that safari of Americans I've heard about lately," Ameur corrected. "They've been wandering from tribe to tribe, studying the native customs."

"Oh, well, then! Bid our guests welcome."

A flicker of surprise flashed across Ameur's face at the unusual command. He masked it quickly. "As you wish, of course," he answered in a formal tone.

Cheira [Cheer-a] raised her hand slightly in answer, then picked up the sheaf of papers she had been studying when he came in. Thus dismissed, Ameur retreated quietly. In the hall he picked up a loose white garment from the bench and swung it over his head. Stepping into a pair of sandals, he hurried off to alert the household. Dinner and rooms must be prepared

1

immediately for the unexpected visitors.

Tiana intercepted her husband at the entrance to the open courtyard.

"They're already here." Tiana gestured toward the door. "It's too late to steer them away."

"We don't have to. Cheira wants us to entertain them. Can you have rooms and dinner prepared?"

Tiana's expression cleared, a sign of relief from the past moments of worry. Ameur saw it and hugged her reassuringly.

"It's not what you think," he said, and prayed he was right.

Two men and a woman had dismounted. Holding their horses' bridles, they stood uncertainly.

"This looks like an old fort of *Les Régiments Étrangers,*" Hardy offered, gazing around with frank curiosity. "They haven't used them for over a century."

"It's much more," the distraught Arab guide interrupted. "It's a place of demons . . . uh . . . uh . . . ghosts." The guide stumbled, trembling with fear.

"Just look at those thick walls," Warren commented, ignoring the gesticulating native. "Too bad it's deserted." The travelers had learned from experience that Charley dramatized everything.

The immense yard was enclosed by high stone walls, the low rambling buildings propped against them. This was the customary manner of construction when safety was a primary factor.

"We go then! Quick!" Charley's voice rose hopefully. He grabbed for the reins of Warren's horse.

"It is kind of eerie," Hilda interjected, half-convinced that Charley was right.

Warren tightened his grip on his horse's reins. "Charley's a superstitious, emotional pessimist." He laughed. "As long as we're here, we might as well camp the night. Another four or five hours in the hot sun is not my idea of a pleasure cruise. Charley and his men can stay outside if that makes them feel better. It doesn't look like they're going to come in, anyway." Warren turned toward the men huddled outside the gate.

"Hey, look!" Hardy grabbed Warren's arm, pointing to a long archway that connected the buildings. "It's not deserted. Some men are over there!" Several heavily burnoosed figures could be seen at the far end of the compound. Their pace was leisurely, unusually quiet and orderly. The strollers paid no attention to the strangers whose horses and frantic guide were making enough noise to be not easily ignored.

2

Charley redoubled his efforts. "Go! Go!" he was nearly screaming now. The escort shuffled uneasily. The horses, picking up the fear in Charley's voice, stamped and pulled at the restraining reins.

Ameur, white-robed and imperious, stepped out onto the pillared verandah.

"Haunted. . . . " Charley's voice hung in the air. In the instance of stillness before he slunk away, the travelers had time to wonder if their guide had eyes in the back of his head, for he sensed the man's presence with his back turned even before they saw him. The effect was to choke off his threats in midsentence, wiping out the exaggeration with which he usually masked his true intentions.

"Anyone who can quiet Charley like that must be a powerful sheik," Hardy commented under his breath as the man crossed the courtyard in long, swift strides.

The newcomers had only a moment to survey their prospective host, but trained observation told them that this was a different manner of desert dweller than they had so far encountered. Although deeply tanned and native-costumed, his clothing was immaculate and his movements purposeful and confident.

"Well, here goes." Warren took a deep breath. "Hope he understands English because Charley sure isn't going to be any help this time." The usually blustery native had faded from sight, indistinguishable from his companions.

As the oldest and most senior member of the party, Warren stepped forward. "Name's Percy Warren, reporter," he said, extending his hand and naming the American newspaper that employed him.

"Welcome to my home." The tall patron smiled, grasping the proffered hand of the visitor with strong, slim fingers, his voice well modulated, his English perfect.

"May I present Miss Hilda Jenkins and Mr. Robert Hardy," Warren stated, ushering his two companions forward with a sweep of his hand and a sigh of relief. Already Warren felt better. The man's speech alone was enough reassurance that they had found a mecca in the wilderness. After months in the strange land, the sound of his native tongue gave the reporter a thankfully accepted point of security.

Well, Charley's wrong this time, he thought. *At least we'll get some civilized hospitality here.*

Ameur shook Hardy's hand and, much to Hilda's surprise, bowed low over hers. She had just time to note, with astonishment, the bright blue eyes.

3

"How may I be of service?" Ameur asked, straightening and returning his gaze to Warren.

"It seems we're lost," Percy replied, somewhat embarrassed. "Our guide has proven unfamiliar with this part of the desert. It appears he has always avoided this area. He thinks there's a curse on it . . . some foolish superstition!"

Ameur smiled sympathetically and shrugged. The superstitions of the natives needed no comment. "Then it would please me greatly if you would accept my hospitality—at least for one night. You must be weary of the inconvenience of desert travel, and there is no suitable campsite within a day's ride."

"We'd be so grateful," Hilda burst out, her feelings the same as Warren's. "We haven't stopped since early this morning. There's nothing out there for miles and miles but the sand and the blazing sun." Hilda shuddered at the thought.

"This is truly the desert, Miss Jenkins." Their host smiled. "But I'm happy to offer you the small comfort of the one oasis in it."

Attendants materialized from nowhere, unobtrusively to take charge of their horses, which the exhausted travelers were more than happy to surrender.

While the tired safarites were accepting happily the hospitality offered and congratulating themselves on the luck that had brought them this way, their outriders were being hustled away quietly. Unknown to their employers, they would be kept under close guard for the duration of their stay. Although fed and sheltered comfortably, the superstitious natives would spend the next twenty-four hours consumed with fear.

The guests gasped appreciatively at the huge, marbled entrance hall, which contrasted so sharply with the ancient weathered stone of the outside. The old assembly room had been skillfully redecorated. The rough walls were smoothed and sanded. Colorful tapestry covered most of the exposed area. The heavy beams supporting the ceiling gleamed dully in the dim light filtering in from narrow slits in the stone, which had been all the windows safety had allowed in the old days when danger of attack was constant. The sparse furniture was ranged along the walls, leaving the marble floor open through the middle of the room. The chairs and divans, interspersed with low tables of what unquestionably was ebony, conformed to the style of the country, although of a better quality than any the travelers had seen in the camps of the sheiks they had visited. A young Chinese girl awaited them at the foot of an immense open staircase.

4

"This is Ching Li, an invaluable member of our household." Their host introduced them.

"A most happy welcome." Ching Li smiled, bowing politely. "May I show you to rooms for rest?"

"Of course, Ching Li," Ameur answered for them. "They've been *à cheval* since early this morning."

"And scorching heat all the way," Hilda added, appreciating the coolness of the stone building.

"Then we'll meet again for dinner." Ameur extended the invitation, then turned away as Ching Li started up the staircase.

"I can hear the clatter of horses' hooves as their riders galloped up to warn of attack," Hardy said, following Ching Li.

"Oh, Bob," Hilda admonished, "this is real."

"Are you sure? Remember what Charley said."

Hilda shuddered and paused to look stealthily behind at the long carpeted hallway with closed doors on either side.

"You both have too vivid imaginations," Warren admonished.

Ching Li opened a door revealing a cozy sitting room with chintz-covered sofa and chairs, a magazine-strewn coffee table, and lacy potted ferns swaying in the breeze from the opened windows.

"Your room, Miss Jenkins," Ching Li said.

"See!" Hilda snapped at Hardy. "It's perfectly lovely!" she said to the Chinese girl. "I'll be as comfortable as a bug in the rug."

"It does look mighty cozy," Hardy admitted.

Hilda wrinkled her nose at him and firmly closed the door.

Hardy and Warren shared rooms connected by a spacious sitting room. The decor was tastefully oriental. The austerity of the heavily inlaid tables and chairs, which the two men had only seen previously at exclusive auctions, was softened by the voluptuousness of the two divans piled high with pillows, the whole coordinated by a genuine Persian rug and heavy damask drapes.

They were still standing in the center of the room admiring the luxury of their surroundings when a burnoose-clad servant deposited their luggage and departed silently with a low salaam.

"To think we almost missed this," Hardy said, walking over to have a look at the bedroom. "There's even plumbing." He raised his voice so his friend could hear. At a loss for words, he had deliberately understated the lavishly appointed bathroom, which combined the most modern conveniences with a liberal use of gold and black fixtures.

"If you and Charley hadn't argued about how to navigate this desert . . . " Hardy returned to the central room.

"That Charley!" laughed Warren, thinking about their incompetent guide whose name he couldn't pronounce nor remember, hence, the nickname, Charley. "If he hadn't been so adamant about not wanting to come this way . . . "

"Why do you really think he was?" interrupted his friend, "and why didn't we hear anything about this place in Algiers?" Hardy was thinking of the maps they had studied when planning their itinerary. The authorities had guaranteed their accuracy, that they were up-to-date and contained the location of all the oases where desert tribes could be found, also all the forts, occupied and abandoned, ancient and modern. His mind jumped to the conclusion he wanted, "I've a hunch we're getting close to our objective."

Warren shrugged, his tone revealing a note of sarcasm, "Your hunches, my friend, have dragged us all over the southern Sahara Desert. Our host doesn't look like your legendary princess to me." Warren paused as a picture of the tall, dark native flashed into his mind. "On the other hand, he doesn't look like an Arab either. Did you notice?"

Hardy nodded thoughtfully, picking up his traveling bag. "Or speak like one, for that matter."

"And much too tall," Warren added, rubbing his chin in perplexity. "He had blue eyes."

"And the silence of the servants! Not at all like the raucous natives who kept us awake half the night. . . . They even had their faces covered. I couldn't get a good look at any of them. Charley's right about one thing. This isn't an ordinary tribal camp," Hardy concluded. "There's more here than meets the eye. I still can't figure out why a fort this size wasn't on any of the maps. This place must cover ten or twelve acres from what I could judge from the approach. How could they lose anything that big?"

Finding no apparent explanation, the unimaginative Warren answered, "Well, I'm for a shower however it came to be here. I'll be glad to get rid of a month of desert sand. Those other sheiks are beggars compared to this!" He disappeared into his bedroom.

Later, escorted by Ching Li, the two men, clean and refreshed, descended the broad stairway and crossed the entrance hall, their footsteps echoing hollowly on the marble floor. Hilda joined them on their way past her room. She emerged scrubbed and rested when the Chinese girl knocked softly at her door.

"Now this is living!" she beamed. "It beats a tent any day!"

"Too much like home," Hardy teased. "I think you materialized it out of your imagination."

"I didn't think of it," Hilda reminded him. "It was that pack-rider who suggested this shortcut to Percy when he was complaining about the long way home, remember?"

"And I did insist, Bob. You must admit that. Even to overriding Charley's objections." Warren defended his colleague seriously, entirely missing the jest.

Ching Li opened rounded double doors set into an archway, obviously a tasteful addition to the original construction.

"Two against one isn't fair," Hardy mumbled, entering the room.

"Come in, my friends," Ameur invited. "I hope you've been comfortable."

"Oh, so nice," Hilda volunteered. "I haven't felt so human since we left home." She gave Hardy a meaningful look.

"My pleasure," Ameur responded. "We have a few minutes before dinner. May I offer you a drink?" Indicating lushly upholstered chairs around a squat, magazine-strewn table, Ameur turned to the small bar nestling cozily under a high row of shelves.

The room was large, but the ceiling-high rows of books proclaimed this a well-used work center. Hardy and Warren looked at each other. Warren raised his eyebrows in questioning surprise as they settled into their chairs.

Hilda casually leafed through the magazines, but her practiced eye noted current issues of what proved to be the leading publications from all over the world.

Ameur handed his guests their drinks. "We're not totally isolated here," he chided teasingly, noting Hilda's puzzlement at the half-dozen languages represented. Her attention was diverted to the selection of books comprising every recognized discipline, or she might have noticed that he seemed to have answered her thought.

Hardy and Warren were having some startling thoughts of their own, especially when they tasted their drinks, the quality of which could not be excelled by the best New York restaurant.

"Now, my friends," Ameur began, seating himself comfortably, drink in hand, "permit me to properly introduce myself. I am Ibn ben Ameur, Sheik of Arx Vetus." He waved his hand indicating the whole fort. "And welcome again to my humble domain. In this out-of-the-way place, we seldom have visitors." After a pause, he added, "But may I ask what brings you so far from the regular caravan and tourist routes?"

"Well," Warren related, "it was sort of a mistake. Our guide, Charley..." *What's happened to poor Charley and the others?* Warren's thought intruded over the narrative.

"Your entourage is housed and fed," Ameur offered.

"Ah, thank you." Warren gratefully discarded the guilt he felt at having forgotten Charley and the others. "As I was saying," he continued, "I wanted to get home as fast as possible. Charley's way would have taken us back over the route we had come. I didn't need to see that again. So I insisted on a direct shot. One of the men said it was impossible. We tried it and became lost. Only by chance we stumbled on this inhabited, hospitable sanctuary."

"Then your purpose is purely sightseeing?" inquired Ameur politely.

"It's turning out that way," Hardy spoke. "But that wasn't our original objective."

Ameur raised his eyebrows, encouraging the newsman to continue.

"You see," Hardy resumed, "for years, rumors have been leaking out of the desert about a woman, a mysterious princess who has all sorts of magical powers. It has been a compelling, fascinating tale and the possibilities for a newspaper to run it as a feature story are tremendous. Our chiefs finally agreed to let us come over here to try to track the legend to earth. We had three months. Our time is almost up."

"There are many such strange tales in the desert, mostly originating in the undisciplined imaginations of..."

Ameur was interrupted by the opening door.

With the arch for the frame and the hall tapestries fading into the background, it was like a Renaissance portrait come alive. The tallish, slim woman belonged in the setting. She wore a simple white gown drawn at the waist by a gilded chain. Her heavy black hair vied in its gleaming with the golden rope that intertwined it. Classically chiseled features contributed to the impression.

Ameur quickly rose.

"Ah, my dear, we've been waiting for you. Come in and meet our guests."

The men awkwardly stumbled to their feet, covering their astonishment with difficulty.

8

"May I present Tiana, my wife," Ameur continued with a stress on the last words. "Percy Warren, Robert Hardy, Hilda Jenkins. They're reporters from New York in search of feature stories for their papers."

Tiana smiled, nodding a welcome to each in turn. "Forgive my tardiness." Her voice was soft and low, perfectly matching her appearance. "It is so seldom that we have visitors that everyone is almost too excited to prepare a proper welcome!"

The two men found themselves grinning stupidly, at a loss for words. Hilda stood, staring openly, a book open and forgotten in her hand.

"You must have come all the way from Tarmquid. That's a very long ride in the heat of the day. You must be exhausted and hungry." Tiana, seeing her guests' confusion, tactfully gave them time to recover.

"We're extremely grateful for your generous hospitality," Warren managed to respond, inwardly cursing his awkward behavior at being caught by surprise. *The desert must be affecting me,* he thought. In his career as a reporter for one of the nation's leading newspapers, he had grown accustomed to interviewing all kinds of people. Surely, the unexpected appearance of this lovely woman was not any more astonishing than what had already happened to them today. *After all,* he reasoned, glancing covertly at his host, *would a young, vigorous man like this sheik live like a monk?*

"Yes, extremely grateful . . . " Hardy echoed Warren while his thoughts, too, were racing, the questions popping into his mind with the rapidity of machine-gun fire. Was this the woman he was searching for? Had he at last found the answer to the restless longing that had haunted him for years? Was she the real goal of the dreams that had sent him eagerly into the hardships of this primitive land? Somehow, as beautiful as she was, he doubted it. His heart was beating steadily, quietly. He felt surprise but not excitement. Even so, he recognized a vague feeling that here was the place where he would find the answer to what had amounted to an obsession. Growing stronger every year, it had brought him to the point where he could think about little else. In desperation, his editor has agreed to this safari, not with any real conviction that it would amount to anything, but in the hope that Hardy would be able to erase the notion from his mind once and for all. His editor insisted that Hardy had a talent granted to only one reporter in thousands: the imagination to write a headline story. At the same time, he admitted that Hardy's overactive imagination led the young man into paths that obstructed the most advantageous use of that talent. Newspapers had little room for undisciplined dreamers. News stories had to be founded on facts. Later, they could be embellished with fantasy. As long as Hardy continued in this way, he was a detriment to himself and his paper. Hardy knew all this. He had heard it often enough, all the way from his chief down to the copyboy. He was more determined than ever to make the most of this chance, not only for what it would mean to the paper, but for his own justification. If this woman was not the one he sought, then he would keep looking. His intuition had been right before, and he felt it now more strongly than ever.

"It's our pleasure that you happened to come this way," Tiana returned, graciously stepping forward. "So without further delay, may I conduct you to dinner?"

Ameur presented his arm to Hilda, gently removing the impeding volume, replacing it among its fellows. With an elegant bow, he murmured, "Miss Jenkins?" She was thrilled and, for once, speechless, but unable to control the gasp of pleasure at the closeness of the handsome face so attentively near. The flex of muscles of his arm at her contact felt like iron under the fine linen of his loose-sleeved shirt. She blushed, the embarrassing color deepening uncontrollably when she perceived a knowing gleam in the vivid blue eyes. Disconcerted, she was certain that he knew what she was thinking.

Tiana led them once more across the great hall. The dining room was entered by an archway of stone.

"This was once the commandant's quarters," Ameur volunteered. "With some of the partitions knocked out, it has made a spacious, comfortable room."

"Indeed. Comfortable and pleasant," Percy agreed, looking around in appreciation at the beautiful dining area. An immense mahogany table dominated the center of the room. The sunlight streaming through the narrow windows cast bright rays across the gleaming surface. Robbed of its blinding intensity, which made travel a misery, the tamed light enhanced the soothing atmosphere.

"You could seat fifty people at this table," Hilda gasped.

"That's correct," Ameur answered, his eyes twinkling as if they shared some private joke.

Hilda felt her skin threaten to redden again. She turned away, prattling on to disguise the feeling. "How soft these lovely tapestries make the austere stone walls."

"It's an idea we picked up from the old castles along the Rhine," Tiana explained. "Then all we had to do was persuade some Persian weavers to follow our designs."

"That was the hardest part," Ameur chuckled, aiding Hilda to her place at the table. "Those people have rigid, traditional designs they haven't changed for centuries."

"Please forgive the informal arrangement," Tiana apologized, indicating their places to the men. "But any other would have us shouting the length of this ridiculous table."

"Being Americans, we're habitually informal," Warren contributed. "And besides, after two months in native camps, this is heaven."

Ching Li appeared bearing a tray with a carafe of wine.

"Mmmm! Excellent!" Percy nodded approvingly after sipping the wine, performing the ritual of a practiced connoisseur.

"Thanks!" Ameur accepted the compliment. "It's from a recipe treasured for generations by Tiana's family. Her father honored me by making me the guardian of it. I have tried to be faithful to that trust. To that grand and very special man." Ameur raised his glass.

After some very casual toasts, the travelers attended to their dinner.

The guests' amazement peaked when they tasted the superbly prepared courses. The dinner was Western-style, highlighted with a rare roast of beef that the Americans, subsisting for the last two months on native fare, demolished enthusiastically.

Ching Li proved to be an accomplished waitress. Along with the help of some white-robed servants silently bringing courses as needed, she offered heaping platters of the hearty fare to the famished New Yorkers.

Hilda, whose life was lived through her assignments for her paper, tried to get a look at the features of the servants. Her unerring instinct for a story quickly perceived the lack of subservience in their attitudes. *Very different*, she mused, *from the attitudes of others we've encountered in the tribal camps. These people seemed to be helping, rather than serving, because they enjoy it.* But try as she would, she could arrive at no explanation nor determine whether or not they were natives.

"This must be a grueling assignment for you, Miss Jenkins." Ameur broke into her thought.

The twinkle of amusement in his eyes brought back the feeling she'd had earlier, that he knew her thoughts. She knew he could enlighten her if he wished; that he would not, she was sure. Her perplexity increased. *Maybe we should have listened to Charley. Maybe these people are only pretending to be cordial. Maybe . . .*

"Oh, no!" Hilda tried to focus on the remark, most of which she had missed. "Those wandering nomads have dirty, cluttered camps; and all the food is boiled in one kettle."

11

Warren and Hardy laughed aloud. Tiana carefully folded her napkin. Hilda stopped in confusion. A red spot appeared on each cheek, unbidden, and slowly spread around to her ears.

"It's that long, hot ride we had this morning, Hilda. We're all about done in." Hardy covered for her. "And she's right," Hardy addressed Ameur. "The food was, for the most part, abominable and the conditions so unsanitary. It's a wonder any of them are ever healthy."

"I agree," Ameur responded, taking up the conversation with Hardy. "We are aware of the situation and are trying through education and example to improve their lot. Tiana and Ching Li spend many hours with the women and children. They suffer the most. It's difficult to believe that some of those chiefs are immensely wealthy, especially in the areas where oil is being drilled, yet they feel no compunction to change their own lives, much less the lives of their followers. Rampant superstition keeps them chained to their ancient ways."

Warren, feeling expansive and emboldened by the good food and congenial atmosphere, ventured, "And you, sir, don't seem to be one of them at all."

"I'm American," stated Ameur tersely. "My wife is Greek."

"Of course, we should have guessed," Hardy agreed.

"But where in America?" Hilda, alert to the trend in the conversation, sought to squeeze any information she could out of their strange host. A familiar locale would provide the security of something known to pit against Ameur's unsettling manner.

"New York." He shrugged, then continued before she could ask more. "I'd be delighted if you'd care to take a turn in the garden before retiring. Evening is the most soul-pleasing time. I'd like to share it with you."

Thus all further inquiry was forgotten in the unexpected pleasure of finding a tropical garden in the midst of the otherwise most sterile part of the desert.

"It's a hobby of mine," their host informed them, as he proudly conducted them on a tour, discoursing at length on the species, characteristics, and points of beauty of the rare trees and flowers, explaining authoritatively the complicated system that enabled him to control the humidity in an open area.

With obvious delight in the achievement, Ameur directed their attention to the fruit trees, carefully selected and imported from Italy. The apples and olives stood like sentries around the perimeter of the garden, allowing only here and there the ivy-colored walls to peep through. The scene was

12

dominated by the two stately walnuts that spread their branches from the center, shading a grassy level interspersed with fountains and flower beds.

The guests exclaimed over the plantings of tulips in full bloom, standing straight in front of rosebushes equally prolific.

Ameur laughed, pleased by the flattering exclamations. "I sometimes feel sorry for them. Out here so far away from their native habitat, they don't know what time of the year it is. I can persuade them to bloom whenever I wish."

"But where do you get the water for all this?" Warren couldn't help asking curiously, remembering that just outside the wall was the bleakest terrain they had traversed, devoid even of the brushy growth that characterized most of the regions they had visited.

"Fortunately, we have plenty of water," Ameur related. "We struck an underground river at 485 feet. The force of the flow itself brings the water almost to the surface."

Warren opened his mouth, but some reason the question didn't come. "Very fortunate," he said instead. He couldn't ask his host how they had gotten the equipment out here to drill so deeply. Ameur seemed not to notice. He continued with an explanation of how the buried pipes fed the water into a time-controlled sprinkler system.

While the weary travelers were gratefully climbing into the first real beds they had known for two months, their host was again in audience with the woman who had instigated his actions that day.

Now she reclined on a divan in the same room, which was brightly lighted since night had fallen. Ching Li hummed a tune to the rhythm of the brush as she drew it along the strands of Cheira's waist-length blonde hair.

The most prominent feature of the room was an imposing ornate chair on a raised dais across from the door. Well away to the right was the cluster of chairs and divans. The low tables were strewn with dossiers, ledgers, and daily issues of a newspaper that specialized in reporting world business trends. A skillfully inlaid pedestal at the side of the reclining figure held a steaming silver samovar on a tray, a cup and saucer of thinnest porcelain nestling at its foot.

The walls of the room, like the great entrance hall, were hung with heavy tapestries depicting scenes from the life of the nomads living in this barren land. Here, though, the stone was covered with a pale greenish substance showing dully between the hangings. Its obvious thickness could be estimated by the smoothness of the surface. There were no windows, hidden lighting automatically provided an imitation of natural light. Now with darkness fallen, lamps were turned on to provide a sense of normalcy. The room was soundproof; only the soft whir of air from a concealed climate-control unit interrupted the unnatural quiet.

Ameur had been silent for some minutes as the woman received the information concerning the guests directly from his thoughts. The telepathic communication, which they employed with ease, a timesaving device, was much faster and more detailed than verbal interchange.

Now he spoke for the first time. "Hans Werner of Zurich begs a personal audience."

"I wondered if he'd ask," she commented. "Give me his record and I'll see him in the morning."

Ameur laid the envelope he had been holding on the table.

"Hans will be most grateful," he said.

"Hans will be difficult as usual," she mimicked, laughing. "But that's my job for tomorrow; yours is to speed your guests on their journey. Give that irresponsible camel driver who pretends to be a guide orders to take his company to the Fort. Advise Siri to offer them hospitality for a few days."

"Siri?"

She frowned slightly. "And make sure he's at the Fort and not away at that stupid oasis." She dismissed him summarily with a wave of her hand. Whatever the reasons for her command, she chose not to communicate them.

She picked up Werner's file and glanced cursorily through it. It was only a formality. She already knew what it contained, as well as his intended request. *Permission granted,* she thought.

"I'm glad Hans is so stubborn and persistent." She smiled at Ching Li. "We need more women in the association. And so far, he's about the only who's had nerve enough to ask." At present, the men outnumbered the women almost one hundred to one. By granting Werner's request, she hoped to encourage the others. All that remained to be done was to assess Mme. Werner's suitability.

Meanwhile, the man in question, unaware of Cheira's decision, paced his apartment. He had been amused earlier to help Ching Li serve Ameur's guests. It had at least occupied the otherwise impossible evening hours. This late at night, however, there was no diversion to take his mind off the course he had set.

He fiddled impatiently with the dial on the wall. The melodies erupting sporadically as he twisted the selector seemed only to increase his restlessness. He switched it off, turning to the table to pour a generous amount of the golden fluid into a glass. The label on the decanter caught his attention. Big embossed letters announced the name of a famous Scottish distillery. In tiny writing at the bottom, the name Capitol Imports, Zurich. With a muttered oath, he downed the fiery liquid in one gulp.

A wry grimace of dissatisfaction crossed his face. This was not what he wanted. He glanced at the round dial of the clock on the wall. The lighted hands stood precisely at midnight. Morning, it seemed, was a century away. He frowned, forcing creases into the normal smoothness of his brow. He picked up the glass and, in a moment of uncharacteristic churlishness, threw it at the defenseless timepiece. The shattered glass fell to the floor, but the hard steel of the mechanism continued to move unperturbed. He laughed at the absurdity of the action.

Werner, tall, well muscled, with just a touch of gray at the temples, displayed a hard-set jaw, determined to go through with his plans no matter what the consequences. He would brave her anger, if that were necessary. His mind pictured the woman who ultimately controlled his existence. He remembered the perfect features, the lovely body; but he thought of her physical appearance as one would admire a work of art. The cold imperviousness of her personality precluded any emotional response from his own warmhearted nature.

After a moment, his confused thoughts rambled on. *Accomplishment of my purpose would be well worth the effort,* he argued as with an adversary. After twenty years as a barrister, his manner had become habitual. It was doubly important that he act now since he was coming up for reassignment. He shuddered involuntarily at the prospect of relinquishing Margo. If Cheira commanded him, there was no question but that he would obey. Yet he loved Margo; his fists clenched in hopeless frustration. She was his wife, the mother of his children, more dear to him every year. *She is more than worth any struggle,* he decided, unconsciously squaring his shoulders.

Ameur knocked, then opened the door.

"Thought you might like to know . . . " he began, then paused as the smell of liquor reached his nostrils. He spied the shattered glass with distaste.

Hans stood, tense, his shoulders drawn up into a stiff line. A muscle twitched just above his jawline.

"Are you preparing for execution tomorrow?" Ameur quipped.

"Did you ask her?" Hans countered, not relaxing his position.

"Sure. And it's all set. So quit worrying."

"Easy for you to say." Hans sagged against the wall.

"I wish I could assure that your request will be granted, my friend," Ameur spoke seriously. "But I can't. You know that. All I can tell you is that Cheira must be considering your proposal or why didn't she refuse to see you?"

"I'm grateful to you, Ameur."

"My pleasure!" Ameur clapped his friend on the shoulder. "See you in the morning."

Alone once more, Hans's thoughts drifted back to contemplation of the woman who would grant him audience in the morning. He had only seen her three times in twenty years, but—and he surprised himself with the discovery—the awareness of her was always with him. *Of course,* he supposed, *it is the same with others.* Those he knew intimated that they felt the same way. In fact, a few were so in love with her that other women meant nothing to them.

He paused in his journey up and down the room, lost in the memory of the events of his first weeks at Arx Vetus. It had been an exciting time. It was then that Ameur's help and encouragement had blossomed into friendship. Hans had met and liked all the members who were in residence at that time. It was his first meeting with Dr. James Connors. Yes, Jim was one of those in love with Cheira; blindly, deliriously in love. That is, until the day of the episode in the garden. Hans was just a casual spectator, there by chance, yet he would never forget Cheira's blazing anger. He had never learned the details nor had he dared to ask. It was apparent though that Jim's love was not dead, only repressed into dull, aching longing.

Hans had learned to feel sympathy for Jim and the others who carried love for Cheira as a burden not to be relinquished. *But why not,* he thought, *after a hundred years or so, they had learned to consider all other relationships as transient.* He could not personally understand their satisfaction in permanently unrequited love. *But maybe they all carry hope in their hearts,* he surmised. *After all, this life is for a very long time.*

He found it, even now after all these years, hard to conceive that his life would go on indefinitely. He paused in front of the wall mirror, dropped his robe and examined his body critically.

There is no change, he decided. His body was mature but still slim and hard with no signs of aging: no wrinkles, no gray hair. He smiled ruefully at the artificial color at his temples. It was a feeble attempt to disguise his perennial youth from his acquaintances. Margo, though, was beginning to notice, especially as her own struggle to maintain a semblance of youth was getting progressively more difficult. *God,* he thought, *she's got to accept Margo as one of us.* The image of his beloved spouse, old and abandoned, rose up in his mind, forcing an audible groan from his lips. Then he saw himself! He saw himself still young. And the years ahead left a bitter taste in his mouth.

The first light was appearing on the horizon and the night breeze, which had cooled the desert, was dying with the coming of dawn before Werner could quiet the turmoil of his thoughts enough to rest.

While Werner was sleeping fitfully, another occupant of the ancient rambling building was just awakening from a deep, restful slumber. Robert Hardy opened his eyes slowly. He had been dreaming of his apartment in New York, his subconscious taking the cue from the comfort of the bed. A part of his mind wondered at the silence, for his ears expected the sounds of early morning traffic indicative of the city. The continuing silence brought him fully awake. He got out of bed and wandered to the slit that served as a window in the old stone wall. He was surprised to find it fitted with glass and screen. Only a small corner of the garden lay open to his view. In the early morning light, it was even more beautiful then he remembered it from the previous night.

At intervals, high spouts of water wavered in the clear morning air, falling into a cloud of mist as they descended to earth. The surfaces of the leaves glistened with drops of moisture as all the vegetation seemed to welcome the refreshing spray. The rays of the sun, not yet the unbearable blaze they would be later, broke into rainbows, captured by the falling droplets. The warm water falling on the chilled earth raised a layer of wafting steam masking the grass and walkways. Hardy's imagination transported him into this dreamworld having no beginning or end.

There you go again, his conscience—ever on the alert for these undisciplined lapses—reminded him. With a shrug of irritation, he returned to reality. *It's just a beautiful garden,* he thought firmly, *made by a very ordinary American like myself. Ha!* his imagination retorted.

Hardy was about to turn away when a movement caught his attention. A golden-haired woman in a softly clinging gown stooped to examine a rose. The loosely hanging hair gleamed in the first rays of light, which signaled the predawn. She turned away slowly, her position making it impossible to distinguish her features. Only the delicate fingers gently holding the flower were visible where the full sleeve of the gown fell back onto her wrist. The long skirt trailing in the grass gave her movements an ethereal grace.

In an instant, she was gone. The journalist wiped a hand across his eyes, realizing that he was staring at an empty spot. Had he really seen anything, or was he dreaming again? There was no one there now, he determined by close examination.

His thoughts leaped back to the events of yesterday. This perfectly amazing establishment in the middle of the desert; Charley's vehement protests against coming this way; electricity, plumbing, all the luxuries of the most modern mansion. *I'd like to compliment the cook personally,* he thought, chuckling aloud. But more astonishing was the American who obviously owned it all—who called himself sheik—and the beautiful woman who was his wife.

As a newspaperman, Hardy searched his memory for an identification of his host. Obviously, the man had access to a lot of money. Since he was young and well educated, he would have to be someone who dropped out of sight in the last few years. It was the only logical explanation; but Hardy's memory drew a blank.

His thoughts reverted to the speculation about the strange apparition in the garden. His attention was drawn to the pounding of his heart. It made him start with excitement. *Perhaps . . .* but the dawning idea was interrupted by the clamorings of his stomach. Prosaically, he began to wonder how long he should wait before it would be appropriate to ring for coffee.

At the same instant, a knock sounded at the door.

"Come in!" Hardy called, grabbing his robe and moving into the center room of the suite.

Ching Li entered bearing a tray. The aroma of coffee wafted out of a steaming silver pot. Hardy was astounded as he watched the girl set the tray down. The coincidence of the girl's arrival as if in answer to his thought awakened more suspicions.

"Breakfast is at eight, sir, in the dining room," she said.

All he could do was stare as she left the room. The sound of the closing door triggered him to action. By the time he reached the hall, however, she was gone. Grateful, but confused, he returned to savor the scalding stimulant, puzzling over what he had seen in the garden. He was tempted to call Ching Li back; but for once, his usual reporter's boldness failed him. There might be other guests here; and he had no right to idle curiosity when he, himself, was a mendicant for hospitality. *Later,* he thought, *I'll find an opportunity.* Adding to the confusion, he noticed that his heart was pounding again.

Percy staggered into the room, sniffing.

"Do I smell coffee?" he mumbled, yawning.

"Yup!" answered Hardy, laughing.

"How did they manage that?" Warren wanted to know. "By magic?"

While they drank the delicious, hot native brew, the two men discussed the peculiarities of their present circumstances, although Hardy—for some reason not clear even to himself—refrained from mentioning the specter in the garden. For one thing, he wasn't eager to bring down Warren's derogatory comments on his head again. The older man was sometimes less than enthusiastic about the whole undertaking, especially when the going got a little rough. Warren was a man partial to the amenities of civilization. If he had ever possessed a spirit of adventure, it was buried now beneath years of easy living. He much preferred the bustle of New York City to the lonely expanses of uncharted desert. He had gamely set out on this safari, however, in the interest of his newspaper; but it was his desire to get quickly back to Algiers that had precipitated the argument with Charley. Only by reminding him that it was his editor who initiated this excursion could Hardy silence Warren's derisive remarks.

Ameur alone joined them for breakfast. Although as courteous and friendly as on the previous day, he announced that their party would be provisioned and ready to leave by ten. Hardy searched in vain for an excuse to prolong their visit.

At the same time that the travelers were departing reluctantly, the woman whom Hardy had glimpsed in the garden was engaged in very different business. Cheira sat imperiously on the ornate chair in the audience room gazing with lowered lids at the man who knelt before her.

The man trembled as her dulcet voice spoke softly. "Well, Hans?" she questioned, giving no hint of her decision of the previous evening.

All trace of the distinguished lawyer that the world knew was gone. He was a mere supplicant here at the feet of the one who controlled his life.

"Mistress," he began, falteringly, "I beg that you will consider my wife, Margo, as a candidate and allow her to join us." He stopped speaking aloud, his voice choked by the emotion constricting his throat; but his thoughts tumbled on, reiterating all the reasons he had rehearsed in his room last night.

Cheira sat rigidly, still effortlessly following what he was thinking. Her mouth tightened imperceptibly and her eyes narrowed as she saw clearly the love he didn't mention, his thoughts busy with a recitation of virtues he assumed she wanted to know. Naively, he could not know that it was his deep love for his wife that brought Cheira to her decision. He could not know the unfulfilled longing that was her constant companion, that she bore as an empty space around her heart, that only of late had she begun to recognize and know it for what it was.

She waited for the wild rush of argument to cease. She wondered what kind of woman could inspire such enduring love in this strong-willed, stubborn man. When Hultz had first suggested Hans Werner as a candidate, she had monitored his activities intermittently for months. She was impressed by the determination, the self-assurance that characterized his manner, and the innate pride that asked favor of no man. That he now begged for his wife was indeed the measure of a great love.

"Very well," she said, quietly. "I agree. I'll come to Zurich next week. As a client, perhaps?" She paused, considering. "As one recently widowed—to settle an estate or whatever else will prove convenient. In that guise, you can invite me to your home. Can you arrange it?"

Werner gasped, his head reeling from the assent she had given so easily. He felt like a man pushing against an immovable barrier only to have it disappear at the moment he applied the greatest amount of pressure.

"Oh, yes. I can do anything for . . ." He stopped, then added simply, "Thank you."

"I'll need a suitable name and background. There's no need to cause Mme. Werner to wonder about me until the decision is made. An appointment at, shall we say, eleven, in your office. We'll proceed from there." She finished, rising. With the grace of one born to authority, she descended the steps to stand before him. "I shall look forward to meeting one who is the recipient of such devotion," she barely whispered. Had Werner been less absorbed with his own emotions, he may have noted the wistful quality of her voice.

"I thank you, thank you," was all he could say.

The little bell sounded twice and Tiana entered, standing silently aside while Werner departed. She nodded to Werner, then turned to Cheira, smiling mischievously, "The travelers have been disgracefully hustled away to Siri's. Of course, they don't know where they're going or why; but the guide has been carefully instructed—or should I say threatened? The poor man will never be the same after a night in Cheira's haunted citadel."

Both women laughed.

"While Ameur was hastening the reporters on their way," Tiana continued, reporting with relish, "Tony Hammond was giving orders to the guide. He used a booming voice and kept appearing and disappearing until the man was frantic."

"Oh, how awful!" Cheira giggled. It was easy to see that the women had a very different relationship from that which Cheira had with the men of her organization.

The morning passed quickly and pleasantly for them. They enjoyed to the fullest the little time they had to spend together.

CHAPTER II

A pleasant morning was not Hardy's fate, however. He morosely jogged over the hot sand, not knowing or caring where he was headed. His thoughts stubbornly clung to the fast-receding pile of ruins that he was so reluctantly leaving behind. That there was something mysterious about the place, he had no doubt, particularly since he had noted the look of genuine fear on Charley's usually deceitful countenance. Their swaggering, boastful guide was reduced to a bundle of nerves, while the pace he set for the party suggested a legion of demons in full pursuit. Repeated questioning could get nothing out of him.

"We go to Sheik Siri," was all he would say; and, clamping his mouth tightly, he'd roll his eyes until he seemed on the verge of a fit. Who Sheik Siri was or why they must go to him seemed beyond the power of the overwrought guide to explain. The outriders reacted similarly, being shifty and evasive to any questions.

The Americans were virtually helpless under the circumstances. Since it would be foolhardy to attempt crossing the desert on their own, it was decided that the wisest course was to continue on with the native escort wherever it might lead them.

The travelers were again weary and disheveled by the time the Fort was sighted. An uncomfortable night in the desert had blighted the spirits of all and it was a silent group that drew up at the gates to ask for shelter and sustenance.

The party was taken in with so little confusion that, had the travelers been less exhausted, they might have wondered if they had been expected. Their quarters, as luxuriously appointed as the ones left two days before, lessened slightly the quality of unreality still hanging over them like a cloud.

As soon as they were settled and alone, Warren spread out the maps.

"Here's the Fort," he pointed. The fact that it was on the map mitigated their apprehensions even more. It was abandoned, they knew, by the Legion about 1835 when the warring tribes had been defeated and moved permanently far to the south. The Fort now belonged to an old family from England and was handed down from generation to generation. Since there seemed to be no mystery about the famous horses raised there, the Fort had not been included in their itinerary. The officials in Touggourt knew the present owner well and were loud in the praises of the special strain of Arabian horses that he sold yearly to discriminating buyers over the world.

"We didn't come here to get a story about horses," Hardy had commented dryly.

At dinner, any reticence felt at their precipitous intrusion was quickly lifted. Sheik Siri ben Ange was an Englishman of the old school, cordial and mundane. About forty-five, six feet three, with a large frame well suited to his height, the sheik was an impressive figure. Immaculate in desert whites, with flashing black eyes and a mouth just full enough to betray a strain of sensuality, he was the most handsome man Hilda had ever seen. Even the two men looked on him with open admiration.

After a hearty meal in the best English tradition, the party repaired to the garden where drinks were served. The journalists delighted to find their host conversant with world affairs and could relate the latest news for which they were hungering after two plus months of isolation. Warren, particularly, kept up a steady barrage of questions, happy to be in his own element again.

For some reason none of them could define, they unanimously refrained from mentioning their experiences at Arx Vetus. It was almost as if they expected their host to tell them that no such place existed. They told him freely and eagerly of their adventures of the last two months. Only the events of the last two days were omitted, and the sheik did not question them closely.

As the shadows lengthened, servants appeared to light the torches.

"Ah," Siri said, "I'd be a poor host if I couldn't provide any diversion before my guests retired. Not the sophisticated amusements of the metropolis, of course, but, perhaps, some local talents to round out your African experience."

The sheik raised his hand, and a drum began to beat quietly in the background.

The travelers hushed expectantly, wondering what new experience awaited, their weariness momentarily forgotten.

A man approached carrying a tall basket from which protruded the hilts of a dozen swords. Siri greeted him in the vernacular, rising to inspect the blades. The sheik ran a practiced thumb along the edge, then demonstrated the keenness by slicing off a nearby bush, the stem of which was nearly an inch in diameter.

"Please be absolutely quiet," Siri instructed the guests, "as one spasm of a muscle could cost this man his life."

They willingly complied, even to involuntarily holding their breaths while the man inserted the blades into his esophagus. Apparently, here was not the mediocre fakers they had been exposed to in the wandering circuses back home.

They settled back into their chairs when, as the next act, wrestlers appeared to lay a mat on the grassy stage. The reporters felt confident of their ability to judge and enjoy this familiar sport.

To the spectator's delight, the performers warmed up with a display of classic holds. Hardy took to naming them, vying affably with his host who gave the native names along with the translation.

Warren was first to notice as the action progressed that this match was more earnest than any he had ever seen. He looked questioningly at his host only to find Siri already watching him intently.

The sheik threw back his head, laughing aloud. "These men will fight to the death unless I stop them."

Hilda gasped.

"This is the desert, Miss Jenkins," he said, turning the full force of his piercing dark eyes on her.

"But you will stop them?" Her voice rose, taking on a note of apprehension.

Siri shrugged, looking back at the struggling duet.

The guests—their initial nonchalance forgotten—watched hypnotically. The contest proceeded endlessly, building a relentless tension from which there was no release. Modern culture and primitive instinct vied for domination within their souls.

Hardy and Warren squirmed, uneasy and embarrassed. Hilda held her hand over her mouth to keep from screaming. At last, when the strain was almost unbearable, one man was clearly the victor having pinned his opponent helplessly. For a moment, all movement stopped. The winner looked at the sheik.

"He's waiting for my instructions, Miss Jenkins; and I'll delegate the decision to you. What is your pleasure? Shall the man die?"

"Oh, Lord! No! No!" Hilda fairly screamed.

"Bah!" Siri retorted, giving the signal for the end of the match with a wave of his hand. "You're too softhearted."

24

The vanquished man was carried from the scene by his conqueror.

For many minutes, silence prevailed. The Americans collected themselves. Then, just as they were breathing easily again, the drum began to beat, insidiously vibrating against their already distraught nerves.

The watchers relaxed with the advent of a group of dancing girls. There were about a dozen, each beautifully perfect in form. Warren sat back, sure that he could enjoy this performance. He glanced surreptitiously at his host when he noticed that two of the girls were undoubtedly Caucasian, but the sheik was sunk in a deep reverie and paid no attention.

The sensuous movements of the dance, however, began to make Hilda uncomfortable. She, who professed to a very high degree of cosmopolitan sophistication, felt painfully aware of the position which the members of her sex held in this barbarous culture. Flushing with embarrassment, she noticed the dancers prostrating themselves, each in turn, at the feet of the sheik. A glance confirmed, much to her irritation, that Percy was enjoying himself immensely. She always suspected he had a streak of lechery in his heart.

The sheik ignored the prostrate girls. Hilda was thankful for that much decorum. She was certain that only their host's indifference kept Percy from offering a few indecent comments. She'd had that experience with him while on assignment in Paris. Her attention was caught by the expressions on the dancer's faces as they approached. Their mouths were tight, their eyes wide. *Could it be fear?* she wondered. The look was only momentary as each resumed her place in the formation. Smiles returned as they took up the steps, which the action had interrupted. Obviously, they were relieved at the sheik's indifference. Did that mean what she was thinking? *That's foolish!* she decided. *This man is too patently a cultured European.* Still, she was puzzled.

The sheik roused and clapped his hands, summarily putting an end to the performance. The girls floated gracefully away, their filmy veils disappearing among the shrubbery. The drum ceased.

Siri turned to Hilda. "You do not approve of my harem, Miss Jenkins?"

She had the eerie impression that he had read her thoughts. "They're lovely," she managed to stammer; but the sheik's attention was already directed to his male guests. They were saying good night, and she was grateful to follow along as a servant led them to their quarters. When she glanced back, their host had already disappeared.

Could a man who appeared so civilized be as barbarous as that? she wondered. And why did she have the feeling that her thoughts held no secrets for him? It was the same feeling she had when the American at Arx Vetus looked at her.

Exhaustion returned full force. *It'll just have to wait,* she thought as she settled into bed. *Too much has happened in the last few days. When I get it all sorted out, what great stories I'll have for the paper.* She sighed and slept.

Siri made his way, not to the seraglio, but to the library. He met Ameur, who was awaiting him with a warm welcome.

"What the hell is this all about?" he demanded, throwing himself into a deep chair and stretching his long legs. "I've twenty acres of irrigation pipe to install at Imla Dun and in two weeks the oil cartel is meeting. Now you call me back here to amuse some vacationing reporters."

"Cheira's orders, not mine," Ameur answered. "And she hasn't seen fit to enlighten me as to her reasons." He grinned. "But, of course, I have an idea of my own. Sam Hackett arranged this safari. I think he's presenting a candidate."

Siri laughed. "You mean Hardy?"

Ameur nodded. "Cheira hasn't been to America for years. What better way to bring a protégé to her attention? Besides, the man is obsessed with rumors of a mysterious desert princess. Rumors? From whom? Somebody has been feeding that young man's very active imagination. Also, he's making a name for himself as a very talented reporter. He works for a rival paper now."

"But why send them here? Cheira's always managed very well without my help before?"

"To get rid of the others, I suppose." Ameur had another thought but suppressed it quickly. It passed unnoticed.

Siri sighed with resignation. "What am I supposed to do?"

"Well, she did some monitoring while they were at Arx Vetus. Now she wants you to keep them here for a few days and find a way to send Hardy back to Arx Vetus."

"So I must aid and abet the falling of some other poor idiot into her clutches. Good Lord!"

"Siri!" Ameur came out of his chair.

"Oh, never mind!" Siri raised his hands, pretending to dodge a blow. "You know I'm always forgetting myself. It must be my heritage. An Englishman finds it galling to bow to anyone."

Ameur sat down, grudgingly accepting Siri's words as apology.

"So Sam Hackett arranged this little drama?" Siri veered the conversation off its dangerous course. He knew from experience that nothing could ever intrude on Ameur's blind loyalty to Cheira. "How did he get him to Arx Vetus?"

"You've met Omar Koria? He came into the organization a few years ago. He's the one who's excavating ruins outside Cairo. Well, he received a note from Sam practically begging him to become part of the escort for the Americans and find a way, if possible, to steer them to Arx Vetus. I only found out when he made his presence known after they were there."

"So Sam's got a little intrigue of his own brewing. And you think Cheira is going along with it?"

"Sam can usually persuade her when he wants to." Ameur shrugged. "And in view of the orders we've received . . ."

Siri rose. "All right! I'll do what I can."

"Farewell, then, my friend." Ameur faded from sight.

For a long time, Siri stood motionless, deep in contemplation, the expression on his face inscrutable. Ameur's order had surprised him. He had been tempted to ignore it, busy as he was, unwilling to place on Mohammed's shoulders the full responsibility for the reclamation project. Still, he was curious. Those at Arx Vetus never interfered with him—in fact, usually gave him a wide berth. It was only through Ameur's friendship that he knew anything of what transpired there. It was unheard of that Cheira would command his aid for any of her projects. Since the censure, she had not even allowed him to see her.

"Damn!" he said softly, ripping off his shirt, the fine silk, the pride of this season's prominent Italian manufacturer of menswear, destroyed by its wearer's need to be freed from confinement: liberty, his basic requirement.

Cheira! The name arose somewhere deep inside, her image floated before his mind's eye. *What would you have me do?* The sharp sword of guilt drove into his heart and twisted there. He groaned. The past paraded unbidden before him. It was more actual now with full realization, more vivid with the added burden of remorse, more painful because the intervening years had offered no solution, in fact had complicated an already impossible situation.

Finally, with a characteristic shrug, he called Ahmed, the native who was his personal servant, and gave a few terse orders. Moments later, a trembling, sleepy Charley was dragged into his presence.

"Tomorrow morning"—the sheik addressed the disheveled heap of quaking humanity in the native dialect, eliminating all chance of the man's pleading noncomprehension—"go to Hardy privately and suggest an excursion—just the two of you—arrange to slip away quietly when the other two are not about—back to the place you have just left."

Charley's trembling increased violently. But before he could protest, the sheik continued, "He's already casting about for a plan. All you have to do is take him as far as the outriders, who will intercept you and take him off your hands. They'll be watching. Take the old trail to Tarmquid, veer off at that campsite the caravans use, then due west. Understand?"

Charley rolled his eyes.

"By riding swiftly you'll meet them in the morning two days hence. Plan to leave at midnight. I'll have two horses prepared and waiting in the courtyard behind the old man's shack. Plan to leave at midnight. Now go!"

Throwing some coins on the floor before the bewildered guide, who stooped to pick up the unexpected windfall, the sheik added in an ominous tone, "Success will bring you twice that—failure . . . " He snapped his fingers, turning away with a lift of his shoulders.

Charley was relieved the sheik didn't elaborate. He was well aware of how the desert chief treated disobedience. He resolved that even his fear of the haunted ruins could not keep him from his mission. The reluctant guide departed, clutching his money and entreating Allah to protect him.

The object of the conspiracy was tossing, wakeful, on his bed. Hardy could not deny that he was deeply disturbed by the evening's entertainment. He grudgingly admired the skill that conceived amusement by playing on the most basic emotions in human nature. His conventional heritage wanted desperately to believe that the sheik's power of life and death over the wrestlers was just pretense, an aptly portrayed climax to the performance; but the strangeness of desert customs to which he had been subjected these last two months made firm conviction impossible, even though their host was not a native. Instances in which men had completely adopted the ways of a strange land were not unheard of.

His thoughts rambled on to a review of the subsequent act. He had been painfully aroused by the dance he had just witnessed, fleeing to the solitude of his room at the first opportunity.

Of course, that was the purpose, he chided himself. Did those girls really belong to the sheik's harem, as Hilda said? Hilda's years of experience as a reporter seldom betrayed her into a faulty conclusion. She had seemed genuinely shocked.

Percy agreed with Hilda, having overheard the sheik's remark. When the two men were alone in their quarters, he had recounted the performance with relish, embellishing it with some obscene remarks of his own.

The predominant thought in Hardy's mind, the apparition in the garden of Arx Vetus, soon pushed the other thoughts aside. The vision—as he now was convinced that it was—rose up in his consciousness, obliterating all other thoughts.

He had to get back there somehow, he decided; but how? Attempting to negotiate the trackless desert alone meant certain failure. Charley, then, was the obvious answer. But how would he convince the shiftless rascal to take him back when the man was patently delirious with fear? *Enough money,* he surmised, thinking of the avaricious native, *would persuade him.*

The obsessed journalist couldn't leave the desert without one last attempt to free himself, especially since his instinct told him he was on to something unusual. If he were ever to rid himself of the phantom of the elusive desert sorceress, he must satisfy his curiosity now. He would probably never have another chance to explore the strange tale, which obsessed him so much that it interfered with his work. There could be no possibility of a permanent commitment in his life while the enchantment lingered in his mind.

The exhausted wayfarer didn't realize that he had dozed off until a steady cracking sound attracted his attention. Unreasonably irritated, he staggered to the window, subconsciously expecting to look into the garden, but a very different sight met his sleep-drugged eyes.

The window opened onto a courtyard, and the scene he beheld sickened him. The sound, which had awakened him, was the cracking of a whip, each stroke drawing blood from the back of the distraught victim. To Hardy's horror, the sheik was witnessing this inhuman punishment, standing immobile, his arms crossed on his chest. When the unfortunate, albeit stoically silent, recipient of this excessive chastisement crumpled into unconsciousness, his master signaled, ending the torture. The sheik walked away without a backward glance.

Hardy sank back against the wall, perspiration beading his forehead, his stomach threatening violent rebellion. *What could the man have done?* he wondered. When he looked again, the courtyard had resumed its silent desolation. All participants in the revolting tableau had vanished. The hard earth enclosed by the stone walls and the side of the building had sunk into early morning quiet. A large shaggy hound busily made his first inspection of the day, scouting thoroughly the two vans and an ancient jeep parked in a far corner. Hardy's eyes wandered along the wall, absently following the dog's circuit. Almost beyond his vision, he noticed an old man asleep against the open flap of a tiny shack. If the man had been a witness to the earlier episode, it evidently hadn't disturbed his repose. Hardy shuddered. He was beginning to understand the barbarity that could be hidden in the vastness of the dark continent.

The reporter's professional conscience, nevertheless, demanded an explanation of the disgusting drama. He knew that desert sheiks held absolute authority over their tribes. But Siri ben Ange was an Englishman! Surely he didn't subscribe to the uncivilized practices of this primitive land. Logic forced Hardy to concede that he wasn't just voicing his own opinion. The entertainment they had seen didn't bear out the assumption. There was little influence of civilization to be seen in that! And how did such a man come to be living here anyway? His intelligence and education were plain; he was well traveled and personally familiar with the world's centers of culture. But there was no evidence or mention of a family, Hardy noted. And what possible justification could there be for the performance he had just witnessed?

Hardy frowned. The last few days of their journey were definitely proving to be the most interesting. He felt now that the months spent wandering the scattered tribal camps had been a waste of time. To a man, the desert sheiks had proved to be ignorant, superstitious leaders who jealously guarded the power they held over their even more illiterate followers; their lives were governed by the fear of the certain future day when some younger, stronger challenger would arise and callously wrench the supremacy from their enfeebled grasps.

A knock on the door startled him, bringing him back to the present. A servant entered carrying a tray with coffee. Hardy hastened to question the man.

"I just saw a man beaten into unconsciousness. What did he do?" Hardy shuddered with remembered horror.

The servant looked at him indifferently.

"You must know about it," Hardy persisted. "The sheik was there."

"My master is just," the man answered noncommittally and unemotionally. By the manner in which he clamped his mouth shut and turned away, the journalist realized that the servant had related all he would on the subject. Hardy was quick to recognize another characteristic of desert people: The loyalty they nourished for their tribes and its leaders allowed no room for criticism. Hardy grudgingly had to admire the potency of this primitive emotion, which was no doubt necessary for the survival of the social unit.

"Wait a minute!" Hardy stepped forward, raising his hand to detain the man. He put the shocking experience aside for later. After all, it was Siri who was responsible for the occurrence, and it was to him Hardy should posit any questions. Now he needed the servant's help to instigate the plan he had formulated during the past sleepless night. "Would it be possible to have a word with our guide?"

"He is waiting in the hall," the servant answered, to Hardy's astonishment.

Hardy brushed aside the ominous feeling that events were accelerating at an uncontrollable speed. With a reckless shrug, he filed the thought for subsequent consideration and signaled the man to admit Charley.

Charley didn't look as if he had fared well through the night. Even the rattle of the cup as Hardy poured coffee made him start and roll his eyes.

"Charley," Hardy began, determined to realize his plan even though Charley's condition made the situation look hopeless, "I want you to take me back to the place we just left."

The guide showed no surprise at this announcement, but he had decided to try once more to evade this distasteful task.

"It is a place of fiends, sahib," Charley ventured hopefully. For if Hardy would change his mind, he would be blameless and consequently free from a frightful chore.

"Nonsense!" Hardy responded. "There is something going on there and I want to know what it is, even if it's supernatural."

"Please, sahib," Charley beseeched, "no one ever returns the same and some never are seen again." He rolled his eyes for emphasis.

"I still want to go," Hardy insisted. "Can you arrange for us to slip away undetected? I'll pay you well," he added, hoping the money would be an incentive.

It appeared that it was for Charley, with an exaggerated though resigned shrug of his shoulders, agreed. *After all,* the native reasoned, *what is the fate of this foolish stranger to me?* The sheik had assured him of his own safety, so it was the will of Allah without doubt.

"At midnight," Charley said aloud, "I will meet you in the courtyard." He waved his hand toward the window.

"Agreed!" answered Hardy, turning his attention to his coffee, satisfied with the outcome of the interview.

Charley had just slipped out when Warren came into the room. Stretching and yawning, he helped himself to some of Hardy's coffee.

"I wonder if there's a way to get a story off from this godforsaken place?" Warren mused, "Two months without a word. Sam Hackett must be having apoplexy."

"Three months was the prearranged limit," Hardy reminded him.

A servant interrupted them with the information that a plane was leaving for Paris at noon. Any communications could be sent then.

Warren beamed. "Good! Send us up some breakfast. Sure wish I had a typewriter," he said, thinking aloud, then added exuberantly, "Give your master our excuses for missing breakfast, but we've got work to do!"

Too bad, Warren mused as he was dressing, *that rumors of the mysterious siren had proven unfounded.* But he was consoled when he thought of the material he had collected, enough to make a byline interesting for many months to come. Why, that entertainment last night was enough to keep readers on the edge of their chairs for two or three days!

The two men were waiting in the sitting room when Hilda joined them. She had "slept like a top," she assured her companions, and was "hungry as a bear just out of hibernation."

"Didn't you get coffee?" Hardy inquired.

"Of course," she replied. "But this desert air stimulates the appetite."

Hardy laughed, thinking of the distaste with which she had picked at the food served them at the various camps.

Apparently the others had not been disturbed by the early morning incident in the courtyard. Hardy refrained from mentioning it, but his resolve to seek an explanation of their host remained firm.

The journalists were pleasantly surprised when servants arrived wheeling three typewriters, reams of paper, pencils, erasers, and envelopes. In short, the room was quickly converted into a press room with all the conveniences.

Percy and Hilda were too anxious to get their stories on paper to waste any time wondering over their good fortune, and soon the machines were clicking away at a furious rate.

It was only Hardy who sat wrapped in thought, sporadically typing a sentence or two. There were many unanswered questions nagging at the edge of his mind that he was reluctant to commit to the eyes of his editor.

Hardy wondered briefly about Sam Hackett. Hackett was Percy's chief, yet Hackett had insisted that Hardy be included in the search. *Strange way for the editor of a rival paper to behave,* Hardy mused. Still, his own chief had jumped at the opportunity, knowing Hardy's obsession with the story.

Since the thought led nowhere, Hardy brushed it aside and forced himself to concentrate on the matter at hand. Rereading, he found that his short report was full of evasions. *The chief will be furious,* he thought, especially when he noted the sheets mounting on the desks of his associates. *But,* he decided, with a shrug in the manner of an Arab resigned to his fate, *my story isn't finished yet.*

The hours seemed just minutes when the servant returned to collect the dispatches. Hilda and Percy protestingly turned over their bulky envelopes. Hardy's single sheet had been ready for an hour or more.

On leaving, the servant extended his master's invitation for his guests to ride with him in the late afternoon before dinner. They accepted, eager for the chance to exercise the cramped muscles of the morning's labor. Hardy alone had the secret motive of wanting to survey the surrounding desert.

Lounging lazily, conversing desultorily, the three safarites, after an excellent lunch, heard the drone of the plane as it passed overhead on its way north.

"Well, at least we won't have to camel out of here," Warren commented. "The sheik seems in no hurry to be rid of us; but I think we might as well wind it up in a day or two, don't you?" he asked no one in particular.

"I could stay here forever," Hilda answered, indolently wriggling deeper into the plump pillows on the divan. "But, I suppose, you're right. What say, Bobby?" She peered questioningly at Hardy.

"I guess . . . in a day or two," Hardy replied, as reluctant as she.

They lapsed into silence. There was no sound but the hum of the fan overhead. The magic charm of the wilderness descended on them all.

Hilda had known Hardy since his early days on the paper when, as a cub reporter, he had shown a talent for ferreting out the angles that sold a story. She had been attracted by his boyish impetuosity and termed herself, half-seriously, his fairy godmother because of the numerous times she bailed him out of the scrapes his unerring news instinct landed him in. She had come to recognize the signs when he was in pursuit of an elusive angle. Watching him now, she felt it, regretting that she hadn't found an opportunity to talk to him alone. *Anyhow,* she consoled herself, *if he is onto something, he won't tell me unless he wants me to help.* Her feeling told her, he didn't want her help this time.

33

She worried over the strange stay at Arx Vetus, but failed to discover a way to dig any deeper into the lives of the inhabitants. The place was lost somewhere far to the south. *It is unthinkable to attempt to return there,* she thought.

Her imagination dredged up an old Spanish legend. It was a tale of a weary traveler who sought refuge late one night at the only house for miles on a dangerous mountain road. He was welcomed warmly by the owner, his wife, and their beautiful daughter. They entertained him lavishly. He had gone to bed congratulating himself on his good fortune. In the light of the morning sun, however, he found, to his everlasting horror, that he had slept in a rotten, rat-infested ruin among the bleached bones of three skeletons.

Hilda mentally shook herself. *Don't be stupid!* she scolded. *Of course, there is actually a place called Arx Vetus.* The thought flashed into her mind, *But you didn't mention it to your English host and you didn't put it in your report.*

Oh, well, enjoy the moment, she cajoled, putting the inexplicable feeling of mystery aside. She was too comfortable; the effort required to think was too great. Besides, the adventure was ended.

CHAPTER III

The last rays of the sun were dancing across the endless sands when the party rode forth.

"Protection against rats," the sheik laughed in answer to Warren's query concerning the large number of outriders. Hilda noted uneasily that the men were well armed.

Hardy dismissed the surmise that the tribesmen were actually guards. *Guilty conscience,* he reasoned to account for the unwarranted feeling. The situation, however, prompted a reavowal of his determination to call the sheik to account.

Drawing up alongside his host, the newsman inquired, as disapprovingly as he dared, about the reason for the postdawn incident.

Siri had waited for the anticipated verbal query, making one of the few concessions to the standards of a society he had long ago abandoned. Now he answered with a shrug, impatiently, "The fool thought he could invite himself to our little entertainment last night."

Abruptly his mood changed, the moment of concession passed. He considered it a weakness. Allowing no chance for further comment, the sheik spurred his horse to a gallop.

As the horses stretched out into the long-strided, tireless gait for which the tribe's animals were justly famous, Hardy found himself lulled into a pleasant state of suspension, content to hold the future in abeyance. He accepted the sheik's explanation with a fatalism that made him wonder idly if he would ever shake off the spell of the shifting sands. The remorseless dominance of the wasted land quelled men into a pattern of unprotesting acceptance.

The ride ended without incident. Hardy gave up his intent to survey the surroundings, discovering after a few minutes that the attempt to distinguish one rise from another was hopeless.

Dinner was a masterpiece, delighting even Warren's gourmet appetite. Much to the relief of the three guests, the entertainment was impeccable. A nomadic band of actors presented a comedy of the misadventures of a camelteer.

When the dancers appeared, Hilda tensed, but was able to relax when she realized that the performance was to be a sedate, although amateur, version of ballet.

Her fellow traveler, however, found—perversely—that his enjoyment was increased by the knowledge that had he been born in another place, he may have had to pay dearly for the privilege of watching the dancing girls of the sheik's seraglio. There was no longer any doubt in Hardy's mind as to their true identity.

Even these pleasant musings could not long claim his attention from the impending adventure. He waited impatiently for their host to bid them good night. Hardy was mentally traversing the route from his room to the courtyard when he noticed Siri's attention focused in his direction. He had the uneasy feeling that his host's keen eyes were following his thoughts and that the midnight escapade was really no secret. His apprehension grew.

But all went as planned; and shortly after parting from the others, Hardy was on his way. He was too excited to notice that they were mounted on two of the Sheik's best long-distance runners. He was happy with the fast pace Charley set and noted with satisfaction the mounting of every rise, the only signposts of the distance covered. The full moon still sailing toward the horizon gave enough light to see clearly. The dry air under the cloudless sky revealed a majestic panorama of twinkling stars. Hardy felt the lightness of exuberance swelling in his chest.

This is what I was looking for, he thought, *and whatever waits at the end of this ride will give me an answer. I know it!*

Dismayed for a moment, he wondered what his friends would think of his disappearance. The feeling of freedom died away as the moon fell out of sight. He had been inexcusably thoughtless, this cursed obsession wiping all else from his mind. His talent for seeing others' views had faded under the demand of his own desire.

He wondered when Charley would stop for the night. It was now almost too black to see. But the silent shadow ahead didn't slacken its pace and Hardy felt once again the inevitability of men's actions under the sway of the impersonal expanses of sand.

One thing was certain: He had committed himself to this course. It had been entirely his own idea. It was too late to change his mind. But as he urged his horse to follow the fleeting outline ahead, he had the curious presentiment that the desert was not alone in making him a pawn. The penetrating gaze of the sheik flashed back to his mind.

By dawn, they had covered almost the distance it had taken the party a day to traverse previously. Charley had made only two brief pauses to rest the horses. Silently, he had offered Hardy a drink from his canteen, but any attempt to draw him into conversation proved futile. The man's expression was so agonized that Hardy wondered what fantastic cabal sulked at the end of the journey to entangle them in its web. Only the surety of Charley's propensity for exaggeration enabled Hardy to keep up his determination to continue. Then, in the face of the native's persistent silence and unrelenting haste, he wondered if Charley would turn back even if he asked him to.

The American was nearly pitched off his horse when Charley reined in without warning. By the time he had regained his balance, Charley had caught hold of his horse's bridle.

"You will wait here." The guide's voice was surly. "Get down!" Charley ordered, giving Hardy a rough shove, not a trace of the usual subservience in his manner.

Surprised, Hardy obeyed. "But you can't leave me out here." Hardy grabbed for his horse when he saw that Charley didn't intend to dismount.

In answer, Charley pointed into the distance where a group of riders were rapidly approaching. "This is as far as I go." Charley wheeled the two horses, making off at full speed in the direction from which they had come, deaf to Hardy's shouts to halt.

Hardy had no choice but to trust his fate to the swiftly oncoming riders. He knew his presence was glaringly evident against the flat land. Charley was already vanishing over the first rise. Hardy waited.

The horsemen pulled up before him, hurling a swirl of sand into his face. The leader signaled for him to mount the riderless horse in their company. Surprised, but knowing the futility of resistance, Hardy complied. Silently, they were off again, the addition to their number having no doubts that he was a prisoner.

The reporter cursed for having been such a fool as to trust Charley when he was well aware of the guide's devious character. Glancing covertly at his escort, he was at a loss to identify them as servants of Ameur. They certainly didn't inspire confidence. Swathed in voluminous garments that protected travelers from the cutting force of the blowing sand, there was no way to judge what sort of men they were. That they had come to meet him was evident. The extra horse proved that they had known their purpose ahead of time. Hardy cancelled the thought that they were an itinerant band of robbers.

37

But how could they have known his plan? No one knew except Charley. The strange feeling came over Hardy again. The sheik's fierce black eyes bored into his brain, making the skin tighten at the back of his neck. *You're crazy!* Hardy rationalized, *the Englishman wouldn't let me walk into danger without raising a hand.* All Hardy's moral standards revolted at the idea of betrayal.

The sun rose and immediately it was hot. The coolness of the night could not be remembered in the presence of the merciless, burning orb rising out of the undulating ground. Physical distress was added to Hardy's other worries. He concluded he would be relieved to stop, no matter where the adventure ended.

His companions seemed oblivious to the heat although the coats of the horses became darkened with sweat. *They can't go on much longer,* Hardy consoled himself. *They will have to halt if only to give the animals a rest.* His mouth was dry; his eyes burning. He was thoroughly miserable.

Even if they are taking me to Arx Vetus, he continued to worry, *how can I be sure of my reception?* The only comforting thought he could dredge up was the knowledge that Ameur was an American. He grasped what assurance he could from that fact. His relief was immeasurable when he glimpsed the walls of Arx Vetus rising out of the distant sands.

No sooner were the horses halted at the steps of the now-familiar stone building, then Hardy was unceremoniously hustled off and thrust into the room he recognized from earlier occupancy. This time, however, he was disconcerted to hear the key turn in the lock. Still torn between relief and apprehension, he sagged against the door. All he wanted was a few minutes to let the coolness of the room seep away the misery of his body.

"My friend," Ameur spoke from where he was standing unnoticed by the window. "Your curiosity is about to be satisfied."

Hardy felt too tired to be surprised, instead he was unreasonably angry despite his helpless position. "After the welcome I just had, I'd say it's the damn least you can do." the prisoner retorted sarcastically.

"Come and eat some breakfast," Ameur replied kindly, ignoring the remark. "You need it!" With a wave of his hand, he indicated the already laid table.

"You knew I was coming!" Hardy glared, accusing.

"I'll explain." Ameur stood his ground, but accepted Hardy's accusation calmly. "Please believe I'm not your enemy. You might as well listen to what I have to say."

Hardy conceded grudgingly, sitting down to a meal he suddenly realized he badly needed.

"Good!" Ameur responded, taking a chair across the table from his belligerent guest. Pouring them each a cup of coffee, he began, "I'm sorry that your journey back was so unpleasant, but you must admit it was of your own making. Your determination to return here would tolerate no delay."

"How did you know I was coming?" Hardy asked civilly, feeling much better with good food in his stomach.

Ameur smiled. "You will understand that when you know the rest. First you must tell me what brought you back here—without an invitation."

Hardy had the grace to blush. He decided his behavior had been abominable, and he owed honesty to his host, who was seemingly doing his best to be cordial.

"I've a feeling you can tell me what I want to know—and my instincts are seldom wrong."

"And what can you want to know so badly that you risk your neck for it?" Ameur asked, quizzically.

"If the rumors are true."

Ameur looked at his prisoner silently for a long time. Then, as if making up his mind to come directly to the point, he said, "The rumors you have heard are quite true. The mysterious princess you have sought is mistress here."

Hardy forgot his breakfast to stare at Ameur. "What do you mean?" Hardy demanded.

"No," Ameur answered his thought, "not Tiana. But you glimpsed her in the garden the other morning."

Hardy felt the air rush out of his lungs, leaving him unable to speak. He gasped, "You know? That's impossible!"

Ameur laughed. "That's what the natives think. They give us a wide berth. Like Charley. Because the state of altered consciousness is totally beyond his comprehension, he is reduced to total collapse whenever this place is even mentioned. Nothing in his experience prepares him to understand what is going on, so he concludes the only thing he can: that it is magic. It was your impetuosity that forced us to use him to guide you here."

Hardy stared. "What are you talking about?" He understood that Ameur had told him something, but his brain refused to register what it was.

Quietly and solemnly, Ameur answered, all the levity gone from his voice, "Transfiguration." The word exploded in the air, although Ameur hadn't raised his voice.

"My God!" Hardy managed to gasp. "You're not serious!"

Ameur waited, experience telling him what a struggle it was to absorb the revelation.

"But there isn't such a thing," Hardy protested.

"There is."

"It doesn't happen anymore." Hardy was incredulous.

"It can."

"Not to ordinary people."

"It does—to ordinary people." Ameur suppressed a smile. "Do you know any other kind?"

"And that's why you're hiding in the desert?" Hardy countered.

"We're not hiding. This is merely a retreat, a place where we can rest and be ourselves without pretense."

Hardy shook his head in disbelief.

"There are almost ten thousand members," Ameur continued. "All, I might add, enjoying that condition because of the power of your 'mysterious sorceress' to confer it. Her name is Cheira."

Hardy thought of Warren's chief, then wondered why.

"Sam Hackett is one of us," Ameur volunteered.

His mind racing on, Hardy missed the implication. "Why are you telling me all this?"

"You don't know yet?" Ameur admonished. "This altered state of consciousness," he went on before the other man could answer, "permits total physical control. Aging ceases indefinitely. We have the power of telepathy."

"Siri?" Hardy interrupted.

Ameur nodded.

"You mean then," Hardy took control of himself, "that you're proposing that for me?"

"Not proposing," Ameur told him quietly. "The decision has already been made."

"Now wait a minute!" Hardy exploded. "Even if I believed this crazy story—which I don't—are you saying that I don't have any choice in the matter? Are all your members recruited by force?"

"Aren't you forgetting that you've been wandering all over the desert looking for Cheira?" Ameur said sternly. "Now that she's accepted you, are you refusing?"

"But what you've told me is madness!" Hardy protested.

Ameur shrugged. "The fact remains that once Cheira has accepted a candidate, there is no longer any choice involved."

Hardy was silent for some minutes trying to digest what he had just been told. The journalist set his jaw. "I won't do it."

Ameur didn't answer.

Hardy jumped up, going to stand by the window. The view of the garden recalled to his mind what he had seen there. Nothing could alter his purpose. "When do I see her?" His voice was low, admitting that if he wished to talk to the woman he had sought for so long, he would have to pretend compliance. His heart throbbed heavily against his chest, painfully aware of the imminence of his goal. He was stubbornly confident that he could resist any mystic rituals perpetrated by these people. What Ameur had told him could be a cover-up for almost anything. In his work, Hardy had come across secret societies before.

"Now," Ameur answered, interrupting his thoughts. Picking up a white robe similar to his own, Ameur ordered, "Put this on."

Before Hardy could comply, Tiana appeared. "Cheira is waiting," she reminded her husband. Hardy gaped.

"Oh, yes," Ameur laughed, noticing the reporter's astonishment. "Teleportation, too."

A few minutes later, Hardy, appropriately clad, meekly trailed Ameur down a series of long halls. He noticed that they were in a part of the rambling old fort he hadn't seen before. The ceilings were low, giving the impression of a tunnel. *This must be the part of the building used for storage,* Hardy surmised. In the old days it was probably dark and unpleasant. Now the walls were smooth and shone with a dull luster. Scrollwork of a dark, polished wood wound along the ceiling, tastefully hiding the wires that provided power to the unobtrusive lighting fixtures. At intervals, doors set into recesses glowed faintly as the light caught the high points of their carvings.

Heavy carpeting deadened the sound of footsteps, but lent a warmth to the otherwise cool passage. There were no windows. Hardy was impressed by the quality of the paintings that camouflaged that lack very decorously.

They passed two burnoose-clad figures deep in conversation. One of the men looked up. Hardy heard the sound of his indrawn breath echoing against the ensuing silence. The man continued on his way, resuming the interrupted discourse. Hardy tried to stop, but Ameur's hand was firmly on his arm forcing him around the corner of the passage, blocking the others from his sight.

"That was Tony Hammond!" Hardy spoke too loud, his voice sounding oddly out of place in the tranquil surroundings.

41

"Yes!" Ameur answered quietly.

"But he's been dead for fifty years." Hardy toned down his voice, but he couldn't control the note of disbelief in it. He was familiar with Hammond because of a feature story he had worked on for weeks a couple of years ago. "He was one of the great silver barons of the last century, killed in a mine cave-in, in Nevada. The body was never recovered."

"Too bad!" Ameur chuckled. "The rescuers didn't look in the right place. They should have searched the gold mines of South Africa."

Hardy was silent. From where he stood, Ameur's humorous quip sounded like dialogue from a nightmare. Hardy was sure he would awaken momentarily. He anticipated the relief he would feel when that happened. But the sensation of the long robe he wore swishing against his bare legs seemed terribly real.

At last Ameur stopped before a door, much larger than any they had passed. Pulling his robe off over his head and discarding it on a nearby bench, Ameur directed his companion to do the same.

Hardy reddened, but stood his ground.

"It's the custom." Ameur explained patiently, "to which we are all bound. It's the symbol of your willingness to serve. That acknowledgement is a small price to pay for the gift you will receive."

"This is crazy!" Hardy refused to believe what Ameur was telling him. "It's the twentieth century! I absolutely refuse to be a party to such nonsense. In fact, I wonder if you're not making all this up. It's a joke, isn't it?"

"When you enter," Ameur continued, ignoring Hardy's remarks, "drop to one knee and keep your head bowed." He demonstrated.

Hardy laughed. His intentions were very different. He was eager to meet the woman he had dreamed about for so many years. *It might be,* he conceded, *that she has the man beside me cowed, but she'll find me not so easily managed.* It wasn't as a slave that Hardy intended to become part of her life.

Ameur rose, studying Hardy gravely. "It's only for your welfare that I instruct you. Do you still refuse?"

Hardy disdained to answer.

"Then you must take the consequences, my friend."

Ameur opened the door. He pushed Hardy inside.

Hardy was startled, surprised by the atmosphere of the room, which seemed to envelop him, forcing him to respond with awe. In the dim light, the long shadows added an air of mystery to the highly charged emotion. The reporter whose flippant quip about the possibility of this happening in the twentieth century heard loudly in his ears the painful pounding of his heart, like a mockery his vision laboring to communicate to his brain the sight it beheld. He walked forward barely aware of what he was doing, his legs operating automatically, drawing him to the figure seated on a dais in the middle of the room, the chair emphasized by streams of focused light.

Hardy knew, at that moment—the realization dawning in his brain from every nerve in his body—that here was the woman he had been waiting for all his life, here was the reason he had found all other woman dull and uninteresting, the reason he had never even been tempted by the many beautiful women who had thrown themselves at him.

He had forgotten everything Ameur had told him and every doubt he had had concerning the reality of the situation. He was filled with the sight of the golden hair framing features of unbelievable perfection. Her eyes were large and almond shaped, a translucent green flecked with the brown and gold of autumn leaves. With the eyes of a man accustomed to the cosmetic masquerades of the women around him, he noticed that her brows were the same color as her hair and that her creamy skin was devoid of makeup.

His gaze fastened on the lovely shape of her mouth. He had no way of knowing that the firmly closed lips indicated a rising anger.

Cheira was busy. She had taken the time to admit Hardy to the society as a special favor to Sam Hackett. Now, noting the man's sophomoric behavior, she wondered if Sam was right, if Hardy was emotionally stable enough to handle such a momentous change in his life. However, she trusted Sam's judgement; still, she decided to bear down hard on the newspaperman and monitor his reaction.

"You have much to learn, Robert Hardy." The usually sweet voice was stern. "You shall never disobey me again."

The flip answer died on his lips, for her body began to glow with such intensity that he was forced to bow his head if only to protect his eyes.

In the next instant, she had placed her hand on his shoulder. Pain shot through his body, dropping him, writhing, to the floor.

"Now," she commanded, her voice low, but with a menacing inflection, "make your obeisance."

Hardy felt that he had stumbled into an inferno. His outraged nerves throbbed dully, now that the intense pain had passed. The ache in his head made thinking impossible. Nothing in his past experience or environment had prepared him to withstand more than a minimum of physical discomfort. The torture he had just experienced eradicated all will to resist. If compliance would spare him further pain, he would willingly obey. He dragged himself into a crouching position, hoping it was what was required.

"Is your power already so great," she continued in the same tone, instilling a cold dread in his heart that he couldn't interpret, "that you appear here as master, fully robed?" She touched him again and the garment he had refused to discard burst into flame. A strangled cry rose from his throat as the blazing cloth scorched his skin. Her touch held him immobile, as though her will now controlled his muscles. There was no way to relieve the agony.

Her hands moving to his temples lifted his head, forcing him to meet her gaze. Totally vanquished and on the verge of unconsciousness, Hardy was only dimly aware of the force penetrating deeply into his brain. All thought was sundered in the pain that enveloped his head. The delicate fingers so fragile in appearance were points of current mangling the unprotected tissues.

His body jerked convulsively, his nerves screaming with the anguish he was helpless to avoid. He could stand no more.

Cheira stepped back, her eyes studying the unconscious figure coldly. Their piercing intensity was the last thing Hardy saw.

When Hardy regained consciousness, he was lying face down on the bed in the now-familiar apartment. Tiana dressed his burns, the deepest of which were on his back where the blazing material had clung. The necessary movement had roused him, despite Tiana's gentleness.

Once oriented, the young adventurer was conscious of an exhaustion so pervasive that any effort seemed beyond the scope of his will. He was as depressed mentally as physically, feeling an emptiness and sense of loss that were seemingly unaccountable, his memory sluggishly refusing to eject the required information. Finally, after long deliberation by his reluctant brain, he managed to open his eyes.

Ameur, lounging in a chair beside the bed, followed the progressive stages of consciousness returning to the prostrate man.

"You have chosen a most difficult path, Robert Hardy," he said, sympathetically.

Just leave me alone, Hardy thought, his brain refusing to put forth the effort required for speech. His body ached and burned. As consciousness again slipped away, he remembered thinking, *She's a witch! I must be dreaming all this.*

Tiana sighed. Smoothing her patient's brow with cool fingers he didn't feel, her pity reached out to the young idealist who had traveled halfway around the world seeking the fulfillment of a dream. That the reality was far different from anything he could have imagined had precipitated an agonizing confrontation with Cheira. Tiana wished for an easier, less painful way for him.

Ameur rose, coming to stand beside Tiana. She turned, laying her head on her husband's breast. Taking her in his arms to comfort her, Ameur murmured, "Sometimes I'm sure this business is harder on you than it is on them. After all, the young rascal is getting no more than he asked for. His impudence had to be squelched sooner or later. You know that Cheira won't tolerate such an attitude. And the society must be protected."

"I know," she agreed, wearily. "But I can't help feeling sorry that it has to be this way."

"You've done all you can. Go and rest," he urged. "He'll sleep for twenty-four hours at least."

The room was bright with sunlight. The heat of the desert sun creeping into the chamber made the efforts of the overhead fan seem futile. The sleeping figure stirred uncomfortably. At last he opened his eyes and looked around.

Hardy sat up, grinding his knuckles into sleep-drugged eyeballs. I've had *enough of the dream,* he thought foggily. *It is time to wake up.*

But looking again, the room hadn't changed; and added, clamoring for his attention, was the itching sensation of his parched, healing skin. *Then it wasn't a dream,* he decided. All the events of the past few days reeled before his mind, only to halt abruptly at the image of Cheira. His head began to ache.

"I hate her!" he said aloud to the empty room. But his pounding heart defied him, until at last with a muffled gasp, he contradicted the statement. "Oh, God! I don't! I don't!"

Tiana appeared beside his bed, bearing a tray. "Feeling better?" she asked, smiling.

Hardy jumped, startled by the materialization. *I must be dreaming again,* he thought, *or unconscious.*

Only since yesterday. Tiana laughed.

Stiffening, Hardy stared at her. She hadn't spoken, of that he was positive.

Yes. She grinned, an impish twinkle in her lovely dark eyes. *You are receiving my thoughts.*

45

"Thought transference." This time he spoke aloud. "I can't believe it!"

You'll get used to it, Tiana assured him telepathically. Then she sobered and spoke. "Cheira will see you in an hour. Be ready."

Hardy winced as Tiana disappeared. *Lord,* he thought, *I'll never be able to cope with this.*

The coming audience soon had his heart pounding again, but the anticipation was accompanied by a new element of nagging, persistent fear. He was so engrossed in his feeling about the impending interview that he failed to notice how quickly the burns were healing. There were only a few red patches left where the burns had been exceptionally deep.

At the appointed hour, a thoroughly converted young man was kneeling humbly with bowed head before the woman who had so changed his life.

"You have learned well, Robert Hardy." Cheira smiled approvingly.

A slight shudder he couldn't control rippled along his muscles.

"You will return to your friends," she continued, "take up your life, study to increase your power until I have need of you."

The shock of her words so disconcerted him that he absolutely forgot Ameur's admonition to refrain from thinking anything that might bring about another session with Cheira's anger. Ameur had warned him that strict compliance with her wishes was mandatory if he wanted to avoid even worse punishment than he had already endured. But the undisciplined nature of Hardy's character hadn't changed overnight. He was still the reckless American in pursuit of his own desires. Although cowed for the moment in his outward behavior, he still stubbornly clung to his original goal.

Hardy refused to believe that she had transfigured him just to banish him. He looked at her, naively revealing the intensity of emotion he carried in his heart, an emotion developed from a dream even before he was aware of her actual existence. To remain here to serve her forever was his only reason to live.

The journalist was too inexperienced to read the warning in the frown on Cheira's brow. She had already summoned Ameur.

"Our friend acquires the habit of obedience slowly," she said. Ameur was alert to the edge of irritation her tone betrayed. "Perhaps three days in the courtyard will give him time to reconsider." She disappeared before Hardy could protest.

Ameur put his hand on Hardy's shoulder.

"Come," he said grimly as a man required to perform an unpleasant task he had hoped to avoid.

Hardy rose reluctantly. "But I didn't say anything," he protested.

"What were you thinking?"

"Oh, God!" He groaned, despairingly. "I forgot!"

"Then you must learn to remember," Ameur told him sternly, taking his arm and steering him into the hall.

"Wait a minute!" Hardy held back, looking over his shoulder at the closed door. "She's got to give me a chance to explain."

Ameur raised his eyebrows, but said nothing. His blue eyes held a look of resignation. He sympathized with Tiana's feelings, but his mind closed abruptly, refusing to allow any critics of Cheira's high-handed methods to take form.

"Come!" he repeated, his voice assuming a tone of command that could not be disobeyed.

In the courtyard, Ameur led Hardy to an iron stake and fastened the metal collar around his neck.

"But," Hardy protested, the surprise of what was being done giving him no chance to resist. "I'm transfigured! I'm telepathic! You won't be able to keep me here like this!"

"You have much to learn," Ameur told him sadly, walking away.

CHAPTER IV

In Zurich, at 11:00 A.M. promptly, a comely widow was being ushered into the office of Hans Werner. She was fashionably dressed in the most expensive style. Werner greeted her cordially.

"Thank you for coming, Madame von Bern."

Only the most observant viewer would have noticed that Werner first extended his hand palm upward and bowed his head. His secretary noticed nothing unusual in her employer's manner. She closed the door quietly.

Twenty minutes later, Werner and Mme. von Bern left to meet with Mme. Werner for lunch. The time had been well spent. Werner's client was thoroughly briefed on her identity.

Margo Werner was a gracious hostess. If she wondered why her husband had singled out this client from the many to invite into their home, she kept her counsel. She did allow herself a twinge of jealousy as she watched her husband's attentiveness to this exceptionally beautiful woman. Her heart sank in the instant the possible reason came to her.

Was this the end? she wondered, seeking the only plausible explanation. She noticed again, as she had increasingly in recent years, that her husband retained all the handsomeness of youth. The smoothness of his skin, without the evidence of aging common to men of middle years, belied the graying at his temples. Today he looked even younger, with a look of helplessness in his eyes that was unnatural in a man accustomed to command. She knew that look. She saw it sometimes when he looked at her. It was an openness that confessed his love, acknowledging the emotions against which he had no defense.

Now he was looking at this woman in the same way.

Impatient as she always was at entertaining such feelings of self-pity, Margo forced her attention back to her guest. She was disconcerted to find that the conversation had ceased. Both Hans and Mme. von Bern were watching her.

She blushed. She had the uneasy feeling that they knew what she had been thinking.

48

"You have a lovely home," Mme. von Bern spoke.

Margo thought she could detect a note of sympathy in the lovely voice. She bristled mentally. If this woman thought she could take her husband and pity her abandonment at the same time—well, she'd see about that!

"Hans has always taken the best care of his family," Margo replied, making her voice sweet and well modulated with an effort. "His primary concern has been for my happiness and that of our sons."

"You're fortunate that his devotion has grown with the years."

Margo was so upset that she missed the tone of sincerity in Cheira's voice. She did, however, notice her husband's frown. That he was displeased with the trend of conversation was clear.

Biting back the remark on the tip of her tongue and making a supreme effort to please him, she suggested coffee in the library. For the duration of her stay, Margo resolved to treat their guest as she would any less-threatening visitor. She politely inquired into Mme. von Bern's future plans and regaled her with stories of the social affairs and attractions of Zurich.

Her effort was rewarded by the relaxation of Hans's frown. Had he been afraid she would make a scene? *Oh, Lord,* she thought, *if I can bear this, I can survive anything.* With the thought came the swelling of her love that would endure beyond any repudiation he could make.

Finally, Mme. von Bern rose. "Such a nice afternoon," she murmured politely. "Thank you for the delicious luncheon. Allow me to reciprocate by inviting you to dinner this evening."

Margo glanced at her husband. In compliance with his nod, she accepted graciously.

"It will give me great pleasure," responded her guest. "I'll expect you at eight."

Margo watched them return to the car, then fled, sobbing, to her room.

How can he be so cruel, she raged into her pillow, *to parade my rival before me so blatantly?*

She had accepted the surmise as true when Hans left her without a word, his attention so caught by his beautiful companion that he had even neglected to kiss her good-bye, an action which had become a sacred ritual during the long years of their marriage.

It's too much to bear, her thoughts raced on, plunging her into despair, *when I still love him so.*

She had no way of knowing the emotional strain her husband was enduring at that moment for her sake. Hans was sitting quietly, giving no outward hint of the tension roaring through his body. He waited for Cheira to speak, carefully keeping his mind clear. The only clue of supplication was the upturned palm resting on his knee.

After what seemed an eternity of silence, she spoke. "I wish to include Tiana in our dinner party this evening. She'll enjoy a little sojourn in the city."

Hans bowed his head in acceptance. This was not what he wanted to hear. Why she wanted Tiana at the evening meeting, he couldn't even guess—although Tiana's presence would ease the painful ordeal, he conceded. Her understanding would be an invisible support against whatever was to come. A consideration for his feelings, however, could not be any concern of Cheira's.

He stopped abruptly, glancing guiltily at the woman beside him, intensely aware that his power was insufficient to hide his thoughts from her knowledge. But if Cheira knew what he was thinking, she gave no indication. She was enjoying the passing scene, noting the changes in the city since her last visit.

"When did they change Lindenstrausse into a boulevard?" she asked, smiling with pleasure at the beautiful street, divided now by a wide median of grass and trees.

"They've been working on it for the last five years," he answered. "They intend to eventually improve it all the way to the Square. Herman Mailer finally convinced the council that the city was growing rapidly in this direction; and if they were going to prevent the ugly, haphazard expansion of the older sections, they would have to act now."

"Oh, yes!" she beamed, her face glowing with pride. "He's so right! He's done a fine job."

Hans flushed with pleasure at the compliment to his friend—the only other man in the city who shared his unique condition. Such praise from Cheira would be highly valued.

"May I tell him what you said?"

She laughed, consenting.

"He'll be very happy to have your approval."

When he dropped her at the hotel, his question was still unanswered. Werner returned to his office, but found concentration on any work impossible. His shoulders ached from the tension of the last hours, a tension he had only become aware of after slumping down into the soft leather chair behind his big desk.

He studied the unusual barrenness of the surface before him. It looked odd. Generally, this time of day, it was littered with the briefs of legal cases in some process of resolution. This morning he had cleared everything away.

He noticed an empty feeling in the pit of his stomach. He wondered if he could be hungry again. With a wry smile, he realized it was his body's shock at the early afternoon inactivity. What was normally the busiest part of his day was today vacant, only the waiting available to fill the void. He sat up.

To his secretary's surprise, he had left orders a week ago that no appointments were to be scheduled on this day. Luckily, he had no cases on the court calendar.

He eyed the only item lying conspicuously on top of the oversized blotter. It was a folder, boldly labeled, "Mme. Erica von Bern." The name in his own firm handwriting recalled to his mind the meticulous care he had taken in compiling the dossier, certain of his friends who held official posts in the city having been persuaded to furnish the necessary documents without their even being aware of their purpose. He had used all his skill, all his knowledge of legal loopholes to make certain that, should the occasion ever arise, no amount of scrutiny would be able to detect any flaws in the fabrication. He had created Mme. von Bern for today and for as long as she cared to exist. When the alias was no longer necessary, he would account for her demise in the same flawless manner of her creation. His object was well worth the effort. He considered the price as nothing compared to the possible reward. His shoulders drew up unconsciously to their former state of tension.

He thought of Margo. He knew what she was suffering. How else could she have interpreted the luncheon but as a threat to her position as his wife. *And,* he groaned, *I am helpless to aid her.* He must stand by and let her think what she wished no matter how erroneous her conclusions.

He cursed the confusion he felt in Cheira's presence, his anxiety so easily misinterpreted by Margo. He had been too embarrassed to kiss Margo in front of Cheira. He was too unsure of Cheira's attitude to risk any indecorous action. The hurt in Margo's eyes haunted him now. He wrestled with the agony of what she was enduring.

He could only hope for a propitious outcome—and soon. Then it would all have been worth the trial. He relied on Margo's strength, knowing how she had borne other crises in their years together. The thought comforted him. He remembered her brave smile when their son was so ill, that time Herman Mailer had called him back from Arx Vetus. There had been no reproaches from Margo for his absence when she needed him most. And before that, when the baby was only a few weeks old, he had disappeared without a trace. She had immediately checked Ameur's story, her instinct telling her it didn't ring true. Still she had stoically carried on, caring for the children until his return, and then welcoming him joyously and never once insisting that he tell her where he had been, satisfied to know that he had returned safely.

His whole being rebelled at the thought that the answer might be negative. There were few women in the organization, he knew. Perhaps he was a fool to think that Cheira would make an exception in his case.

What if—he shuddered at the possibility—*the lack of female members was intentional? If, womanlike, Cheira jealously wanted the undivided love of the men under her control for herself? Then my admission of love for Margo had been a stupid mistake.*

No, you're wrong, he objected, by habit his own adversary. *Hadn't she sanctioned the marriage of Ameur and Tiana? It was obvious how much Cheira loved them both. There had never been a hint that she was envious of their relationship to each other.*

He shook his head. *Admit,* he chided himself, *that you're not familiar enough with any of them to make a judgement. They could hide an unpleasant situation as effortlessly as they withhold their thoughts.* He regretted now the contented attitude that had made him neglect the study necessary to increase his power.

At last, when he could endure the waiting no longer, he phoned Margo. His heart ached when he heard the evidence of grief in her voice, which she courageously tried to conceal. He couldn't trust himself to acknowledge his awareness of her suffering. Deliberately, he made his instructions terse and impersonal.

"Meet me at seven-thirty in the main lobby of the Bremen Haus," he told her, hoping that some of the love he felt would show in the quality of his voice.

Hans was not mistaken. Margo knew her husband well. *What hold, then,* she wondered, vigorously scrubbing away the ravages of her tears, *did this woman have over him?* She was determined to discover the trouble and unreservedly fight for her husband—to the death if necessary. With firm resolution, she set about devising a plan.

Margo was in the hotel lobby promptly at the appointed time. She was not too preoccupied, however, to notice the admiring glances of the men and the envious looks of the women. Intentionally, she was a picture of carefully contrived beauty and high fashion. The flawless impression was the result of hard work. Satisfied by what she saw in the eyes of the strangers looking at her, she felt strong and confident, able to meet the enemy—if so her husband's client proved to be—on her own terms.

"You are a vision of loveliness this evening," Hans whispered, admiration shining in his eyes as he took her arm.

In the elevator, she permitted herself one moment of weakness. "Darling, please tell me what's wrong. Let me help!" she begged.

"You are helping," he responded, stopping her lips with a kiss.

They were welcomed by a petite Chinese girl. Margo was surprised to hear her husband address the girl familiarly.

"Good evening, Ching Li." He smiled.

Ching Li bowed in reply. "Madam is awaiting you." She stepped across the small foyer of the suite to open ornate double doors.

Mme. von Bern came forward to greet them. "Good evening, Hans," she said, smiling. "And Margo—may I call you that?—you are lovely. No wonder Hans feels as he does."

Werner reddened, but remained silent. He bowed low over their hostess's hand. Margo noted the action, which took a second longer than etiquette required. At the same time, she wondered if there was a veiled threat in the compliment. But she had no time to consider. Her hostess led her into the room. A comely, dark-haired woman stood at the fireplace. Margo's senses sharpened; she inhaled quickly. If this was combat, she was ready.

"May I introduce my companion, Tiana," Mme. von Bern stated. Margo noted the absence of an introduction to her husband. She saw just a flicker of greeting as Tiana's eyes strayed to Hans's face. The look held an inexplicable note of understanding. *That's the wrong reaction,* Margo thought. She found herself liking the woman immediately. *Whatever is going on,* she decided, *Tiana is an ally.*

Margo murmured a polite response to the introduction. Against her better judgement, she surrendered to the feeling that this woman was her friend. She permitted it to show in her eyes. Then she wondered if she had moved too quickly, making her defense vulnerable. She would have to be doubly cautious, she determined.

Tiana responded by taking her arm, leading her to the couch that was part of an arrangement commonly referred to as conversational grouping. Margo had an irrelevant vision of the suites that made up the hotel, all looking the same. The exception, however, her experienced glance told her, was that this was one of the most expensive. Unobtrusively, she dropped her hand to rest on the rose brocade, allowing her fingertips to confirm the richness of the heavy upholstery.

Nonchalantly, she widened her vision to include both women. She recognized their gowns as part of the spring collection of a very famous Parisian. Her mind clicked off the obvious price tags. The clicking changed to a whir as she estimated the price of their jewels.

But neither woman had the pinched look about the mouth that could be noticed only by another knowledgeable woman. *Evidently, whatever the woman is after, it is not money,* Margo concluded. Her mind drew a blank. She could come up with no conceivable motive.

Hans was describing the politics of Zurich to Mme. von Bern. Margo's attention sharpened when she heard the details he was relating. Astutely, Margo realized that what he was saying would generally be considered confidential. Hans was not naive. *Was intrigue the answer?* she wondered, knowing her husband's affiliations and remembering his unexplained absences.

Ching Li served drinks, then dinner.

The conversation shifted subtly to Margo, but not without her awareness of the maneuver. She shouldered the burden of talk willingly, hoping to give Hans a necessary breather. She had confidence in his ability. She determined to give him time.

Soon, however, she was fighting her own battle. She had to use all her skill to counter the probing attack. Margo grudgingly admired the stratagem of her opponents. She was dismayed that Hans didn't come to her rescue as she had to his. Increasingly, she got he impression of being on trial—and with Hans's consent.

Guiltily, Margo felt she could like the two women—if they were not her husband's enemies. More and more perplexed, especially since Hans was actually encouraging her to answer any and all questions, she was gripped by the fear that her husband had capitulated. She returned with renewed determination to her original plan. She'd engage the contest for them both. *They'll get no quarter from me,* she decided.

Subtly, using all the ingenuity she had acquired over the years as hostess to her husband's important clients, she led the conversation away from herself into the small talk so acceptable at social events where personal noncommitment is the prime requisite. She ignored the secret signal from Hans, which was their private mutual sign to desist, when he discovered her strategy.

Margo was well into a lengthy description of the prize-winning roses at the last garden show when Mme. von Bern stood up abruptly, laughing. Hans winced, his face ashen. Margo hesitated, looking from one to the other. Mme. von Bern's action was an inexcusable breach of etiquette. Tiana was openly grinning. Margo was completely nonplussed when Mme. von Bern gasped, still laughing.

"Yes! Yes! Delightful! Smile, Hans. It's what you've been waiting to hear, isn't it? Margo is a treasure." She turned to Werner, who had also risen.

"I hardly dared to hope," Werner's voice was so low as to be barely audible.

"Bring her to Arx Vetus. Are two weeks enough to wind up your affairs?" Werner inclined his head in assent. "You will, of course, be relocated afterwards."

Werner bowed low, kissing her hand. With a smile at Margo, she left the room.

Tiana, silent during the exchange, came forward now, kissing Hans. "Congratulations!" she said.

Margo, recovering from her initial astonishment, demanded, "What is this all about?"

"Our eternity together," Hans told her, beaming. "Let's go home, my darling, and I'll tell you all about it. The ordeal is over. I love you." Werner hugged his wife so tightly she gasped, amazed as always at his strength.

CHAPTER V

In contrast to Werner's happiness that night, two thousand miles away Hardy was doing some sober thinking. Still pinioned ignominiously by the iron collar and chain to the post in the courtyard at Arx Vetus, he had been exposed all day to the hot desert sun and the cold, bone-chilling night.

Although he had suffered intensely from exposure to the elements and had had nothing to eat, he was in surprisingly good shape.

I ought to be dead, he thought ruefully. So far, extraordinary endurance seemed to be the only benefit of transfiguration. Repeatedly, he had tried to teleport out of his predicament, but his body had remained obstinately earthbound.

The chafing of the collar on his raw skin increased his misery, but no more than did the humiliation of his position. He was learning self-control along with endurance and submission without protest. That obedience could be forced upon him, he no longer doubted. His great love was of no consequence to his beloved nor was it likely ever to be.

Hopelessly, his heart still pounded violently when he thought of her, compounding his discomfort. The gentle undulation of the golden hair persistently moving away from him would rise in his mind to increase his agony. No matter how he concentrated, he could never see her face.

He dozed fitfully for a while, half-reclining against the post until the night chill made rest impossible. Pacing the circumference of the chain-limited circle, Hardy vacillated between cursing the fate that had led him this way and doubting the sanity that accepted the whole episode as reality. Perhaps, he was, after all, actually wandering delirious in the desert. Why then was he still alive? *Two more days,* he thought, *if this is real.* Then what? Back to the States, with the days stretching endlessly before him. The prospect made the present situation almost desirable.

Hardy watched tirelessly for a glimpse of Cheira. Although many people passed within his range of vision, Cheira was not among them. Only Ameur spoke to him, coming in the evening to bring water, lingering to give instruction on his new life.

"When you go back," Ameur advised, "go to work for Sam Hackett. He's wanted you for years. I think, though without proof, that he was instrumental in your candidacy. Everyone has been expecting it anyway. Your exceptional talent has become widely known. You will be of great use to the organization. We have needed a good man in the States for a long time who is not hampered by his position as Sam Hackett is."

Hardy shrugged. The use of his ability in some distant future was of little interest to him under the present circumstances.

"Then you don't think Cheira will change her mind?" Hardy asked expectantly.

"Our mistress never changes her mind." Ameur was certain, adding with a warning note in his voice, "I would recommend that you dismiss what you are thinking."

"That's proving difficult." Hardy flushed. "Don't you think I'd rather hate her?"

"What you must do"—Ameur was sympathetic—"is neither to love nor to hate, but to be loyal and obedient."

The young man looked so miserable that Ameur encouraged him with a smile. "It can be done."

Hardy wondered fleetingly if Ameur spoke from experience, but the sheik's clear blue eyes gave him no hint.

The night air, rapidly cooling in the absence of the sun, brought Hardy's thoughts back to his helpless condition.

"If this is reality, why don't I have any supernatural power?"

"In the first place, none of it is unnatural," Ameur answered. "Every human being has the potential. How you realize it is up to you. Your consciousness has been heightened so that with concentration you can accomplish whatever you wish quickly and easily. When you go back, ask Sam to help you. There are many others in New York, too. You'll find all of them glad to help."

Hardy cringed in embarrassment as a group of burnoose-clad riders returning from a late ride walked their horses past.

"Are all these men members?" Hardy ventured to ask.

"Yes. They are not permitted to speak to you or help you, but you have their sympathy," Ameur explained. "Some of them have also suffered for indiscretions. They are here now to be assigned to new positions. Agelessness, for such a small segment of the population, can present a problem. After thirty years or so, one's associates are noticeably older. It is necessary, then, to seek a new identity in another part of the world."

Hardy was distressfully aware of his own sparsely clad body and the shameful position that exposed him to the gaze of all. The men passed by silently and, to Hardy's great relief, apparently took no notice of him. He watched until they passed from sight under the huge stone arches that marked the entrance to the stables.

He turned back to Ameur, the man's sympathy evident in the stillness of his posture.

"At least, they didn't laugh," Hardy said.

"No," Ameur answered softly.

"I appreciate it."

"Yes. They understand."

Hardy was silent. The moon had risen over the edge of the enclosure. He thought it peered at him contemptuously. Its rays mercilessly illuminated his ignominy, reflecting brightly on the metal stake that held him pinioned, denying him even the comforting anonymity of darkness.

Ameur waited, following Hardy's thoughts. He knew the sense of confusion which led to the next question.

"What do they do here?"

"After many years, this is the only permanent sanctuary that exists for them, a place to meet their friends without pretense.

"With heightened intelligence, they do a great deal of good in the world. The natural leaders of their fellowmen, they work in government, business, scientific research, and many other fields. Doubtless, you would recognize most of them."

"Like Tony Hammond?" Hardy interrupted.

"Yes. You may meet him one day soon, if you wish. You are welcome to come here any time you're free. It will give you a chance to make friends without the necessary strain of relationships outside."

"But how can they lead two such different lives?" the reporter puzzled.

"It gets easier with practice." Ameur grinned. "By comparison only a small part of their time is spent here—about two weeks a year is mandatory, and, of course, longer between assignments. Some members are able to get away for a weekend or two at other times."

"But their families . . . " Hardy mused. "How do they keep it from them?"

Ameur's expression saddened. "There are no families for most of them. The price of our enlightened state is sterility. It tends to dampen permanent alliances, especially on the part of male members. A union of such intimacy is nearly impossible when the most important aspect of one's life

58

must be concealed. There is no satisfactory way to explain such a state to the uninitiated. In any case, it is forbidden. To maintain such a guard over one's actions even in privacy would prove an unbearable burden for most."

The reporter's mind jumped to the obvious. "But . . . Tiana?"

Ameur smiled. "We only have increased the ability to control our passions, not dispense with them. Each of us copes according to the culture of his origin. For me, marriage was the obvious answer, happily coupled with love . . . and Cheira's gracious consent to Tiana's transfiguration. I'm afraid the other members haven't been so fortunate, although a few of them were married before receiving the altered state." Ameur added, thinking of Werner, "If at all possible, their wives are accepted if they request it."

Hardy thought about Siri, certain now that his interpretation of the dance had been correct.

"Yes," Ameur answered his thought, "Siri's harem is exactly what the name implies."

There was one more question so important to the young man that he hardly dared even to think it for fear of the answer, but not knowing would be equally unbearable.

"And Cheira?" he asked, his voice just audible.

The answer was long in coming. Finally, Ameur said, "Our mistress has no personal relationships. Her whole life is devoted to the association."

Perversely, the relief Hardy expected to feel was not forthcoming.

The third day proved to be the most difficult, the beat of the sun relentless on his already parched skin. By noon, Hardy's head was reeling, his lips dry and swollen. The relief he had enjoyed with the first warming heat of morning had long since turned into an agonizing burning that penetrated the already baked layers of his skin until the bones themselves seemed parched. It was painful to move. Even the morning shadow of the metal post, which had afforded a small pillar of shade, was denied him now as the sun stood directly overhead.

He felt that the flesh of his shoulders was being peeled off, leaving exposed to even greater torture the more sensitive layers beneath. The feeble attempt of his body to cool itself only added to the agony as sweat trickled under the cracking skin. The direct rays of the sun heated the metal of the accursed collar, so that even the effort of breathing increased the chafing.

Ching Li brought him a cup of water. Completely demoralized, he cowered away from her.

"It is permitted," she insisted, putting her hand on his shoulder. Coolness flooded over him and a pleasant hum ran along his nerves.

"I'm sorry my power is so small," Ching Li apologized.

Hardy was incredulous, forgetting his misery in the shock of discovery. Of course, he chided himself for the stupidity of not realizing it before, if one had the power to induce pain, why not pleasure?

"Can anyone do that?" he asked.

"Better than I," she nodded. "You, also, when you have studied some and are well."

She went away, but left him comfortable enough to endure whatever time was left.

Ameur came in the late afternoon. While he freed Hardy and handed him a burnoose, some similarly clothed riders were bringing up horses.

"You will be left within walking distance of the Fort," Ameur told him. "When you get there, your ordeal will be over. Good luck, my friend."

Before Hardy could respond, Ameur was gone. In the next moment, he was mounted and galloping out the gate. The men were silent, but by the way they rode in close formation around him, he knew that he was still a prisoner.

At the Fort, Percy and Hilda were having an uneasy time of it. Hardy's disappearance seemed inexplicable. Their fears were somewhat allayed by the size of the search party that the sheik sent out immediately after the reporter was discovered missing.

But as the days stretched into a week, Hardy's companions began to fear he might never be heard from again. The desert was vast and cruel. The disappearance occasioned strange tales from the servants, surreptitious whisperings behind closed doors that were intended to reach the ears of the foreigners.

A short respite to worry occurred with the return of the supply plane. Percy and Hilda were pleasantly surprised by the arrival of a fellow journalist.

Julie Crown introduced herself as a correspondent for the *Portland Globe*. She explained that her chief was a friend of Sam Hackett's. After a lot of pleading, he had agreed to let her catch up with the safari. When Sam received Warren's dispatch, she knew where to find them.

"And here I am," she added, tossing her golden hair.

Enchanted as always by a fresh young face, Warren proceeded to flirt outrageously with her, at the same time watching his host covertly to forestall any advances by the degenerate Englishman.

"If that man makes one move toward her, I'll kill him," Percy stormed to Hilda.

"Sure you will," Hilda replied, mockingly. She couldn't help contrasting the paunchy man beside her with their bronzed, broad-shouldered host.

It was the day after Julie's arrival. The sheik had invited them for a swim in the harem pool. Hilda wondered idly what the sheik had done with the women, for none were seen. Lounging at poolside, she dreamily admired the pair in the water: the sheik, hard muscles rippling under the tanned skin as he dove off the board; and Julie, whose suit couldn't conceal the soft voluptuousness of her young body. Hilda sighed. She always had had a romantic bent.

Percy interrupted her thoughts. "The nerve of him," he said peevishly, "bringing her to his harem."

"She doesn't know that's what it is," Hilda replied reasonably.

A patently agitated servant motioned his master to poolside. After listening a moment, the sheik followed him out, pausing only to throw a towel around his neck, leaving his guests staring after him in wonder.

Peremptorily abandoned, Julie swam around listlessly for a few moments, then came over to Hilda and Percy.

"Well," she said, climbing the ladder and picking up a towel, "is he always so rude?" Not waiting for an answer she continued, "I'm for a shower and a nap before dinner."

"Fine!" Hilda agreed, rising to accompany her. Percy trailed behind, feeling unaccountably dejected. He was beginning to wish he had never come to this godforsaken place.

A servant tugged at his arm, motioning him to silence with a nod toward the retreating women. Percy followed the man into a room nearby.

"Hardy just came in," the sheik informed him without preclusion. "He's in pretty bad shape. Ahmed is putting him to bed. Let's see what he has to say."

"My, God, man!" Percy gasped when he saw his friend. "What have you been through?"

Hardy was lying face down on the bed, his skin burned and peeling; his hair and eyebrows looked singed.

"I'll be all right," Hardy's voice grated, raw and hoarse through his cracked lips. "Got lost . . . been wandering for days . . . caravan picked me up. Lord, the desert is hot!"

The sheik said nothing. Percy looked at him questioningly.

"He's in excellent hands." Siri motioned toward Ahmed competently dressing Hardy's raw flesh. "Let him rest. He'll explain more later."

Reluctantly, Warren left his friend; but once away he sped off to the girls' room to break the news.

"Hardy's come back!" he shouted, bursting into the sitting room.

Hilda dropped the magazine she had been reading. "Thank God!" she murmured over and over as Warren rushed on with the details.

With the promise to keep them posted, the excited journalist hurried away to be with the injured man.

"I'm sure you're greatly relieved," Julie offered sympathetically.

"Oh, my dear, yes," Hilda lamented. "I hope he'll be all right."

"I'm sure he will," answered Julie, resuming her reading unperturbed.

It was three days before Warren invited Hilda and Julie to go with him to see Hardy.

"He's so much better," explained Percy, "that he wants to meet our new colleague. Maybe you girls can get more out of him than I can. He insists that he spent the time wandering around in the dessert, but he won't give any reason for going in the first place." Warren gave Hilda a knowing glance, thinking of the place far to the south that was never mentioned. Warren was betting that Hardy had tried to find it and was now too ashamed to admit it.

"He might have died," was Hilda's only answer.

When they entered, Hardy was propped comfortably on a divan.

"Well, well," beamed Warren, rubbing his hands together in satisfaction, "I do believe you're going to get better. Fit as a fiddle in a day or so, huh?" Warren chuckled. "And here's our new member. Bob, let me present Miss Julie Crown of the *Portland Globe*."

Hardy rose stiffly, not looking up. His hand was already extended when he raised his eyes to meet those of the young woman standing before him. For a moment, he stood as if paralyzed. His startled eyes saw nothing but the mass of golden hair framing an expression his senses refused to credit as possible. She was smiling at him with the interested look of a stranger meeting a man she had heard a great deal about. She extended her hand, her smile broadening to expose even white teeth enhanced by lips painted the color of frosted coral.

It was the sight of her mouth that broke the effort of control. A shudder passed visibly along Hardy's muscles. Then spasmodically retracting his hand, he stood with bowed head, his whole body shaking.

"Not as well as you thought you were, fella." Warren stepped to his friend's side, solicitously. "Ladies, why don't you come back later," he suggested meaningfully.

"Okay," agreed Hilda, "take your time getting better, Bobby. We'll wait. We're just thankful you're alive." And taking Julie's arm, Hilda left the room.

As soon as the door closed, Hardy looked up, his face ashen, his body still trembling. Warren had gotten him back on the sofa, when Hardy hissed through clenched teeth, "Get the sheik up here right now!"

Warren was surprised and puzzled. "What do you want him for? You need rest, not more company."

"Get him!" Hardy grabbed his lapels threateningly. "Now!" His eyes had a wild gleam.

"Okay! Okay!" Warren conciliated, thinking Hardy delirious.

"I'm not crazy," Hardy muttered, forgetting in his agitation to conceal his telepathic ability.

Warren rushed to the door. "Be right back," he flung over his shoulder. "Don't get excited!"

"Please come," Warren begged the sheik. "I think he's had a relapse. Delirious. Crazy. Demands to see you right now."

"What happened?" questioned Siri.

"He was feeling so well this morning that I took Miss Jenkins and Miss Crown to see him," Warren explained. "Just as I introduced him to Miss Crown, he was taken with a violent shaking. I had to send the girls away. It was then he went nuts, insisted that I get you."

"You're a fool!" Siri snarled, venting his anger irrationally on Warren, although he was at a loss to understand why he cared how Cheira treated Hardy. Long strides took him quickly to the sick man's room. Percy, half-running to keep up, was proclaiming his innocence for whatever it was the sheik seemed to be blaming him for.

At the door, Siri commanded, "Stay here until you are summoned." The door closed firmly before Warren could protest.

Hardy sat with his head in his hands, his body still shuddering sporadically.

At the sound of the sheik's entrance, he looked up pleadingly. "What am I supposed to do?"

"Are you telling me," Siri laughed mirthlessly, "that a female correspondent from—where is it? Portland—was too much for you? Granted, she is uniquely lovely, but after all, it's my understanding that you're a man of the world."

"Stop it!" Hardy fairly shouted. "I thought all the members were supposed to be so helpful. You're making fun of me."

"And myself as well." Siri's expression of sadness puzzled the young reporter. The sheik's voice softened. "Look, you're going to have to get used to this. She's liable to turn up at any time—in any guise."

"But, why?"

Siri shrugged. "Her reasons are her own. You play it her way or suffer the consequences. And you look like you've already had about all the consequences you can take for a while."

"You mean," Hardy asked incredulously, "I act like she really is a cub reporter from Portland?"

Siri nodded.

Like a test, he thought.

"Well put." Siri grinned.

"Thanks for your help," Hardy said sarcastically. His shoulders sagged. *I'll never be able to do it.*

"You have no choice, comrade," Siri answered his thought.

"Ameur said exactly the same thing." Hardy's lip curled upward despite the distress and confusion he felt.

The next afternoon, when the introduction took place again, the young journalist was able to shake the hand of his colleague. Only the sheik noticed the slight tremor that Hardy was unable to control.

They talked of Hardy's adventure. Hilda did her best to prod her friend into an admission of she knew not what. There was something he was not telling, she was sure. She failed.

At the end of an hour, Warren hustled the visitors away, admonishing lest the patient become overtired and suffer a repetition of the previous day's collapse.

Their host volunteered to escort the ladies to their quarters.

I must see you. Siri directed his thought to the girl masquerading as Julie Crown. Julie listened attentively to Hilda expound her theories of Bobby's absence.

Siri received no reply. Cursing the power that enabled her to shut him out of her thoughts, the scowl deepened on his face. Hers was the only mind that could resist his probing. *One day,* he swore, *my power will exceed hers.*

For the five days she had been at the Fort, she had given him no private word. He chafed under the humiliation that granted him no acknowledgement and struggled unremittingly with the feelings her proximity aroused. He could endure the torture no longer.

He had waited with a patience foreign to his nature, a patience that no one else in the world could expect to elicit from him. He had been filled with hope at her arrival. It was the first time she had visited the Fort. He took it as a sign that her attitude was softening.

At times, he was blind with jealousy, sure that Hardy was her only reason for coming here. The thought that she might entertain a personal feeling for the callow youth inflamed him. It was only the absurdity of the idea that permitted him a minimum of civility toward the reporter. He could even, at times, feel compassion for the struggle Hardy was having in the difficult adjustment to his new life. As usual, Cheira wasn't helping to make it any easier for him.

But now that Hardy was back, did she intend to leave without a word? He surmised that it was her intention to use the newsman as a reason for visiting New York. And he couldn't hope to detain them for more than a day or two. Hardy was almost well. If Siri was going to act, it had to be now.

Surely her visit meant more than an excuse, when there were many other guises ready to her hand. She had always avoided the Fort. Her appearance had been a shock. She must know what her being here was doing to him. Hardy wasn't alone in suffering from her methods. He would gladly have traded the subtle torture he was bearing for a concrete punishment like the stake.

He was astonished at his capacity for self-control. If only he loved her less, he would challenge her power and finally learn his chance for mastery. He wondered if she knew that he had long since ceased to fear her power. Physical possession alone had become distasteful. She must want him as much as he wanted her. Nothing less would ever satisfy him again.

It was the dominance of that desire that turned his pride to humility, his impatience to endurance. But, God, he could not let this opportunity pass without seeking a chance to at least determine the trend of her feelings. Even if she despised him still, he had to know.

His thought was interrupted when, seemingly by accident, she brushed against his hand. The pain shooting up his arm would have felled a lesser man. He winced, bowing his head slightly in submission to the reprimand.

Hilda chatted on unaware that anything unusual had happened. The proximity of the handsome desert man provoked in her a coquettishness for which she would soundly denounce herself later.

At the moment, however, as soon as the sheik departed, she was unable to resist voicing her feelings. "Don't you think he's the most handsome man you've ever met?"

"Possibly," Julie said, showing little interest.

"But he's so wicked," Hilda confessed, warming to the subject. "Do you know he has a harem?" she confided, watching to see if she was shocking the girl from the West.

"Really!" Julie commented. "How do you know?"

Satisfied that she held the girl's interest, Hilda continued conspiratorially. "He had them dance for us before you came. It was positively degrading the way those women threw themselves at his feet. It was the worst spectacle I've ever seen—and I've seen a lot. Even the European girls—two of them are, you know. The blonde hair is a dead giveaway. You'd think that they, at least, would have more pride."

"Maybe they're afraid," Julie offered tonelessly.

"You could be right," Hilda conceded. "I did notice expressions that might have been fear on their faces. But the motions they went through . . . anyway, he ignored them."

"Are you sure?" Julie showed the first sign of real interest.

"Of course!" Hilda asserted. "I could tell by the bewildered yet relieved looks on their faces. I suppose they have mixed emotions. He's so handsome, yet he can be so cruel."

"What makes you think that?" Julie questioned.

"One morning," Hilda explained, "in fact, the morning after we arrived—I saw him have a man beaten unconscious. I've never found out why. I guess I was afraid to mention it."

"The man may have deserved it," Julie said. Hilda failed to notice Julie's surprise at the statement that had popped out involuntarily.

Hilda frowned. "Possibly. He's been so nice to us."

"Hmm . . . yes." Julie nodded, reaching for a scarf to wrap, mantilla-like around her head. "I think I'll take a walk in the courtyard before dinner. It's so lovely this time of day." Abruptly, she decided to see Siri.

"Go along, dear." Hilda agreed. "I'm for a nap."

Siri joined her on the steps of the old stone fort. She ignored his presence until, strolling down the long avenue that led to the main gate, she stopped to watch some of the tribal children playing in the sand.

66

"So beautiful," she murmured. "Perhaps the reason for agelessness is that without creation, destruction is meaningless. Our existence is outside the order of things. We are nothing."

She turned to look at him for the first time. Julie Crown was momentarily forgotten. Cheira stood before him. The sadness in her eyes, tears glistening on her long lashes, startled the man beside her. He had never seen her in such a mood.

Impulsively he raised his hand to touch her. She recoiled instinctively, a look of fear flickering for an instant in her eyes before she could control it.

Imperiously, she turned to resume her walk, failing to note the expression of remorse her action produced in her companion.

"You wanted this meeting to plead for Hardy?" Her usually sweet voice heavy with sarcasm made him wince. "Have you learned pity at last or is it his manhood you wish to protect?"

Her words contorted his face more than any physical pain she might choose to inflict could ever do.

"I only wished for a moment alone with you," he said, his voice self-deprecating in a tone only Cheira had ever heard.

"Well?" she threw back at him, her voice cold.

"The years are endless without a moment in your presence." All trace of the usual arrogance was obliterated as he walked humbly beside her, betraying the love he felt by the tone of his voice. But Cheira didn't hear.

"You seek the opportunity to test your power perhaps?" she asked sharply, dismissing the implication of his explanation.

"Never against you. I swear it," he protested, wondering why he should foolishly have considered her ignorant of his determination to become the most powerful man in the association.

They had reached the huge iron gates set into the stone of the bulwark. The blocks were warm when Cheira put her hand on the wall. In an attitude of daydreaming, she wondered idly if the men, almost two centuries dead, had placed these stones about the same time she herself had been given shelter by Wang Lu.

Leaning with her back against the rough-hewn stone, she gazed out onto the sand stretching endlessly toward the horizon. *Am I as eternal and as barren as the rocks and the sand?* she wondered sadly, remembering the children in the courtyard.

Siri, standing silently beside her, gazed—for once freely—on the only woman he had ever loved. His throat constricted painfully at the sight of the slightly parted lips and the gentle rise and fall of her breasts synchronized with the even breathing. His hands clenched at his sides as his body remembered.

Cheira sighed. Lost in her own thoughts, she paid no attention to her silent escort. Unable to penetrate the barrier of her mind, he could not guess the line of thought that had prompted her statement. He would like to think her remark meant that her attitude toward him was softening, but her subsequent reaction made that seem unlikely.

The questions returned to nag him: Why was she here now? Was Hardy so important to her that she had come to the Fort—the once place she had avoided all these years—to be with him? Or had she come to challenge his power? She knew what he was doing. Did she have some way to assess his increasing ability? He had seen the flicker of fear in her eyes, although she suppressed it immediately. Whatever her reasons, he decided he must accept the fact of her hatred for him. That much was obvious—too obvious to doubt.

Now, turning back the way she had come, Cheira resumed her usual behavior.

"I will require the use of your study at midnight," she said, her voice soft, but imperious, "to grant Hardy an audience. See that he's there."

The sheik, shaken from his mood abruptly, reacted with flaming jealousy. "Am I to provide accommodations for another man's tryst?" His control vanished; his voice was a growl of frustration.

Cheira swung round to face him, her eyes blazing. "Do you still think yourself the master of my actions?" she challenged him. Their eyes locked for an instant, then Siri turned and stalked away.

That night, Hardy joined the others for dinner—the first time since his adventure. He was able to participate in the polite conversation without betraying the emotion that raged inside him. Percy and Hilda were pleased to note traces of his old gay self.

Hilda observed with satisfaction how often he glanced at Julie. Her matchmaking instinct leaped to the fore. *How romantic,* she thought, *the simple country girl captures the heart of Gotham's most eligible bachelor.* At that moment, she began to contrive a strategy.

The sheik invited his guests to an evening of entertainment in honor of the newly restored member of the party. Hardy alone seemed to notice the hard gleam in his eyes, but try as he would he could not penetrate the sheik's thoughts.

The young reporter was horrified at his host's audacity in inviting

Cheira into his harem. *Would the sheik dare,* he wondered, *let the women dance?*

He worried unnecessarily, however, because Miss Crown declined to attend, pleading a headache. Hilda was grateful for the excuse. She would keep Julie company, she told their host, happy to absent herself in view of her past experiences that, in retrospect, had become an ordeal.

Much later, under cover of the music, Siri told Hardy, "At midnight Ahmed will conduct you to a meeting with Cheira. Be ready!"

Hardy stepped into the room and made an obeisance—this time, eagerly. Now his only desire was to obey her. All doubt as to the reality of the situation was obliterated from his mind. He accepted her control over his future unquestioningly and no longer rebelled at the thought that she would never return his love.

"You have conducted yourself well this evening." Her voice floated to him from across the room.

He was happy to have pleased her at last, but the highly trained, inquisitive mind of the reporter doubted that she had called him here for that reason.

"My reason," she answered his thought, "is to encourage you to continue that conduct when we return to New York."

His heart began to pound painfully as the meaning of the plural pronoun sank into his mind.

"Go with Ahmed now," she interrupted his thought. "Follow him and submit to the ministrations of Haji."

Puzzled, he obeyed. Ahmed led him out of the building, across the courtyard, and into a low shelter, which leaned tiredly against the stone of the rampart. Inside an old man sat at a table, the only light being laboriously cast by an exhausted candle sputtering in a dish nailed to the wall. Hardy remembered seeing the old man the morning after his first arrival at the Fort.

The ancient one motioned Hardy to be seated on a low stool beside the table. It was only then that the reporter noted the array of needles and ink set out neatly on an immaculate white cloth. Unceremoniously, his burnoose was slit with a sharp knife to bare his right shoulder. Working swiftly and skillfully, the old man had completed the minute symbol in just a matter of minutes.

Without having uttered a word, he shoved Hardy out the door, closing it firmly. Ahmed was waiting, with a hooded lantern, to light his master's guest back to his own quarters. The whole operation had taken so little time that Hardy was back in his room before he had time to wonder about the meaning and purpose of the tattoo.

CHAPTER VI

It was decided that the adventurers would terminate their sojourn via the supply plane due the following day. The fruitless search was over, they all agreed. Warren voiced the hope that it was the last they'd hear of the "phantom princess of the Sahara."

Hilda was anxious to return to New York to continue her matchmaking without the proximity of the handsome sheik, whom she considered a constant threat. *An innocent girl like Julie could be swept off her feet if their knowledgeable host decided to charm her,* Hilda mused.

Hardy was made to promise that he would discard his romantic notions permanently and begin to appreciate the joys of reality. The promise was duly made to his two friends in all sincerity by the young journalist.

The party bade their host a reluctant farewell. The sheik, with his always irreproachable manners, gave them repeated assurance that they were welcome at any time.

Hilda was thrilled when he kissed her hand. Only Hardy was aware of the communication when the sheik repeated the courtly gesture with Julie. The young man cursed his inability to use his new power and vowed to remedy the situation as quickly as possible.

Go to London, Cheira telepathized. *John has a matter of utmost importance to discuss with you.*

The sheik turned to Hardy to shake hands. When their eyes met, Siri noted the look of frustration. *Increase your power if you don't want to miss anything.* Siri's eyes twinkled as he sent the thought. Aloud he said, "Goodbye, old chap. Don't remember the desert too harshly."

"It's been the greatest experience of my life," replied Hardy sincerely.

For the first hour after takeoff, Hilda took advantage of the opportunity to appropriate Julie's undivided attention. She was lavish in her praise of the virtues of "dear Bobby," as she was fond of calling Hardy.

"He's the most eligible bachelor on the entire continent," Hilda exaggerated. "And I've never seen him so attentive to any woman as he has been to you. Why, he never takes his eyes off you."

Julie murmured noncommittally something about her work being her major interest.

"Don't be foolish!" Hilda brushed away her reason impatiently. "You have the whole world before you. Bobby will be the leader of the profession in a few years. You'd be the envy of every girl on the East Coast. I can name several right now who would give anything to get as much attention from him as you do.

"And look how handsome he is," Hilda pushed her case with every lure she could think of. "I do believe he looks even better since his ordeal in the desert."

Julie glanced politely in the direction of the young man under discussion.

"Come on!" said Hilda, rising. "You just sit with Bobby for a while. You really haven't had a chance to get acquainted. I'll get Percy to make some drinks. We'll be in Paris soon and that calls for a celebration."

Hilda dragged Percy out of the seat next to Hardy's and deposited Julie in the vacated chair. She sailed off with Percy in tow, deaf to his protestations.

"Sit down." Julie laughed at the young journalist standing stiffly beside her seat. "Did you follow the conversation?"

Hardy flushed, shaking his head. "I'm sorry. I can't seem to manage it yet. While Percy was talking, I couldn't concentrate."

"Your skill will improve with practice," she reassured him, her manner kinder and less haughty than at any previous time. "It seems Hilda has made up her mind to strike a match between New York's most eligible bachelor and the innocent little girl from Portland. She's very determined. She's spent the last hour trying her darnedest to brainwash me.

"No," she answered his thought, "I'm not angry . . . only amused."

Hardy relaxed, the look of apprehension leaving his face. He liked Hilda and didn't wish to see her suffer because she had ignorantly blundered into a situation beyond her comprehension.

"I'm not such a monster as you seem to think," Cheira said in a low voice. "Only those who are mine ever suffer from my displeasure." Laughing quietly at his look of consternation, she continued, "You don't wish to disappoint Hilda, do you? It will give me an excuse for lingering in New York while I visit a few of our too-long neglected members."

"How can I pretend such a role?" he asked, his eyes pleading.

72

"It will be good for your soul," she answered, with a tinge of irony, just as Hilda was returning with a tray.

Hilda, misunderstanding the look of pained confusion on Hardy's face, beamed, congratulating herself with the progress of her plan.

In Paris, the travelers' first duty, as always with people of their calling, was to file their stories. Over Hilda's halfhearted objections, but to her inner satisfaction, Hardy insisted that Julie report through his office. He thought to forestall an embarrassing situation for her.

To his surprise, however, she seated herself at the typewriter and, two hours later, handed him copy that even the most meticulous editor would be proud to print.

"How did you learn this?" Hardy asked, astonished.

She shrugged. "One learns a lot in a couple of centuries."

"I'll never be able to understand." He shook his head hopelessly.

"Fortunately, understanding doesn't seem to be one of the requirements," she told him ruefully, remembering how many years she had spent exploring the facets of her condition. "How much satisfaction you obtain from your state is up to you." She placed her hand on his arm to encourage him.

Hardy trembled uncontrollably at her touch. He tried hard not to pull away.

"One of the first things you must learn, if you are to succeed in this new life," she instructed kindly, noticing the reaction, "is to live your particular role. Right now, we're going to oblige Hilda for a few days, remember?"

Hardy closed his eyes, a groan escaping his lips.

Julie chose to ignore his reaction. "It's time to meet Hilda and Percy for dinner," she said, preparing to leave.

Hilda was very pleased as she took note of "dear Bobby's" behavior at dinner. He was tense, unable to concentrate, and had a feverish gleam in his eye. Progress was more rapid than she had dared hope, she decided. On impulse, she suggested adjourning to one of those intimate little clubs for dancing.

"How delightful!" Julie, with a little tinkling laugh, seconded her suggestion.

Percy claimed Julie for the first dance. Hilda danced with Hardy.

"You look like you could kill Percy, darling," she chided.

73

"I'm sorry, Hilda. What did you say?" He frowned in an effort to listen to her.

"Never mind, dear," she said. "It wasn't important."

"Hilda"—Hardy seemed to have decided to confide in her—"do you believe in fate? I mean, do you think that our lives are predestined from birth?" He hesitated. ". . . And loves, also."

"Don't try to analyze love, dear."

"But can a person be in love even before the loved one is known?" Hardy persisted.

"You're being too serious, darling." Hilda evaded the question. "If it happens, it happens. Time doesn't matter." She was beginning to understand why Bobby had never fallen in love before. At least, when love came—and she was sure it had—her favorite protégé had fallen in love with a nice, wholesome girl. Hilda resolved the question the way she thought best. At the beginning of the next dance, she took Julie's hand and put it in Hardy's in a deliberately dramatic manner. Then she laughed nervously, doubting the wisdom of her boldness when Hardy glared at her.

The young reporter, fighting to control the trembling of his limbs, led Julie onto the floor when she eagerly accepted Hilda's prompting.

"You're a terrible actor," she whispered, nestling against him, responding naturally to the slow, intimate tune. "Haven't you realized that the biggest advantage of being the way we are is that we can experience everything? And," she added, grinning impishly, "more intensely than ordinary people." She slid her fingers up to his shoulder, her fingertips just touching the skin above his collar. A tingling sensation began at the roots of his hair, spreading rapidly along his nerves. His body relaxed, surrendering to the pleasurable sensation. A picture of Ching Li that day at Arx Vetus when she had alleviated his suffering flashed into his mind. "My power is small," the girl had apologized then. He was painfully certain of the immense power of his partner now.

"Oh, my God! Please don't!" he groaned.

She laughed softly and stepped away. Returning to the table, she asked Hilda, "Do you mind if we go back to the hotel? Suddenly, I'm awfully tired."

Relieved, Hardy felt grateful and guilty at the same time.

The next afternoon Sam met them at the airport in New York. Hardy watched him carefully but could not detect by any word or glance that Sam knew Miss Crown to be other than a cub reporter from Oregon. In fact, he gave most of his attention to Warren, who was not only the senior member of the group but also the only one on Hackett's staff. Julie seemed perfectly satisfied at being treated as a neophyte, remaining unobtrusively in the background, speaking only when spoken to. Hardy was plunged into confusion. Again the doubt assailed him as to the reality of his experience. He wondered if he were delirious.

After they had dropped Warren at his apartment and left Hilda to make their visiting colleague comfortable—a task she insisted upon—Hardy demanded of Sam, "Do you know what really happened out there?"

"Of course," the older man chuckled. "You got lost in the desert for a week." At the look of dismay on Hardy's face, Sam laughed. "You've had a rough time of it. My advice is a hot shower and twenty-four hours in your own bed."

"Don't evade the question." Hardy was irritated, his experiences still too fresh to appreciate the editor's levity. "Do you know who she really is?"

"Yes," Sam answered, sobering.

"Then you're a damn good actor." Hardy exhaled sharply, sinking back against the seat of the taxi.

"I've been at it a long time," Sam explained. "I've seen her in many guises. Some much more surprising than this one. And also at Arx Vetus. There alone is the pretense entirely absent." His usual gruff tone softened. "But always, her coming is like the first rays of the morning sun heralding a bright new day. Her presence is the personification of our reason for being. We owe her our lives. It's by her power that we live." Sam paused, looking sharply at the young man. "Bob, do you have any idea how old I am?"

"Three months ago, I would have said fifty. But now, I don't know."

Sam grinned. "In 1860, I was a reporter for the *Atlantean* down in Georgia. I had already worked there for twenty years. Ed Peterson, who was my partner, is just a few years younger."

Hardy's eyes widened in disbelief, but his interest quickened.

Sam continued. "You aren't old enough yet to understand; and maybe you never will because you won't have to experience it—but look around you. Most men spend fifty years making a life for themselves, acquiring some sort of security so they can enjoy a little leisure. However, they discover too late that their best years are already spent. Their bodies are deteriorating rapidly and they have nothing to look forward to except senility and death.

"Conversely, look at what I have had. I went out to Australia around the turn of the century. The country was just beginning to open up. I went to work for Tony Hammond, prospecting for whatever minerals might be there. Ed Peterson, who's always game for adventure, came out a year or so later. We found some of the first gold ever shipped out of that country. It was a hard life, but ours were charmed, so we enjoyed every minute of it. We got back into newspaper work during the war.

"In a few years, I'll have to leave here, but I already know what I want to do. I'm going to slip off to some secluded place, like some island in the Pacific, and write history. I've seen things that will never be recorded otherwise.

"So you see, life can be pleasant and rewarding. When you're physically vigorous and mentally sound, you can do anything. And we owe it all to Cheira."

Hardy sat up. "You love her," he accused.

"Is that so surprising?" Sam countered. "We all do—each in his own way. Where do you draw the line between love and gratitude? If you can make a definite distinction, you're more astute than most of us."

Hardy grimaced, his own turbulent emotions demanding that he concede the point. He did not, however, apply Sam's observation to himself.

Resuming his normal tone, Sam asked, "Did she say how long she'd be here? The others are waiting to know."

"Two or three days, at least. Hilda has a romance concocted. Cheira wants to use that as an excuse." Hardy shook his head dubiously. He paused, then added, "She's already accused me of being a poor actor. I'll never be able to pull it off."

"Sure you will." Sam was reassuring. "We've all gone through this at one time or another. Besides, there's hardly any way to botch it. No one would believe you if you tried to tell them the truth anyway."

"I guess you're right," Hardy replied. "I can hardly believe it myself. But you spoke of others. Very many?"

"About a hundred here in the city," Sam informed him. "A thousand around the country."

"And they all have these powers?"

"Yes, in varying degrees, depending on how long they have enjoyed the condition. How much power one develops depends also on the individual's innate ability to concentrate and how much time one is willing to spend practicing. Cheira doesn't have anything to do with that. In fact, she has little to do with our daily lives. Except in a situation like this, we rarely see her. As mature, intelligent men we live our lives as we see fit."

The enormity of the experience made Hardy feel weak.

"Will you help me?" he asked, humbly.

"We'll all help you," Sam averred. "You're very welcome among us." Putting his hand on the young man's shoulder, Sam grinned broadly. "Now will you come to work for me?"

"You bet!" Hardy responded.

Back in his apartment after almost three months, Hardy savored the change that had taken place within himself. Surveying with satisfaction his personal premises, he realized this was the first time he had been entirely alone since he locked his door to begin the adventure of his life. That it had been successful beyond his wildest dreams there was no doubt.

Sprawled on the big oval bed, the young journalist grinned wryly. Reality had made a mockery of his puny imagination. He had dreamed of finding a woman, beautiful beyond description, but pagan and primitive. His coming was to change her life, to sweep her into the modern world, and to watch benevolently as she discovered the wonders of the twentieth century—and as it discovered her. He imagined the envy of his contemporaries as he paraded her through the most exclusive salons, her blooming naivete the quality that all modern women had lost somewhere in their childhood without even understanding that a precious attitude toward life had vanished.

Though early afternoon, Hardy fell into a sound sleep. A long time later, he dreamed: a single perfect rose drifted against a background of clouds, its fragrance so heady as to be almost unbearable. He felt an encompassing desire to grasp and possess the exquisite blossom. He hungered to own its beauty, to know the ecstasy of it, to be fulfilled by it. Reaching upward to catch the stem as it hovered just above his head, his fingers closed tightly—on the razor-sharp thorns. The excruciating pain shot along his arm, pervading his chest. He gasped, dragging his hand away. The warmth of something sticky prompted him to open his clenched fist. He exhaled sharply, horrified. His palm was covered with blood.

A quick, involuntary contraction of muscles caused the sleeper to roll over. The hand that had been crushed against his belt buckle as he lay on his stomach showed a dent from the prong. The image in his mind faded and the exhausted adventurer continued sleeping, undisturbed.

77

CHAPTER VII

About midnight, Dr. James Connors still sat in his office, going over the results of the tests completed the previous day. Several times he passed his hand across his eyes, but was too absorbed to break his concentration.

The research laboratory that he headed was famous for its experiments in preventive medicine. The case holding his immediate attention was a study of 450 inhabitants of an isolated Maine farming community whom he and his colleagues had succeeded in keeping disease free and without physical malfunction for a decade. He was trying to determine how long the condition could be maintained. How much of the experiment's success had to be attributed to luck and to the cooperation of the people? He felt that the isolation would have to be maintained for at least another decade before any scientific conclusions could be drawn. The natural hardiness of the people was a factor not to be overlooked.

Two problems had arisen recently. While there had not been a death in the village since the inception of the study, the oldest resident was now ninety-six. He was aging very slowly, less than half as fast as considered normal. He had good health and was still able to support himself. Connors smiled, remembering the old man's insistence on chopping his own wood for winter, irascibly refusing his neighbor's help.

The researcher puzzled over the manner of this man's death. Did a body die just from old age or would some unforeseen anomaly hasten the end? Did Connors dare increase the old man's hormonal dosage? He frowned. The lab had failed to devise conclusive tests that could be used on animals. However, it was a decision that could not be postponed too long. He made a note to speak to his chief assistant. Perhaps together they could discover something that had been overlooked.

To further complicate the problem, the villagers were about to place the whole program in jeopardy. Envying the prosperity of their neighboring villages from the tourist trade, they were growing more and more restive at the confinement. Ever since Harry Pritchett got himself elected mayor last year, he'd been filling the people's heads with visions of affluence, telling them what a perfect ski resort Mountain Oval would make. Without the help of the more conservative oldsters, the project would have blown sky-high before this.

If those proud fools could only be convinced to take compensation for their participation in the experiment, they could have everything their neighbors enjoyed and more. The institution was well endowed and the money had been offered repeatedly. But none of them would accept a penny. All the lecturing he had done seemed to give them no conception of the importance of the program. They persisted in viewing it as free medical care, which their rigid moral standards just grudgingly allowed them to accept.

Superstitiously, they had begun to believe that the medical skill, which had kept them healthy for so long, could continue to protect them against the influx of numberless gangs of disease-ridden humanity.

He resisted rigorously the idea of abandoning the experiment. *Maybe the two problems could solve each other,* he thought. *If I can keep the old man alive and vigorous, I can pressure the people into prolonging the isolation. I'd have a concrete example of the experiment's worth.*

"Does your work never allow you to rest, Doctor?" a soft voice whispered at his shoulder.

Connors looked up, annoyed, unsure of what had disturbed him. Purposely, he used the late night hours as the one time he could work without interruption.

"Am I really so unwelcome?" the voice questioned.

Connors eyes widened in disbelief at the sight of the woman standing beside his chair. His expression changed to one of pleasure and welcome as recognition dawned. She smiled.

Gathering her hands to his lips, he knelt before her.

"Cheira, mistress." The words were formed against her palm. "So long, so long."

"Your concentration is admirable," she commented, but the tone of her voice was more critical than extolling.

"It's my work," he answered, the inflection in her voice easily interpreted by his knowledge of her character. "What you sent me to do."

"But I didn't ask you to work without rest," she stated, defensively. "Your associates have told Sam that you spend more nights than not going over the details of all the experiments conducted here, doing work that could be easily delegated to someone else."

"What else have I to do?" he murmured, his voice husky.

"You have been missed at Arx Vetus, too," she added with just a hint of irritation, lifting her hands so he would rise.

"Of what use," he retorted bitterly. "You are never there . . . for me."

Silently, she turned away, confirming his statement. He could not know her thoughts, or see the flicker of fear in her eyes.

Sighing, but accepting the rejection that was now only a familiar emptiness, replacing the aching despair once endured, he led her to the sofa he kept in his office for the many nights he worked till dawn. *It was so long ago,* he thought, dropping to the floor to sit at her feet.

Wisely, she steered him back to the present, postponing the concern that had brought her here. "Tell me about your experiment in Maine. The report Ameur showed me sounded very exciting. I'd like to hear more."

His expression returned to its normally preoccupied frown as his mind recovered the details of the project, which absorbed all his waking hours. He explained how the villagers had been totally quarantined for a year before the actual experiment began. During that time, extensive tests were compiled, as well as a comprehensive medical profile for each individual. Since then, they had been allowed limited freedom to come and go as long as they submitted to thorough examinations before reentering the village. At first, they received massive doses of the endocrine extract by injection. (She already knew how many years it had taken to synthesize the elusive hormone and then to produce it in sufficient amounts.)

Cheira noted the medical man's increasing enthusiasm with satisfaction. She relaxed, allowing her interest to devolve onto his words. She had her own reasons for wanting to know the outcome of this particular experiment.

"At present," he continued, "the health of the villagers is maintained by diet control, annual examination, and the hormone extract in pill form."

"Would it help Wang Lu?" she interrupted.

"I don't know." He shook his head helplessly. "He won't let me try it. Perhaps you could persuade him?"

"No." she objected, "You know he has my promise. He must be allowed to go his own way. I just thought maybe he would agree. But suppose there were others? You know about Mott's experiments in London?"

He nodded.

"If one of us were to return to the status of ordinary humans, would the same regimen have similar results?"

"I think so," he answered, thoughtfully. "If the restrictions were put into effect immediately after the change had taken place, the same results should occur."

"Then the only aspect of ordinary life that we would be subject to is aging?"

"Yes," he replied regretfully. "I'm afraid we have a long way to go before we can do more than retard that."

The implication of her questions leaped into his mind like a flash. "Are you saying that I may begin such an experiment?" He jumped to his feet excitedly.

She laughed softly. It was his boyish enthusiasm, along with an aesthetic quality and his innate gentleness, that had always appealed to her. It lent a note of incongruity to the character of an exceptionally brilliant scientist. It had taken her a long time to discover why she had rejected him and longer still before she realized how much she had hurt him.

"All I am saying"—she brought her thoughts back to the present with an effort—"is that you may set up the preliminary project so you will be ready when the time comes."

"What an idea!" he responded, pacing up and down the open space between the oversized mahogany desk and the couch. The small office seemed too confining now and his thoughts strayed momentarily to wishing he had succumbed to the suggestion of the directors when they had offered him a bigger office—more suitable to his position, they had said.

Without pause, his thoughts jumped back to the proposed experiment, racing so far ahead of possible speech that he simply allowed her to follow, enjoying the effortless means of communication, which was so seldom his privilege to use, working as he did exclusively with ordinary humans. A million details spilled out of his mind, methods, controls, possible subjects.

It was not until after she had gone and the first flush of excitement for a new project—felt only by a dedicated professional—had subsided that he realized her whole visit had been spent talking about the experiment.

He cursed softly as the vision of her arose in his imagination. She had been dressed in the customary manner of Arx Vetus, her exquisite loveliness only partially concealed by the loose folds of the garment. In retrospect, he felt the soft material as it brushed against his cheek and his lips recalled the warm satiny texture of her skin.

What unrealized inadequacy did he possess that had made her finally reject his love? She had wavered on the point of surrender for months, then suddenly had sent him away.

Those months. He had been blind with happiness. He remembered the day they walked in the garden at Arx Vetus. One of the infrequent rainstorms had suppressed the usually suffocating heat. The air held a freshness indigenous to a tropic island and all the vegetation was responding enthusiastically. Their blooming was almost visible. The flowers smiled with the voluptuousness of life. They complemented his own joy. Catching her hand, he ran with her across the damp grass, swinging her into his arms when they reached the privacy of the arbor; her laughter swelled his heart.

He never learned how Siri happened to be there. He saw only the black eyes flashing with intransigent hatred and felt the sheik's fist ramming into the side of his head. There was no time to defend himself. He staggered from the force of the blow.

Cheira acted before he could recover. She leaped at his assailant, screaming with indignation. He had never seen such a display of unleashed power. Siri fell to the ground writhing from the pain of the grasp, strangling his will and paralyzing his muscles.

"Get out of my sight," she spat at the prostrate man when she finally loosened the grip on his shoulder. The revulsion on her face was unmistakable.

The joy of that moment before Siri appeared was never repeated. For weeks she avoided him. He felt again the hurt and confusion. A shudder passed through him. At last, she summoned him to a formal audience, handing him the assignment that made him a researcher at an important laboratory in the States. At any other time, it would have been the answer to a lifelong dream. But the cold, impersonal way she looked at him turned it into a nightmare.

It was weeks before the numbness subsided and he could think clearly; and many painful years passed before his love was reduced to a bearable aching throb. He had learned to live with the hopeless memory much as one can learn to live without an arm or a leg. He survived only because he could not bear to leave the world she lived in, managing to use his work to drug the unwanted emotion.

Connors stopped his thoughts, shaking his head in self-disgust. What profit was there in reliving that long-past episode?

"Stop wallowing in self-pity," he said aloud. The words seemed to hang in the air long after they were spoken, mocking him. Squaring his shoulders, he summoned the discipline that had become second nature, so much so that he was unaware of the energy he continually expended on the suppression.

Obediently, his mind turned back to the project. It was not until the sounds of the staff beginning a new day's work reached his ears that he noticed the sunlight streaming in the window. He realized then that he had spent the night pacing the cramped space.

Two hours later the laboratory was alive with new instructions issuing forth unremittingly from the office of the chief.

He frowned with irritation when the desk buzzer persisted. Flicking the switch, his voice harsh from exhaustion, he barked, "What?"

"There's a Miss Crown on the line, Dr. Connors," his secretary explained apologetically. "She says she's a reporter from Portland, Oregon."

He felt his annoyance increasing. "Why bother me?" he snapped. "You should know by now how to handle the media."

"She insisted that I relay a message," the secretary explained, puzzled. "She said to tell you that you have her ring."

Dr. Connor's brow smoothed and the corners of his eyes wrinkled with the semblance of a smile. But the shape of his mouth betrayed sadness.

"Put her on," he instructed to the astonishment of the woman in the outer office. She had never heard that tone in her employer's voice.

"Good morning."

He recognized the voice that held the power to make his breath catch in his throat.

"Are all researchers so busy that their minds are impenetrable?"

"I'm sorry," he answered. "I've been preoccupied with a new experiment."

"Has your secretary introduced me properly?"

"She said something about a reporter," he replied lamely, trying to recall the information.

"Exactly," the voice affirmed. "My name is Julie Crown, correspondent for the *Portland Globe*. I'm visiting New York. Some colleagues of mine refuse to believe that the famous Dr. James Connors would grant an interview. He's practically a recluse, they say. His only loves are his guinea pigs. Are they correct?"

"Not quite." With an effort, he matched her bantering tone. "Rumor has it that there is an old, unrequited love somewhere in his past. It explains why he's so temperamental—a bad trait in a scientist."

"Imagine that!" she gasped, pretending astonishment. "What a scoop for a cub reporter. Will you come for an interview, then, Doctor?"

"Anytime," he answered without hesitation. "It is my firm belief that neophytes should be encouraged."

"That's very good of you, Doctor." She laughed.

The melodious quality of her laughter constricted his heart, making it agony for him to continue the light interchange.

"Will you meet us for dinner at the Four Horsemen at eight?"

"All right," he agreed and she hung up.

He took only a second to note the time and place in his appointment pad before he plunged back into his previous absorption in the new experiment, forcing the unwanted—because hopeless—emotion into quiescence.

In New York, Julie was just turning away from the phone when it rang.

"I took a chance that a call might be included as part of the role," she heard Hardy say, timidly.

"Why, yes, it is," she answered pleasantly. "You may even escort me to Sam's office. I have an appointment right after lunch."

"May I take you to lunch!" the amateur actor asked, hopefully.

"Of course, Bobby! You've been reading the script carefully, I see." The tinge of sarcasm in her voice made him wince. "Eleven-thirty." She hung up without waiting for an answer.

Cheira stood frowning at the phone for a moment, then laughed. She was thinking, *Even with the power of telepathy, I still had to use the phone twice this morning.*

Hardy knocked on the door of the hotel suite. It was exactly two hours since he had spoken to Miss Julie Crown on the phone. He had spent the interval instructing himself in the art of self-control. By the time he handed over his car to the doorman, he was convinced that the excitement he felt was what any man would feel who was about to escort a beautiful woman to lunch. But when he stood before the door, his resolve cracked. His body began to tremble. Rocking back on his heels, hoping the movement would relieve the tension, he waited.

"Good morning, Mr. Hardy." Ching Li surprised him by opening the door. "Miss Crown will be ready in a moment."

"What are you doing here?" Hardy blurted out.

"I'm very fortunate," she answered, "in having been permitted to accompany Miss Crown here. I dearly love New York. It has been many years since I have been privileged to visit. I have many relatives and friends here," she added shyly.

Julie came, smiling, into the foyer. "I'll be back before dinner," she said to Ching Li. She turned to Hardy and took his arm. "Shall we go?"

Fighting desperately to control his shaking, which had returned full force with her proximity, Hardy concentrated on the appropriate movement. He struggled with his thoughts, trying to decide how to ask her where she preferred to lunch.

"The Tea Garden," she said, solving his dilemma.

Hardy started the car and pulled into the traffic, flushing violently, afraid to think at all, lest his thoughts betray him.

"You must be the most unhappy member of our organization, Bobby," she said, laying her hand on his arm. It was the first hint she had given that she understood his struggle.

Why am I finding the change I wanted so desperately so difficult to achieve? he wondered. Hardy felt his throat contract with emotion. No words were possible. He concentrated on negotiating the heavy lunch-hour traffic.

Once in the Chinese restaurant, Hardy cursed under his breath for not thinking about the impossibility of getting served at that hour. The waiting line was ridiculously long.

The first time she trusts me to do something for her, I fail, he thought, then mentally winced, as he remembered her telepathic power.

She was standing quietly, unruffled by the jostling crowd. Just as Hardy was about to suggest they go elsewhere, a waiter approached. Bowing, he asked them to follow.

To Hardy's surprised relief, they were ushered into a small superbly furnished room, decorated like an ancient oriental pagoda. The waiter showed them to a table in a small alcove.

Hardy was just congratulating himself on the luck that rescued him from a tight spot when he noticed his companion's preoccupation. It was only by focused attention that Hardy discovered the powerful, angry thoughts being sent to someone outside the room. The young reporter quavered in sympathy for the unseen recipient of Cheira's displeasure.

I will not discuss the matter further, Wang Lu! Her thought was so powerful that Hardy winced. Then to his astonishment, he saw tears glistening on her long lashes as she sank back against her chair in an attitude of despair.

"Wang Lu, Wang Lu," she murmured aloud, a tear coursing its way unheeded down her cheek as she pictured in her mind the ancient Chinese owner of this famous restaurant who resided in seclusion on the premises. Unknown now to all but a few, he had served Cheira for over a century. Fifty years ago, he had returned to the mortal state that he might eventually join his ancestors in death. His desired goal, however, was to be long sought. With Cheira's reluctant permission, he had absented himself from Arx Vetus and her sustaining presence. Slowly, his power had begun to fade, except his ability of thought transference, which clung stubbornly to his otherwise aging body. Apparently, he was not to be afforded the comfort of mental senility. Cheira had never allowed any other member to follow Wang Lu.

Brushing aside the tears impatiently with the back of her hand, Cheira's eyes took on the hard gleam of anger. *Ching Li will not follow her father in untested experiments.* The message shot out of the room to its unseen target.

Without a backward look, lunch forgotten, Cheira stalked out of the restaurant. Hardy couldn't help wondering why the object of her anger was spared her vengeance. Intuitively, the newsman understood that it was not Julie Crown who sat silently beside him in the car traversing the short distance to Sam's office. Fear, he admitted, condemning himself for a coward, made him respect her silence. A vision of his ordeal at Arx Vetus was still too vivid in his mind for him to wish to transfer any of her anger to himself, although the curiosity of the reporter tempted him to brave the emotion that hung over her like a cloud.

She was still angry when they entered Sam's office. Hardy was in for another surprise as he witnessed the editor's greeting.

"My dear," Sam took both her hands in his, kissing her cheek affectionately. "I've been counting the minutes till you came." Leading her gently to a chair, he continued in a conciliatory manner, evidently aware of what had just transpired. "Don't be angry with Wang Lu. He is still your loyal, loving slave."

"The old man's a fool." She vehemently spat out the words. "He presumes to tell me what not to do. Then, when he can't change my mind, he offers his own daughter to take my place."

"What better proof of his love?" Sam's voice was still patient and gentle.

She looked up at him as he sat perched on the end of his desk. "You agree with him," she accused, understanding dawning in her eyes. "I suppose you are all united against me and have delegated Wang Lu to speak for you."

Sam guiltily dropped his gaze.

A moment longer she was angry, then her face cleared and she laughed. "You are all cowards hiding behind an old man."

Sam, not able to deny her accusation, answered defensively, "Your safety concerns us deeply."

"I suppose John has alerted the entire organization?"

"Yes. Did you think he would not?"

Hardy waited silently in the background. He couldn't make any sense out of what was transpiring. Resentfully, he felt like a new boy at school. Conversely, however, he was glad to be left out of whatever had caused Cheira's anger.

"Enough!" She dismissed the subject with a wave of her hand.

Sam acquiesced. But Wang Lu was not the only self-delegated member with an unpleasant task. The newsman squared his shoulders to withstand another onslaught. "Stuart Mervin begs for reassignment or, if it would please you, permission to withdraw from the society. He cannot continue much longer in his present state."

"My stay in New York is supposed to be pleasant," she stated, ignoring the statement.

Sam's long acquaintance with Cheira enabled him to decipher the true meaning behind her words. He could be of no help to his friend nor could he dissuade her from the insane course she intended to take.

"Well!" Sam took the cue. "I've got Bob on my staff at last." He motioned Hardy away from the window where he was standing. "I promise he'll be the best newspaperman you've ever known. I've watched him for years and his natural talent is outstanding. When he can operate with full power, it will be phenomenal."

Cheira nodded, smiling at the young man's embarrassment. Sam went to the wall, slipping back a panel to reveal a well-stocked bar.

"You've a lot to live up to, Bob," Cheira postulated, eyeing the young man with mock severity. "Sam's been singing your praises for a long time."

Hardy's gaze met Sam's as he took the glass from the older man. He knew, then, who had actually planned the expedition and why. His startled memory dredged up incidents of Sam's subtle references that had kept his imagination fired with the desert legend. He remembered now belatedly that it was at a regional seminar for newsmen that he had first met Sam and Ed Peterson. They had related the legend. And he knew now it was intentional.

"Sorry?" Sam quizzed, watching him closely.

"Good Lord, no," Hardy burst out, blushing at the vehemence of his words. Then he subsided into the confusion of mixed emotions.

Sam held his glass up in a gesture of salute and with the satisfaction of an aim accomplished.

Unknowingly, the two men fed Cheira's conviction that her plans were the right course to take. They epitomized her pride in what the organization could contribute to the welfare of society.

"What are your plans now?" Sam asked, turning to Cheira.

"Dr. James Connors is honoring us with an interview this evening at dinner," Julie Crown, cub reporter, announced proudly to the seasoned newsmen.

Sam laughed, the change immediately apparent to him. "Us?" he questioned.

"Hilda, Percy, Bob, and I," she enumerated. Noticing Hardy's quizzical look, she remembered that he hadn't been present last evening when she had wagered with Percy and Hilda. "You will join us, won't you?"

Reddening, Hardy stammered affirmation.

Sam smiled. "So, Miss Julie Crown, the unknown from the West, is going to flabbergast the metropolis by the execution of a coup."

"Hilda said it couldn't be done," she announced, grinning, looking like a mischievous child. "Percy has wagered the outfit of my choice from the best boutique in town if I can get Dr. Connors to show. You wouldn't expect me to pass up a chance like that, would you?"

Laughing, Sam joked, "Serves Warren right, the pompous ass. I wish I could tell him what he's up against."

"Go ahead," Julie challenged, looking at Hardy for confirmation. "He'll never believe you."

Sam turned to Hardy, the smile still on his face. "Bob, let me tell you about our august leader. Whimsical as well as beautiful. Mysterious and awesome. Profound and venerable. She will never cease to fascinate you." Sam raised his glass to her.

Hardy fidgeted in confusion, at a loss to locate the proper bantering response.

Cheira yawned obviously, but her eyes twinkled.

"I'll see you both this evening," she stated, putting down her glass.

To Hardy's bewilderment, she vanished. He stood, mesmerized. Dragging his eyes away from the empty spot with effort, he asked Sam, his tone hopeless, "How do you people cope?"

Sam motioned his new employee to a chair.

"A little humor helps," Sam advised. "And a lot of practice. Don't take it so seriously."

Hardy rubbed his neck, squirming uncomfortably. Suddenly, his clothes chafed his skin. Although the physical damage had been quickly repaired, the imprint in his memory would remain for a long time while polarized to that experience was the deep emotion boring into his soul with a singleness of purpose which threatened to be permanent. He couldn't see, under the circumstances, how he could take Sam's advice.

"I can't keep up," Hardy despaired. "I act like a fool when she's around." He envied Sam's suave performance. "Besides, I'm a lousy actor."

Sam smiled sympathetically. "You'll learn," he reassured the young man. "Right now the memory of your experience is still too fresh in your mind, but it will fade in time. I'm sorry I couldn't warn you, but you know that was impossible. I gambled that you'd be able to handle it. And you did! Give yourself some credit, Bob. Sometimes Cheira acts arbitrarily. Then we all suffer." Sam paused.

"You're in a difficult position, Bob," he continued. "You've probably seen more of her in the last week than most of us in twice as many years. Myself, for instance, I haven't seen her for ten years. Most of the time, we go about our business, study a little in whatever field interests us, especially if we want to try something new for our next assignment, and work at increasing our power the way ordinary men try to improve their golf games."

"Improve!" Hardy's voice rose in helpless desperation. "I don't have any to start with."

"We'll take care of that!" Sam assured him. "We have a member who is very old and powerful. He specializes in guiding the rest of us."

The young man was somewhat encouraged by his chief's indication that he, too, needed assistance. "How much power can you have?"

"No one knows that," Sam answered.

"Who, do you think, is the most powerful, besides Cheira?" The reporter wanted to know.

Sam thought for a moment. "Siri, probably."

Questions kept popping into Hardy's inquisitive mind. "But what if someone became as powerful as Cheira?"

"I don't know that either. So far no one has. And even if someone did, why would anyone challenge her position? I shudder even to think of the consequences." Sam frowned.

"Wang Lu, or whatever his name is, apparently defied her today, yet she did nothing. Why?" Hardy remembered his own punishment for what seemed a far less grievous offense.

"The old man holds an honored place in the organization. He is the only one who has ever returned to the common human state. He has lost almost all his power. Cheira won't take advantage of his helplessness."

Hardy, silent at last, sat musing over all he'd been told. Involuntarily, his pulse quickened as the concept of his new life opened before him.

"Come on." Sam resumed his normal jovial manner. "Let's go to dinner. Let me exercise the prerogative of my seniority and escort Cheira this evening."

Hardy grinned, ashamed at the relief he felt.

At eight-thirty, Julie, Hilda, Percy, Sam, and Bob were well into their second round of drinks. Dr. Connors hadn't appeared.

"It was a game try," Percy sympathized, looking at his watch. "What made you think he'd go for a setup like this when we can't even get five minutes with him in his office?"

"He promised he'd come when I talked to him on the phone this morning," Julie answered, lamely. "He probably forgot until the last minute. He's so wrapped up in his work."

The Four Horseman Restaurant was a large, barnlike structure, half-timbered with a vaulting gambrel roof. It had been a carriage house at the turn of the century. The restaurant took its name from the four giant statues marching down the main aisle. The open-sided partitions had been retained, covered with heavily embroidered burlap enhancing each dining party's illusion of privacy. The clientele was upper middle class, mostly young professionals. A versatile quartet provided dance music for the late evening crowd.

Sam excused himself on the pretext of making an important phone call. *I'll shake him up a bit,* he telepathized to the frowning young woman.

"Don't feel too badly, dear," Hilda tried to soften Warren's triumphant attitude. "We're all carried away by our enthusiasm sometimes."

Julie made an effort to smile. Sam had scarcely returned when the eminent scientist joined them, apologizing for his tardiness. Warren was flabbergasted. Torn between astonishment at Dr. Connors's appearance and disgruntlement at being bested by a neophyte, he struggled to regain his professional poise. Sam winked at Julie, bringing an engaging smile back to her face.

Hilda was entranced by the distinguished physician. *Early forties,* she appraised mentally, noting the streaks of gray in his hair. She was fascinated by the long, capable fingers, which he used to emphasize his remarks and which expressed so well the slender build and the unworldly quality of the dark brown eyes.

For half an hour, Hilda and Percy plied him with questions about his work. He answered politely and directly, neither evading nor offering information. Hilda liked the quality of his voice—firm and businesslike, yet with a hint of gentleness. She decided he was one of the nicest people she had ever met.

Why is he so shy of the press? she wondered. *Is there something about his personal life that he wants to hide?* Finally, she could resist no longer; the romantic bent of her character demanded satisfaction.

"Is it true, Doctor, that you have never married?"

For the first time, the man was visibly ruffled. "My work keeps me very busy," he stammered.

"I think Dr. Connors is too dedicated to his work," Julie interrupted, faintly stressing the words.

Dr. Connors looked directly at her for the first time. His eyes widened imperceptibly. Whether that statement was a threat, he failed to determine.

The exchange didn't slip past Hilda; she interpreted it in her own way. She was certain now that they knew each other. It answered the question of why he had granted an interview so willingly. Fear gripped her heart. Had she made a mistake in her judgement of Julie? Was he in love with her? The very possibility made her shudder, but the aptness of the judgement alerted her to watch more closely.

The matchmaker wanted no interference with the smoothly developing progress of her plan. She conceded grudgingly that Dr. Connors might be a threat to its satisfactory completion, although the man seemed totally oblivious of his own charm and attractiveness. That at least was a favorable point. She knew from experience how dangerous a male could be when he was fully aware of his power, especially to an unknowledgeable girl like Julie.

Hardy, also, had detected the communication. Jealously, he wondered if there was something intimate in their relationship. Now that he had seen her very human reactions to situations, he was less sure of Ameur's estimate of her personal life. The idea irritated him and increased his feeling of inadequacy. A hard stare from Sam stopped the thought before it could take definite form.

"Well," Sam broke the silence which was becoming patently out of place at a social gathering, "an old bachelor like myself can't pass up the opportunity to dance with a beautiful lady. May I, Miss Crown?"

Julie accepted docilely. Dr. Connors, recovering his poise, danced with Hilda.

"What did you make of that?" Warren asked his fellow correspondent when they were alone.

"He means nothing to her," retorted Hardy before he realized he'd been trapped into an admission. He smiled sheepishly.

Warren raised his eyebrows. "You'd better make sure of it, then, my friend," was his advice. "Hilda's got her heart set on a match between the two of you. From the way you act, I'd guess you feel the same way."

Hardy looked away, neither confirming nor negating Warren's observation.

"Can't say I blame you," Warren continued, taking Hardy's silence as an admission of agreement. "She's a mighty beautiful girl. Should be in the movies." Warren paused thoughtfully. "There's something different about her, though. Can't put my finger on it. It's more like something I can feel. When she looks at me, I swear I don't have a thought she doesn't know. You've noticed those eyes of hers—that green, I can't describe it, with flecks of gold and brown that catch the reflection of light like a . . . "

"A goddess," finished Hardy, his voice barely above a whisper. He seemed unconscious of having spoken aloud.

Warren chuckled. "Now don't let your imagination carry you away. We've just gone through that. But, yes, that's a good description." Warren fell to musing, talking as much to himself as to Hardy. "Wonder what trick she used to get him on the phone. I've tried for years. Can't get past his secretary."

"Maybe you don't have the right power," Hardy commented, dryly.

Before Hardy could put forth the resolve to ask Julie to dance, he intercepted her thought to Connors. The doctor complied by leading her onto the floor. Hardy was puzzled by the expression of uneasiness on Sam's face, but he could detect no thought to clarify it. Disconcerted, he ordered another drink, the now familiar feeling of depression overwhelming him.

How have I displeased you, mistress, Connors telepathized, taking her in his arms. The slow tempo of the music defied the tension between them.

It would seem, her thought came back clearly, *that science is an all-encompassing passion.*

His body stiffened at the rebuke. "My work is ever yours to command," he spoke softly, the hurt demonstrating in his eyes. "It fills a life otherwise forever empty," he added, his lips just touching her hair, his arm involuntarily drawing her close against him.

Ameur tells me you haven't returned to Arx Vetus for five years. Her thought was accompanied by a flash in her eyes as she pulled away. *Now you don't even remember an appointment.*

"What use?" he replied, his voice and his mind forming the same words. His tone conveyed the defeat he felt.

Don't be a fool! You will soon begin to lose your power, if you haven't already. I don't suppose you spend any time increasing it? No wonder I have to use the phone to reach you, like an ordinary person. Her thoughts jabbed at him mercilessly. *Can you even understand me now? Of what service will you be when your mental ability begins to decline?*

Connors was visibly crumpling under the onslaught. "The situation shall be remedied immediately, Mistress," he murmured, humbly.

Cheira ignored the stricken expression, refraining from making a comment that would temper the unfeeling discipline. The omission would surface later to haunt her.

When they returned to the table, Dr. Connors excused himself, signifying that he must get back to his work. Percy and Hilda thanked him profusely and promised flattering coverage in their papers.

Hilda felt relieved. As much as she liked Dr. Connors, she was happy to see him depart. Something had transpired on the dance floor that had obviously not improved the relationship. Hilda hoped it was other than she surmised. She'd hate to think she'd chosen the wrong girl for "dear Bobby."

Weren't you a little hard on him? Sam remonstrated telepathically, hoping even belatedly to soften her attitude.

I'll not have another Wang Lu, Cheira blazed at him, the thought physically perceptible by a widening of her eyes.

Sam bowed his head, acquiescing. He felt a sort of paternal concern toward the little community of members in the vicinity of New York. Since he was a senior in the society, he assumed a responsibility to smooth their relationships with Cheira as far as he was able. Sometime he succeeded in swaying her—not often.

He recalled what Wang Lu had said when he complained of her high-handed methods: "When she discovers love, it will be different." Sam waited for years to see it happen. At first, he was sure she loved Ameur. But when Ameur married Tiana and brought her to Arx Vetus, Cheira seemed happy for them both. She and Tiana became close friends. No matter how diligently Sam watched, he could detect no conflict of feelings.

93

Later, when Jim Connors came into the organization, Sam was sure that here was the right man. His hopes were nourished when Connors took up residence at Arx Vetus. Then something happened. Whatever it was, Connors came to the U.S. His reluctance to return to Arx Vetus increased with the years. Somehow, the fact that Cheira had come after him wasn't encouraging. Sam was inclined to believe the reason she had given. He knew how deeply she regretted Wang Lu's return to ordinary life.

And now, this new project. There was certainly no chance of love for her there. In fact, he feared just the opposite. She could never find happiness with a man she hated. He experienced a wave of helplessness. He could think of no way to swerve her from this outrageous course.

Hardy was triumphant. He had understood the entire exchange. When the party broke up, he asked permission to escort Julie back to her hotel.

Once out of hearing of the others, Cheira suggested, "Let's teleport."

"I don't think I can," Hardy replied doubtfully, a chill running up and down his spine. He recalled the fruitless efforts he had exerted at Arx Vetus.

"You'll never know unless you try, and it's just a short distance," she added persuasively.

Eager to please, the reporter promised to try if she would tell him what to do.

"Remember," she instructed, "your will is immeasurably stronger than it was in the unaltered state. Use it. Concentrate on the objective to the exclusion of every other thought." She paused. "Let's see. How about the sidewalk in front of the hotel. There are no solid obstructions in between. There are few people out walking this time of night so no one will notice."

Hardy nodded. She stepped beside him, taking his hand. In a flash, she had changed from angry goddess to adventuresome child. Hardy was amazed at the change. He tried to decide how to react.

"You're not concentrating," she accused, grinning.

He reddened guiltily, remembering too late how transparent his thoughts were to her. Making an effort to concentrate, he closed his eyes and pictured the hotel entrance in his mind.

"Hold the picture." She whispered the command. "Now will yourself to be there. Concentrate on the sidewalk."

He felt a light tingling sensation through his body, a faint humming in his ears. He squeezed his eyes shut, petrified of the chance of seeing himself floating through the air above the traffic of Manhattan. At that instant, a siren wailed. The conditioned reflex of the reporter leaped to the fore. The image vanished from his mind. He felt, too late, the heaviness of his body hit the sidewalk.

He sat up cautiously, wondering how many bones were broken. When he looked up, Cheira was standing over him choking with laughter.

The doorman rushed over to offer assistance, wishing wholeheartedly that people would at least wait to get home before getting falling-down drunk. The reporter's dismay when he deciphered that thought brought renewed convulsions of suppressed laughter to his companion.

By the time the disgusted doorman had Hardy on his feet and dusted off, Cheira had herself under control enough to say, "Come on. Ching Li will make you a hot cup of coffee."

"That's a wise decision, miss," the doorman said approvingly.

It was the next evening that Hardy got an idea of the extensive membership of the organization on the East Coast. Sam had arranged a private banquet for the members, giving them a rare opportunity to greet their leader. Many of them visited Arx Vetus while Cheira was absent and consequently hadn't seen her for as long as fifteen or twenty years.

As a newspaperman, Hardy was in his glory. There was hardly a leading figure in any field who wasn't in attendance.

When Cheira appeared, the young man caught his breath. She was dressed as he had first seen her at Arx Vetus. Her gown looked like it was made of pure gold, but light as chiffon, for the folds swayed softly with her movements. The aura that visibly surrounded her body was so bright that the eyes faltered.

Hardy was reminded of some ancient deity returned to receive the homage of modern man. The illusion was heightened when the entire assemblage knelt with bowed heads.

At an inconspicuous signal, they approached her individually. All communication was by telepathy. The room was devoid of sound. The heavy carpeting even muffled footsteps.

Watching the proceedings, Hardy wondered at the overall order being maintained. He had been at other gatherings where several hundred people spelled uncontrollable chaos. No one seemed to be in charge, yet no two started forward at the same time although they came from different parts of the room.

They all know their order of seniority. Sam came to stand beside him.

The neophyte, still unused to thought communication, almost spoke aloud. Sam put a restraining hand on his arm.

It's hard to believe that we're in New York City. Sam read Hardy's thought. *It would be easier to think this was happening in some temple of antiquity.*

An organization of men who have so much power at their disposal have no need of elaborate rules of conduct, only some single point of unity, which is what Cheira provides. That's only logical because we all owe our capacity, the root of our power, to her. These formalities are just symbols of our acknowledgement and gratitude.

Hardy hadn't missed a thought. With his ability to concentrate heightened, he grew aware that the room was a cacophony of thought.

Only a few of the members are women, he noticed, surveying the groups scattered around the room.

Yes, Sam responded, *but I understand that is going to change in a few years if plans move ahead on schedule.*

What plans? his companion wanted to know.

I'm not at liberty to reveal that specifically, Sam answered. *The sciences have made some great advances in the last few years. We're learning more about the physical aspects of transfiguration. Someday, everyone may be able to enjoy it. But the cost will be great. Perhaps, too great.* Sam looked worried.

Hardy failed to grasp the meaning of Sam's final remarks. His interest was caught by an old man who stood apart, motionless, his head bowed. Hardy recognized Stuart Mervin, the financier. Mervin was noticeably older than anyone else in the room. *What was it Sam had said about him during the meeting in his office?* Hardy wondered.

Let him be a lesson to you, came the thought of the man beside him. *The appearance of age is a skillful use of cosmetics.*

Hardy looked at his employer questioningly.

Many years ago, Sam explained, *Cheira ordered him to finance some oil exploration in the Near East. I've never learned any of the details except that he refused, telling her that such a move would eventually disrupt the economy of the entire world. As a consequence, the development of that area was almost completely halted. Cheira stubbornly built her own company, but it has taken many years. It's only in the last fifteen years that a considerable amount of oil has been coming out of the desert regions, as you know. It could have happened twenty years earlier.* Sam shrugged. *You've already seen a few examples of Cheira's displeasure.*

And felt it, Hardy thought wryly.

Ha, yes. Sam smiled. *Anyway, she has never forgiven him. She forces him to make regular visits to Arx Vetus, but won't grant him reassignment. He resorts to artificial aging to appear normal. He's outlived—if I may use the word—all his contemporaries. He's here tonight in the hope she'll relent. Of course, he doesn't know I spoke for him this afternoon. He would never have permitted it. A proud man! But, she'll have to do something in a year or so. He can't very well appear to live more than a hundred years.*

Hardy's sympathy went out to the lonely man. He was seeing him in a new light, this aging millionaire who was the bane of the press. Reporters Hardy knew fought for special assignment months ahead so they could be out of town when it was time to cover Mervin's annual birthday celebration. It was the only time he appeared in public. The news media was always on hand, if only to prove the old man too cantankerous to die.

Can't anybody defend him? Hardy wondered, noticing the men whom he knew to be the old man's friends from stories about them. They were now ignoring his presence.

They bear their own scars. Sam shrugged. *Besides what can they accomplish except to bring her wrath upon themselves? He understands.*

Hardy thought of the wide berth the members had given him at Arx Vetus. No matter how seldom Cheira saw some of the men in her organization, there was no question but that hers was the final word when she so desired.

The young reporter continued to scan the room making mental notes of the important personages in attendance.

Where's Connors? His mind marked the famous scientist's conspicuous absence.

At Arx Vetus, Sam informed him silently. *Didn't you notice how she sent him scurrying last night? He's been so wrapped up in his experiments that he hasn't paid a visit to the home port for a long time.*

Teleportation, Hardy thought, wryly thinking of his own single attempt to teleport a few city blocks. The idea of teleporting halfway around the globe struck him as an awesome accomplishment.

His thought was interrupted by the sudden stillness of everyone in the room. The ceremony was about to be concluded. Cheira stood for a moment gazing into the familiar faces. A sad smile played about her lips. Those who knew her intention recognized the farewell she was extending, acknowledging the possibility that her existence might cease if her plan miscarried.

The aura around her began to brighten until it filled the dimly lit room

97

with a blinding light. All knelt and for the first time a sound replaced the silence: an audible sigh.

The light faded; she was gone.

Conversation sprang up throughout the room as men and women relapsed into the familiar manner of communication that dominated the major portion of their lives. Hardy was amused to learn that thought transference was as unnatural for them as it was for himself.

The young newsman was flattered that so many notable personages took the time to congratulate him on becoming a member. Sam beamed with pride.

"Thank the Lord, we'll at least have a favorable press on this coast," a relieved senator commented, voicing the common sentiment of politicians and businessmen alike.

"Does that mean that I'm never to disagree with your policies?" Hardy frowned fearing the revelation of some secret rule. He had had grievous differences of opinion with this particular man in the past.

"Heaven forbid!" The jovial denial relieved the reporter. "It just means I'll be able to explain the reasons for my actions and hope that, with mutual understanding, we'll see eye to eye more often." The senator paused, his tone becoming confidential. "Remember that pipeline that you denounced so loudly in your paper because it meant taking on obligations to another country that you felt were out of proportion to what we'd be getting in return? Have you thought about it lately? That line is carrying a third of the oil the East now consumes. Originally, it was Cheira's idea. Do you think knowing that might have softened your attitude?"

Hardy reddened. Laughing, the politician put his hand on the reporter's shoulder. It was the promise of future cooperation.

"Thanks," Hardy responded earnestly; and the word contained all he wanted to say.

Sam attracted his attention. "Cheira wants to see you now. At the hotel."

Hardy departed at once. Resisting the temptation to try teleportation, he hailed a cab.

By the time Ching Li ushered him into Cheira's presence, the now familiar excitement had taken hold of him. The ceremony had added a deep, pervading awe to the commingled emotions of love and fear, which had been born at Arx Vetus. All doubt that he had found the purpose of his existence was erased forever.

"Come in," she smiled, motioning him to a chair. Instead, he knelt beside the davenport on which she reclined. She noted the action, but said nothing.

"I must leave tomorrow. You and Percy and Hilda will see me off on the plane for Portland. I'm sure that Hilda, for one, would never rest if I just disappeared." She ended laughing.

Although he knew better, Hardy extended his hands supplicatingly, "Must you go?"

"The plane leaves at ten." Her voice held an inflection he had learned painfully to identify. Recoiling reflexively, the young dreamer had learned a lot in the last weeks. He was shocked that he still had the audacity to protest any of her actions, no matter his feelings. But the question had burst out before he could stop it.

Seeing the stricken expression on his face, Cheira, for once, relented, her voice softening. "We'll meet again soon."

Hardy bowed his head in acquiescence. The headstrong reporter had been replaced by a mature individual who could accept unpleasant orders without undue protest.

"Hilda will be disappointed when I fail to return," she continued. "You'll have to invent some plausible story should she question you. Wire Ed if you need corroboration."

Hilda stood with tears running unashamedly down her cheeks. It was dramatic, she knew, but she didn't care. Hoping still for some miracle to bring Julie and Bob together permanently, she was fighting a premonition. *Why did Julie feel it necessary to return to Portland so soon?* Maddeningly, Bobby was failing to protest the departure.

Until the last moment, Hilda searched for a way to detain the girl. An ominous foreboding that she'd never see Julie again grew stronger by the minute. Frantically, she cast about for a means to ensure the relationship. Since the moment of doubt the night they interviewed Dr. Connors had passed, her determination that Julie was the ideal girl for Bobby had concreted. She envisioned them walking through the years hand in hand, the envy of all their contemporaries, the delight of her own old age, while Bobby reached over higher heights of success in his profession. And she would know she had been responsible. She hated to give up that satisfaction.

She hugged Julie tightly, holding her in the embrace unnecessarily long, hoping by the gesture to communicate the feelings she couldn't voice. An arm still around the girl, she drew Bobby close, her intention obvious.

Julie obediently put her arms around his neck, smiling at his discomfiture, and with an innocent twinkle in her eyes, pressed her lips to his.

You always were a terrible actor, she thought.

Hardy's panic was lost in the sensation spreading along his nerves, her thought the only words echoing in his mind.

She drew away and ran for the plane.

Hilda sighed. "That was beautiful! See that you don't let her get away!"

The young reporter, fighting to regain some semblance of self-control, smiled ruefully.

CHAPTER VIII

Hans and Margo had been at Arx Vetus for three days. Hans had worked day and night to meet Cheira's impossible deadline. Having managed it somehow, he was free now to revel in his wife's enjoyment. Everything delighted her. It was the adventure of her life.

From the moment they stepped aboard the plane until it landed in Oran, Margo had changed. With the progression of miles southward, she threw off successive layers with which the years had covered her personality.

The decrepitude of the old shuttle plane, which was a converted fighter left over from the war, made Hans concerned about ever reaching Touggourt. Margo was uncaring. She sat with her face pressed against the window, with childish wonder watching the undulation of the scrubby hills. She insisted Hans watch with her as they passed over flocks of grazing sheep, their woolly bodies like tiny mounds of pebbles dotting the landscape, the shepherd like a forgotten doll shading his eyes to squint into the sun to observe the plane passing overhead—concrete evidence of a world of which he was only dimly aware.

The snaillike progress of a caravan wending its way toward the desert outpost held Margo's undivided attention until it passed out of sight behind the low profile of hills. The ancient trade route emphasized the intimate link between the past and the present.

"I'm going to love it," she sighed, sinking back into the seat for the first time, a new youthful sparkle in her eyes.

"This is only the beginning," Hans told her, smiling happily.

Ameur and Tony Hammond met them in Touggourt with the horses.

"Welcome," Ameur said gravely when Hans introduced them.

Margo gasped. Even after more than two decades, it was impossible to forget those clear blue eyes. "You're the one," she blurted out impolitely in surprise.

Ameur grinned. "I hope the amount was adequate."

Margo wrinkled her nose, her eyes sparkling. "Only now is adequate," she retorted.

"I may never want to leave Arx Vetus," Tony Hammond commented, winking at her when they were introduced. "There will be too many beautiful women around."

Margo blushed happily.

Hans had dreaded the last wearisome lap of the journey. It was a hard trek and he feared how much it would tax Margo's strength. But she took to riding a horse with the greatest ease. The desert exhilarated her; she thrived on the camp fare the nights they spent out. She was entranced by Ameur's chivalrous manner; and she and Tony Hammond became mutually admiring comrades, their relationship based on a light, steady banter.

Margo was enchanted by Arx Vetus. Within hours of her arrival, she and Tiana became fast friends. Every inch of the old ruin had been explored before she was satisfied. Her lively enthusiasm brightened the whole atmosphere.

Margo had accepted all that her husband had told her with only slight skepticism; but by the time they were settled into a plush apartment at the old fort, she was fully convinced, eager to begin a new life.

Now that he was free to reveal his power, Hans enjoyed the pleasure he could give her. Her dark eyes would widen and she'd shiver at his touch. The indescribable ecstasy she felt when he made love to her made her impatient for the power to reciprocate.

Margo was lying on a divan in their suite dreaming of the paradise to come. Hans had just stepped out of the shower. Hans wandered across the room, naked except for the towel around his neck. He stopped, absently tracing the line of his jaw with gentle fingers searching out any errant whiskers. He stared into space, frowning. The time of Cheira's arrival had become a dread. He wondered if the anxiety was caused more from his fear of the ordeal of transfiguration or a wish to get it over with as soon as possible.

Margo watched him, admiring the hard muscles rippling under the bronzed skin when he moved. His hair had returned to its natural color. Catching her breath at his youthful appearance, she sighed contentedly. Just a few more hours and this existence would go on forever. Her imagination failed to conceive of anything greater.

Hans called, "Come in," in response to a knock on the door. Tiana stood in the doorway.

"Cheira has arrived," she announced. "I'll let you know when she wants you," she informed Margo.

"At last!" Hans spoke to the closed door.

Margo was too embarrassed to speak. The hot blood rushed into her face, staining the white skin a deep red even to the roots of her hair.

"Darling, you're shameless," she chided her husband who hadn't moved when the unexpected visitor entered. She was shocked at his non-chalant behavior.

Hans laughed, crossing the room swiftly to take her in his arms. "Tiana has taken care of me when I was as helpless as a baby. Modesty with her would be a little ridiculous."

"But you're mine," she persisted, brushing her lips sensuously against his chest.

"And soon, forever and ever," he whispered huskily, allowing his body to respond to her touch.

At lunch, Tiana informed Margo that Cheira would see her at two.

"Oh, now, I'm scared," Margo confided, her eyes getting large and round. "Hans says he was sick for weeks. Even after he was recovered enough to get around, he was plagued with blinding headaches and nausea."

"What did he tell you that for?" Tiana was annoyed.

"Because I insisted." Margo jumped to her husband's defense. "I wouldn't let him alone until he told me everything."

"Hans exaggerates," Tiana stated flatly. "Besides, you know how stubborn men can be. And unreasonable. They bring it on themselves."

Margo stared at her, only partly convinced.

Tiana grimaced. "Admit that Hans heads the list. He fought like a tiger. Right to the last minute. What can you expect?" Tiana's kind heart never became inured to suffering of any kind. That she was helpless to prevent the struggle that took place at transfiguration before strong-willed men would submit did nothing to lessen its impact. *Hans had been one of the worst,* she remembered, *fighting Ameur to the limit of his strength and cursing me for cooperating in what he considered a barbarous practice. Never had Tiana seen her husband angry, but that day it was only Cheira's intervention that prevented Ameur from murdering Hans. But it is unnecessary for Margo to be subjected to such details!*

However, the memory of the ordeal was still vivid in Hans's mind. His nervousness increased with each passing minute. Now that the time had arrived, he cursed himself for subjecting Margo to what he knew was to come. Perversely, he wished fervently that he hadn't been in such a hurry. He could have, possibly, discovered another way to keep Margo with him. *It will be years before she is really old,* he rationalized.

Visions of his own transfiguration leaped back into his mind in vivid detail, haunting him, condemning him for the decision to subject the woman he loved to like torment.

He had thought he was in good physical condition, even had proven it a few times in bouts with his coworkers; but the punishment he had taken from Ameur that day was beyond anything he had ever experienced. Such strength and speed of movement was inconceivable. Reinforced by anger, Ameur had withheld nothing.

He remembered how it all began. He had been living in Berlin, a young law student, going to school days and working nights. It was just after the war, when the whole country was struggling to build a new economy. The old order had collapsed and the common man was determined to carve an independent, prosperous place for himself, free from the ancient bonds of oppression. He found himself in the vanguard.

Margo had just given birth to their second son only two weeks before. Since she was unable to work, his job was necessary for their sustenance. Unwillingly, he had gotten involved with the newly formed labor union. Before he realized it, he was one of the leaders.

That particular night was one of the coldest of the year. He shivered involuntarily at the recollection. About two in the morning, he was trudging homeward, exhausted by the hours of wrangling which had just ended. His mind doggedly rehashed the arguments over the settlement of the upcoming contract. The men didn't seem to agree on anything. He knew that unless he could unite them around some central idea, the cause was lost.

The city was sleeping. Except for the crunch of his feet echoing in the empty street on the brittle snow, there was no sound. He hurried as the sharp air began to penetrate his thin coat. He frowned. It had been a choice of extra fuel to keep Margo and their babies warm or a new winter coat for him. He had considered dropping school, but Margo wouldn't hear of it. He felt his heart swell with love now as he remembered how she had denied herself every comfort so their dream of a better life could eventually become a reality.

No sound had attracted his attention, but suddenly two men were beside him. Before he could cry out, a car pulled up and he was hustled into it. He had no doubt but that it was the hired thugs of the opposition who held him captive. Cursing his carelessness, he struggled blindly.

Oh, God, Margo! He thought despairingly of what would happen to her without his support and fought with all his might to no avail against the unnatural strength that held him.

His captors were silent as the desolate streets. Muffled as they were in heavy overcoats and fedoras, it was impossible to identify them in the darkness.

When he was thrown aboard a plane, which proceeded southward, he began to wonder if his first conclusions had been correct. Why would they go to this much trouble to get rid of him?

He was lying in a sort of narrow closet. As the hours passed and the plane droned on, the numbness of his bound wrists and ankles, along with the weariness of twenty hours without sleep, made him cease his struggle to get free. He might as well save his strength for whatever was to come, he reasoned. It must have been about three in the morning when he was kidnapped.

The puzzle was compounded when they landed in the desert. It must be somewhere in the Sahara, he concluded, although his mind was too beclouded for certainty. With the coming of dawn, he could see his captors clearly. They were dressed now like Arabs. A burnoose identical to theirs was thrown over his head and he was tied to the saddle of one of the waiting horses.

The company had increased to eight. They rode full gallop in tight formation, heading due south into the vastness of the uncharted wilderness. He was thankful that he had learned to ride as a youth in the little Hanoverian village of his birth, for the pace was never slackened. Once past the few crumbling buildings of the landing strip, the horses settled into a tireless, ground-covering canter. Despite his worry, he admired the sleek coat and rippling muscles of the beautiful animal who moved so effortlessly beneath him. The superb condition of the animals was comforting. Renegades did not possess such perfect creatures.

The temperature rose rapidly as the sun climbed higher overhead. Waves of heat danced over the sand. He wondered if they meant to ride the horses to death. He must be the prisoner of madmen, he decided, forgetting his previous estimation.

His misery increased unbearably; the perspiration poured into his eyes, making them sting and blur. The rivulets of sweat trickling down his back caused intolerable itching. His body, unprepared for the extreme change of climate, reacted violently. Consciousness was departing in surging billows of dizziness.

The abrupt halt would have pitched him over the head of the horse if he hadn't been tied securely. He was only dimly aware of being hauled down and thrown roughly into a dark place. It wasn't until the coolness started to penetrate his overheated body that he regained his senses.

"Feeling better?" a deep, quiet voice beside him inquired civilly. The bonds had been removed. He felt relieved by the restoration of circulation. Restraint, he understood, was no longer necessary, since the desert itself furnished an insurmountable barrier to escape.

Hans lay on a mat in a small tent. He forced his eyes to open. The man standing over him was tall, broad shouldered with the deeply tanned skin of a desert dweller. Strangely, Hans noticed, there was no malevolence in the bright blue eyes. His expression betrayed genuine concern. Hans stared at him, trying desperately to remember if he had ever seen him before The sullen expressions of the hired thugs who hung around the labor meetings paraded before his mind's eye. None of the drawn, dissipated faces even remotely resembled this robust desert man.

"I am Ameur." The stranger spoke flawless German, although Hans had an intuitive doubt that it was his native tongue. There was something indefinable in the inflection as the sound struck his ears. "We have never met before." The man seemed to answer his thought.

Hans eyed him shrewdly, astonished at the accurateness of his captor's guess. "Why have you gone to all this trouble?" Hans inquired wearily. "You could have killed me just as easily back there."

Ameur chuckled. "It's not to kill you, my friend, that we've brought you here, but to give you limitless life."

Ameur indicated a tray of food on a little table beside the mat.

"Eat," he ordered kindly. "We won't stop again for twelve hours."

Unable to make any sense of what the stranger told him, certain only that he didn't have much choice, Hans complied without protest. For the moment, his depleted strength could summon no further resistance. He had had no sustenance since noon of the previous day, skipping dinner last night in favor of the meeting and instead drinking numberless cups of hot black coffee and smoking as many cigarettes. Now his arteries felt flaccid, moving his blood sluggishly, increasing the general weakness of his body. His stomach, used only to the basic minimum of food at the best times, was outraged at none at all. But as the first mouthful slid down his throat, the image of Margo leaped into his mind. The food, at one moment delicious and welcome, transformed into a dose of bitter revulsion. He threw down the fork. By now, Margo would be frantic.

"It's been taken care of," his captor informed him. "A message has been delivered to your wife stating that you've been called by the local in Stuttgart on an emergency. She's been given enough money to last until your return."

Hans found it hard to believe what he was hearing. For the second time the man had divined his thoughts. "How could you have known what I was thinking?" he blurted out.

Ameur's eyes narrowed with humor. "I'll explain all that when we reach our destination. For now, finish your lunch."

Hans knew he was probably a fool for allowing the man to persuade him, but Ameur's eyes looked so unflinchingly into his that it was hard to mistrust him. Silently, he resumed eating.

Satisfied, Ameur left him to his thoughts.

More perplexed than ever, Hans tried to find a reason for his predicament. He was convinced now that his abduction wasn't related to labor activities. There was something different about his captor that he couldn't define, but he was sure the man didn't fit the type he was familiar with.

Ameur returned in a few minutes.

"It's time to go," he said. Hans knew it was an order. Stiffly, he rose. Ameur took the opportunity to study the man being brought to Arx Vetus at Cheira's command. Hans Werner was exceptionally intelligent, he concluded with admiration. However, he decided, frowning, a strong will was evident in the candor of his look and the set of his jaw. Ameur sighed. Experience predicted a struggle ahead. Cheira would need to make good use of her power to bring this man to submission.

"We head south," Ameur volunteered.

Hans stood alertly, neither accepting nor rejecting his captor's offer of compromise.

"It's a long, hard ride," Ameur continued. "You can make it as difficult as you choose."

"Where are you taking me?" Hans stalled.

To Hans's surprise, Ameur seemed to be willing to explain. Hans listened—with reservations.

"To a place called Arx Vetus. It's the headquarters of our society. You have been selected to become a member. How rare a privilege that is, you will only fully realize later!"

"What society?" Despite his caution, Hans was interested.

"That also you will learn later. Let the information I have given you suffice for now."

Hans clenched his fists, fear beginning to churn in his stomach. Surprised, he tried to identify it. He wasn't a coward. He had survived the war years and often only because his courage held firm in many a tight spot. But here was an unknown element with which he couldn't cope.

"I'm not being mysterious intentionally," Ameur interrupted his thought. "It's only a matter of finding the best way to explain it to you."

The third time, Hans noted. "You know what I'm thinking. How?"

"Because I'm transfigured," came the quiet reply.

Now as Hans sat waiting in the library of Arx Vetus, the fantastic horrors and the ultimate indescribable happiness of those two weeks marched across his mind. Sometimes, he still doubted it had happened.

He had resisted with every ounce of his strength and will what he had been convinced was the effort to take control of his mind. He had been filled with the stories, which had leaked out after the war—for the most part unfounded rumors of inhuman experiments that lingered in the imagination ready to leap forward at the slightest hint of an unusual occurrence. Ameur had been unable to convince him. Submission had come only after a long and bitter struggle. He had never regretted his transfiguration, of course, but his heart ached for the woman he loved now undergoing the same torture.

"It won't be like that for her," Ameur volunteered sympathetically.

Hans looked gloomily at the man who lounged across from him. In the twenty-four years that had elapsed, Ameur had changed from jailer to valued friend. Hans was grateful for his support. It made the waiting bearable.

Had his own memories not clouded his reason, Hans might have been able to accept Ameur's correct summary of Margo's experience.

Tiana led her off to the right of the impressive dais, which stood in the middle of the large, rectangular room, to a cluster of low, comfortable chairs and divans. Huge pillows were strewn over the thick carpeting. Ching Li perched in the middle of a deep red, satin-covered hassock, plucking an ancient lyre to the accompaniment of her sweet, soft voice.

As the two women approached, Cheira rose from one of the chairs and, laying aside her book, came toward them, smiling a welcome to Margo.

"Are you happy now, my dear?" she asked, kissing Margo's cheek.

"Oh, yes," Margo answered shyly, taking the chair beside Cheira, which she indicated.

"And your children?" Cheira inquired.

Margo needed very little prodding to tell of her sons in detail. They were now men, but with a mother's heart, she still regarded them like the babies they were so many years ago. The eldest was a lawyer in Zurich just beginning a promising career. The youngest was in Paris studying art.

"He's a romantic. Hans says he takes after his mother." Margo blushed.

From any discussion of the sons, it was only a natural step to speaking of their father. Margo's listeners could have no doubt of the intensity of the love she bore her husband even after more than a quarter century.

Margo, though naturally a loving, extroverted individual, had learned through the years to keep her own counsel. She was surprised at how good it felt to be able to confide her most secret hopes and fears to the sympathetic companions who surrounded her now. In the short time she had known Tiana, she had learned to love and trust her. Now her instinct told her she could extend unreservedly the feeling to Cheira and Ching Li.

"You're so fortunate to have the love of a man like Hans. He's been willing to risk everything to stay with you." Cheira's voice betrayed a wistful note, but it went unnoticed by the others.

Margo responded quickly. Slipping to her knees before the woman she had once thought she hated, she looked up at her with tears welling in her eyes. "I thought you were trying to take him away from me. You're so beautiful. I wouldn't have blamed him, but . . . " She gazed earnestly at Cheira. "I love him so much. I'd do anything to stay with him."

Cheira put her hands on Margo's temples, her eyes probing deep into the other's brain.

"I'll do anything . . . " Margo's voice trailed off as she surrendered to the penetrating force that burned deep inside her head. An irresistible drowsiness took hold of her. She was unconscious when her body slumped to the floor. Ching Li and Tiana raised her, adjusting her comfortably on a divan. They waited silently. The time would be short, they knew. Margo had offered no resistance.

The shock to the brain by the sudden stimulation produced varying periods of incapacity, the prior degree of resistance usually being the determining factor. A willing candidate, therefore, experienced only an ordinary fainting spell followed by a short restorative sleep to effect total recovery.

In a little while, Margo sat up, yawning with the first flush of awakening. Then she wilted in chagrin, remembering where she was, vexed by her own rudeness. Tiana smiled reassuringly, bringing her a cup of tea. Cheira shrugged, lightly dismissing what Margo insisted was an inexcusable breach of etiquette.

However, after their reluctant acceptance of her apology, Margo was able to reclaim her original enthusiasm. They became absorbed in a discussion of the couple's future plans. Margo wanted to go everywhere. She picked a dozen favored spots. At least one of the others had been there. They vied with each other, detailing the attractions of each pet city. Margo couldn't decide.

Finally, she said, "I'll go wherever Hans wants to go."

It was the thought of her young, handsome husband that prompted Margo to confess her most secret fear.

"I've been aging so rapidly," she confided, blushing. "These last few years, I've been frantic. Hans has been so kind. He never hinted that he noticed; but I knew he did. I'd catch him studying me, especially in the evening when we were alone. The frown on his face would make my heart stop." A tear popped out of each eye, glistened for an instant on the dark lashes, then traveled unnoticed down her cheeks.

"You realize now what he was thinking?" Cheira asked gently.

"Yes," Margo murmured with bowed head. "I'm so grateful. I know he loves me, and if I don't get any worse . . . " She paused doubtfully. She couldn't quite believe that the aging process could be arrested.

Cheira cupped her chin with the palm of her hand, her elbow propped on her knee. "Well," she paused dramatically, frowning, making a pretense of perplexity. "What can we do for our friend?" She winked at Tiana.

"Make her young and beautiful again?" suggested Tiana enthusiastically. She grabbed Margo's hand, leading her to the corner where mirrored panels joined to cover two walls.

Ching Li unclasped the fastening that held Margo's tunic at her shoulders. Margo flushed violently, squeezing her eyes shut. She had eagerly adopted the traditional attire of Arx Vetus, convincing herself that the looseness of the dress hid the sag of her breasts and the ugly protrusion of her stomach. The floor-length gown masked the lumpiness of her thighs, and she had made a determined effort to ignore the loose flesh of her arms.

Now, as the dress dropped around her ankles, she trembled with shame at having these beautiful women examine her aging body.

"I think your description of yourself is greatly exaggerated," Cheira said critically, answering Margo's thought. Tiana and Ching Li hastened to agree. Margo was grateful for their kindness; but even at their urging, she hesitated to open her eyes.

Finally, gritting her teeth, she took control of herself, admitting that if she was to learn the secret of eternal youth, she would have to cooperate fully. She turned her gaze bravely to the mirror. Her eyes widened slowly in astonishment at what she saw. The wrinkles that she had tried in vain to hide were just faint, barely discernible lines. Her skin was smooth, fine grained, just tinged with the pink she had been so proud of years ago, which set off so nicely her almost black hair.

She stepped closer to the mirror to better inspect herself. Her breasts had already begun to firm, she was sure; and when she stood erect, the muscles of her stomach tightened elastically.

The first noticeable changes from transfiguration occur in the skin and muscles, which exhibit a remarkable improvement. Almost immediately, the skin takes on the clear glow reminiscent of youth. For those who are able to see it, the aura is bright blue, changing through the years to gold as the individual's power approaches its peak. Muscle tone is restored simultaneously, contributing to the youthful appearance. Within a day or two, the subject has returned to the look of full maturity, the state enjoyed just before the onset of aging. The body, thereafter, is able to maintain that most desirable condition indefinitely.

In the pleasure of discovery, Margo had momentarily forgotten her companions. Now she looked around. They were grinning broadly at her.

"In a few days, you'll be as beautiful as you were twenty years ago," Cheira told her.

"Oh, thank you! Thank you!" she burst out, sobbing with abandon. Ching Li refastened her gown, performing the task the other's trembling fingers could not accomplish. They were sympathetically silent, understanding the tears were happy ones. Cheira put her arms around Margo, murmuring softly and stroking her hair. The years of tension were washed out of Margo's soul by the tears she shed.

Gulping, she whispered, "I'm sorry for being such a fool."

"It's all right," Tiana soothed, leading her to the divan.

"No one ever had such good friends." Margo smiled, brushing the wet streaks from her face. "What must I do to become like you? I'll do anything!" Now more than ever she was eager to endure any ordeal necessary to achieve the altered state.

"It's already been done." Cheira smiled.

"But Hans said it would be terrible. He's been so worried," Margo objected.

"It was terrible for him," Cheira agreed. "He struggled like a wild man. We couldn't convince him that we weren't trying to take over his mind. You see, no one can be transfigured without their consent. The altered state can only be realized with the agreement of the subject."

"My poor darling." Margo saddened. "He can be so obstinate!"

"Which makes him all the more valuable," Cheira completed the thought. "Timid personalities can't be trusted to accomplish their goals. You're lucky, Margo. You'll never be subjected to the pressures Hans has had to withstand these last years. Had he been weaker, do you think he could have concealed his altered state so well? Surely you can imagine how you would have reacted had you known. And not only yourself, but everyone he came in contact with. There was never a respite, except the short time he was able to spend at Arx Vetus."

Margo interrupted, "Those business trips . . . "

Now Margo understood what had puzzled her through the years of her marriage. Whenever Hans went out of town, he always took her along, except one week a year. She never knew when it would be, but she had come to expect it. It was the only time she didn't know where he was.

She had discovered the singularity of that week accidentally. Jeremy, their oldest son, became violently ill without warning. The physician diagnosed a ruptured appendix, recommending immediate surgery. Margo called the number Hans had left. To her surprise, it was the home of Herman Mailer, a political friend of Hans whom she barely knew.

At the time, she was too distraught to wonder about it, but later when Jeremy was out of danger, the peculiarity of the incident struck her. Mailer hadn't told her where Hans was, but offered to reach him for her. Hans walked into the hospital waiting room less than an hour later. When she questioned him, he vaguely implied that he had returned early, by chance having completed his business quickly. What that business was, he declined to elucidate.

For the next twenty years, she was able to identify those weeks by the telephone number he left. Because she loved and trusted him, she had come to accept the annual disappearance. It became identified in her mind with Herman Mailer. Therefore, she assumed it was some sort of political activity. At first she worried, fearing for his safety, remembering the activities during the war; but as time passed and nothing happened, she ceased even to speculate about it.

Now she recalled it was after Hans's return from one of those weeks that she noticed how young he looked. The contrast had emphasized her own aging body.

Ching Li rose to switch on lamps as the artificial lighting, mimicking the sun, signaled the advent of evening. The afternoon had passed quickly, unheeded by the happily occupied women.

"There'll be no more unexplained separations," Cheira said, having followed Margo's thoughts. "Your love can grow forever and ever." This time, Tiana detected the wistful note in Cheira's voice; but she was at a loss to interpret it. She would remember it later.

"When will I have power?" Margo's thoughts seldom left her husband.

"It will increase gradually as you learn to control concentration. With practice, you'll have all the powers the members enjoy."

Margo blushed, thinking of the power she wanted most. She shivered, recalling the ecstasy she felt when Hans made love to her. She wanted to be able to return that heightened pleasure. She wanted him to experience what she felt.

Tiana interrupted her thoughts. "Shame, Margo," she teased. "Must your friends be exposed to such indecent imaginings? You have deceived us," she continued, mockingly serious. "We thought you were a lady, and instead, we find in our midst a common harlot."

Margo had forgotten about the telepathic talents of her companions. The look of mortification that spread over her face sent them into peals of laughter.

"Enough!" Cheira raised her hand, pretending sternness. "One little test and we are finished. I will give you a telepathic command. If you can understand, carry it out."

Cheira directed Margo to the other end of the room where stood a huge chest. It had to be opened by a series of concealed springs and dials. The fledgling member proceeded without hesitation. She was able to follow Cheira's instructions as clearly as if she were standing at her side.

Easily the complicated mechanism was mastered. The chest opened. Cheira directed her to a bottom drawer. Margo gasped in astonishment as she pulled it open. Necklaces were piled in confusion. Jewels of every cut and description gleamed as their facets caught the light.

Bring me the rubies, Cheira's thought came to Margo clearly.

Carefully untangling the unique piece from its fellows, Margo lifted it out of the drawer. Executing the reverse combination, she closed the chest and made her way back across the room to lay the gems in Cheira's hand.

Very well done, Cheira thought.

Margo smiled proudly. "It's so easy!"

"And you shall have this for a reward." Cheira fastened the necklace around her neck, the red ovals dripping from a golden chain. "Now, let's go to dinner."

The men in the library were instantly alert when the door opened. The audience room was extraordinary in that the impenetrable sustenance that lined the walls allowed no communication to pass through it. The substance had atoms so closely packed that their movement could not be detected even by the most modern instruments and so stable that it was impervious to any outside influence. Telepathy was out of the question.

Hans's agitation had increased as the afternoon deepened into twilight. He could get no hint of what transpired beyond the closed doors. Having spent hours pacing the hall, he had just allowed Ameur to persuade him back into the library for a drink.

Hans stiffened as his mind detected the first movement of the door. He waited, scarcely breathing, forcing himself to still his thought lest it betray his anxiety. Cheira might now interpret his worry as criticism. If the torture he had endured were a necessary part of transfiguration, might she not think him ungrateful that he was unwilling to allow Margo to suffer a little when the reward was so great? Did he expect his wife not to pay for such a great gift, just because he loved her? That was the last eventuality he desired at the moment.

After a seeming eternity, the library door opened. Cheira entered the room. According to the custom at Arx Vetus, both men bowed deeply.

"We'd be pleased to join you for a drink before dinner." Cheira spoke to Ameur. Only after he moved to obey, did Ameur realize that the afternoon had been as trying to his nerves as it must have been to Hans. He glanced understandingly at his friend as he passed.

Hans stood, immobile, his head still bowed. Ameur marveled at the control the man had acquired that permitted no thought-laden energy to emit from his brain.

"For heaven's sake, go to him, Margo"—Cheira laughed, taking the drink from Ameur—"before he has apoplexy."

Margo ran to her husband, flying into his arms. He clasped her tightly, his eyes closed, savoring the first hint of relief.

"I'm all right," she assured him, laying her hand against his cheek, looking up into the beloved face. "I've been having a wonderful time—and after all the terrible stories you told me. It was easy," she chided playfully.

Relief flooded over him with the certainty that she hadn't suffered. He held her at arm's length, studying her expression intently, trying to understand what she was saying. The sparkle of her eyes convinced him. After all, the process was a mysterious one which he couldn't hope to understand.

He made a decision. Dragging the burnoose over his head and clad only in the loin cloth, he crossed the room swiftly to kneel before Cheira, indifferent to the astonishment his actions caused to the others.

"From this moment," he declared earnestly, "I dedicate myself without reservation to any service it may please you to require of me."

Appreciating what it cost this proud, strong-willed man to surrender so completely, Cheira rose. Standing before him, she offered her hand, solemnly accepting the vow he made in gratitude. He placed his lips against her palm, a token of final, total submission.

A festive air pervaded Arx Vetus that evening. At dinner, the four conspirators made plans for a party. Hans raised his eyebrows quizzically when his gaze met Ameur's. The only answer he received was a noncommittal shrug. Ameur was as puzzled as he was.

With about fifty members in residence, there was an adequate number of guests, the instigators decided. In a serious moment, Cheira asked Ameur if Siri had yet returned from England.

"Yesterday, mistress," Ameur answered.

"Be sure to invite him, then," she ordered, a look of surprise flicking across her face, which Ameur could not interpret.

Margo, without a moment's hesitation, cast off the air of dignified matron, which had characterized her demeanor for so many years. Relishing to the fullest her rejuvenation, she was determined to celebrate accordingly. Cheira and Tiana seemed to have caught her enthusiasm and were enjoying themselves as much as she.

Since there were no professional entertainers at Arx Vetus, volunteers were sought. They spent hours signing up amateur jugglers, acrobats, comedians, singers, and anyone else who had a talent to contribute. Ching Li volunteered to play the lyre of which she was so fond. Margo remembered a little tap dance she had performed in school. Cheira and Tiana decided to execute a serail dance, despite objections raised by Ameur who was the only member who realized the implications.

It was after midnight when the self-appointed committee postponed final preparations until the next day.

Hans was pleased and surprised by the instant change in his wife's behavior. He had forgotten the spontaneous gaiety that had first attracted him so long ago. That she embraced her new life wholeheartedly, he couldn't doubt. It was as if the intervening years had never existed.

115

When they were alone at last, she unfastened the clasps of her gown, letting it fall unheeded to the floor. All trace of the reticence she had shown in the last few years vanished.

"Look! Look at me!" Her laughter tinkled like chimes in the wind. Pirouetting before her husband, her dark hair floated on her shoulders and the rubies hung like drops of blood at her throat. Throwing her head back, she cupped her breasts with her hands and, whirling again, sucked in mightily the tiny protrusion of her stomach, which was rapidly vanishing.

"I shall be beautiful again," she declared proudly, scampering away to the mirrored panel in the bedroom to minutely examine the reappearance of youth in her body.

Hans watched her capers silently, his face sober, his heart bursting with gratitude to the power that had granted him such happiness. Although pleased with Margo's comeliness, the prospect of limitless existence was far more important to him. The bleak pall that had hung over their relationship for the last few years was lifted forever. Now no separation would ever be necessary nor the unbearable pain of watching her inexorable senility and death. There would never again be any need to hold part of his life secret from her, or to watch the pain of doubt cloud her dark eyes at his evasiveness.

What an idiot he had been to have waited so long! All his fears had proven groundless. Of all the possibilities he had tried to foresee, the ease with which Cheira had accepted Margo was not one of them. His own experiences had overshadowed his reason. It hadn't occurred to him that the simple, joyous goodness he loved would appeal to anyone else. In fact, he had cursed her obvious display of loyalty. His disbelief, he now realized, was an affront to Margo as well as to Cheira and everyone else at Arx Vetus.

"Darling, why are you looking so glum? Aren't you happy?" Margo's face clouded as she noticed his silence.

Purposefully casting off the somber thoughts, he scooped her up in his arms. "Such beauty should not be wasted," he murmured with a soft chuckle. Nestling his face into her breasts, he carried her to the bed.

"Have you taken leave of your senses?" Ameur snapped, slamming the door of the apartment.

Tiana was taken aback. She had failed to notice Ameur's agitation. She was reminded how greatly her husband's power exceeded hers and how easily he could conceal his feelings from her. But she remained calm. "Why are you disapproving so vehemently?"

"I've never seen Cheira act like this," he confessed. He walked swiftly around the room as if activity might give him an answer. Suddenly aware of its pointlessness, he threw himself down on the sofa.

Tiana came to sit beside him. "It's a celebration for Margo. That's all."

"And the dance?" Ameur growled.

"In the desert, a serail dance is acceptable entertainment, isn't it?"

"Not for you—or Cheira," Ameur retorted.

"But it was Cheira who taught me," Tiana protested.

"And it's something she should never have known. The responsible party will surely pay for it one day," Ameur prophesied, bitterly.

"What are you talking about?"

"Just that the dance is indecent and most unsuitable for your party," Ameur altercated.

"My dear, are you forbidding me to participate?"

Ameur shook his head grudgingly. Even now he couldn't countermand Cheira's wishes; the habit was too ingrained. "But I still don't like the idea. And," he added, surreptitiously revealing the real reason for his anger, "Siri will be furious. Don't you understand? He'll think Cheira is taunting him."

"Nonsense!" Tiana laughed, relieved, thinking she understood what Ameur referred to. "He'll think Cheira has finally ceased to hate him. Do you expect her to beg his forgiveness? What better way to show her feelings than through a custom of the country?"

Ameur frowned, remaining silent. He could say no more without telling Tiana more than he felt she should know. His loyalty to Cheira allowed no concessions, even to his wife.

"All right!" he said, closing the discussion.

The sound of preparation for the celebration could be heard shortly after dawn. An air of gaiety pervaded the atmosphere. Rooms were robbed of divans, chairs, pillows, and tables to be placed in a circle in the garden. Ameur's irritated tones could be heard periodically above the constant clamor as he tried to protect his prized shrubs and flowers—not always successfully—from the careless revelers.

Throughout the day, amateur entertainers could be spotted in secluded corners practicing furiously. The program informally allowed each guest to be a spectator until taking his turn as performer. As the sun dipped toward the horizon, activity reached a hectic pace. The usual last-minute changes in scheduling were made with all the sobriety and concentration of professional producers.

117

Then just as the flares were lighted, order asserted itself. The pseudobacchanalians took their places. Supper was served and the festivities began.

"Siri isn't here," Cheira complained, frowning as she took her place.

"He'll come," Ameur responded, his voice so low as to be almost inaudible.

"Your disapproval is very apparent," she accused impatiently.

Ameur bowed, but made no denial, his action an admission of the attempt he was making to conceal the premonition that had nagged at him all day.

Cheira laughed, refusing to become infected with Ameur's doomsday attitude. "Then we'll start without him." She clapped her hands in signal for the performance to begin. In the excitement, she forgot Ameur's dire mood.

Tony Hammond's imitations were a highlight of the program. His talent extracted the simplest foibles of a character and submitted them to gross exaggeration without distorting their identity. It was executed with such exuberant innocence that even the embarrassed objects of his mimicry laughed wholeheartedly. Ameur, of course, whom Tony worshipped with the crystal idealism of a small boy for his one great hero, was the object of the most discerning pantomime. He caricatured Ameur's habitual wide-legged stance, which had once betrayed his identity despite the most meticulous costuming. The audience blatantly encouraged him with raucous cheering.

The entertainment was almost over. The sheik appeared just as Ching Li was finishing her song. He silently took the vacant chair at the foot of the divan on which Cheira reclined. Her heart leaped despite the pretense of ignoring his lack of greeting. With determination, she maintained absorption in the performance.

Margo danced. While the crowd was applauding, Cheira stole a glance at the taciturn figure beside her. The scowl on his face rebuffed her intended overture. It was evident that he was treating her invitation as a summons, his presence an indication of obedience rather than personal inclination.

Cheira's expression clouded. She was puzzled. Siri obviously was far from pleased. *Wasn't this what he's been waiting for?* She'd expected him to come to her immediately on his return from London. According to Ameur that was two days ago. Now he was here grudgingly, the heavy scowl on his face revealing clearly the annoyance he felt.

Was he angry because she hadn't told him herself? She'd wanted to, had hinted broadly the trend of her thinking, but the fear that still nagged her made her delegate the explanation of her intention to John. *Cowardice,* she admitted ruefully, *had kept me silent at the Fort, even though I'd had plenty of opportunity.* Siri had heard only her words; the meaning she'd wanted to convey escaping his attention.

And as usual, some chance remark had caused her to flare up at him. Would he ever understand that finally she had realized she loved him? That what she had thought was hatred and revulsion hadn't been identified correctly because of her stupidity, the true nature of her feelings masked by the dominance of a fear she couldn't control?

She made a feeble effort to probe his thoughts. Her mind, coming against the barrier of his, recoiled. She hadn't the courage to try to overcome it.

The fading, sporadic applause brought her attention back to the performance. The grassy circle of the impromptu stage was empty. A movement at the edge of her vision told her that Tiana had risen. She hesitated, recalling Ameur's disapproval. But it was only for a moment. *He didn't realize how much the new interpretation of my feelings has changed me,* she rationalized. There could never again be any misunderstandings which would cause her to lose control, wielding her power with wanton vengeance.

A hush fell over the spectators as Cheira rose. She joined Tiana in the spotlighted circle. They wore identical, traditional harem attire. As they took their positions, backs to each other, heads thrown back, the mingling of golden hair and black presented a breathtaking contrast.

The drums like heartbeats sounded from nowhere and everywhere. The tableau was prolonged unbearably. The onlookers held tense. Ameur stirred uneasily. He had informed Siri of Cheira's invitation; but he hadn't told him of her intended participation, silenced by his own disapproval, yet reluctant to give Siri a chance to voice a criticism—a criticism which long association told him would be forthcoming, especially under the circumstances. Siri was on the verge of erupting. The trip to London had shocked him. He had yet to regain any equanimity. Now this. Ameur confessed he could only wait to see what happened and, if something did, try to temper the situation.

Ameur tried futilely to determine his friend's thought. He was surprised at the strength of Siri's ability to resist the probe. For years now, there had been no reason for a confrontation. He was unaware of how much the man had increased his power. He had a wild urge to stop the dance, but the habit of more than a century was not to be broken under the first stress.

Cheira would do as she pleased. His duty was obedience, no matter his personal convictions. Long ago, he had forfeited the will to judge her actions. *Besides,* he reasoned, *it is only a vague premonition and guilt at not having warned Siri that worries me.*

A single pipe began a thin, monotonous cadence. The dancers moved, sensuously following its lead; the wavering light gleamed on the skin revealed through the transparent material of their trousers. The diminutive vests, one black, one gold, strained at their delicate chains, making only a minimal pretense at concealing the creamy mounds of their breasts.

They separated, each wending her way around the circle in opposite directions, whirling, bending, swaying. The beat of the drums increased almost imperceptibly, and the pipe grew louder and more insistent.

The grace of the dancers was heightened by the sylvan setting. The majestic walnuts, their top branches swaying gently in the freshening night breeze, created an earthy awareness in the spectators, enhancing the gestures of the dancers, emphasizing the symbolism of the ancient ritual, demanding acknowledgement of the most intimate function of living things. The movements were an identification first recognized by totemistic primitives—as strong today as in the first man at the dawn of time.

The absorption of those seated around the circumference of the sky-vaulted stage, the unconscious attitudes in which they were suspended, exhibited plainly the universality of the basic emotion regardless of the disparity of the cultural backgrounds represented. They were caught—some with only partial acquiescence—in the web of their most primal feelings. This was the purpose of the dance patterns, whether they were aware of it or not.

Only Siri was outwardly unaffected. He watched; but as a man can be coerced by his own code, more rigid than any torture. There was no relaxation of the blackness of his expression, nor any movement to release himself from the anguish he was experiencing. His knowledge of the objective of the dance increased the agony he felt at Cheira's performance. For him there was no veil of ignorance to soften the intensity of reality.

Completing the circle, the dancers tarried, the swaying of their bodies mingling the long tresses of black and gold, their bodies touching, caressing and withdrawing, only to reconverge, a second and a third time.

The drums penetrated, commanded, separating the dancers, momentarily allowing the tension to subside as they whirled around the circle. Their motions elaborated until they came together again, the swaying and bending at last so pronounced that they were kneeling.

120

The drums and pipe ceased abruptly, leaving an electric silence in the still vibrating air, deserting the two women prostrate on the ground. Only Siri and Ameur knew that there was yet one movement to complete the ritual; the blatant invitation which no onlooker could misinterpret.

Siri moved first. In one violent motion, he was beside the dancers. Roughly grabbing Cheira's arm, he lifted her to her feet. His normally exceptional strength increased by the release of the anger he felt toward her for what he considered a deliberate public humiliation.

"You brought me here to mock me," he hissed through clenched teeth.

Ameur, close enough to see the fear leap into Cheira's eyes as she gasped with the pain of Siri's tightening fingers, knew the sheik's reaction to be all that he had expected—and what Cheira had not.

"Siri," he said, his voice low and ominous, "you go too far."

The sheik, fighting to regain control, responded to his friend's hand on his shoulder.

Shaking herself free from Siri's loosened grip, Cheira met and accepted the challenge she saw in his eyes. Lunging at him with the ferocity of a jungle cat, she dug her nails into his shoulders. There was no longer now a guest who didn't understand the unscheduled drama taking place. Each sat rigid, staring, the energy emanating from Cheira's body so potent that the air crackled.

Siri dropped to his knees, but his gaze never wavered. Only the tensing of his jaw muscles and the drops of moisture gleaming on his forehead gave an indication of the wrenching pain that was making his nerves scream in outraged protest.

Time stopped, suspended, the scene frozen, the participants victims of a nightmare from which they were helpless to extricate themselves. Ameur, his concern growing as the connotation of the contest manifested itself, finally interfered.

"Please, mistress, stop—unless it is your intention to kill him," he whispered. His words broke the spell. A look of horror spreading over her face, Cheira stepped back.

"I leave for London within the hour," she announced in a strange, breathless tone and fled into the darkness, leaving the man to savor the depths of despair, interpreting her action as irrevocable detestation.

CHAPTER IX

Instantly, every member of the manor household was aware that her lady-ship had returned. Only a slight attitude of excitement, however, would have alerted the chance visitor that any change had taken place.

Jennie was first to welcome her.

Jennie—the little north country peasant girl whose dreams of princesses had lured her to the city where her wild escapades had caught the attention of Lady Pemberly—had paid uninvited visits to the houses of the rich, at night or in their absence. Once she had stayed two weeks in an occupied residence. Although she had made friends with no one, she had been too busy to be lonely. Each house she explored inch by inch. When she was satisfied that she had learned all she could, she would turn to the library and read voraciously until circumstances interrupted her.

It was not until Jennie decided one night to visit the stronghold of the Pemberly Petroleum Interests that she was captured. She had no way of knowing that all the servants were transfigured beings, never even having heard of such a state.

From the moment they met, her ladyship liked Jennie and Jennie loved Lady Pemberly. The little peasant girl was transformed into the handmaiden of one of the world's most influential women.

"Call John immediately," her ladyship directed brusquely, barely returning Jennie's greeting.

Since the personal quarters of Lady Pemberly were impervious, Jennie stepped into the hall to send the telepathic message to her mistress's chief deputy. The most important man in the Pemberly Conglomerate, he answered to no one except Lady Pemberly herself. In her absence, the routine affairs of the gigantic organization rested on his shoulders. There was never a question but that he executed his charge perfectly, the ultimate administrator.

"You spoke with Siri?" Lady Pemberly asked without preliminary when he arrived. He nodded. "Then tell me!" she ordered.

"He agrees to comply with your wishes," John replied, "but reluctantly.

He resents the basis on which such a personal contract is extended. I implied that the union would be used to consolidate Pemberly influence in the Arab nations."

She grimaced, remembering the scene her cowardice had already produced. *Was their relationship destined to be fraught with misunderstanding and conflict? Nevertheless, the marriage could be postponed no longer, and since he was the only man . . .*

"Does he know about the experiment?"

"Yes, but not how it will affect your arrangement. I'm sure he'd be opposed as we all are."

Ignoring the last remark, she pursued her own thought. "He thinks, then, the marriage is a matter of politics only."

John shrugged. "Yes."

So that is the reason for Siri's behavior at Arx Vetus, she thought. *A platonic union is an effront to his masculinity; in his mind, a gross display of my power. He assumed that I was taunting him; and I had responded to the fear his actions aroused in the only way I knew, even though I had vowed only moments before that I'd never use my power against him again no matter how he acted.* She sighed. How could she overcome the dread that had been spawned so many years ago and had so colored her attitude that reason and knowledge were powerless to dispel it? In spite of that, she loved him regardless of how much she fought it.

"It wasn't my intention that he should think that," she said, her voice betraying the confusion she felt. Her realization that the true cause of the misunderstanding stemmed from her own evasiveness depressed the natural tendency to lash out at John. "You should have told him all as I requested," she ended lamely.

"It gives you a chance to change your mind, my lady. This move is most unwise."

"So you keep telling me. So everyone keeps telling me. I don't want to hear anymore." Cheira's voice rose nervously.

"But the man is unpredictable," John protested, pressing the advantage her attitude gave him. "The life he leads certainly makes him dangerous. I fear for your ladyship's safety."

She frowned. *I fear, also,* she thought, *but even that will not allow me to choose anyone else. I have tried.*

"He arrives in two weeks," John interrupted her thought, the long years of association warning him to pursue his objection no further. "It has already been agreed."

"Good! See that the press is notified. Have him entertained by the right people. Pemberly Enterprises must receive real benefits from this also." She put aside the disquieting thoughts, taking refuge in the business that occupied most of her time.

"It is arranged, my lady." John was offended that she would think it necessary to remind him of such basic protocol. Cheira failed to notice.

Immediately returning to the privacy of his own residence when Lady Pemberly dismissed him, John allowed himself the luxury of unguarded thought.

In all the years he had been employed by Pemberly Enterprises—first in the States and later, when it seemed expedient to expand worldwide, at their headquarters in London—he had been loyal to Cheira's purpose. Her directions had always been in the best interests of not only the company, but of all those connected with it.

Fifteen years ago, when she wanted to assume a more public role, he had arranged for the smooth transfer of leadership in the giant corporation. He had learned by chance that the reason for her action was the refusal of Stuart Mervin to continue backing the company. That Mervin had dared to take a stand against her still dismayed him. He was sure he could never act in such a manner, even now.

But for the first time, he disagreed wholeheartedly with her intentions. There were other ways to consolidate Pemberly holdings in the Near East. There were others who would be more than happy to participate in Mott's experiments. There were others much better suited to her purpose than a wild horse-breeder from the uncivilized stretches of Africa.

The resentment that had risen like gall in his throat when he learned of her choice of a partner had been conquered with great difficulty. He had always disliked the arrogant posturings of the owner of the Fort. Whenever they met, the conversation was barely cordial, only their common allegiance to Cheira preventing open hostility. Now he felt dislike crystallizing into hatred. The anticipation of Siri's assumption of a dominant role in his life added a bitter coating to the hatred.

Nevertheless, his presumption of a close bond between herself and Cheira was his own fault, not hers, he admitted. He had never regarded her as a woman like any other. He beheld a vision, unique, apart from the flesh-and-blood world. His failure to name the emotion he felt was now belated.

He recalled instances that were forever lost because he had not attempted to capitalize on them. The hours they had worked side by side until physical exhaustion quenched their enthusiasm and the camaraderie of a common goal had set up a link between them were opportunities missed. He had no right now to complain that he was not her choice. Self-pity must not be allowed to interfere with his loyalty or color his actions.

So, he decided, *if she loves that infernal nomad of the Sahara, I must accept the fact.* Her involvement in Mott's experiments, though, worried him more. He had an uneasy feeling that she was jeopardizing her life by the course she persisted in taking. So far, his best efforts, along with those of other members of the society, had not budged her. He wondered that he had never noticed before how single-minded she could be.

Of course, he could keep trying whenever she gave him an opening. And there was always the possibility that Siri would refuse to cooperate. *Very slim,* he reminded himself, imaging the sensuous Arab. Siri, in his opinion, was amoral, arrogantly holding his desires above the limitations accepted by civilized men. It was foolish to even consider that he'd decline the relationship even under the terms offered. He shuddered to think of Cheira at the mercy of one who had never even learned the meaning of the term.

Siri's only redeeming feature in John's eyes was his inviolable sense of honor. It was only a small straw on which to rely.

Characteristically, the possibility of open revolt never occurred to John. The habit of obedience to the power that sustained his existence was too deeply ingrained.

An astute business sense forced him to concede the points in Siri's favor. Even Cheira didn't know that Siri was the son of the last Earl of Zetland, the chief of the fierce island race that claimed direct descent from the Vikings. Further, Siri's present position of influence in the oil lands couldn't be denied. His tribe was highly respected and Siri held a prominent place at any international meetings.

He shuddered with revulsion as he pictured the life of the sheik. *How can the man stand to rot away in the desert?* he wondered. *He is too proud for his own good,* John decided, *and obedience to him is a bitter crust to be continuously resisted.* John wondered uneasily if even Cheira could control Siri, or if she too would suffer when resistance exploded into open defiance. He had no confidence in Siri's regard for the feelings of others. In fact, he doubted that the sheik even considered them.

He silently reavowed his allegiance to Cheira. He would acquiesce to her plan if there was no way to dissuade her; but he would remain close, ever vigilant, a buffer between her and the sheik.

As usual, John had done his work with perfection. Two weeks later, when the sheik arrived in England, he was promptly acclaimed the highlight of the social season, eagerly scooped up in a whirl of teas, balls, and hunts. The ranking matrons vied for the attentions of the handsome desert chief. They were titillated with the romance of his life and charmed by his courtly manner.

The younger set swamped him with invitations to sports events, dances, and a few more intimate activities. The former he politely accepted; the latter he consistently refused.

Everyone who could wangle an invitation did so the night of the Duchess of Yerby's ball. Sheik Siri ben Ange, the guest of honor, was to be presented to Lady Pemberly. The appearance of both of them caused a high level of excitement and curiosity, for despite Lady Pemberly's influential position in the business world, she seldom attended social functions. Rumors, of course, vanguarded the event.

Constance, Duchess of Yerby—one of the few female members of the society who was also a leading civic figure, her husband being the chairman of the board of Pemberly Enterprises—was instructed by Cheira personally. It was felt that a public meeting would pave the way for what was to follow. If Pemberly Enterprises was to benefit by the course Cheira had set, it was necessary to carefully engineer the staging of events.

Lady Pemberly arrived late, well after ten. In accordance with her instructions, the Duchess hastened to introduce the pair.

"Your humble servant, madam," the sheik murmured, bending low over her hand with the courtliness that had set many a heart fluttering in the last few weeks.

The Duchess, as tastefully and speedily as possible, ushered the couple onto the dance floor so the ball could begin.

"Welcome to England, my lord," Lady Pemberly was overhead saying as the turbaned visitor escorted her into the ballroom. "It is said that the charm of the desert is irresistible . . . " The melodious voice was drowned out by the sound of the orchestra.

For the first time in her memory, Cheira doubted her ability to act her self-appointed role. The advice she had given so coolly to others flashed through her mind, but did little to quell the panic when Siri's arms closed around her. In all the intervening years since she had been captive at the Fort, she had never allowed him to touch her. Now, through her own decision, she had to permit it.

As if cognizant of her thoughts, his arm tightened. She trembled. The fierce, dark eyes demanded a response. Involuntarily, she tilted her head.

"I . . . I'm sorry." Her lips formed the words, her thoughts referring to the incident at Arx Vetus, her voice humbly sincere in a manner so foreign from its usual imperious tone.

"I must learn to obey without question and to submit without protest," he countered, smiling mirthlessly. Though his thoughts matched his words, his eyes shone with the challenge. He'd never been able to see her as other than an exquisitely desirable woman. His look told her that now, along with the certainty that he had not been defeated, the contest only postponed.

She attempted to draw away, to mask the crumbling of her composure, but his arm was like a steel band imprisoning her.

"It's your cooperation I'm asking for," she defended lamely.

"Of course, my lady." The arm around her loosened as if in obedience to her wishes, but his eyes remained fierce, telling her that it was his will that initiated the action. He would cooperate only insofar as it suited his purpose.

Siri held her gaze steadily as he effortlessly guided her in the intricate steps of the waltz. "Do you still think I comply from fear of your power?" He spoke the words slowly, tonelessly, after a long period of silence.

The dance ended before she could reply. Lady Pemberly was claimed by various hopeful suitors for the rest of the evening. The sheik obligingly danced with scores of wide-eyed admirers. Cheira dutifully smiled, danced, and carried on polite conversations with jewel-laden dowagers; but her mind was occupied with far more personal problems.

Had he meant that he obeyed her out of love? Or was it repentance? Or—she shuddered to think of it—*just plain physical desire?* She couldn't decide. She hadn't dared to ask him. How could she make him believe that she loved him after all the times in the past when her actions had been instigated by a desire for vindication?

For a long time she had believed it herself, thinking she hated him for the merciless way she had been treated; but when they'd meet again, her heart would skip with the joy she felt. Then when he looked at her, her body would quiver, remembering; and the old, deeply buried fear would return. She would resort to humiliating him or inflicting pain to assuage her own.

Now, the success of Mott's experiments had made a decision necessary. She could not sacrifice any other member to such a revolutionary procedure. Once she had decided to be the first to undergo the transformation, her direction was determined.

Knowing that she could never give herself to anyone else, marriage to Siri was the only course she could take. That she was deliberately withholding the true reasons for precipitating the union at this time caused her great distress and uneasiness; but, if he knew, he would certainly refuse to cooperate. *If he only loved me a little, if the light I see in his eyes when he looks at me is more than just desire; if, if . . .* she thought irritably. She had never been able to understand his way of life or what motive drove him to equal her power. She was a fool to even think he might love her. If he did, how could he keep those other women? She winced at the thought. She envied Margo her gentle, faithful husband who was willing to give his life for his beloved.

When they met again at Baron Cavoren's hunt, the sight of Siri provoked the thoughts that were making her life an agony. Cheira's greatest desire was for the love of this strange man. She hated the overtly obedient, but subtly defiant attitude that he adopted toward her.

During a lull in the chase, Siri rode up beside her. She jumped guiltily, wondering if he were able to probe her thoughts. But if his power was great enough to penetrate the barrier she erected, which was more than effective against even the most powerful members of the association, he apparently had not chosen to test it. He was fully occupied with the nervous thoroughbred he was riding. She smiled. It was perceptive of their host to understand the desert man's restlessness at the confinement of British society and provide him with the most fractious animal in the stable for diversion.

"Your ladyship is enjoying the hunt?" Siri asked, bowing politely, momentarily holding the horse quiet.

"Yes, thank you," she answered, matching his tone, relieved and reassured by his relaxed manner and friendly smile. There was no hint in his expression that he remembered the unfinished conversation at the Duchess's ball. Moreover, he'd made no attempt to see her in the intervening days. She'd had to be satisfied with Constance's reports of his activities. The separation she'd imposed seemed to have no effect on his enjoyment. She couldn't reconcile his behavior with what he'd said that day at the Fort. She was sure, even without any solid ground on which to base her assumption, that when he knew her plan, he'd hasten to declare his undying love.

She was disappointed; but, she admitted, it made her role easier and conveniently postponed the confrontation she feared.

"And will your ladyship honor me by attending the 300 on Saturday? Billingham has offered to let me drive his car." He grinned like a schoolboy on a new adventure.

"But that's so dangerous." She gasped involuntarily. She barely noticed when his horse had reared almost perpendicularly, whirling on its hind legs. She knew his unequaled skill as a horseman, but the idea of his driving a racing car fired her imagination with fearful scenes. She knew, too, the reckless daring that disregarded his own safety. "Jared Lang was killed when his car exploded. Cremation is not one of the things your altered state will protect you from."

The grin vanished from his face, a frown taking its place.

"Is your concern with the life of your humble servant, or do you wish to avoid the inconvenience of selecting a new consort should there be an accident?" His voice was heavy with sarcasm.

The cry of the huntsman and the clamor of the hounds as the chase was resumed prevented her answering. The sheik's attention was forced back to his mount, prancing and pulling, catching the excitement from his galloping stablemates.

Siri failed to notice the tears welling in her eyes. *Is there never to be an end to our misunderstandings?* she wondered hopelessly.

Spurring her horse to a gallop, Cheira used the violent motion to throw off the unpleasantness of the cutting remark. Disgusted with herself for what she considered an uncharacteristic weakness, she wondered if acknowledgement of her love was turning her into a simpering female, whose helplessness provoked such emotional responses.

If only she dared use her power to break through the barrier of his thoughts, maybe she could be better prepared for his reactions. But, in the same instant, she admitted that her courage would dissolve before such an attempt.

Gossips were abuzz with the news that Lady Pemberly had, for the first time, attended the auto races. Only a few spectators recognized the unusual crest on the sheik's car. Had the gossips been able to identify it, they could have ceased their speculations. The symbol was a blazing sign to those familiar with it.

Sir John fumed at Siri's audacity. He was shocked at the profane display of the sacred emblem. But Lady Pemberly defended the sheik and forbade any reprisal. After all, she reasoned, no one would recognize it anyway, except members. That she was fanning John's enmity toward the fearless adventurer, she was blissfully unaware.

Cheira had her own explanation for the sheik's irreverent use of her secret crest. He wanted her to understand that it was not fear of her power that was causing his acquiescence. Unable to determine his motive, her days were filled with confusion and the nights with restlessness. If she accepted the obvious explanation, she knew she'd not have the courage to continue her course.

As the car sped around the oval, the sheik received thunderous ovations from the crowd in appreciation of his skill. None of them would have believed that his expert handling of that precision machine had been acquired in one practice session, that the power of his intellect and the perfect condition of his body made possible that which took ordinary men years to acquire. Only Billingham fully realized the enormity of the accomplishment.

. . . And Sir John. "He should not be allowed such a public display of power," he exclaimed with disgust.

Two months later, the betrothal was formally announced. Siri, true to his word, uncomplainingly played his part—a role he detested, docilely embracing a way of life that he had fled many years before. Cheira vacillated between a compulsive desire to declare her love and fear that his response to her was prompted by purely sensuous tendencies. Consequently, she cowardly evaded private meetings, never exercising the prerogative to summon him.

Drawing the obvious conclusion from her actions, Siri obdurately smothered his feelings, burying them deep in his heart, accepting her conduct as his just desserts.

Siri was not a man prone to the minute examination of his motives. Once he recognized that what he felt for Cheira was not physically based, he sought any artifice to win her over. When he failed, he turned in desperation to the increasing of his power as a means to finally overcome her resistance, to force her to recognize his love and sincerity. He had never considered a direct challenge as the way to mastery, intuitively knowing that was not what he wanted. Even now he didn't attempt to penetrate the barrier protecting her thoughts. He thought the meaning of her actions apparent enough.

"You're determined to play this damn charade to the end," he accused one day when they met at a party, the frustration that was his constant companion particularly sharp after hours of listening politely to the inanities of empty-headed socialites.

"I don't understand," she answered. "I thought you would be pleased."

The look of puzzlement in her eyes tempted him to believe her. She must know what sort of impossible situation she was creating. There were too many men in the organization for her to claim innocence. Moreover, if she were relying on her power to control the situation, he had warned her often enough that he did not fear it.

"You know how much I despise this life, yet you condemn me to it. And you wish me to believe that your motives are solely political. How long do you expect me to tolerate this?" He allowed his glance to travel over the room with open distaste.

Despite her vows to the contrary, Cheira reacted. "Your suffering touches me," she replied stiffly. "Perhaps we can learn pity together." He winced as the arrow hit home. With bowed head, he granted her right to seek atonement. He accepted it as her true motive.

Now he realized that the close association she proposed was to be more tortuous than all the years of banishment. The hardest to bear was the look of contempt in her eyes. No matter her efforts to mask it, her body of itself recoiled from his touch. *How much she must despise me!*

Siri lived by a strict code of justice. He accepted that it was right for a man to pay for his transgressions, the law of cause and effect unmitigated by ignorance or blind passion. The reality of the action was unchanged. When he recognized his own behavior as deviant from this norm, he was even harder on himself than on others—and his reputation did not include mercy. Cheira, as the victim, had every right to any redress of grievances she chose. That her demands were tearing him apart was his concern.

He was doubly glad for the time spent increasing his power. It was only this that could give him the control he needed to bear her scorn while complying with her mandate.

The *New York Currier* sent its promising young reporter, Robert Hardy, to cover the sensational story. He was personally picked for the job by his editor, Sam Hackett. Hardy joined a number of his colleagues who had gone to London to report the visit of Sheik Siri ben Ange to England. The Arab was the cause of so many conflicting rumors that the paper wanted a first-rate man on the scene to sort them out. Hardy was happy to oblige, having a personal reason for wanting to see the sheik. Naively, he never inquired into Sam's reason for singling him out. It was his job to verify the story that the sheik was about to execute a merger with Pemberly Enterprises.

By the time Hardy reached London, the rumors had added another facet: the merger with the giant corporation was to be effected through the sheik's marriage to the Pemberly heiress. Hardy's instinct for news sharpened.

A skillful reporter soon unearthed the fact that the sheik was actually a Northman, a descendent of the last Earl of Zetland. Droves of reporters and cameramen descended on the ancestral manor when it was discovered that it was being renovated. For days, pictures of Lamborn Heath appeared in all the papers, its somber outline in everyone's mind.

Hardy's curiosity grew as he tried to determine what sort of woman could interest the sheik enough to make him submit to such a blatant invasion of privacy without complaint, even apparently with consent. Many pictures of the manor included the sheik in the role of manor lord.

Hardy spent his first three days in London trying to catch a glimpse of Lady Pemberly. Until this assignment, he had never really noticed the infrequent pictures that had appeared. Most were in Sunday supplements, foggy reproductions that were unidentifiable, accompanied by some dry nondescript review of her business accomplishments. Disinterestedly, he had regarded the stories as unimportant fillers, necessary because of the influence of the position rather than any newsworthiness of the individual's personality. In fact, if he had thought of the Pemberly heiress at all, he had assumed her to be an old maid whose position was the accidental result of birth.

Now his instinct told him he had missed something. Siri's behavior alone would support the contention.

Finally, he had turned to the London office's morgue for whatever standard glossies they could find in the files. He wasn't satisfied with the secondhand accounts he had gleaned from the staff. The general descriptions of Lady Pemberly lacked the clue he knew he needed to unravel the mystery. He had tried several times to reach the sheik, both by phone and telepathically. His efforts were unsuccessful.

An office boy delivered the thick envelope of photos and clippings to the pressroom. Leaning back in his chair, his feet on the desk, Hardy settled comfortably to study the material on Lady Pemberly.

Only a glance precipitated the involuntary reaction: His heart began to pound annoyingly against his ribs.

"My God!" he groaned, dropping his feet to the floor with a thud.

"What's the matter, Bob? Are you ill?" Karen Benedict looked up in alarm from her adjoining desk, surprised by Hardy's pale, expressionless face. She had been thrilled when Hardy came to work for the *Currier.* It meant she could wangle assignments with him. Secretly in love for years with the dashing young newsman, she had jumped at the London trip. It was a chance to attract his attention in the most favorable circumstances: the romance of a foreign land and with all the competition left far behind.

"Are you ill?" she repeated.

Hardy sat with his head in his hands.

"I'm all right," he answered finally. Gathering up the material, which lay strewn across his desk, he stuffed it all back into the envelope. "Come on," he said, making an effort to maintain a normal tone. "Let's get some coffee."

Confused, but determined to make the most of the invitation, Karen Benedict grabbed her purse and trailed out of the office after her distracted coworker.

"Have you ever seen her in person?" Hardy asked when the elevator door closed behind them

"Who?" Karen puzzled, wondering what she had missed.

Having controlled the initial shock, Hardy was overcome with such a feeling of hopeless longing that he turned on his companion irritably. "Lady Pemberly, of course! Who else?"

Karen flinched. "Yes," she answered, at a loss to understand what there could possibly be about the English peeress to provoke such a reaction. "At the race the day Sheik Siri ben Ange drove Sir Billingham's car. She's very beautiful! Haven't you heard?"

"Mm!" Hardy hesitated, appearing to be deep in thought. "Excuse me a minute!" Leaving her standing at the door of the coffee shop, he hastened across the lobby. Outside, he wondered if he dared try teleporting in a strange city.

What the hell! he thought, a feeling of recklessness flooding into his muscles. *Even if I miss the manor, I can always catch a taxi.*

Hardy had been faithfully practicing his new powers, especially teleportation, which particularly fascinated him. Now he daringly decided to try to get into the Pemberly stronghold. *If I can only have a minute with her,* he reasoned, *it will be well worth the effort.* Closing his eyes, he concentrated.

"Good afternoon, Mr. Hardy." The man who spoke was standing over him, greatly amused.

Hardy had landed on a carpeted floor. He was grateful for that, at least. *One of these days I will concentrate long enough to materialize at my destination standing on my feet,* he promised himself.

"My name is Stevens," the man said, helping him up. "May I be of service?"

"I want to see Lady Pemberly." The reporter was still too disconcerted to be devious.

"Well, that may be a little difficult," Stevens replied kindly. "One only sees Lady Pemberly when her ladyship wishes it."

"But I know her," Hardy persisted, childishly. "I know her . . ." A fleeting thought noted that the man had called him by name.

As if in answer to it, Stevens rolled up his sleeve and thrust his arm forward for Hardy's inspection. Tattooed on the inside of his forearm, the familiar symbol could easily be mistaken for a mole. To the reporter, however, the minute mark was as glaring as a neon sign.

"You, too?" he whispered.

"Everyone here at Pemberly House," Stevens informed him. "Did you think that in the place where Cheira spends the most time she would be left unprotected?"

"I must see her." Hardy tried to brave the doubt beginning in the pit of his stomach.

"She knows you are here. You must be satisfied with that," replied Stevens. "In any case, I will allow you to go no farther."

Stevens's voice remained friendly, but Hardy sensed the veiled threat by the firmness that came into it.

"Okay," Hardy conceded defeat, realizing that his incipient power was probably no match for this trusted retainer. "Show me how to get out of here."

Lady Pemberly, accompanied by the sheik, appeared personally before the board of the giant Pemberly Enterprises to formally announce her intention. The Duke of Yerby arranged for the restoration of Siri's ancient title.

Afterwards, Lady Pemberly met with the press. Her graciousness, frankness, and beauty won the hearts of even the most seasoned.

Hardy sat, stone-faced and silent. No one, of course, noticed—except Karen. She was increasingly puzzled by his behavior and worried, as the only rational explanation seemed to be that he was ill—perhaps mentally rather than physically. The thought chilled her.

Oblivious to his coworker's concern, the *Currier's* leading correspondent had forgotten his job, indeed his very surroundings, in the presence of the one who held his exclusive allegiance. In desperation, when he received no answering thought, he dared remind her of the promise she had given that last night in New York. Hardy writhed in helpless frustration as the conference dragged toward its finish. Her unruffled demeanor distracted him.

He doubted his ability to contact her. He doubted the power he was supposed to possess. He wondered again if the whole thing had been only a dream.

Rising at last, to terminate the meeting, Cheira paused. Looking directly at the forlorn reporter, she sent the message he had begged for: *Midnight*. He understood clearly.

Siri returned with his fiancée to Pemberly House. It was his first visit since coming to England. He came reluctantly, maintaining a silence that made Cheira apprehensive, her ignorance of his thoughts producing an unnatural vacillation in her attitude, the more so when a newly discovered timidity made a serious effort to overcome the barrier in his mind out of the question.

Tea was served in the small dining room overlooking the garden. The sheik's taciturn mood remained. With difficulty, Cheira listened to John's explanation of the maneuverings necessary to affect a transfer of stock that would ultimately lead to Pemberly control of one of the largest manufacturers of pipelines in Germany. At any other time, such a discourse would have held her interest for hours. Now her concentration was totally destroyed by Siri's dark eyes watching her across the table.

He gave her no respite from the surveillance. The torture was exaggerated by her uncertainty. She understood his behavior as a means of forcing a commitment from her. It only made her more reluctant, the threat of latent strength causing her to recoil. *If I could only detect a spark of love in his eyes,* she alibied, *it would give me the courage I needed.* The full-blown fear, which her memory conjured up, strangled even the desire to speak.

Finally, John lapsed into silence, giving up the struggle to obtain any coherent decisions from his distracted employer.

Then Siri spoke, his manner indicating that he had reached a decision after prolonged reflection. "With your ladyship's permission," he announced formally, "I will return to the desert for a short time. I'm needed at Imla Dun." His arrogant attitude belied the humility of his words. He rose abruptly. Looking directly at her, he added with a characteristic shrug, "This place suffocates me!"

"I think it would be proper, my lady," John hastened to insert before she could respond.

Cheira lowered her eyes. It was all the assent Siri needed.

"My plane is waiting. I can be in Touggourt for dinner." So saying, he precipitously fled the room.

Cheira didn't move, the unexpected action shocking her into immobility. Her mind was stunned. Then her attention was drawn to an unfamiliar throb beginning at a point in her chest. She caught her breath.

"Let him go," John spoke softly. "Since you don't want him to know the whole plan now, it's better if he's away."

Jealously, she wondered if he was so anxious to return to the desert because of the oda at the Fort. Although, she conceded, he had made a point of revealing his destination: Imla Dun, the big oasis where he raised the famous strain of Arabians prized by equine connoisseurs throughout the world. *There is no doubt,* she thought resentfully, *of his love for his horses.* And whatever else he did, Sheik Siri ben Ange never lied.

"Are you certain you don't want him to know? Shouldn't you know how he will react before you go too far?" John interrupted her thought, grasping quickly the chink he detected in her attitude.

She shook her head sadly. "If all the others object, how can I expect Siri to agree?" She was thinking of the violent argument with Wang Lu and the multitude of objections raised by the members in New York.

John tried another tack. "But, my lady, is it safe to wait too long? Siri is the most powerful man among us, you know that. He's potentially dangerous."

"So are we all." She dismissed the objection.

"But his temper," John persisted, "and his streak of cruelty. You know how he rules those poor devils out there." He waved his hand indicating the direction of the desert.

Cheira winced. "It's a very primitive society," she said in a small voice.

"Perhaps Mott could do something," John suggested, unwilling to give up the opportunity of obtaining her permission to put some sort of restraint on the sheik. Once the ceremony took place, he would be almost helpless to protect her. He shuddered to think of her at the mercy of the tribal leader's unbridled passion.

"It will come soon enough." It was all she would say.

Later alone, she frowned, thinking of John's patent dislike of Siri. Keenly cognizant of her chief deputy's obsessive loyalty toward her, she knew that at all cost the two men must be prevented from open hostility. She needed them both for the success of the experiment. Mott's procedure would make it possible to raise all of mankind to the state of transfiguration. No sacrifice was too great to accomplish such a goal. An unidentified urge demanded that.

Her thoughts returned to the immediate future and the gulf widening between herself and Siri, threatening unforeseen complications to the fruition of her plan. She had defended him to John: now she defended him to herself. *He never acts from temper or cruelty alone,* she rationalized, countering John's insinuations. *They may be instruments, but only that. He is always in control.* She probed for the basis of the conviction, but the reason she tried to find evaded her.

Her mind tended wistfully to the gentleness she had witnessed in him, handling a foal or playing with the children of his tribesmen. *Am I expecting too much,* she wondered, *to hope that, when I am his wife, he can also be kind to me?* She felt optimistic, magnifying the unimportant reasons on which she based the feeling. In that mood, she vowed to declare her love and her intentions as soon as he returned.

It was after midnight when Cheira appeared in Hardy's room. He was sprawled in a chair, sleeping. A look of annoyance crossed her face, until, on closer inspection, she detected that he was drugged. Her hand was on his shoulder to stimulate him to wakefulness when the door opened. Discreetly, she withdrew to watch.

Karen entered with a porter in tow.

"Help me get him to bed," the girl ordered. "I had to give him something," she explained defensively, as much to herself as to the old man. "He was so nervous—couldn't sit still a minute. I had to give him something. And at the Pemberly interview, he just sat there—in a trance. I think he's having a nervous breakdown."

With the clumsy handling of the girl and the old man, Hardy began to revive.

"What time is it?" he asked groggily, spying Karen. "What are you doing here?"

"About one," she answered. "But what difference does that make? You're ill."

"Get out of here," Hardy growled, struggling up to push her toward the door. "Get out of here," he repeated, his voice breaking with a sob of despair.

There's no need for her to leave, Bob. The thought came into his mind. *She's a very lovely girl and concerned for your welfare.*

He staggered, tottering between Karen and the disgusted porter, the combined effects of drugs and alcohol making his speech thick and slurred.

"You're ill," Karen repeated. "Please go to bed. You must rest." Karen spoke soothingly, taking his arm and trying to coax him in the direction of the bed. At the look of absorption on his face, as though he were listening to an inner voice, her worry increased. She, too, stood still, undecided on any logical course of action.

You're still a terrible actor, it seems. Your emotions are so transparent. What else could she believe? Pay attention to what she's thinking for a moment. She's about to decide that you're insane.

Hardy sank onto the floor, half-crouching, half-kneeling, his drug-numbed limbs only making a clumsy approximation of the position he tried to assume. His mind was a misty, aching morass; but Cheira's telepathy came to him clearly. He understood, only his brain refused to respond. His body trembled from the superhuman effort he was exerting to bring himself under control.

Karen dismissed the porter with a wave of her hand.

The old man was glad to escape. In a lifetime of service, he had seen all kinds of drunks. He accurately diagnosed this one as potentially violent if triggered by the right provocation. He felt sorry for Karen, but experience warned him that it was a waste of time to try getting her away from the man. He shrugged, closing the door softly. *There's nothing new in the world,* he thought, *and a drunk is a drunk no matter where he comes from.*

Hardy's shoulders sagged even lower when he understood the porter's thought. *But I didn't drink that much,* his mind protested.

Karen drugged you, Cheira informed him. *You'll be all right in an hour or so. She thought she was helping. You certainly must have been acting strangely. No matter. Your mind is clear enough to understand.*

Karen was too frightened to move. She remembered the sight of the mentally deranged she had once seen in an institution while doing a story for the Sundays. Her instinct told her to remain quiet lest she provoke him to violence.

Listen carefully, Cheira channeled the energy forcefully, helping Hardy to function as normally as possible. *We shall probably have no more personal contact. We both have much work to do. In the next few years, I want you to give Dr. Connor's experiments on aging as much publicity as possible. Try to plant in the public mind an acceptance of longevity. However, until we know how that experiment turns out, don't focus attention on Mott's work. Some of your inquisitive colleagues may want to discover their own information, if you give them a lead. Jim Connor's Maine experiment can be safely investigated by anyone.*

"You!" Hardy said aloud, stiffening as the implication of what she was telling him became clear. . . . *Intend to undergo the transformation,* he finished in his mind.

Yes. The silent affirmation came back.

Hardy knew then what the older members were objecting to so vehemently. He also knew that he didn't have the audacity to voice his objections, but that he wanted to.

Then you understand what I want you to do? The question pushed aside his own weaker thoughts.

He assented. *It's what people have always wanted, but never had any real hope of achieving. It will be easy,* he thought.

One other, and I hope, also a pleasant task . . . She paused, hesitating at the possible consequences of a hasty decision, the hesitation a new and alien characteristic. Impatiently, she cast it aside and continued. If Hardy were the man she thought he was, he'd handle what she was about to propose competently. If not, she might as well find out right away.

You know we want more women members. Karen is a lovely, intelligent, responsible girl. Sam has recommended her with the most glowing praise. I can see that she loves you. Within the next year, bring her to Arx Vetus—as your wife.

"No! No!" Hardy groaned.

Do you reject the first service I ask of you? Was your promise of obedience given so lightly?

The cry of agony wrenched from the lips of the man she loved mobilized Karen to action. She called a doctor, exhorting him to come to the hotel with the utmost haste.

By a curious empty feeling which left him light-headed, Hardy realized that Cheira had gone. Dragging himself upright, he fell across the bed. It was all over. He was sure he'd never see her again. He regretted having lost the years before he knew her. They were less painful than the knowledge he now possessed. A feeling of limitless frustration swept through him, making even breathing a conscious act. There was nothing he could do to alter the course of his future. He observed as from a great distance the mechanical pumping of his heart. He wondered why it bothered. He no longer cared.

Karen was sure the worst had happened. He lay so still.

But the doctor pronounced him "fit as a fiddle" except for what he termed "a very heavy dose of sleeping pills."

Karen was frantic as she showed the doctor the capsules She had only given him three.

"But these react especially potently with alcohol," the doctor informed her, noting the half-empty bottle of Scotch on the dresser.

"You mean I could have killed him?" she gasped, recalling how she'd slipped the powder into Hardy's last drink. "Is that why he acted so odd when he was coming out of it?"

"It might very well have been a reaction. Hallucinations are common in a case like this," the medical man agreed, snapping shut his bag. "If you should need me again, just call. But I'm sure the worst is over."

Karen only nodded, her attention already reverting to the prostrate figure on the bed. Kneeling beside him, she whispered, "I'm sorry!" Timidly, she put her hand on his hair.

Raising his head, he looked searchingly at her. She had the queer feeling that he was really seeing her for the first time. A lost expression lingered in his eyes, yet a new firmness was forming around his mouth. Confused, Karen looked at him questioningly.

"It's all right," he said, his voice betrayed sadness and resignation. Leaning on his elbow, he took her face in his hands, kissing her experimentally. She submitted quietly, but with growing dismay.

"Do you know," he continued in the same tone, "that we will be married?"

"Oh, darling," Karen responded happily, "of course we will." Her smile faded as the manner of phrasing reached her consciousness, making her frown. "Why did you say that?"

"Now it's my turn to be sorry," he apologized; his head was clearing rapidly.

He sat up, feeling better. "As you've probably heard, I've no experience with courtship." He smiled, ruefully.

"I don't mind," she answered, "if you really meant it."

Recoiling inwardly, Hardy cursed the fate which had fulfilled his dreams beyond his wildest imaginings, only to snatch from his grasp forever the only woman he could ever truly love. He couldn't blame Cheira for not returning his love, but how could be obey her command? He really had nothing against Karen. In fact, he liked her. But the years of obsession had precluded interest in any other woman.

The words he was using to frame his thoughts hit him with extraordinary clarity. He swung his legs over the side of the bed. Karen froze, stunned by the sudden movement. Was the strange behavior starting again? She watched him, wide-eyed.

Hardy stared at the wall, his eyes unfocused; his mind hammering the words over and over again. Like a flash, he saw. He knew what he was doing.

It was not Cheira, the reality, that haunted him, but an ideal liberally laced with imagination that resided only in his mind. By obeying Cheira, he would be unfaithful to no one but a phantasm. Ameur had tried to tell him that at Arx Vetus, but the cloud of his own emotions had been too dense for the words to penetrate. And Sam! Sam had told him many times since then that the whole story was only a ruse. Sam! Sam had sent him to London knowing all the time that Cheira was Lady Pemberly. How many times and in how many ways had he been told that his imagination was his greatest asset, but that his lack of discipline negated that, that he would never reach the heights until he learned to use his talent, not be used by it. The realization lifted a great weight off his shoulders, permitting him to anticipate the future with optimism.

"How about some breakfast? Order some up," he suggested in a normal tone. Grabbing a towel, he headed for the shower. He needed some time alone to spell out to himself the flash of insight he had just had. Yesterday, he would have ordered the girl out without a second's thought. Now he decided he might want her to stay.

Karen Benedict. She was one of the most intelligent women he knew. He grinned, even if she acted ridiculous when he was around. Her behavior wasn't any worse than his own. If her feelings stemmed from the same deep emotion . . .

She certainly was beautiful—soft bronze curls, lovely figure. Chuckling, he thought how easy it was going to be to surrender at last. Suddenly, he realized what he'd denied himself through the years. Still smiling, he turned the shower on cold, quelling the unexpectedly eager response of his body.

Face it, he mused, *you've been a damn fool, pursuing a dream for twenty years.* Then the unimaginable reality. Did he think that Cheira would accept his continence in some primitive ritual of sacrifice? *You damn fool,* he accused himself again. It made the laughter bubbling in his throat burst into sound.

He frowned deprecatingly, examining his slender body and mild features. Did he imagine he could compete with the extraordinarily handsome desert chief who exuded masculinity and power with every movement?

"Hey, breakfast is here," Karen yelled, pounding on the door.

Watching him curiously when he sat down and dove hungrily into the hot food, Karen concluded that his actions were normal.

Finally she ventured, "Did you really meant what you said a little while ago?"

"What did I say?" Hardy picked up a piece of toast.

"You said that we'd be married." Karen's voice was little more than a whisper.

"Well?"

"Did you mean it?"

"Yes," Hardy stated with conviction without interrupting his meal. He concentrated on spreading jam meticulously on the toast, acting as if the task required all his mental power.

"Is that all?" Karen's voice betrayed the disappointment she felt. This was certainly the least romantic proposal she'd ever received. The fact that it was the only one she'd ever wanted made it even harder to bear.

"For the moment." Her companion grinned. He had himself under control now, and, as Cheira had predicted, was learning to enjoy his appointed role.

"You're maddening!" Karen pounded the table with a small fist, her voice rising. "What sort of proposal is that?"

He stopped eating, laying aside the fork with slow deliberation.

"It's what you've been wanting ever since we came to London," he said, with mock severity.

Karen gasped. "I haven't been that transparent."

"Maybe I'm a mind reader," he retorted, laughing outright. "I also know that your intentions haven't always been honorable," he teased.

Karen blushed, the color spreading into the roots of her hair. She answered earnestly, in a soft voice, "But I love you."

"I know," Hardy admitted simply, his tone matching hers. Rising, he came around the table and drew her into his arms. "I can't lie to you," he continued seriously. "That would be too unfair. I don't love you, but we must be married. There are reasons that I'm not at liberty to reveal at present; but I can promise that you'll know one day soon. I swear that I'll be a good and faithful husband." The last words came in a strangled whisper.

"That's why you've been acting like you have?" She searched his face, willing now to accept any explanation that had a reassuring tone of rationality. Hardy had always been different than any man she had ever known: his strangely celibate life that she had seen as a mark of a strong character, but others had seen as a ridiculous snobbery; his great talent that was usually hampered by an unbridled imagination; and the naivete with which he faced the world and was to her the dearest trait of all. But her love was strong enough to withstand all the peculiarities, even the fact that he didn't love her in return. Yet he wanted to marry her. If that was all she could have, it was enough.

Hardy nodded, kissing her mouth experimentally.

"Do you expect me to believe that?" Karen couldn't help asking.

"You know my reputation," he reminded her. "I've never proposed to anyone before. That I do it now, honestly revealing how I feel, must give you some indication of my sincerity."

"But why now?"

"I told you. I can't tell you the reasons. You must accept that they are good ones. Anyhow, you've plenty of time to think it over. You needn't give me an answer right away. But I can promise you this much: You'll never regret it. As soon as we're married, then I'll explain." He looked directly at her, meeting her gaze steadfastly. "I swear it!" he added firmly.

"Well, this isn't exactly the way my dream went." Karen discarded romanticism quickly for reality, being a very practical girl. "But if it's that important, okay."

This wasn't in my dream either, he thought. But strangely he felt light and happy.

CHAPTER X

Hasi burst out of the small tent pitched proudly beside the sheik's larger one. He rubbed his eyes roughly, driving away the sleep which had claimed him just minutes ago. His keen young ears had picked up the distant drone of a plane, the sound streaking through the silent morning air. The camp was still asleep, only the shaggy hounds were already making their rounds.

Hasi ran for the big sorrel gelding tethered handily near his tent. Throwing on the bridle, he jumped on the horse's back, urging him toward the stallion paddocks, scattering squawking chickens, ignoring their cries of indignation at being so summarily awakened.

Within minutes, the boy was industriously scrubbing nonexistent dust from the already gleaming hide of the black stallion. The horse fidgeted between surprise at the unusual dawn grooming and the excitement he sensed in the boy.

Hasi ceased his labor to critically inspect the animal. Satisfied that the horse was spotless, he carefully lifted the silver-studded saddle onto Skotias's back. The horse, sure now that something odd was afoot, snorted and stepped away. Hasi spoke softly to him, the tone soothing, while his deft fingers flew unerringly to accomplish their work.

By the time the boy returned to the tents, leading the stallion, others were milling around excitedly. They, too, had been awakened by the swelling drone of the plane. As one, the tribesmen headed for the landing strip, Hasi in the lead with his master's horse.

Siri's greeting matched the enthusiasm of his men. He was as glad to get back to the oasis as they were to have him. When he complimented Hasi on the excellent condition of the stallion, the boy beamed, the light in his eyes showing clearly the love he had for his master. The cheering tribesmen corroborated Hasi's sentiment.

The black stallion, by this time trembling with the excitement of the boisterous welcome, plunged at the end of his line, rearing perpendicularly as soon as Siri was mounted. Siri laughed, letting the horse have his way. Whirling on his hind legs, Skotias was in full gallop when his forelegs

144

touched the ground. Siri shouted, for once dropping the reserve he usually maintained before his followers, letting them see the delight he felt in returning to the desert. He let Skotias full out, leading the madly yelling group in a circle around the giant oasis, recklessly disturbing the mares in their pasture and chasing the yearlings in a wild dash along the fence, their long legs sending them sprinting ahead of the older animals.

Siri had discarded the last restraints of the city by the time he pulled up before his tent, shouting an order for breakfast as his feet hit the ground. As fast as he moved, Hasi was before him, holding open the flap of the over-sized structure.

The sheik stopped just inside, allowing the dim, familiar coolness to wash over him. He surveyed the canvas enclosure with pleasure. He felt his identity enveloping him. His heart beat stronger in recognition. This was his life: essential, direct, natural.

Flopping down on the spacious, leather-covered divan, he let Hasi pull off his boots. The thick animal skin rugs, souvenirs of hunting from all over the world, felt soft when he walked across them to the curtained partition that concealed bedroom and bath.

Sprawled in the big tub, which was the one luxury he considered nec-essary even in this remote part of the world, Siri let the hot, soapy water soak away the tension that the last few months had generated. He grimaced as an endless procession of silly women and effeminate men paraded through his brain. In idle amusement, he marched the images out of the tent, out of Imla Dun, and into the merciless expanse of barren desert. With his mind's eye, he watched with satisfaction as they disappeared beneath the line of the horizon, wandering off without protest or provision, clothed only in their civilized ignorance.

Refuse! The word cracked inside his skull, snapping his body rigidly upright. *Challenge her!* But at the same instant that the thought flashed in his brain, the answer crowded it out. He lay back again, forcing his will to submission by the inactivity of his muscles. It was the one thing he would never do, he was certain. Even if he disregarded the oath that bound him, he could never again lapse into that state of unbridled passion of which she had borne the brunt. He was younger then, less disciplined. The years he had spent acquiring the power he possessed only narrowly allowed him to seek atonement for that transgression. Another such episode could earn him nothing but eternal damnation, which he would perpetrate by his own hand. His strict code of honor would allow a mistake if expiation were made in full measure, but never a repetition of the same error. The method of atonement was clear; he would not evade any of it.

Hasi interrupted his thoughts, speaking solemnly from the other side of the curtain, "Your breakfast is ready, master."

Siri smiled at the boy's precise English. "I will be there directly," he answered distinctly.

While he ate, Siri quizzed his protégé on his lessons. He admired the boy's brave struggle to pronounce the unfamiliar syllables of a foreign tongue, and Hasi's obvious pride in his accomplished task delighted him.

"Very well done," Siri told the youngster at the end of the recital. "Perhaps, if you continue such scholarship, in a year or so, you can go abroad to a university as Gamiel and Ahmed have done."

Hasi could only stammer and roll his eyes in reply. Such a promise was too great for any normal expressions of gratitude. But his master's recent unexplained absence darkened even this unspeakable joy. The worry urged him to elicit a further condition to the magnificent pledge.

"If you are in England, may I go to a university there?" the boy asked, with a spasmodic inhalation of breath.

Siri laughed. "We'll see. Now fetch Skotias before the morning is gone. I want to take a closer look at those yearlings. And tell Mohammed, I'm ready to ride."

Hasi fairly flew out of the tent.

When the sheik emerged a few minutes later, Hasi was holding the black stallion, already saddled and bridled. Mohammed, the headman, stood respectfully waiting.

The days slipped quickly by, filled with hard work. The proud, nervous horses required all the sheik's skill and concentration. The daylight hours passed too soon.

It was the long hours of the night when the hands of the clock seemed to stand still, when his mind would grant him no rest despite the protest of his aching muscles. Then his footsteps would trace an endless path in the fur of the rugs, and he would rage against the emotion that held him. The flickering flame from the dying lamp marked with wavering illumination the monotonous progress of his shadow on the canvas walls.

His followers, ever alert to their master's mood, whispered worriedly around the campfire. Instead of the usual raucous bragging and loud singing, the older men told tales they had heard from their fathers. For once the younger men listened.

The youths had paid scant attention before when the oldsters uttered ominous predictions concerning their master's absence. Now they listened with bated breath as the old men told of the far-off island that was the true home of Siri ben Ange. They watched intently as the men drew rough maps in the sand to show where it was. The youths furrowed their brows trying to recall the half-learned geography lessons, which they had resented for the time it took them away from the horses.

The tale was the legend of the tribe. There was magic in it and super-human feats. It had happened in the time of their great-grandfathers. They were poor in those days, the stragglers of wandering nomads living as best they could off the scraggly herds of sheep that scratched an existence from the skimpy brush surviving in the dry sand. Only a fierce pride in their hearts enabled them to bear the cruelties of the desert and its even more barbarous conquerors.

Then, one day, a warrior came, riding a magnificent black stallion. "Just like Skotias," Mohammed assured his audience. The warrior challenged the leader to combat, as was the custom. When he had despatched the hated leader, he invited all those who were brave enough to join him. "The timid ones slunk away," Mohammed intoned. "Only those strong and fearless could brave the fierce manner of the warrior. They followed him."

When a great number of men had been gathered in this manner, the warrior took them to an oasis. "This one," Mohammed waved his hand at the few ancient palms overhead. "And he told them to call it Iula Dun. He taught them to be horsemen and to raise and train the offspring of the great black stallion."

Then, a strange thing happened. The warrior was now old. Leaving the headman in charge, he went away. One year later, to the day, a new, young warrior came. He resumed leadership of the tribe, in the same way as the old one. "He looked the same and acted the same," Mohammed related in a hushed tone.

The same thing had happened again when Mohammed was just a child. He remembered the time when his father was leader of the tribe in the sheik's absence. Now, the headman was certain it was happening again. The signs were there. The sheik had gone to the mysterious fort one hundred miles to the south, the place where no one ever went, the place where it was possible to vanish forever.

Years ago, some of the men had stolen away to investigate the place. Only the bravest men of the tribe had undertaken the adventure. It was while their master was absent. But they were discovered by the inhabitants at the gate. Then the sheik came and dragged them home in disgrace. His anger

147

was fierce and the men were severely punished. No one had ever dared try it again. How the sheik knew they were there, they could not even guess.

But their master always seemed to know what they were doing and thinking. It was this strange power that made them take the punishment for errors honestly admitted no matter how harsh, rather than face the murderous rage of a master to whom they had lied.

Mohammed predicted that the restlessness of the sheik presaged his departure. The headman waited now only for the summons that would tell him so.

Siri came out of the tent to stand at the edge of the awning. The confines of the canvas enclosure were particularly suffocating this night. He noticed the men still huddled around the fire. Their thoughts came to him clearly; but the pity he felt for the bewilderment of his faithful followers carried no desire to enlighten them, even if he were free to do so.

The men, nevertheless, slunk guiltily away to their tents, leaving him alone under the star-filled sky. The encompassing stillness of the earth cloaked in the blackness of night brought his restlessness to the acute point. The time had come to test the emotion that held him prisoner.

The next morning he ordered horses and provisions for the journey to the Fort.

The west wing of the main building at the Fort was like an extension of the garden. The spacious atrium was filled with tropical plants, their gaudy blossoms filling the air with a heady fragrance. Music from concealed speakers pleasantly drowned the monotonous hum of the big fans overhead. A twenty-foot-square tiled pool dominated the center of the room. Lilies of such exquisite workmanship that only the sense of touch could determine their artificiality floated on the still surface.

A dozen women lived in the seraglio, in a state of oriental luxury. With all their needs provided, they were free to follow their personal inclinations. The women were permitted to leave whenever they wished, the only stipulation being that as long as they remained they accept the limitations of a cloistered existence; and once they chose to depart, they were never allowed to return. Their voluntary stay, therefore, was a tacit admission that they belonged to the master of the Fort. It was a custom of the country.

Dira Sadi, the widow of a tribesman and mother of Hasi, acted as a sort of housemother. She was the women's only liaison with the outside world. Dira's sympathy for her countrywomen was responsible for the presence of most of them. She had rescued them from cruel masters or irresponsible, abusive fathers. The ancient status of women in the desert remained unchanged, despite the influx of foreigners.

Dira encouraged the women to spend a major part of their time on education. The sheik's extensive library provided an inexhaustible supply of books on every conceivable subject, and the office in the main wing generously supplied materials and magazines. Many a former resident had gone eventually to the university in Cairo, there to become nurses, technicians, or secretaries. The sheik's generosity to women he had never even seen was long and gratefully remembered by successful women whose lives would have otherwise ended as the drudge of some ignominious nomad.

The two European girls were daughters of Swedish missionaries who had fallen victims of a tribal war. Lilith and Blanca were rescued by Simbar Abu, a member of Cheira's organization and longtime friend of the sheik's. Abu sent them to the Fort, confident that Siri would see to their futures. The girls had never seen their guardian, except the single time, shortly after their arrival when he had welcomed them. He had been courteous, but distant. They were preparing now to leave for Sweden where a cousin had been found to care for them. Bianca was eighteen, her sister two years younger.

The girls were dawdling by the side of the pool, listening to American rock blasting from a tiny recorder, when the sheik burst in. They were too astonished to move.

Still clad in a voluminous burnoose, he looked gigantic. His unusually handsome face was drawn into a series of sharp angles, the skin stretched tight over the bones. He stood still on the steps leading into the atrium, the sound of the door he'd slammed behind him still echoing against the walls. He surveyed the room with narrowed eyes.

At the noise, the other girls ran from their chambers. The looks of curiosity on their faces changed to one of dismay. The shock was understandable. None of the present residents had ever seen the sheik. He was almost a mythical figure in their lives, their only knowledge of him was what Dira chose to tell them. The obvious reason for their living in the seraglio had become only a symbol. The aging sheik spent his time with his horses, on the affairs of his tribe, and on the mysterious studies that even rumors didn't explain.

Siri's glance moved over the tableau, traveling over the silent figures as if they were part of the decor. Not until his gaze encountered the blonde girls at poolside did he walk forward. His foot kicked aside the blaring recorder sending it sputtering into silence in the depths of the water, making the lilies bob frantically on the widening ripples.

149

The girls rose uncertainly as he stopped before them. Their skimpy European swimsuits concealed little from the fierce black eyes. Siri's head jerked back in the characteristic gesture of surprise as Lilith's green eyes met his look unflinchingly, an apparent act of will conquering the fear lurking in their depths.

Dira Sadi hurried up, the garment she had been mending still hanging in her hand.

"What do you desire, master?" she asked, making a deep curtsy. One glance at his expression told the old woman what she could not believe. In a fleeting thought she wondered if the sheik had gone insane.

Lilith shifted uncomfortably, her courage failing fast under the sheik's unwavering stare.

He turned abruptly. "Send her to my quarters," he snarled at Dira Sadi as he passed her. She had only heard that tone in his voice before when he was meeting out punishment to a recalcitrant follower. Now, mustering all the daring she possessed, she acted quickly.

"You must not, master," she pleaded, trotting at his side to keep up with the long stride. "These girls are here under your protection. They are not one of us. Please, master, chose one of the others."

He stopped and she caught her breath as the full power of his gaze rested on her, but she would not retreat.

"Do you refuse to obey me?" His voice was so low she barely heard, but the tone sent a chill to the very depths of her soul. Without waiting for an answer, he mounted the steps and walked out.

Dira Sadi stared at the door, her mouth pressed into a thin line of defiance, her lips white, her mind making a frantic effort to grasp what had happened. The sheik's actions were unprecedented. She couldn't decide what to do; she was torn between fear and the necessity for protecting her charges.

It was Lilith who moved first. Running to the old woman's side, she said breathlessly, "It's terribly exciting. Did you see the way he looked at me?"

Dira turned to the girl. "Dear child, you don't know what you're saying."

"Of course, I do." Lilith laughed, to cover her nervousness. "Do you think I'm that stupid? He wants me. And he's the most handsome, most masculine man I've ever seen."

"You don't know what you're saying," Dira repeated, looking sadly at the girl. She was only a child by the standards of her cultural birth, that culture which idealized women, which made no provision for this type of existence.

Dira wondered if she dare defy the sheik. She could send the girls away immediately, before he discovered they were gone. She pushed out of her mind the pictures of the sheik's vengeance. Deliberately she accepted the consequences of her actions in order to save her charges.

"You must go away now," she said, turning to Bianca who had come up to stand beside her sister. "Pack at once. You leave within the hour."

"No!" Lilith stopped her sister as she moved to obey. "Help me to get ready. I'm going to the sheik."

Bianca hesitated, looking from one to the other.

"Speak to her," Dira wailed. "She doesn't know what she's saying."

Bianca smiled, more aware than her sister of the attitude the old woman held. "I think she does," she explained. "You're judging us by your standards. We don't consider such an encounter as the end of the world or as an irretrievable ruination, only as a pleasant interlude. I wouldn't miss the chance if I'd been chosen."

Dira's eyes widened, shocked. "You must not," she whispered.

Lilith's scornful laugh was her answer.

"You're old-fashioned," Bianca retorted.

Lilith's heart was hammering against her ribs and Dira Sadi's sobs of protest were still ringing in her ears as she opened the door to the sheik's quarters. She was acutely conscious of the long cloak that swished against her bare legs as she walked. She felt the soft silk lining clinging to her back and the unaccustomed contact of the flesh of her arms on the warmth of her breasts as she held the voluminous folds tight about her body. This was an adventure such as she had only read and dreamed about. That it was actually happening left her breathless. She thought of the times she and Bianca had whispered in the night recounting everything they remembered about the sheik, giggling in embarrassment as they confessed to each other the fantasies in which he exercised the right which their presence in his harem implied.

Siri was standing at the window when Ahmed motioned her into the room, closing the door noiselessly. Lilith felt her bravado vanish with the departing servant. Her eyes flicked automatically around the dimly lit room;

she noted the divan upholstered with leopard gaudily astrew with satin pillows, flanked by heavily padded chairs. She thought how incongruous it looked next to a huge mahogany desk piled high with books and papers. An expanse of thick carpeting drew her vision to the alcove, which partially concealed an immense bed. She stared at it for seconds before she could pull her eyes away.

Siri hadn't moved nor in any way acknowledged her presence. She looked at him now. The fading light outlined his shoulders as he stood with his back to her. She saw the muscles bunched on his arms, folded across his chest. Her peripheral vision heeded the discarded shirt lying across the back of a chair. He wore the loose trousers secured by a wide sash and the high boots customary in the desert.

She trembled, suddenly aware of the tension in the silence and painfully conscious of her own inexperience. What was she supposed to do, she wondered. She knew now that he was aware of her presence. She saw the tautening of the muscles in his back. But why did he hesitate?

"Come here," he said. The words rupturing the silence of the room turned her legs to water. He had repeated the command before she summoned the strength to obey. He still did not move.

Lilith felt the hysteria rising up from her stomach. She clamped her lips tight together to suppress the scream gathering at the base of her throat. *Only concentrate on moving your legs,* she told herself. Somehow, she managed to make the journey across the carpet and come to a halt beside him.

An eternity passed in the time it took him to turn his head. His face bore the same expression she had seen in the seraglio. In the instant their eyes met, she wondered why now it looked like an expression of torture. She forgot her fear in a quick response of sympathy. She stepped closer, knowing a desire to assuage the loneliness and torment an unguarded moment had allowed her to see in his eyes.

But his next words shocked the impulse into quiescence.

"Take that damn thing off." His tone was cold, brutal, reminding her of the purpose for which she was here. With one hand clutching the opening of the cloak, she reached up with the other to throw back the hood still concealing her totally, revealing only her eyes.

"My name is Lilith," she whispered, needing to prod his acknowledgement of her as a person. The tensing of a muscle in his jaw gave her confidence. She started to recapture the feeling of sympathy, but it died when he spoke again.

"I know your name," he said in the same cold tone. "And many other things about you. And also that you have not obeyed me."

She trembled, no longer caring if he noticed. Her eyes widened in horror.

"But I can't," she protested. "Not just like that."

Her thoughts were too apparent to avoid despite his resolution to keep the counter impersonal. He laughed mirthlessly. He could find no pity in his heart.

"You have read too many novels and have had too little instruction from Dira Sadi." He paused, letting the silence wear down her resistance.

"Obey me," he said finally. He spoke softly, barely above a whisper; but she perceived an inflection in the tone that brooked no defiance. She was helpless before the power in the flashing black eyes. Her nerveless fingers opened the clasp of the cloak; the heavy material slid off her shoulders.

Lilith forced herself to stand straight. She was here because she wanted to be, refusing disdainfully Dira's plan of escape. It was too late to regret the consequences of her decision. At least she could keep from cringing; but she could not control the hot blood that rushed into her face, spreading down her neck and shoulders. She saw his hand come up, the long fingers reached out to touch her. She closed her eyes, a wave of dizziness swept through her brain. She waited, holding her breath, only partially controlling the queasiness of her stomach.

But the touch never came. Siri had ceased to see the girl standing before him. Cheira's image blotted her out. He saw the mistress of Arx Vetus in the flashing sequences of a kaleidoscope; in the white tunic she wore at Arx Vetus, her golden hair cascading down her back; in the trim suit of a newspaperwoman leaning against the stone wall of the Fort, lost for the moment in contemplation; in a décolleté ball gown, the wide skirt catching his legs as he led her in the steps of a waltz; in the severe cut of a riding habit, which only intensified the constant ache of desire that haunted him. The pictures halted abruptly as he saw her in the costume she wore that last night at Arx Vetus. His consciousness focused on the green eyes that mocked him no matter what the circumstances or the costume, the flecks of gold and brown highlighting the irises, presaging not the warmth of autumn but only the bitter cold of winter.

With an oath, he flung himself into a chair, the precipitant movement dissolving the spectre. In the last decade, he had come to accept the recurring images as the price of his increasing power. It was this that forced him into a kind of tortured celibacy. That he had chosen to test the spectre's strength once again was his own folly.

Absorbed in the anguish of his thoughts, Siri had forgotten the girl. Wide-eyed, Lilith stared at him, caught between confusion and panic. She could make no sense of his actions. Slowly it dawned on her that she had been rejected. She looked with almost scientific objectivity down at her young body, but could find nothing wrong with it—her skin was smooth and soft, her legs long and slim, her stomach flat, her small breasts firm and erect.

She looked at the sheik. He was leaning forward, his hands bracing his bowed head. Her attention was drawn to the heavy black hair that curled at the nape of his neck. She noticed the streaks of gray at the temples and her practiced eye, so deft at detecting the use of dye and bleach in women, told her that it was not real. But the thought led nowhere. She dropped it for another puzzle. Her glance traveled to the bowed shoulders. Her keen eyes discovered the minute circle of a tattoo. She took a step forward, succumbing to the irresistible curiosity of youth.

Her movement brought Siri out of his reverie. He stood up, turning to look at her in surprise. She saw that he had forgotten her presence. The humiliation of her position pushed all other thoughts out of her mind and a reckless anger took its place.

"Go back to the women," Siri said, his voice kinder than she had yet heard it. But the pride that gripped her would not allow her to recognize it. She wanted to hurt him, to penetrate the distance between them, to make him desire her.

"What's wrong with me?" she spat at him. "Or is it you?" Her voice rose hysterically. "You're not a man. You're . . . you're . . . "

His hand flew at her so swiftly she had not time to react. He slapped her face.

"You may think what you like," he said, quietly, "but keep your thoughts to yourself."

He turned away, walking deliberately across the room to jerk the bell cord.

Lilith sagged against the chair, the sobs she could no longer suppress shaking her thin shoulders. The cloak lay unheeded where it had dropped.

"You'd better cover yourself before Ahmed comes," Siri spoke, his voice resuming the kindly tone.

With a sigh of defeat, Lilith obeyed.

Wrapped up to the eyes in the flowing cloak, the girl silently followed Ahmed back to the west wing. She noticed the astonished looks of the servants they passed and the knowing winks they gave each other burned her with humiliation. She wanted to scream at them and scratch their eyes out. Then, in an about-face characteristic of her fickle personality, spoiled by the years of being her doting parents' darling, she decided that no one need ever know. Her tearstained face could just as easily be proof of the sheik's passion that her outraged innocence had endured. Her fingers crept up to the welts on her cheek. Disappointed, she felt no satisfactory swelling. In a flash of inspiration, with her teeth clenched to silently withstand the anticipated pain, she dug her nails into the tender flesh, leaving long red streaks that oozed tiny drops of blood. Her vivid imagination had conjured a graphic version of the experience by the time she returned to the seraglio.

When the girl had gone, Siri resumed the restless pacing he had interrupted when he left Imla Dun. The episode had proven only his own helplessness to control the emotion that possessed him. If what he felt for Cheira could not be conquered, it could at least be resisted. That he must submit to the course she required of him, he conceded; but he resolved that she would never know what it cost him. He would not allow her the satisfaction of seeing his frustration. No code of honor demanded that much. He would meet the cold hauteur of those beautiful green eyes with an arrogance of his own. He accepted the fact that she detested him, that she had good reason, and that the position into which she had managed to maneuver him was devilishly clever. He had seen often enough the unerring deftness of her revenge descend on anyone who dared to defy her. That she had ignored his behavior for so long should have warned him.

He was due back in London day after tomorrow. But why wait? The house at Lamborn was ready for occupancy now. He grimaced at the irony that it was a woman who was responsible for the opening of the ancient manor. *What would be more fitting,* he thought, *then that she should be his first guest?*

He stopped the steady striding that carried him back and forth across the room, halted by the spectacle: Cheira in his father's house. He almost wished the old man were alive. How he'd enjoy watching the tyrannical earl try to dominate her! His imagination failed to even attempt to see the outcome of such a contest.

CHAPTER XI

"Please, my lady," Jennie begged. "You must eat something."

Lady Pemberly sat with chin in hand staring dreamily into space, ignoring the tray of food on the little table. Jennie fidgeted, her brow creased with worry, torn between her mistress's obvious unhappiness and her own helplessness to alleviate it.

Cheira had had no communication with Siri since the day he'd walked out, fleeing to the desert to escape an intolerable situation. That was three months ago. But now the official ceremony was less than a month away. He was due to return to England. The manner of his precipitant flight bothered her. Was his yearning for the desert an indication of his true feelings?

She longed to send him some message. She had even been tempted to monitor his thoughts surreptitiously or to secretly observe his activities. What was he doing in the time he was away from her? What held his devotion? The old feeling of timidity paralyzed the impulse for action, instead prompting an indecisive, debilitating frustration of worry.

Siri was too powerful to arouse open defiance now, she reasoned. That he would comply with her wishes, she had no doubt. He had given his word. But it was his willing cooperation she craved. *How far would he feel obligated to hold to his promise when he learned the real basis of the union?* She dared not insert any additional complications into an already explosive affair. If he thought she was spying on him, if he thought she doubted his word . . . She shuddered. *Might it not destroy the reluctant concession she had wrested from him?*

He didn't love her. And without love to temper his dynamic character, what nightmare was she creating for herself? *Well,* she thought, sitting up and squaring her shoulders, *my love will have to sustain us both.* She would take the full responsibility since it was she who had initiated what was to follow.

With a determination foreign to her nature, she vowed to openly declare her love at the earliest possible opportunity, realizing fully the vulnerable position she was accepting.

Why am I doing this? she wondered. Were the noble motivations she had declared to the others truly the reasons she was driving herself into such an uncertain future? There was a tiny suspicion that she didn't want to admit even to herself that she wasn't that unselfish. Was the personal reason more important than her duty to the society? She couldn't decide. She only knew that the question was there.

The question of her own humanity had become a growing preoccupation that gnawed continually at the edges of her consciousness. She had to know! Science had finally given her the opportunity. What had seemed purely miraculous a century ago was now submitting to the scrutiny of the laboratory.

I can fulfill both aims, she decided, *as long as I insure the continuity of the organization.* She was sure she knew how to delegate her power to transfigure to someone else. Some of the others had had plenty of time to develop to the point of being able to produce the required amount of energy.

She reviewed the most likely possibilities: John, of course; Ameur and Tiana; Sam Hackett in New York; Ed Peterson in Portland; Siri, obviously . . . She chose John, mentally reciting the reasons for her choice.

Frowning, her thoughts turned to Wang Lu. Why had he been so obstinate? He could have helped her now. She would never forgive herself for allowing his lapse into the ordinary human state. *But then,* she wondered honestly, *could I have actually stopped him?* Were his stated reasons the true ones? In those days, no one's power even approximated her own; but Wang Lu had guided and encouraged its acquisition. It was only logical, therefore, to believe that he knew as much about it as she did, or more. She remembered how he had refused transfiguration, maintaining that he was already too old to tolerate the input of energy required. Finally, when she and Ameur had continued to insist, he had submitted. She sat up, an intuitive light flashing in her mind. Wang Lu had had no reaction whatsoever from the transfer of energy. She hadn't thought of it before. Now she remembered that there had been no practice on his part to learn the use of power. She had assumed that it was because of the time he had spent helping her that he already knew what to do. Now she was not so sure.

Then, suddenly, he had decided to relinquish his state. He had told her that if they separated, his power would gradually fade. She had accepted that. But now she wondered. Could that really happen? That premise had been the reason for the rule that all members must spend some time each year at Arx Vetus. She shook her head, unable to find any answers.

Had he deliberately removed himself from temptation, fearing his own ability to control such great capabilities, which his knowledge would have made it easy for him to obtain? Had his oriental wisdom cautioned him against creating a situation that could possibly have led to an outright challenge for supremacy?

Perhaps he had been even more aware than she of the weaknesses in her character. She thought guiltily of how quickly she had accepted Siri's challenge that night at Arx Vetus, even though she had sworn only moments before to control her temper.

Of course, the members had proven Wang Lu's fears—if such were his motive—groundless. With the increased ability to absorb knowledge quickly and easily and hence to acquire anything the world had to offer, they had shown little inclination to misuse their power. An indefinitely prolonged lifetime made overindulgence unnecessary. There was no frantic hurry to experience all the facets of life while life and youth still remained. Time became a friend and each moment an experience to be savored.

In the process, destructive activity became meaningless. There was no need to circumvent the creative process through unlawful acquisition of another's labors. The ultimate threat, death, was no longer an excuse for avaricious behavior.

She had never had any doubt that it would be so. She had always had an all-pervasive faith in the tendency of humanity toward good. *Was it ignorant innocence,* she wondered, *this conviction that intelligent men would naturally aim higher and higher when the insidious threat of extinction was removed?* How or when she had come by this conviction, she didn't pause to question.

It must be admitted though, her thoughts continued, *that most of the members had reached middle age and, therefore, the stability of maturity, before they were admitted to the society. They pursued their chosen careers, leaders in their fields, with no help from me.* She never inquired into their personal lives beyond the injunction to study and practice to increase their power. On this point she was adamant, making it Ameur's chief duty to see that everyone obeyed.

As the organization grew without her constant and direct supervision, her attention had turned inward, to herself and what she was. The need to know had become more and more insistent. No matter what method she employed to nudge her memory she could remember nothing before that day in Darjeeling. And then she was just like she was now. The void in her memory had become a source of annoyance, underlying and interfering with everything she did, intruding distractingly on her duties.

With the organization running automatically and the scientific means available, she clearly had no valid reason to wait. Her thoughts supported the validity of her actions. *And bolster my courage*, she thought wryly, smiling to herself.

"My lady," Jennie spoke softly, hesitating to interrupt Cheira's meditation. "Lord Siri has arrived. He's waiting with Sir John in the library."

"But he wasn't due till day after tomorrow," Cheira protested, jolted out of her reverie.

Jennie responded sympathetically to the startled look in Cheira's eyes. The country girl's unqualified love made her sensitive to the moods of her employer. She felt the conflicting emotions that were making her mistress suffer. Willingly she would have born the burden had she known how to do so.

Making her way to the unexpected meeting, Cheira was surprised to feel her heart pounding. Having grown used to considering herself cold and impassionate, she was unprepared for the feelings that Siri's proximity evoked. The feelings she had were new and startling.

She left the suite immediately, but her footsteps slowed as she walked down the long hall. She walked, discarding the idea of teleportation because it was time she needed. It took an act of will to summon the composure that usually was second nature. Pride came to her aid; and by the time she descended the winding staircase into the great hall, it clothed her like a suite of armor, her feelings concealed beneath it, safe even from the most probing eyes.

At the door, she smoothed her hair, an outward gesture of the act she was assuming and settled her features into an indecipherable, expressionless mask.

The two men rose as she entered.

"We were just discussing the itinerary for the next couple of weeks," John explained, handing her a glass of sherry when she was seated. In his customary brusque manner, he resumed the conversation with a discussion of prenuptial events. Again, Cheira was grateful for John's businesslike attitude. It gave her an excuse for silence in a situation that, she was finding out, demanded the utmost in. self-control.

Cheira listened with as much concentration as she could muster. She found Siri's silence disconcerting and squirmed under the bold appraisal of his gaze. Although he hadn't greeted her—his manner implying that such a formality was an unnecessary gesture between them—he seemed to challenge her to set the terms of this meeting.

It was subtle torture not to know what he was thinking. An acute infection of timidity made her dismiss the temptation to attempt to find out. There was also the dread that the barrier in her own mind might prove insufficient protection should he decide to test it.

"Does this program meet with your ladyship's approval?" John concluded, refusing to react to the tension he sensed between his listeners.

"Oh, yes," Cheira's attention snapped back to what John was saying. She agreed because she hadn't heard a word. *If need be, I can change it later,* she decided. Glancing at Siri, she was met with a look of amusement. Irritatingly, but beyond her control, she felt the hot blood rising into her face.

"There's still a few days before the formalities begin." Siri spoke for the first time. "I've had Lamborn Heath opened and renovated. The workmen are nearly finished."

Cheira could not fail to notice the contrast between the two men, each a representative of his respective culture. Although both men were nearly the same height, John looked slender in a dark, expertly tailored business suit; while Siri exuded the strength of a man able to subdue the elements and manipulate them to his advantage, dressed as he was in the native costume, the spotless white material emphasizing the free spirit of the wearer.

"May I have the honor of your ladyship's company? You shall be my first visitor," Siri continued, lounging indolently in the formal, brocaded chair. His manner obviously flouted the protocol required and accepted without question by others.

John cleared his throat.

"You, too, of course." Siri laughed. "I didn't expect Lady Pemberly to come without her duenna . . . er, entourage."

John glared at him, but said nothing.

"This weekend, then?" Siri turned to Cheira for confirmation, ignoring one of the most important men in the organization. John reddened, compressing his lips to keep back the angry retort. It was only Cheira's presence that prevented a confrontation.

Cheira nodded assent.

Without another word, Siri left the room.

"That barbarism is intolerable," John burst out as soon as the door was closed. "He hasn't even the excuse of ignorance to speak on his behalf. He knows very well what he is doing. How much humiliation must we bear?"

Cheira was silent during John's tirade. He stopped in front of her, waiting for a reply.

"I'll see you at Arx Vetus," she said slowly, "in twenty-four hours."

John started, surprised. He hadn't expected her attitude to have changed so much, so quickly. The anger faded out of him. Deflated, he sat down, absently gathering up the papers lying scattered on the coffee table.

"I'm very busy," he protested weakly.

Cheira waited.

"In twenty-four hours," John sighed, surrendering, "as your ladyship commands." But his hatred of Siri grew.

Tiana had long ago learned to take Cheira's appearances in her stride. She was always pleased with any time they could spend together. Although she loved her husband and Arx Vetus, Cheira's visits meant direct contact with the world she had forsaken and the female companionship that Arx Vetus lacked.

Conversely, it was only with Tiana that Cheira threw off her natural reserve and the regal manner that had become habitual.

"For the first time," Cheira confided, when they were alone, "I'm frightened." The two women were settled comfortably on the sofa in Cheira's suite. The room was small and cozy, ideally suited to the intimate confessions they periodically made to each other. "The enormity of what I'm doing is finally becoming real."

"I know." Tiana took her hand n both of hers, lending comfort and support through the gesture.

"I wish Wang Lu were here," Cheira said, plaintively.

"We all love you and we'll use all our power to protect you. Wang Lu couldn't have done more."

"I appreciate your help very much. Without it, I couldn't go on. Especially the way John and Siri act . . . " Cheira related the episode at Pemberly House and her realization of the enmity of the two men most directly involved with the fruition of her plan. She told Tiana what she intended to do.

"I'm a coward," Cheira confessed. "I've never realized it before. It's always been so easy. There has never been any question of anyone's loyalty. Now I find my wishes in conflict with the others."

She sat up, shaking her head, her thoughts swinging to the one problem that seemed to be unmitigatingly selfish. "And I'm the only one who can't remember what it was like before. Maybe there wasn't any past for me."

"Of course, you had a past," Tiana reassured her, hiding her own shaky

161

confidence. "Just because you can't remember doesn't mean anything. And this is your opportunity to find out."

"Do you think they'll still hate each other if I die?"

"Oh, my dear"—Tiana squeezed Cheira's hand tightly—"you won't die. Ameur has thoroughly researched Mott's procedure. And although he doesn't like it, he has admitted that it's not dangerous. And they love you, too." Tiana's voice was firm.

Cheira looked at her doubtfully.

"Please believe me," Tiana said earnestly. "Siri does love you, but he's a proud man. And you must admit your actions haven't been encouraging. There is much misunderstanding between you. Remember no one can read your mind, not even he."

"I'm not so sure of that," Cheira returned, then added defensively, "I can't help remembering—and . . . "

"Surely, Siri has more than made up for that," Tiana admonished. "And you're not the innocent child you were then, either."

"I know," Cheira agreed. "But I guess I'm still afraid of him. I can't seem to control that."

"Nonsense," Tiana's voice was firm. "You have decided to trust him. Now do it! Come," she added, rising, "let me have dinner served in the garden. Ching Li will play for you, and the desert night will soothe your spirit and bring a promise of hope with the dew of evening."

Cheira followed meekly, content for the moment to let Tiana bear the responsibility for her immediate actions. Sometimes it was a comfort to be taken care of, and she hadn't known it since Wang Lu's desertion.

A long while later, Ameur came into the garden to sit with her. He sat cross-legged in the grass next to her chair. She saw the worry in the expression on his face.

"I beg you to reconsider before it's too late." He spoke so softly that she wasn't sure if she heard his voice or was receiving his thought. Ameur was repeating again the objections she had heard from the others. Only Tiana seemed to understand her need and her duty. All this opposition was undermining her determination. She summoned all her courage to withstand Ameur's arguments.

"The process is too new," he continued emphatically when she didn't answer. "A mechanical device is always risky."

"Tiana said you had examined the procedure thoroughly and had found it safe."

"It is safe; but there is always the chance of a slip. Why not let someone else try it first?"

"You know why," Cheira whispered, masking her uncertainty.

"Well, even if that part of the experiment is successful," Ameur admitted grudgingly, "you will have proved your point and you needn't go on."

"But that is only the beginning of the plan," she reminded him. "The reversal of itself proves nothing."

"Siri will never agree." He shook his head. "He's changed, you know. Despite his seeming antagonism, that's just his pride. He really loves you. He'd never cooperate in any way that would endanger your life."

"There's no reason to believe my life will be in danger," she interjected, refuting that argument with a vehemence that betrayed her own trepidations. "And besides the reward will be more than worth any risk." Her chin came up firmly, but Ameur wasn't looking at her. "I appreciate your concern," she added, almost formally, "but my mind is made up." Her voice softened. "Please don't make it any harder for me."

Ameur shivered; and she knew it was not the freshening breeze of evening or the fear that she might be endangering her life, but the agonizing knowledge that she would finally belong to another. The relationship between them, although settled for years, still lingered in their memories. This action of hers would put the stamp of finality on it. Siri's spectre stood between them then and now crystallized permanently with her approval.

"You know why Siri is my choice," she said, referring to the episode that had never been discussed between them. "You more than anyone know how I've struggled to free myself from the emotion that binds me. I've given up trying to understand, but I know it's stronger even than the fear I haven't been able to conquer. Ameur, my dear, dear friend, you cannot save me this time—if, indeed, it's saving I need.

"Sometimes I have the feeling that this was meant to be, that I've known it, but that I just can't remember. That this is the beginning of some grand plan even though we are nascent. Yes, it's more than an impression. It's a compulsion that's been growing stronger every year.

"Stand by me, old friend," she pleaded. "Perhaps there is salvation in this somewhere for all of us."

Ameur bowed his head without answering. It was his acknowledgement and acceptance. He would no longer oppose her.

They didn't speak again. He sat with her through the night. Ching Li played softly, her fingers like the desert breeze floating across the strings of her instrument.

Ameur's presence was comforting. She was glad that he stayed, especially since this would be their last time together, perhaps forever. Just having him near her just as he had so many years ago when, frightened and humiliated, she had sought refuge at Arx Vetus.

It was then a partially abandoned outpost of the Foreign Legion. The young American lieutenant had discovered her while on a routine patrol. She had been too shaken to hide her plight from the sympathetic mercenary, spilling out the story of her disastrous initial attempt at rectifying the misery of the world. She was huddling in that forsaken place because of her reluctance to return to Wang Lu and admit the failure of her mission, undertaken despite the Oriental's dire predictions.

Ameur, with characteristic optimism and a strong bent for adventure—traits which accounted for his being in the Legion in the first place—suggested she make Arx Vetus her headquarters. By skillful manipulation of his unwary superiors, he had been able to reroute the patrol, virtually leaving her in isolation. He arranged a clever ambush by a usually hostile Arab tribe whose chief had succumbed to the American's charm. As a result, his men reported him killed, thereby freeing him to stay at Arx Vetus.

Voluntarily and enthusiastically, Ameur submitted to her first confused attempts at transfiguration. Uncomplaining, he had endured the agony of her untutored power, encouraging her to continue when the enormity of what she was attempting intimidated her.

Together, they had devised the formulas that determined the level of concentration needed for the direction of the energy her body could generate at the behest of her will. She practiced teleporting to certain prearranged points. Many times Ameur set out to bring her back when she had not returned within the allotted time. He insisted that she must have perfect command of the ability to teleport so that never again could she be held prisoner as she had been at the Fort.

They experimented with mental pictures to form an impenetrable barrier to the violation of her thoughts in anticipation of the day when an organization would be formed, and she would need always to be on guard against any attempt to challenge her power.

She discovered that she could direct the energy emitted from her body. That by directing it through her hands, she could produce pain or pleasure in anyone she touched through an act of will, that by diffusing the energy her body would glow.

Through an arrangement with the tribe that had helped him execute his demise, Ameur provided for their needs and insured their solitude. He drew up the plan that set the organization in motion, collected a list of candidates for Cheira's inspection, and suggested a method of bringing them to Arx Vetus without undue publicity.

Ameur instigated the accumulation of books, which enabled them to acquire a working knowledge of every major science and profession. The ease with which their expanded consciousness retained information made study a pleasure; and Ameur insisted, if their grand plan was to be workable, they needed to know what the world already knew.

It was many years later before Cheira realized how much she owed to the American's common sense and single-minded loyalty. And by then she knew that the one payment he wanted she could never grant him.

She notified Wang Lu, two years later, of her whereabouts and what she was striving to accomplish. In all that time, Ameur had never tried to take advantage of their necessary intimacy, nor did he ever refer to the devastating experience which had brought them together.

When dawn came, she bade him, "Go to Tiana. She awaits you."

He rose to one knee, twisting to meet her gaze, expressing in his eyes the acceptance of her decision made endurable by the undiminished love which would always conceive her wishes as one with his own. She could be sure of his loyal support.

She leaned forward and kissed him gently, her lips lingering on his mouth. For a moment he remained immobile. Then, with a low moan, he pulled away and disappeared in the direction of the buildings.

Cheira sat on the ornate chair in the audience chamber. Gowned in gold, a faint aura emanating from her body, she was every inch a goddess of antiquity. It was intentional.

"From this day," she questioned the man before her, her voice imperious, denying by her tone any informality that had ever existed between them, "will you employ your great power only in my service, even when my status is no higher than the lowliest human?"

"I will," John answered without hesitation, solemnly matching the tone of impersonality in her voice. "That has always been my only desire," he added voluntarily.

Cheira took a deep breath and plunged on. Only half of the vow she wanted from John had been given. "And will you pledge never to use your power against Siri ben Ange, for he will be my husband in fact?"

His shoulders sagged as if a weight were being placed upon them. He had anticipated Cheira's intention, but found himself still unprepared when the actual words were spoken. Cheira had daringly placed his allegiance in the balance against his hate for the desert man.

After a long moment of hesitation, he said clearly, "I will."

Cheira sighed, relieved.

John knew that in her anxiety to protect the man she loved she had placed him at Siri's mercy. Siri, he was certain, despised him for the position he held, especially his continuous proximity to Cheira. Now he would be helpless to defend himself in any future confrontation. Nevertheless, now that the pledge had been given, he felt better. Despite the personal danger, he welcomed the opportunity to prove his loyalty. It was the one avenue open to him to declare the love he would never otherwise reveal.

"Return, then, to your duties," Cheira commanded, determined to maintain the formal tone of the meeting to the end. Unknowingly, Cheira had defined their future relationship, breaking forever the camaraderie of the past. By her action, she had taken a fork in the road, which separated her from John. The future would unfold to haunt her with it.

After John had gone, she sat thoughtfully for a long time. She wondered at the relief she felt when she heard John's pledge. Was there any doubt in her mind concerning his compliance? Why had she insisted he come to Arx Vetus to a formal audience to pronounce the words? Her subconscious mind supplied the answer, but in a manner she couldn't recognize.

She recalled Wang Lu's first arrival at Arx Vetus. It had taken her two years of rationalizing the humiliating events of her failure before she had the courage to notify him of her whereabouts. He arrived, thankful for her safety; but his worry was not alleviated until he had spent hours grilling Ameur privately and cross-questioning Tony Hammond and Simbar Abu.

Wang Lu approved their plans for the organization and suggested the formality, which was to become a tradition, concerning the members' dealings with Cheira. The others agreed, over Cheira's protestations, realizing the need to protect her from men whose ability to acquire power they had no precedent with which to gauge. Even Ameur bound himself to comply with the rules they adopted.

Over the years, the role she played became her identification of herself, without question. It was only with Tiana and Ching Li that the rigid formality was ever relaxed. The ritual had become a refuge, she decided; but she did not realize that it was intentional.

Wang Lu, wise in the aims of oriental psychology, had cleverly created an atmosphere of awe and reverence to surround Cheira. He directed the construction of the audience chamber with an eye to its effect on the members. They felt that they were entering a temple. No one, including Cheira, ever discovered that it was Wang Lu who subtly implanted the idea in all their minds that submission of the will was necessary for transfiguration to occur. He meticulously arranged the ceremony, including the elements of surprise and mystery so that the idea was never questioned. The expert psychologist that he was knew that once the basic premise was accepted, there was little likelihood that it would be questioned by even the most astute members. Herein lay Cheira's real protection through all the years of the future—and in a manner far more infallible than the most modern army. It was Wang Lu's gift to the waif whose uniqueness could never be duplicated and whom he loved with a paternal love even greater than that which he bore for his own daughter.

Cheira arrived at Lamborn Heath as the Arctic twilight settled over the moors. Siri welcomed her warmly, whisking her off to ride across the heather in the half-light, which never became wholly dark, their only attendants two huge wolfhounds who answered to the names of Thor and Odin.

"Such grand names," Cheira commented, laughing, matching her mood to his. "Aren't you afraid of the wrath of the gods?"

"I'm not only unafraid," he answered boastfully, "but I challenge them. Any trial they can devise cannot match the one I'm about to undertake."

They had reined in their horses and dismounted.

Cheira swallowed hard, fighting down the gasp that rose unbidden to her throat. Siri wasn't going to make it any easier for her; that was obvious.

The ground felt soft and spongy underfoot. *Yielding,* Cheira thought. Purposefully yielding, as she must be now. She could no longer evade the necessity to speak. Her time had run out. She stole a glance at her companion.

Siri walked beside her, yet not close enough for intimacy. The indifference of his manner hurled her mind back into confusion, her decision waving on the brink of flight. His attitude was one he would adopt with any casual friend, definitely not the way a man would walk with the woman he loved.

Why, then, has he brought me out here alone? she wondered. She had been sure that at last he would tell her what she wanted to hear. Timidly, she let her mind drift toward him, ready to retreat at the slightest resistance. To her surprise, his mind was open. The expected barrier was not there. He was thinking only of the beauty of the moors, and she felt his exhilaration as he watched the romping hounds. So, his indifference allowed him to discard any defense of his thoughts. *He cares so little,* she winced, *that no protection is even necessary.*

A wave of irritation rescued her fleeing decision, perhaps because his behavior left nothing to resist. He gave her no avenue of escape, no way to continue the pretense of impersonality or to sidestep the commission of her feelings into words, unless this was the pattern she intended their future relationship to take. He was giving her the choice.

Never before had she been face-to-face with a situation unsolvable by the use of her power. She took a deep breath.

"Will marriage to me be so distasteful, then?" she murmured, barely whispering.

"A *mariage de covenance* will be unbearable," he admitted, his voice husky, "but I have accepted the terms. I make no complaint."

She caught her breath. "That was not what I asked," she chided softly, stepping closer to his side.

He stopped, for the first time looking directly at her.

"Do you realize the meaning of what you've just said?" he demanded sharply, searching her expression.

"Yes," she nodded, averting her gaze.

"My God!" he groaned, the words wrenched from deep in his throat. Dragging her horse around roughly, he ordered her to mount, his expression inscrutable as he assisted her. Then, leaping onto his own horse, he spurred the surprised animal into a headlong gallop.

Cheira's confusion resulted in an attempt to read his thoughts. It was the strongest effort she had made. But coming hard against the barrier now erected there, making its presence more clearly intentional in view of the recent openness, she quailed. Her resolution failing to support the thrust, she surrendered to the derangement of her own thoughts.

Dismayed by Siri's reaction, Cheira despaired of ever understanding this desert-dwelling Viking. Did he think she was deriding him? Or had he come to despise her so much that the intimacy she offered repulsed him?

He allowed her no opportunity to speak to him alone again, neither during the ride back to the manor which Siri accomplished without slackening the pace nor later at dinner. Afterwards, in the library, Siri and John played chess. Cheira and Jennie, left to their own devices, made a survey of the ancient volumes which the shelves had housed undisturbed for decades.

Cheira struggled against the habit that demanded her prominence in every situation of which she was a part. Being ignored like this was galling.

She wanted to scream, to command Siri's attention, to imperiously punish his indifference. But she had committed herself; and it kept her silent. An alien feeling of humility undermined her usual surety.

She found herself watching him. Standing, dwarfed by the high, book-filled shelves, frozen for the moment in contemplation with her heart pounding from the sight of him, she was overcome by a desire to touch him. She tried objectively to examine the wish and, further, to wonder what it would be like. Then a flood of memory made her shudder and turn her attention to the book in her hand.

As the hour latened and the men seemed far from completing their game, Cheira excused herself. Perversely, they made no effort to detain her.

She retired, feeling restless and distraught. The creaking of the anti-quated manor jangled her nerves, seeming like the mocking laughter of wandering spirits who resented her efforts to conquer their bastions.

One thing altered consciousness does not do, she thought ruefully, *is reveal the future.*

Once Cheira departed, the game was swiftly ended, the ruse no longer needed. Both men knew that the real purpose of the evening was to arrive at a mutual, workable understanding, if possible. The fruition of Cheira's plan mandated some sort of cooperation between them, whatever their personal feelings toward each other.

Over glasses of unbelievably old Scotch whiskey, the antagonists got down to business.

"Did you know," Siri asked bluntly, "that it's her intention to consummate this marriage?"

John nodded.

"You knew the first time I came to see you?"

"Yes."

"Then why was I led to believe otherwise?"

"To see what your reaction would be." John's tone was obviously unfriendly. "Cheira felt you might refuse to cooperate, refuse to give up that life you lead. I felt it wise to obtain your word while committing Cheira to the least defined course of action. I still hoped to persuade her to change her mind. Besides, she's afraid of you, you know."

"Damn it!" Siri brought his fist down on the mantle of the fireplace he was leaning against. "I've given her no cause, despite the humiliation I've endured. Is there no end to atonement?" Siri's head fell forwards in a rare moment of self-pity.

"Then there is a reason for her fear?"

"You don't know?" Siri was incredulous.

John shook his head.

"But surely," Siri persisted, "the intimate relationship you've enjoyed all these years has provoked confidences?"

John leaped out of his chair, his face white. "There has never been any intimate relationship. How dare you insinuate it?" He shook with anger, his voice an ugly snarl, his eyes glaring at his opponent.

Siri stared at him, clearly taken aback. He hesitated. The man's vehement outburst hardly left room for doubt. *If John speaks the truth,* the thought flashed into his mind, *is the reason for my hatred of this man only the product of my own imagination?* Siri conceded the possibility.

"Let it go, then," he said, quietly. "I'm sorry."

John sat down again, the color slowly returning to his face. Realizing that little could be accomplished by continuing his attitude, he accepted Siri's apology, though still burning from the implied insult to Cheira.

"So she's devised another form of torture," Siri mused, staring into the fire, his shoulders sagging.

"What do you mean?" John was genuinely puzzled.

"You don't expect me to believe she'll go through with it? I'm not that big a fool, John," Siri snapped.

"She will," John averred, disapproval and resignation coloring his tone, but his conviction apparent.

Siri laughed—the mirthless laugh of one viewing his own torment and accepting its justice. "If you actually believe that, then you're a worse fool than I am. Cheira loves nothing but her damned organization, and me least of all. Do you want a recital of the humiliations I have suffered over the years? It could take all night," Siri ended sarcastically.

"She loves you," John answered defensively, even though the words stuck in his throat.

"Most of the time, she doesn't even allow me to speak to her," Siri contradicted. "Her actions could not show more plainly how much she hates me. Now suddenly, I'm supposed to believe that she loves me?" Siri shook his head. "One of us is crazy!"

Siri paused, caught by a new line of thought. He looked slyly at John, trying to discover what had not been said. "Toward what purpose is this union actually aimed?"

"She loves you." John stuck to his story. "How could you believe otherwise? There are a dozen other men she could have chosen. You do her an injustice."

Siri lapsed into silence, his conclusions wavering in the light of the other's seeming certainty. Could he be wrong? His instinct warned him to be wary, but his reason could find no valid reason for it and his heart clamored for belief.

"But why now?" Siri made one last effort.

"You ask me to reveal a woman's heart?" John laughed bitterly. "You're the experienced one, remember?"

Siri winced.

"Be certain that I have voiced my objections repeatedly," John continued, pressing the advantage. "In my opinion, marriage for a woman like Cheira is unthinkable; and to someone like you, preposterous."

Siri, half-angry, half-amused at John's comment, yet accepting its truth, refrained from the cutting retort he was tempted to make. Instead, he said, surprised at his own humbleness of tone, "Believe that I have loved her for a long time. It was only the hopelessness of her ever reciprocating which has nearly driven me mad. And her actions have enforced my convictions . . . yet tonight on the moor . . . I had made up my mind to accept whatever terms she outlined . . . and to abide by them. That she'd go so far was the one possibility I'd never considered . . . but because I want it so much, I'll accept it. I'll believe that what you say is true; but I'll never be able to understand it."

"Since when is Cheira obliged to explain her actions to you?" John retorted. "Besides, understanding is unnecessary. Just be worthy of the trust she places in you—or I'll find some way to avenge her."

Siri heard the threat; but the manner of its wording puzzled him. He had always scoffed at John's strict adherence to the etiquette society outlined, yet he had never once considered that it stemmed from cowardice.

"Some way," Siri mimicked. "I'll wager that your power at least equals mine, as you must know. Does that mean that you're too much of a coward to test it?"

"It simply means that it shall never be used against you," John admitted sullenly.

Siri stared at him. "Isn't that stretching your civilized code of honor too far?"

John answered reluctantly. "It hasn't got anything to do with a code of honor. Cheira has my pledge."

Siri had no answer for the unexpected reply. He turned thoughtfully to the fire, dancing and crackling on the ancient stone hearth. For some reason, he realized that his standing thus was the way he remembered his father. It was a habit of the old earl's whenever he wrestled with some complicated problem that was defying his best efforts to solve it. He watched the flames, mesmerized by their journey over the defenseless logs, leaving total destruction wherever they passed. He moved restlessly, evading the image.

"So she has effectively tamed us both," Siri mused.

"Criticism is uncalled for." John's voice was hard.

Siri laughed, the laughter heavily laden with irony. "Is it love or fear that makes you so loyal?"

"That's my affair," John growled. "What concerns us here is your behavior."

"Instruct me, then." Siri bowed slightly to the seated man, the irony still sharpening the look in his eyes.

"You must convince her that you love her," John said, seriously.

"Are you going to describe for me the proper method of making love?" Siri sneered.

John ignored the remark. "Assuage her fear—by a little gentleness, if you can. And control that damnable temper." John raised his eyebrows, forgetting that it was his temper that had nearly ended the discussion. He added, threateningly, "And remember, I intend to see that you do. I mean to make sure by any means handy—to make certain that her trust is not abused. I'll protect her somehow; you need never doubt that!"

"Well," Siri replied, "I thank you for your candor. Our positions are clear it seems: you, the protector; I, the perfect suitor."

Filling their glasses, Siri raised his in a toast, "To the beautiful, unpredictable, unfathomable Lady Pemberly."

John rose, touching Siri's glass with his own. The antagonists eyed each other warily above the rims of the heavy goblets.

The bleak, old mansion settled into the artificial quiet of night. The slumber of the occupants allowed the amplification of the creak of the aged timbers and the groan of the ancient stone. It stood somber in the half-light, its darkened windows catching here and there a darker shadow. The movement was only an illusion caused by the broken rays of a never-setting sun hiding just below the horizon. The eerie glow of the moonless sky produced a shadowless landscape resenting still, after many centuries, the man-made buildings.

There were no trees to break the sense of isolation. Only the few outbuildings and the low stone fence provided a modicum of separation from the endless monotony of the moors. The outbuildings, drab and gray as the manor itself, looked like huddled waifs against the ragged skirts of an ancient mother.

Even the few scattered piles of new lumber left by the workmen and the patent newness of the net stretching across the freshly mown grass of the tennis court did nothing to alleviate the air of desolation. The renovations only added to the feeling of eventual decay, like a decrepit oldster surrendering to the frantic efforts of a physician fighting stubbornly the inevitable. His ministrations only delayed the final end.

The manor emitted the air of knowing that this latest onslaught was only temporary, that the time drew inexorably nearer when the moors would reclaim its own, that its master's life was only touching in passing its own. The sound of the timbers was like a tired sigh.

Cheira spent a disquieting night. The awakening emotions she felt were a new experience. Seldom had she been even slightly conscious of her sex. It had been incidental to the more important aspects of her life. She was only vaguely aware of the response her presence aroused in the members of the organization, and it had always been a simple matter to either ignore or quell the unwelcome advances. Her power was an unchallengeable deterrent, as Ameur had predicted. The ritual surrounding her was an effective barrier that even the most aggressive dared not cross.

The only times she had come close to personal involvement was with Ameur and, many years later, Jim Connors. Both times the spectre of Siri loomed up, marring the relationship, demanding her withdrawal, even though she was convinced of her hatred for the fierce master of the Fort. Just recently, since the success of Mott's experiments had forced a decision, had she realized that the intensity of feeling that swept through her whenever he was close was not hate.

Failure to decipher the meaning of his actions following her admission precluded any rest until the early hours of the morning.

Jennie, noting the rumpled bed and the faint shadows under her mistress's eyes, refrained from disturbing her. Consequently, it was almost noon before Cheira awakened. Her breakfast tray was accompanied by a note from Siri inviting her to a game of tennis that afternoon on the newly renovated court.

"A tennis court?" she commented to Jennie. "On the moors!"

"I found the plans for it in the library," Jennie replied, her old habit having revived immediately after she set foot on the premises of Lamborn Heath. "An Englishman who was leasing the estate had it installed the summer of 1885. He was a friend of Major Winfield who imported the game from the continent."

"Oh, Jennie." Cheira laughed, interrupting the girl and making her blush.

"Tennis?" Cheira queried, doubting the seriousness of Siri's invitation.

"Of course." He laughed, meeting her in the central hall. "Isn't that a perfect pastime for a hotheaded recreant reduced to a docile thrall?"

He saw the anguish leap into her eyes and was immediately contrite. "Forgive me," he murmured with unaccustomed gentleness. "You know me well enough to realize that chivalry is not one of my virtues, if indeed, I have any. You have chosen a poor prospect for a husband, I fear."

Impulsively, she put her hand on his arm, intending to deny his words; but when their eyes met, she was silent. His dark eyes held hers, and she saw the light begin to burn in their depths.

Withdrawing from her touch with discernible effort, Siri continued, reverting to his original tone of banter, "I'm serious about the tennis match. In fact, I'll wager the gray you rode last night that I can win in three sets."

"And what will I wager?" she asked lightly, her confidence returning. "I have nothing so grand to offer."

His eyes denying the frivolity of his voice, he suggested, "Like a true knight of old, I only desire a kiss from my lady's lips. The promise of such a reward would spur me to superhuman effort and insure my victory."

Blushing and flustered, Cheira fled in confusion, a novice at the art of badinage.

On the court, Siri lost no time making good his boast. The few times Cheira had played before, her opponents were ignorant of her power to move swiftly to meet the oncoming ball, the power behind the racket that of her mind rather than her muscles. She had won or lost as the purpose suited her. Now she was too frightened of discovery by her knowledgeable opponent to dare to compensate for her lack of practice, especially since Siri was obviously using only his natural skill. By doing so, he had laid down the terms of the handicap. He was watching her vigilantly, defying her to accept his conditions.

All right, Cheira thought, gritting her teeth. But she would not surrender so easily. She'd put up a fight to lessen, if she could, the humiliation of a total rout. Siri intended to give no quarter, using the game to test the truth of her commitment. He recognized her reluctance to be bested in any situation. Now he was daring her to use her power.

Cheira's determination dwindled rapidly as the ache in her legs turned to pain, her shoulder and arm protesting the outrage of being required to meet the force of the relentlessly oncoming ball with an equal thrust. She felt her heart pounding from the strain. It was only her pride that kept her from conceding. She was thankful when the ordeal ended. Siri won swiftly and effortlessly, but she had demonstrated the sincerity of her commitment.

Jennie was waiting when they finished, impatient to show Cheira the manuscript dating back to the late fifteenth century, which she had unearthed in a tower of the old mansion. The payment of the wager, the acknowledgement of Siri's victory, remained uncollected.

Succumbing to a mood of resentment and self-pity precipitated by the rout of the afternoon, Cheira dined in her room with only Jennie for company. She was still piqued when John's request for her presence in the library was delivered.

She decided to comply, but in her own good time. Even with the realization that what she was doing was a childish display of temper, she continued to prolong the preparations with unnecessary attention to the details of her appearance.

Actually, she finally admitted, she was reluctant to face Siri. Her commitment professed, she was finding it impossible to determine how to proceed. Siri's behavior was impeccable; but she knew he was secretly testing her, doubting still her change of attitude. Honestly, she couldn't blame him.

Did she really think she could force him to do what she wanted? Was she clever enough to trick a man of Siri's intelligence? *But I'm not really tricking him*, she corrected the thought. "Because I love him," she murmured softly.

It was early evening when Cheira came down to the library. John had returned from London bringing several members of the board of Pemberly Enterprises with him. These men had worked for months to create a program that would remain within the guidelines of good taste insisted on by Lady Pemberly, yet would promote the greatest amount of goodwill for the giant corporation.

Pemberly's rapid growth to its present position of leadership in its field posited public relations problems not encountered by smaller companies. The board members worried that the corporation's size would give it a reputation for impersonality. They wanted especially to formulate the impression of humanness through Lady Pemberly's marriage. They wanted to give their customers a sense of identification with the head of the company, while at the same time solidifying their relations with the oil producers through Siri.

Cheira appreciated the importance to Pemberly Enterprises, yet she did her utmost to keep pomp at a minimum knowing Siri's dislike for such ceremonies. What the board wanted now was her final agreement. To John's annoyance, she insisted on Siri's consent to every event. *John can't be expected to understand how important Siri's opinion is to me,* she thought.

Her worry was unfounded, however, for Siri agreed willingly to all the festivities the council proposed. He even took an active part in the finalization of the plans, spending time meticulously reviewing the guest list to insure the inclusion of every important sheik.

In fact, Cheira thought, with an obstinacy singularly feminine, *he acts like he's enjoying this. As if his public position were more important than being my husband!*

Her irritation increased as the evening wore on. She had steeled herself for the coming meeting and now he was being as indifferent as when he had let Jennie claim her company in the afternoon. Cheira was rapidly reaching the end of her patience. When the discussion drifted into the choice of a tailor and the proper style for the Earl of Zetland's wardrobe, with Siri acting as if the subject really absorbed his interest, she could stand it no longer.

Rising, she interrupted the conversation in which she had taken no part, deliberately revealing by her tone the pique she felt, "I'm going to walk in the garden. Siri?" she half-asked, half-commanded.

"Delighted, my lady," Siri responded with alacrity, offering his arm.

"How can you stay so interested in that nonsense?" she accused when they were away from the house.

"My behavior is determined solely by my lady's pleasure," he stated formally. "I'm sorry if I misinterpreted your wishes."

She tried to detect a tone of mockery, but failed. The meekness of his manner gave rise to a reckless forwardness in her own.

"Can't you do anything but apologize?" she snapped. "Why don't you collect your wager from this afternoon?"

"I thought perhaps," he replied, looking into her eyes, "that you preferred to forget that frivolous moment. If so, I would not hold you to it."

"Once you accused me of mocking you," she whispered breathlessly. "Is this your revenge?"

176

"Shall I ever learn to please?" he returned with a question of his own, his voice betraying an unnatural humility.

Obediently, he drew her into his arms. He felt her tense. He waited. Then she stood quietly. With a finger under her chin, he covered her lips with his mouth. The gesture was simple and very gentle, but he did not withhold his energy.

The pleasure that coursed through her body made her sag limply against him. His arm tightened around her.

Abruptly, he let her go. "My role of courtier is still very new," he said in a low, unsteady voice. "Do not tempt me too far."

She stared at him, wide-eyed, an incredible truth dawning in her mind. She had never, before this moment, been the recipient of the power of a transfigured being. She allowed few people to touch her and never in a situation where a display of power was called for.

In the shock of realization, she had forgotten to conceal her thoughts. Siri was looking at her with a flicker of amusement in his eyes. "Then you must have made a poor choice of lovers," he said.

Before she could reply, John and the others joined them. She was sure John had come out intentionally; and the casualness of his manner infuriated her, the more so when she noticed the laughter still lingering in Siri's eyes. He seemed to be enjoying her discomfiture.

Late into the night, Cheira lay sleepless in her bed, reliving the experience of Siri's kiss. Her nerves tingled deliciously as her imagination recreated the touch of his mouth. Frowning in the darkness, she was amazed at her own naivete. How could she never have thought of the power which she had given to so many and not of herself as the recipient? Perhaps, she smiled critically, from the same stupidity which had failed for so long to identify the special feeling she had for Siri as love. And if Mott's experiments hadn't forced her to think about it, she probably still would not have known.

Could the intimacy that she had dreaded for so long actually be something like the pleasure she had felt tonight? But her body answered with trembling, remembering the terrifying weeks spent at the Fort so many years ago.

CHAPTER XII

Cheira returned to London the next day. According to plan, she would not see Siri again until the day of the ceremony.

The city took on a festive air. People were coming from everywhere to witness the social event of the season. However, if the population had been aware of the difference, they would have noted no influx of association members. Only those whose work necessitated their presence were there. The outward trappings of the occasion were politically oriented and suited Cheira's purpose, but it did not influence the lives of the other members.

Accordingly, all preparations were made in the ordinary way. lady Pemberly spent hours being fitted, the gown designed by one of the leading couturiers imported from the Continent especially for the event. The dress was white, a watered silk which casted to blue in the folds, giving the impression of the sea in sunlight. To Cheira, the long train was heavy but—she finally acceded to the designer's instance—mandatory. It was traditionally necessary, the pompous little man convinced her. By the time he had adjusted the veil of similar length, Cheira cheerfully detested the famous Frenchman as well as the uncomfortable demands of tradition.

When the last tuck was taken, she was happy to turn her attention to a final check of the guest lists. Since this was Cheira's first experience with a major social event for which she was responsible, she found herself enjoying even the tedium of preparation.

Siri, meanwhile, true to his word, adhered strictly to the protocol of the coming occasion. He entertained lavishly all the important personages of the realm, as well as attending foreign dignitaries. In a highly contrived, but colorful, public ceremony, he accepted the ancient title of his ancestors and swore his allegiance to the Crown.

As the bells tolled high noon, Cheira entered the vast and ancient cathedral. Standing quietly beside John while the long line of prelates proceeded down the aisle, she was struck by the enormity of her undertaking. She thought of the forlorn waif Wang Lu had sheltered that day so long ago in Darjeeling. She longed for his support now, in the fulfillment of the great power she possessed, but which might never have developed without his wise guidance.

That loving support had forsaken her. Her heart pounded. Her thoughts turned to the man waiting for her at the foot of the altar. There was uncertainty . . . courtesy . . . allegiance . . . but no love.

As her steps picked up the solemn cadence of the music, she was appalled by the no longer avoidable realization that she was putting herself in a position where her power would be meaningless. Was it this dread that had made the members object so vehemently to her plans?

The full impact of her helplessness assailed her as she took her place beside her chosen mate. He towered over her, even the conventional clothing he wore unable to conceal the powerful physique.

She interrupted her thoughts, the piercing look of her partner confusing her. She was almost certain now that the barrier, which kept even the most powerful members from monitoring her thinking, was ineffective against him. So frightening was the realization that she was barely conscious of the solemn words being spoken by the archbishop.

Siri turned her to him as they exchanged their vows. The twinkle in his eyes belied the solemnity of his countenance. *See what an obedient slave I have become?* he sent the thought to her. *I endure this pomposity without a murmur simply because you command it.*

There are other members here, her eyes widened in warning.

They can't intercept my thoughts without my consent any more than they can yours. He was unabashed. *Do you think you have given your hand to a neophyte?*

She lowered her eyes, refusing to accept any further communication. The ceremony was ended.

Walking down the aisle, smiling graciously in answer to the approval of the beaming faces of the guests, she felt reaffirmed in the soundness of her course. Her mind picked up lively, intelligent thoughts at random from different parts of the immense church. Her attention was arrested by a young boy of about fourteen who was staring at her unblinkingly. She nearly burst out laughing with delight when she discovered that he was actually wrestling with the problem of the proper fuel mixture for his model airplane. Her own sacrifice, if indeed the future would prove it to be such, was insignificant against the possible preservation of such a mind. The very real fear gripped her that accident or disease could cause her to lose him before he developed his full potential. It had happened with others.

If the experiments were successful, the waiting would be unnecessary and with it the increased risk. The need to delay the altered state until maturity would be erased when a proven procedure existed, when the transformation could safely return the transfigured to full fertility whenever it was desirable. It was her anxiety of producing a static society that stayed her hand. Above all else, it was her sole responsibility to correct the deficiency her power had created. To make permanent sterility the price of unlimited life was to make the gift a mockery.

Siri handed her into the waiting limousine and the long procession of cars moved slowly into the street. Waving now to the crowds that lined the sidewalks, she thought again of all the reasons, both public and personal, that had brought her to this moment. Finally, all doubt disappeared and she knew her decision was right and irrevocable.

The reception proved to be interminable and exhausting. Public relations in the Pemberly interests made it necessary to receive long lines of visiting emissaries. No one must be allowed to feel slighted. As the hours wore on, she was increasingly grateful for Siri's support. His constant attentiveness made bearable the tedium of accepting congratulations in a dozen different tongues. His unflagging tact rescued her several times when the inattention caused by fatigue trapped her into an incoherent mixture of languages.

It was after two in the morning, having somehow dragged herself through dinner and an elaborate formal ball, that she repaired with the members of the board to Pemberly House. All those intimately concerned with the event wanted to celebrate its success. It was Siri who thoughtfully suggested that it would be proper for her to retire. She gratefully acquiesced, leaving him to host the lingering well-wishers. She went to her quarters alone.

It was late afternoon of the following day before Cheira called Jennie. She voiced the question, which had lingered in her mind all during the sleeping hours and which rose to the surface with insistence immediately upon awakening, "Where is Siri?"

"He did not wish to disturb you, my lady," Jennie answered. "He has left word that he awaits your convenience."

So the time she dreaded had come. Cheira felt excitement mixed with trepidation. The feeling rose from the pit of her stomach in a physical churning. She prayed for courage. With her commitment, she had relinquished all her defenses. There could be no masquerading behind an assumed attitude, no retreat to the safety of her position either as Lady Pemberly or mistress of Arx Vetus. She had discarded all in order to realize what had become the sole purpose of her life.

She caught herself giving Jennie numberless needless tasks. It was an unnecessary delay to the meeting she still feared, but a futile tactic.

Quit procrastinating, she thought. *He's keeping his word to the letter. He won't come unless I summon him . . . and that I must do.*

She trailed Jennie aimlessly as the girl put the sitting room in order. Her mind lapsed into a vacillating enumeration of excuses. Once or twice, she decided to discard the whole plan. Her gaze was arrested by the gold disk above the mantle. The light caught and emphasized the raised letters. Somehow, it gave her the courage she needed.

"You may call him, Jennie," she said, aloud, surprised at the firmness in her voice. She failed to notice the brightened glitter of the disk.

Jennie stepped into the hall to send a telepathic summons to her new master.

Siri came immediately.

Cheira stood uncertainly in the middle of the room. Her first impulse was to flee ignominiously to the sanctuary of her bedroom, until—and the thought made her catch her breath—she realized it was no longer a private haven. By her own decision, she had given him the right to be there. Helplessness swept through her, riveting her to the spot.

Siri was across the room in a few long strides. Always astonished at his stature whenever he was close, now she was overwhelmed. Her mind registered involuntarily the movement of his muscles beneath the silk shirt and the length of his legs, emphasized by the slim trousers. The contrast to the voluminous desert costume in which she was used to seeing him stressed the robustness of his body. Her heart pounded painfully.

He knelt before her, head bowed. She stepped back, astonished. She had tried to imagine what he would do when he came, but it was not this. His action forced her to speak, to put into words that which she feared most. Tears of frustration welled up in her eyes, the drops clinging precariously to the long, thick lashes.

"A long time ago"—her voice was a strangled, hesitant whisper—"I implored you to spare me. Now must I beg you to possess me?"

He rose, his eyes searching her face; the disbelief was apparent in his face.

"I love you too much," he spoke softly, his manner without a trace of the usual arrogance, "to ever force you again. It is the only atonement I can make."

She sighed. At last he had spoken the words she wanted to hear most. Simply and so directly, he revealed his intention. She believed him. It gave her the courage to accept the inevitable consequences of her commitment.

"If love is violence, I can accept that now," she spoke hesitantly. "I have never loved anyone but you."

"You don't believe I meant that," Siri protested, surprised.

"I don't know," she whispered. "I have no way of knowing."

He grasped her arms, making her shiver at the first touch. He didn't seem to notice. "Have all your lovers been so incompetent that they have given you no pleasure?" His voice was harsh, demanding.

"I have had no lovers, my lord," she murmured, blushing.

"My God!" The words escaped involuntarily from his throat. "All these years. I have seen your intimacy with . . ." He paused. "You have forced me to witness it. And you expect me to believe that?"

"I have had no lovers," she repeated, the tears spilling out of her eyes, making shimmering droplets on her cheeks. "The times when I wanted to," she admitted, seeing the doubt on his face, "you were always there. Even when I thought I hated you, I could see you so clearly that the other one was blotted out. I could only flee before the menacing specter." She caught her breath in a sob.

He knew the strength of the experience and no longer doubted her admission. He took her in his arms, his lips against the soft mass of her hair. "My love, my love," he murmured soothingly. "I believe you."

She sagged against him, surrendering unreservedly the burden she had carried for so long. "But I'm still afraid." The confession was muffled, her face pressed against the silk of his shirt. "Please be kind." The words were no more than a catch of her breath, but he heard them as loud as a scream.

Realizing finally the terror she still felt and the emotional scars she carried from his thoughtless actions, he swore anew his vow of atonement, binding himself to her more absolutely and permanently than any threat of her power could ever do. The compassion latent in his character rose now to guide his actions.

He whispered softly, "I'll show you the beauty of love, the unmatchable pleasure it can give, the joy, the fulfillment—and you'll forget the other. Love isn't fear or pain or violence, only unlimited sweetness and ecstasy. It will be the highest expression of our feelings for each other."

She trembled, but made no answer; her mind and body were quiescent, obedient to the previous decision of her will. Each cell of her being waited expectantly for the impulse to flight. It did not come. She stood, poised with bowed head. Holding her at arm's length, his hands moved caressingly to her shoulders; his hands described the limit of the space that was hers. There was no escape possible.

He walked away, leaving her standing in the middle of the room. Selecting a chair by the fireplace, he sat down.

"You needn't go through with this," he said, his voice containing a gentleness foreign to it.

She couldn't move. A shudder passing visibly through her body was the only indication that she heard.

He cursed silently. "Why don't you ask Jennie to bring us some supper?" The suggestion was a means to relieve the tension.

Like an automaton, she obeyed, the order issued mechanically.

Siri poured a double Scotch for himself and one only a little less strong for Cheira. Her fingers closed automatically around the glass. However, the tension was unrelieved, its waves buffeting her like the surf against an open shore. She watched Jennie serve the meal and wondered idly at the stiffness of her motions. *Why, Jennie's frightened,* she thought, amazed. It had been a long time since she had identified with the feelings Siri's presence prompted in others. Now she remembered and the sympathy she felt for Jennie alleviated somewhat her own tension.

"Cheira," Siri tried again patiently as they sat across from each other at the table, "I will understand if you want to change your mind. I can see how you feel. No matter how closely I've questioned John, he assures me repeatedly that your reason is to further Pemberly; and you have given me no better reason. But that reason is not equal to what you're putting yourself through."

She picked at the food on her plate, nervously pushing it back and forth, forgetting to put it in her mouth. Her lips trembled. She couldn't answer.

"I love you, believe me," Siri continued in the same gentle voice. "I have accepted the terms of our relationship. You can leave it at that."

She shook her head, her eyes riveted unseeingly on the plate before her.

"I love you," Siri pursued, attempting to find the words which would make it easier for her. "But I won't force you. It can only happen if you want it to." Patience was an unnatural exercise for Siri and gentleness a facet of his character well rusted from disuse. Now he suppressed the irritation which was the more natural response.

"My darling, shall I leave?" he tried again.

"No." Her mouth formed the word, but there was no sound. Raising her eyes finally to look at him, he saw the fear, dominant now that she had relinquished all her defenses.

With the realization of the scope of the damage that had been done to her emotions, he was able to exhibit an unnatural compassion. He came to kneel beside her. Taking her hands in his, he kissed them. She felt the sensation travel along her arms. She closed her eyes.

When he took her in his arms, he willed her to relive the moments in the garden at Lamborn. She sagged against him, forgetting the fear, forgetting everything but the memory of his kiss, blending now indistinguishably with his lips on her mouth. She never questioned the origin of the picture in her mind, instead she was lost in the thrilling of her nerves.

He opened the clasps of her gown. It fell to her waist, held there by a thin cord. With his fingertips he traced the swelling of her breasts.

"You are so beautiful," he told her simply, his voice husky with controlled emotion. The picture in her mind sharpened in focus. She could smell the earthy scent of the heather subtly overriding the odor of the cultivated plants. Her arms stole around his neck; the image faded. She no longer needed it.

Lifting her in his arms, his lips seeking the hollow of her throat, he carried her into the bedroom.

The pleasure of his arms around her; his lips on her mouth causing an unbearable sweetness to sweep away even the memory of fear; his hands moving over her body imparting sensations never experienced, the possibility of which she had not imagined, could not have imagined: She drifted in a realm of bliss.

A low humming sounded far away. It was familiar. She tried to listen, to identify it, to draw it closer. Her nerves vibrated to the distant song. Somehow it synchronized with Siri's breath at her ear. She accepted that, searching no further. Unnoticed, the sound faded away.

Spontaneously, she moaned. He guided her response skillfully, using the energy he could summon with care but unstintingly to increase her enjoyment. Intuitively, he knew he owed her this, that his own satisfaction would be measured by what she felt. If his body could be the instrument of her pleasure, now in greater measure than it had been the means of her torment, he would be satisfied. Once more, he was grateful to the power that gave him such control.

Her body arched instinctively toward him, demanding the union that only minutes before she still dreaded. He possessed her gently, joining his body to hers in total consummation. A convulsion exploded within her, traveling up her spine into every nerve of her body.

He was surprised by the release of her power, hurling him to dizzying heights of sensuality, more intense than any he had experienced. For an instant, he was swept away by the passion, forgetting entirely the resolution to subordinate his feelings to hers.

Control returned quickly; his first thought was of her. She lay limply beneath him, her breath coming in shallow gasps. He withdrew from her gently, lowering himself beside her. Taking her in his arms, he fondled her hair, twining the long golden strands in his fingers.

She stirred. "I didn't know," she murmured, raising her eyes to study his face.

"And have I given you pleasure, my love?" he questioned, smiling.

"Oh, so much—so much," she affirmed, timidly touching his cheek. "Does it sound so awfully stupid that I never knew?"

"You know now," his lips formed the words against her mouth.

"I was so afraid." She smiled, plaintively. "If I had only known . . . "

"If you had known, would you have chosen another lover?" he teased, tracing the curve of her thigh with his fingertips, stimulating a trail of tingling nerves.

"No! No! Only you sooner," she declared, reaching up to pull his head down. For the first time, initiating the caress, she deliberately sought his mouth in newly discovered passion. Aligning her body with his, she emanated an energy which set his nerves pulsing.

"Cheira," he gasped helplessly, surrendering to the union she offered. Their bodies fused in the rhythm of ecstasy.

Later, they lay side by side, their energy spent.

"Will it always be like this?" she asked, in wonder.

"It need never be any other way."

"But . . . "

"Don't!" He interrupted. "Don't think about any other time than this. Now is the beginning! And nothing must ever be allowed to come between us."

"I love you," she whispered in answer.

She nestled trustingly now in the shelter of his arms. In a few minutes, he knew by her even breathing that she slept.

Sleep is an arbitrary condition to one of altered consciousness. It can be postponed indefinitely by an act of will. However, with any great expenditure of energy, a period of rest is necessary. Cheira, happy and contented, made no attempt to resist the drowsy sensation which overcame her so pleasantly.

Siri let himself float into a restful state of relaxation. He remained quiet so as not to disturb Cheira. His thoughts drifted aimlessly. How he had hoped for this moment! After she had disappeared that time when he first knew her, he had been restless and irritable. Even then, he had failed to identify the feeling that rushed back over him. While he had known her, the restlessness that had driven him his whole life was absent. He was like a man whose illness was of such long duration that he had forgotten how it felt to be well. In fact, having never known other than the unfulfilled yearning, he was oblivious to its presence.

Only when she was gone was he able to recognize it. And in his stupidity and senseless passion he had driven away the light of his life, the only peace he had ever known. There was no question in his mind but that he had driven her, defenseless, into the merciless desert, to die in a way with which he was thoroughly familiar, a way of horror beyond description, a victim of thirst and the burning sun.

There was only one alternative to that fate: that she may have been picked up by a passing caravan. That could have been the reason his men failed to find her. The thought was even more intolerable than the visions of her death. He knew well the fate of an unprotected woman in the barbarous land.

Lira had finally intimated that he was in love. He had flown into a rage, cuffing her for her insolence, sending her fleeing hysterically. His mood, nevertheless, remained undiminished. The vision of the golden-haired girl haunted his dreams and distracted his waking hours. For the first time since he had come to the desert, he lost interest in his horses and the affairs of the tribe.

It was five years before he found her again, at the tiny oasis a few miles from Arx Vetus. He smiled at the memory. Naively, he had assumed that it would be a simple matter to get her back.

She had already begun to build her society with Ameur's help. He remembered his shock that day at the appearance of Ameur and Wang Lu, but his flaming jealousy of the American had blocked all other considerations. He would kill the man who dared to take Cheira from him.

But a direct confrontation had quickly established the advantages of transfiguration. The humility of being bested so easily made him eager to accept Cheira's offer of his own transfiguration. He saw it as a means to accomplish his purpose. It had become his only ambition.

He hadn't at first realized that he was submitting to her power, that her offer was the means by which she could gain revenge. But her cold, imperious manner brought him quickly to that conviction. In fact, his persistent advances had resulted in banishment from her presence for years at a time.

It was during those years that he had devoted his time to increasing his power, his only goal to match or exceed her strength and thus have the ability to make her his again.

There were times when he was certain Ameur was her lover. The vehement denials of the American never wholly obliterated the surmise. He recalled the hours of agony spent wrestling with the belief, facing the stark realization that he was powerless to change it. When the chains of the emotion coiled about him most mercilessly, his tribe suffered, the helpless victims of their master's substitution.

It was only Cheira's prolonged absences in England that transferred his jealousy to John. He was able to accept Ameur's repeated offers of friendship. Then was planted the seed of hatred for John, which bubbled beneath the surface of a thin veil of tolerance.

Now he gazed at her sleeping form, the lashes casting shadows on her cheeks, a strand of hair curling wantonly on her breast. He recalled their love, smiling wryly, remembering the time he had raged helplessly against the men he was so sure held her favor. His eyes narrowed.

He recalled the time he had come upon her with Connors in the garden at Arx Vetus. He was surprised, doubly so because Ameur usually forbade his presence if Cheira was there. But this time, Ameur was absent. The unexpected sight of her in Connor's arms, the happy laughter ringing mockingly in his ears: His rage flared murderously. He would have succeeded had Cheira not brought him writing to the ground by the unbearable pain she sent through his body, her fingers on his shoulders like the searing of a brand. She had summarily dismissed him then; he was forced to obey. The episode solidified his determination.

His household paid dearly for the abasement; his wounded pride wreaking vengeance on all in his service. He vowed to match her power, resolved that a like occurrence should never take place again.

But he had failed to reckon with Cheira's telepathic powers. Under threat of permanent exile from Arx Vetus, she had demanded his pledge. She left him no choice, knowing that permanent exile from Arx Vetus would rob him of altered consciousness and consequently any means of ever accomplishing his purpose.

I have stayed true to my oath, he thought with satisfaction, *even the night of that blatant display at Arx Vetus.* But it had been long before that that he had realized that the pledge was unnecessary, that love was the real deterrent.

It was what he wanted her to know, too, when he had first accepted the terms of their marriage. But her manner had precluded the declaration. *Does she really believe me, even now?* he wondered.

He frowned. He had been so certain that the admission she made at Lamborn was just another form of torture. The many obvious expressions of her hatred and his conviction that she was entitled to it had made even the possibility of the last few hours seem inconceivable. His mind reeled at the accomplishment of what he had longed for for so many years.

He drew Cheira's sleeping figure more closely against his body, heightening the sense of the smooth, warm flesh in contact with his own, savoring the fulfillment.

But why has she, at this particular time, chosen to reveal her love? The thought intruded, making him stir restlessly. Stray comments—on his part deliberately ignored in his desire to believe, but which had caught his passing attention—from John and the other members of the board came back to him; but he was slipping into deep slumber and they passed unnoted from his mind.

The artificial lighting was imitating the first hint of dawn when Siri awakened. Cheira was leaning up on her elbow studying him, a soft smile on her lips.

I love you, he thought. She jumped, startled from her reverie. Before she could answer, he pulled her face down, his lips finding her mouth, the kiss an expression of the yearning of all the past years.

Drawing away to look at him, she asked seriously, "Can you ever forgive me for waiting so long?"

"Are you asking my forgiveness?" he retorted. "After what I have caused you to suffer? Wasn't it that experience that caused such a long separation?"

"But I should have known." She refused to let him take the blame. "I was so busy interfering in the lives of others that I never had a life of my own. Siri, do you realize that at this moment there are more than five hundred people who qualify for transfiguration and probably many more that we haven't even heard of? It's not right to deny anyone when they are ready."

Siri drew his brow into a mock frown. "And must I share you forever with the organization? I'm a selfish, jealous man who shares nothing which is his."

"I am yours, forever." She smiled, softly. "Only for a little while yet will I have to see to the organization."

Siri missed the implication.

"And it's time to see John," she continued, her mind back to her duties, the habit of years strong.

"Wait!" he said, pulling her down into the crook of his arm. "Be mine just a little longer. I've waited so long for your love. It can't be unreasonable to want to be alone with you. Or will I always have to share your love?"

Not waiting for an answer, he jumped up, lifting her in his arms. The positive movement banished the world from his mind. He carried her, laughing and squirming, through the dressing room. He kicked the door shut and deposited her under the shower, turning it on full.

She clung to him, painfully aware of his appraisal as she stood naked, trembling from the shock of the water. She closed her eyes to avoid looking at him.

He laughed, turning her face to his, pretending to be stern. "Have you forgotten that it's a passionate barbarian you have taken for your lover?"

Flicking the handle of the lather tap, he smeared her with handfuls of suds. She watched, fascinated by the white patterns his tanned hands made upon the intimacy of her body. Her eyes widened as her body responded.

"Now," he ordered, in a tone of mock severity, "you do it." Not giving her the opportunity, in her timidity, to refuse, he put a mound of foam into her hand and, holding her wrist smeared it on his chest. She smiled then, caught the spirit of frolic, and began to lather him vigorously.

The touch of her hands aroused him, making his body ache for satisfaction. He put her arms around her neck and lifted her until, holding her astraddle his hips, the joining allowed free release of the energy of his power, heightening the impetus of passion.

Lost in the sweetness of sensations coursing along her nerves, she arched her back, eyes closed, lips drawn away from her teeth. She trembled, surrendering to the expanding intensity of feeling until a violent paroxysm released her own power, making him grown with a pleasure that drained him.

The water poured over them unheeded. She gasped, struggling for breath as the water ran into her mouth and nose.

"Oh," she choked, laughing, "what shameless advantage you take of me!"

Grabbing a towel, she ran into the dressing room. He lazily took his time, toweling himself dry, enjoying the aftermath of sensation as it ebbed out of his quieting nerves. When he joined her, she was already dressed. She evaded him skillfully when he reached for her and darted out of the room. *For this time, I have won,* he thought, satisfied.

He dressed slowly, content to listen to the subdued tone of her voice as she ordered Jennie to bring their breakfast and notify John that she would see him. His eyes narrowed, thinking of the fool he had been to have tortured himself endlessly by imagining that her relationship with her chief executive was more than formal. He understood now that he had judged her by his own passion, which had often clamored for release without any necessity for love to sanction it. He had failed completely to recognize the strength of the fear implanted by his own brutality. *Mon Dieu,* he thought, *let me make it up to her now.*

Jennie was deftly arranging the table when Siri entered the outer room. She allowed herself one shy glance at him. The smile on his face as he looked at her mistress reassured her. She could report to Sir John that all was well. Cheira was radiant with a tinge of color in her skin, sparkling eyes, and more contented than Jennie had ever seen her.

When John entered, Siri was standing apart, smoking, leaning against the fireplace mantel at the end of the room. Cheira rested nonchalantly on the sofa. The arrangement was contrived by Cheira in deference to John's feelings. Siri cooperated grudgingly.

"I trust your ladyship is well?" John greeted her, bowing low. No hint of the hours of trepidation he had just gone through showed beneath the formal mask.

Siri winked at Cheira when their eyes met.

"Very well, thank you," she told John solemnly, ignoring the silent mocking laughter in her husband's glance. "Proceed," she commanded, hoping to avoid any familiarity that Siri might notice.

With customary brusqueness, John recited, "The Duchess of Conmoor has planned a reception for this evening. Madame Bentley extends an invitation to a grand ball tomorrow evening—that was okayed by your ladyship at Lamborn Heath. And Baron Caveren would like you to join his hunt this weekend. They are all most anxious for your ladyship to attend—and his lordship." Up to this point, he had ignored Siri. Now he was forced to acknowledge his presence. He glanced in Siri's direction, but his glance as their eyes met was cold and noncommittal.

Siri laughed. John had the grace to blush uncomfortably.

"I do only what your ladyship commands," Siri told him, unabashed.

"Glad to hear it," John answered icily. The understatement provoked Siri to more insinuating laughter.

"Very well," Cheira interrupted the exchange between the two men. "You may accept for us. Anything else?"

"That is all, my lady." John's words covered the thought he directed to her: *Dr. Mott wishes you to come to the clinic tomorrow afternoon at two.*

Siri took a step toward them, instantly alert. The maneuver was unexpected, making him miss most of John's thought.

"The Duchess's reception is at nine," John continued in a flat businesslike tone. "May I attend you at an early supper?"

"Of course," Cheira assented.

Bowing, John departed. "Until then," he said.

Cheira sat very still. She had noted Siri's attention to the thought passed between her and John. The time had come to make the explanation she knew he would demand. That was his right, but she still dreaded it.

The silence lengthened painfully.

Finally, he came to her and stood looking down impatiently.

"Well?" His voice was so stern it made her tremble with the old fear she thought the last hours had eradicated forever. She felt the power of the will that made his tribesmen die rather than disobey him. She could identify with the lowliest camel driver at the descent of the sheik's displeasure. And this time she couldn't defend herself by an imperious show of power.

"I have something to tell you," she began weakly, her voice pleading.

His attitude remained unchanged.

"Please, please, my love," she begged. "Don't be angry." In her agitation, she failed to recognize her own premature reaction.

Siri sat down beside her, softening enough to stroke her hair.

"I think you had better tell me what it is that you're so sure will displease me. I've heard rumors that, perhaps in the joy of your love, I chose to ignore. Tell me," he commanded, but not unkindly.

Taking a deep breath to bolster her courage and gripping his hand in both of hers, pressing it against her heart, she began. Her words were like a recital. "A nonpublicized department of Pemberly Research has been conducting extensive experiments for many years. They have uncovered the physical difference between a transfigured individual and an ordinary per-

191

son. They know how to reverse the process. Someone must be first." She paused lamely, waiting for a word of encouragement; but Siri's gaze did not relent. Only the tenseness of his posture and the tic of a muscle in his jaw told her he had already anticipated her next words. She had borne the result of that attitude before and the memory made her shrink from continuing. But continue she must, knowing her decision was made and that he had to accept it no matter how great his disapproval.

She rose to stand before him. Straight and proud, she mustered her authority to be better able to withstand his reaction.

She knew he did not intend to help her. "I am to be first." She spoke each word distinctly, her voice clear and firm now. "Our state of being is too precious to endanger anyone else. I have carefully analyzed my procedure. I'm confident that I can teach John to transfigure, in case the experiment should fail or while I have no power. The organization will not be impaired."

Absorbed, Cheira failed to notice Siri's frown. The statements she intended to be persuasive had the opposite effect. The seed of doubt of her love grew.

"There is also a very selfish reason why I must do this," Cheira admitted, giving first the cause she felt was least controversial. "The need has been growing with the passing years to know who or what I am. I can't refuse the opportunity. I've no memory before the day I awakened in Wang Lu's home. He found me wandering in the street and took charge of me because I was Caucasian. He intended to return me to the European community. But, after extensive inquiry, he was unable to establish my identify. I remained under his protection for many years, discovering my power gradually. At first, Wang Lu was astounded at how quickly I could learn. Then one day, I discovered I had the power of telepathy. Wang Lu is a very intelligent man. He guided and helped me."

She paused. Siri volunteered no comment.

"There is another important reason," her voice dropped to a whisper. "If the experiment is successful and if you will agree, you shall undergo the reversal. In a short period of time, we can expect to become fertile. The true and final consummation of our love will be possible." She ceased speaking. Her eyes wavered under his penetrating stare, until unable to stand it longer, she looked away. The strain showed in the flush of her cheeks, while the skin around her mouth and eyes took on a startling pallor.

She continued bravely, knowing she must say it all now before her courage failed irretrievably. "If we are successful, our society need no longer be sterile. We can welcome younger people and avoid the danger of losing them while waiting for their reproductive years to pass. You know that has happened. We'll have the best of both worlds."

Her gaze returned to his.

He rose. She caught her breath, awaiting his reaction.

"So your love has qualifications." His voice was even and cold. "Your decision is unalterable?"

Quaking before the force of his power, his statement cut like a knife in her heart; but she determined to remain firm in her decision. She whispered, "Yes."

Without another word, he turned and left the room.

Jennie rushed in. "Are you all right, my lady?" she asked, unable to hide the concern she felt. Siri had rushed past her heedlessly. She was shocked by the look on his face: the expression distorted into a gaze which saw an impossible mission; the cheeks drawn inward in distaste; the usually sensuous lips pulled back into a thin line of resistance. His body moved of its own volition—in headlong flight.

Cheira stood where he left her, the cold determination still in her eyes. Jennie entered her field of vision as a different actor on a stage. There was no need to shift the focus.

"Jennie," she spoke like an automaton, "get Stevens. Tell him to monitor Siri's actions. It's very important. Go quickly. I want to know where he goes and what he is doing. Caution Stevens to be careful. If he is detected, he must suffer the consequences. Then call John here immediately." The last order was an afterthought. She paced the floor.

John entered in a few minutes, his face white. "What happened?" he demanded, for once forgetting his usual respectful demeanor.

"I told him everything," she answered, her journey up and down the room uninterrupted. "He listened in silence. He asked if my decision was final. When I said that it was, he left without another word."

John's first sensation was relief for Cheira's safety. He had come to believe in Siri's love, but without doubting the violence of which he was capable. That love necessarily would produce the feeling of frustration when he learned of Cheira's disregard for her own well-being. His imagination failed to envision Siri's reaction to the rest of the plan.

"None of us approves," he reminded her. "Did you think Siri would accept your decision without protest?"

"I believed in our love. I thought that would help."

John suppressed a smile at such a viewpoint, totally in opposition to his own and—he was sure—Siri's.

"I was prepared to argue, if need be, to convince him . . . " she added.

" . . . With the full knowledge that he must submit in the end," John completed her thought. "You know Siri realizes that there is no point in discussion. The only choice he has must be made alone—either to obey or defy you."

The little affinity between the two men sparked momentarily. Pity and understanding formed a tenuous link.

"Let me talk to him," John volunteered.

Cheira hesitated, the ache of separation already growing in her heart. She wanted to go to him, to use her love to sway him. But could she? Emotion could never affect his will, she was certain of that. He could exercise perfect control. It was foolhardy of her to believe she could overcome that iron discipline by any feminine wiles. Even her power was ineffective against him. He had demonstrated that on too many occasions.

"Very well," she said at last. "I'll wait until I hear from you."

John learned from Stevens that Siri had gone to Lamborn Heath. *That's a good sign,* he decided. If Siri had returned to the desert, his task would have been immeasurably more difficult. It would mean that defiance was almost certain. John felt he had retreated to the ancestral manor simply to cool off.

At Lamborn Heath, John found that Siri was riding. He had been gone about three hours, Stevens reported. Ahmed, Siri's servant from the desert, was with him.

John settled down in the library with a drink to wait.

It was already dark when Siri returned. He came directly to the library where he poured a straight Scotch. His clothes bore the evidence of hard riding.

"Why, my comrade in bondage," he asked, his voice expressionless, without greeting or showing the least surprise that John was there, "of all the women in the world must it be my fate to love only that one?" He laughed bitterly.

"That's a rhetorical question!" John relaxed. The choice had been made.

Siri slumped into a chair opposite his visitor.

John, encouraged, added, "She's waiting for you now."

"I imagined as much," Siri sighed, the prospect, now, not giving him any pleasure. He had been maneuvered into a trap and cursed his own willing blindness. "As usual, Cheira considers no one's position but her own."

John frowned at the criticism, but refrained from comment, reminding himself that Siri's cooperation was necessary, no matter how it was obtained.

Siri continued, "I suppose I must listen to endless persuasions and explanations, at the end of which I will submit gracefully. I can think of no pleasanter way for a man to lose his self-respect."

He grinned mirthlessly, refilling his glass, examining the golden contents with the air of a man beholding his one salvation. He turned back to John with cutting insinuation, "You envy me, old chap? Perhaps, for you submission comes easier. But, then, a weak man couldn't hold her."

John winced, but said nothing.

Siri shrugged, half-regretting the thoughtless jab.

"So this is what I wasn't told before," Siri mused, swirling the liquor in the bottom of his glass. "Cheira's intention to take part in Mott's experiment is what triggered this charade. I'm being used to further the aims of the organization after all."

The memory of the hollow victory he had thought he had won this morning left a bitter taste in his mouth that even the smoothness of the aged Scotch could not dissipate.

"You have been chosen because she loves you," John corrected.

"You make me sound ungrateful," Siri sneered, his voice heavy with sarcasm.

"Aren't you?" John retorted. "I didn't think you'd be so squeamish about circumstances. After all, you've got what you wanted."

"She's given herself to me as the means of insuring my compliance, is that it?" Siri eyed his adversary. "If it was just a woman I needed, I've got a harem full of them just for the asking."

"You're a rotten bastard!" John accused, hatred in his voice.

Siri persisted, ignoring the remark. "Has her power already failed that she must resort to such devious tactics?"

"Would you have preferred that way? You would deserve it, if I had my way," John countered, his patience and fleeting sympathy eradicated by Siri's perversity. He considered the exchange senseless and unnecessary. *He's stalling,* he thought, with a wave of irritation.

"I would have preferred honesty," Siri answered, his shoulders slumping. His voice was dull and lifeless, defeated. "It's an insult to both of us if she thinks possession of her body is all I desire. It's her love I have longed for and fooled myself into thinking I had."

"I didn't realize you had such high ideals," John snapped, unsympathetically.

"Does my profession of a noble emotion stretch your credulity that much?" Siri laughed, refusing to take offense, robbing his antagonist of an anticipated victory. The enmity between the two deepened.

"Your ability to appreciate Cheira's sacrifice does, though," he retorted.

"Sacrifice!" Siri was exasperated. "Revenge would be a better word."

Now, John was puzzled. "What does that mean? What possible reason could she have for wanting revenge? Only the powerless need such an emotion. How could that apply to Cheira?"

Siri studied the man sitting opposite. He saw the rigid austerity that characterized a life of conformity with the standards of European civilization. *No,* he thought, *this man would never be guilty of the savagery of which I, myself, am capable.* He was convinced that John didn't know about the past.

Siri laughed. It was his only answer.

"She's waiting for you," John repeated, refusing to abet a trend in the conversation he didn't understand.

"Tell her I'll come back tomorrow."

"But she wants you now," John protested. "And the Duchess's reception. You've got to attend that. The invitation has already been accepted."

Siri glared at him for a moment, then turned and stomped from the room. He took the stairs two at a time.

Since his return, he had occupied the master suite in the old manor. The rooms retained the familiarity of childhood. Now his thoughts took refuge in that far-off time. He remembered the hours spent there, his mother sitting in the rocker by the fireplace while he played with his toys on the floor. It was a time of silent companionship they shared. He felt the coolness of her hands smoothing back his hair. Her touch drove away his childish problems.

He remembered, too, the resentment he felt when his father interrupted the serenity they shared. He recalled the awe he felt for the formidable giant. He was sure his mother felt it, too, because she always laid her work aside to wait humbly on the Earl of Zetland. He resented his mother's humiliation with all the ferocious loyalty of his young heart.

After his mother was gone, he never entered the rooms that his father continued to occupy alone. The old man's moroseness grew as he aged. The harshness of his manner repulsed his son. Siri gave him as wide a berth as possible, busying himself in the stable, tending the animals to whom he gave all his love.

Now, when it was too late, he understood the old man's loneliness. How empty his life was without the woman he loved! How he covered his vulnerability with gruffness as the only way he knew of dealing with the love he bore for her son! The lad never understood until he was grown the inhibitions which had been interwoven into his father's character by the laws of the culture in which he was raised.

In that instant, Siri almost grasped a clear comprehension of himself. He shook his head, trying to stabilize the idea but it slipped away. The essence he could have withdrawn from the content of the thought failed to form in his mind because of his simplistic view of the comparison. He was only acquainted with the surface of his parents' relationship.

John knew that further attempts at persuading Siri would prove futile. He returned to Pemberly House and Lady Pemberly. *Be thankful,* he told himself, *that it has turned out so well.* He paused only long enough to order Stevens to the residence of the Duchess with regrets that the last minute indisposition of Lady Pemberly . . .

Cheira rose quickly when John entered. The strain showed in her face and in the tenseness of her movements.

"What happened, John? Have you seen him?"

"Good news, my lady," he hastened to reassure her. "Siri went to Lamborn Heath. I have spoken to him. His love for you has overcome his reluctance. He gave me his word, he will return tomorrow."

"Tomorrow!" She repeated the word vacantly, attempting to conceal the disappointment she felt.

"Yes," John repeated firmly. "Tomorrow!"

"But why?"

"He'll cooperate, but he's a proud man. It must be on his own terms. You can't rob him of his dignity, too," he chided.

"I never intended that."

"Then you must be patient."

She sighed. It was assent.

Lost in thought, unconscious of her own change, Cheira was unaware of the contrast between her customary cold, businesslike attitude and the softly feminine picture she was presenting now.

Seeing her standing there with her golden hair loosely falling about her shoulders and the material of her gown clinging to her body, John felt despair rising unbidden in his heart. The resentment he had thought conquered returned full force. That he must accept another's possession of her was almost too much too bear.

"The Duchess!" she exclaimed.

With an effort he controlled his thoughts, thankful that she had been too occupied with her own to notice.

"I've sent Stevens with the message of your indisposition. I have promised to go instead."

"You serve me well, old friend," she said, smiling. "I am grateful."

He bowed low in acknowledgement but actually to hide the guilty flush rising to his face. He wished never to burden her with the knowledge of his true feelings.

"That's the purpose of my life, my lady," he answered in a muffled tone and hurried from the room.

She left word with Jennie to admit Siri at whatever hour he might choose to come; but she spent the night alone, sleeping fitfully, her empty arms aching to hold him, her body yearning for his touch. The intimacy she had dreaded had become an insatiable hunger. In intervals of dreaming, she saw his face smiling at her, felt his arms around her, his mouth on hers; but the incipient sweetness of sensation turned into pain, her memory dredging up the past brutality of unbridled passion. The very real sob rising in her throat jarred her into wakefulness.

With the first light of dawn, she rose. Convincing herself that this was tomorrow and he would come at any minute, she dressed carefully. She astonished Jennie by the detailed care she took to enhance her beauty, a condition previously ignored. She personally supervised the ordering of breakfast, fidgeting with housekeeping details, which made Jennie smile at her ignorance. When everything was ready, she waited.

He did not come.

By noon she was frantic. Waiting, submitting to the will of another was a new experience. Patience was a virtue Cheira had never before needed.

She summoned John. He assured her that Siri was still at Lamborn Heath.

"Wait!" he told her sternly, in a tone that Cheira would never have tolerated under ordinary circumstances, a tone that John would never have believed he would dare use in addressing her.

Finally, she demanded that Stevens be brought in to give a direct report. The man came, trembling and uncertain. He had never entered Cheira's private suite. In fact, she had only spoken to him directly on the day she had transfigured him. The awe he felt then was undiminished.

"What is Siri doing?" she demanded.

"He's riding, my lady," he stated, managing to keep his tone normal. "Ahmed is with him."

"He did that yesterday," she spoke petulantly.

"And today, also."

Irritation rising in her voice, she snapped, "Get out then, if that's all you can say."

Stevens scurried away, glad to be out. Cheira stood glaring at the door, her fists clenched, willing to blame anyone but herself for Siri's behavior.

"It's time to dress for your appointment, my lady," Jennie ventured to remind her.

"What good will I be without a husband?" Cheira lamented, overcome by self-pity and the novel sensation of incompleteness. The ache in her heart was a real physical sensation. It made her feel weak, unable to concentrate.

"He will come," Jennie reassured her, "as he promised. A Northman always keeps his word." Jennie allowed a note of pride to creep into her voice for her countryman.

Cheira was waiting in the great hall for her car when Siri appeared, bowing formally.

"Your humble servant returns, my queen, obedient to your wishes."

She gasped, joy leaping into her face.

"I love you so," she whispered, voicing the thought uppermost in her mind. She raised her hand to touch his cheek. Siri grasped her wrist, stopping the movement.

"Then give up this madness." His voice was stern.

The pleasure of his coming died out of her eyes, leaving only barren determination. She shook her head slowly.

"Do you think I'm such a fool to believe your avowal of love under such conditions?"

"But it's true," she whispered, her lips trembling as she fought to hold her decision against the severity of his attitude. He couldn't know that her surrender was shaking the very foundation of her character, that the woman she had discovered within was battling for supremacy over the founder of the most unique organization the world had ever seen. She clung desperately to the course she knew she must take, but Siri's disapproval made the task almost impossible. Her breath caught in a sob.

Siri relented enough to try another tack. "And if Mott fails?"

"It's a chance I have to take," she responded.

"Even if I ask you not to—in the name of that love you insist that you bear for me?" His hold on her wrist tightened.

"It's not that way," she answered, summoning the last of her failing courage. "Now that I know the full meaning of love, it's more important than ever that I do this. Please try to understand."

"I've spent the last twenty-four hours trying to understand," he retorted. "I understand that your love is a pretense to ensure my cooperation, that you allowed me to have you as the price of it. Because you doubted my love—thinking me capable only of blind passion—you were willing to do this despite the fear you couldn't conquer. You chose me because the chance for revenge was too sweet to pass up."

Cheira winced at every phrase, head bowed, accepting the pain inflicted by his words like physical blows. The accusation was so unjust she had no defense to make, only a stubborn determination to cling to the course she had chosen. She saw the chasm widening between herself and Siri. She couldn't reach him and the ache returned to her heart.

"I do love you; and I must do this," she whimpered.

Without another word, he led her to the car and took the place beside her. The heavy scowl on his face made her afraid to break the silence.

CHAPTER XIII

Dr. David Mott met them at the steps of the clinic. Ushering them into his comfortably furnished office, he greeted Cheira and introduced himself to the earl. He explained the purpose of their visit, "Today we will give you a thorough physical examination, your ladyship. Dr. Irene Carpenter, who will perform the examination, is a brilliant physician. You may have the utmost confidence in her ability."

The young scientist was acutely conscious of the dissension between his patients. Accurately, he judged its cause. He had been barraged by protests from all the senior members of the organization. The experiment was proceeding only because Cheira sanctioned it. It was not surprising, then, that the man Cheira had chosen as her companion in the project was exerting all his influence to dissuade her. In the face of so much opposition, David failed to understand Cheira's determination to continue. Objectively, the experiment would not be hampered by the use of another subject. He realized, however, that he had no authority to refuse if she insisted.

He wished he knew her better. He had spoken to Cheira only a few times: at his transfiguration; and more recently, when he had outlined the progress of the experiments that had led them to this moment.

He had not met Siri before.

"If your ladyship will come this way," he spoke deferentially, indicating an adjoining room. "I will be back directly, my lord." He bowed to Siri whose only acknowledgement was an expression of hostility.

David hurried back. Siri was standing at the window, staring into space, a heavy scowl settled on his face.

"What can I do, my lord, to make it easier?" the younger man asked candidly.

Siri turned to look at him. David was conscious of the dark eyes boring into his mind. The scientist had never met a man of such commanding presence. Here was a man indifferently aware of himself, but acutely conscious of his environment—not in the manner of fear, but in the attitude of challenge. He would never doubt what his senses perceived, nor hesitate to make a judgement. He would discount any physical weakness in the face of that judgement, using his body as the instrument for the execution of his will. He would expect others to do the same, having only contempt for anyone who did not continuously require the best of himself.

And should a decision of his prove to be incorrect, he would be fully prepared to bear the burden of consequences, disdaining mercy, demanding justice. The evident pride of his being would be sated by nothing less, for no action of his would ever be realized without the full knowledge of his mind and the sanction of his will.

That the physical perfection of his body matched the excellence of his spirit was only a factor so long as it served his purpose. Even under these trying conditions, his joy of existence was apparent.

He looked, David thought, like the model the famous sculptor had used when he chiseled the marble for the statue of his namesake. David did not frame these words. They were all contained in the imagined conception of the sculpture.

David felt a great awe for the legendary figure. The one man in the society who defied convention, leading a life that flaunted all the rules of society and seemed only an exaltation of his own ego. The note of similarity to his own life was responsible for the admiration. The mastery of environment which Siri had accomplished was a symbol of the possibility of victory to the young man.

"I want to know everything," Siri stated, a threat in his voice.

"Yes, sir," David responded, eagerly.

For the next two hours, David conducted Siri on a thorough tour of the clinic. He was impressed by Siri's scientific knowledge and his quick grasp of the most complicated procedures. Even for one of altered consciousness, the man's intelligence was astounding. In his work, David had tested thousands of individuals, but none came close to the intellect that Siri possessed. The scientist found himself looking forward eagerly to an association with this exceptional man.

"In two days, your ladyship," the young doctor told Cheira when she was ready to leave, "at the same time."

"Mott explained the experiment very thoroughly. I'm impressed," Siri volunteered when they were in the car. "It's dangerous, but he seems to be using well-tested procedures. I could find no flaws."

Cheira turned to him eagerly. "Then you approve?" she asked hopefully.

"Of the experiment—yes. Of your part in it—no. Mott says he's got fifty applications and could have a thousand any time. There's no reason for you to risk your life."

She sagged back onto the seat, her determination again threatening to be swamped in a sea of hopelessness.

"But I must," she insisted stubbornly in a low voice. "We are all the way we are because of me. I'm solely responsible."

"The advantages far outweigh the disadvantages. There isn't a single member who regrets his condition or who isn't grateful to you for it," Siri responded, demolishing her argument. But he reckoned without her blossoming femininity.

"That's a man's point of view," she countered. "Women enjoy transfiguration, too; but not if the price is sacrifice of their womanhood."

"There aren't enough women in the society to matter," Siri said in exasperation.

"But there will be," she retorted, "as soon as the experiment is successful."

Siri's mouth drew into a thin line. He didn't answer.

The silence deepened and lengthened between them. Siri was reminded that he also had made a commitment.

"As you wish," he said finally.

Siri was reserved but attentive the rest of the day and in the evening at Madame Bentley's extravaganza. Charming and with impeccable manners, he was received with unanimous approval by the leading members of the slightly decadent, highly overcivilized culture. If any of the desert man remained, the vestiges were undetectable.

Cheira found herself in the uncomfortable position of supplicant. She was experiencing the vulnerability of the lover. Her misery was a burden only partially concealed. Siri was making her bear the weight of their difference of opinion by ignoring her telepathic messages of devotion.

The maternal concern of sympathetic but ignorant dowagers only made matters worse.

It was late when they returned to Pemberly House. With mixed emotions, Cheira anticipated the time when they would be alone. With the moment at hand, she was grateful for the respite when Siri poured a drink and sank morosely into the chair by the fireplace.

She detained Jennie longer than usual, finding a dozen odd chores for the little maid. All the time Cheira's thoughts searched for some sign from Siri. She wanted him to come to her, to cast aside his convictions to be with her, to show her that his love could surmount all barriers.

At last she could find no excuse to delay longer. Dismissing Jennie, Cheira went to Siri, her desire destroying the separation her pride tried to erect. She knelt at his feet, her cheek against his knee, no longer caring that her action was a contradiction.

"You cannot be sovereign and subject at the same time, my love," he said sadly, raising her onto his lap, "nor can I be master and slave, too."

"But love makes all things possible," she murmured. Putting her arms around his neck, she took the lobe of his early gently between her teeth, biting just hard enough for emphasis.

"Is that the logic of the sovereign or the woman?" he chuckled, despairingly, his mouth warm on her breast through the material of her thin gown. Her body arched against him in quick response, impatient for the pleasure it was in his power to bestow.

"Oh, my darling! Love me! Love me!" she pleaded.

You're a fool, he thought. *Why deny yourself possession of this woman you have desired for so long?* With a rationalization foreign to his nature, he deliberately put the thought of the impending experiment out of his mind.

"Huriyah," he whispered, putting her down on the cushions in front of the fireplace; the flaming desire obliterated all their differences.

Briefly she cried out as the buttons of his shirt cut into her flesh. Still, she clung to him, her body straining to accept his.

His power flowed unrestrainedly along her nerves. She gasped as the convulsive movement precipitated the flow of energy he expected, demanding the release he did not try to withhold.

She lay quiet, unresisting when he picked her up and carried her to bed. A faint smile played about her lips as she watched him undress, openly enjoying the sight of his nude body, while surrendering to the fatigue of her own spent nerves.

Contentedly, she nestled in his arms when he stretched out beside her. He pulled her close, enhancing the recent memory of union, crystallizing the sensations to store in his memory.

"I want this moment to last forever," Cheira whispered, identifying with his mood.

"We can do it," Siri fantasized. "We will build our love into a shield, impenetrable like the substance on the walls, unbreachable because we will always stand together."

"Oh, yes," she agreed. "That's all I'll ever want." She closed her eyes, savoring the peaceful communion, the warm glow of happiness that was still a new experience. Drowsily, she accepted the moment for an eternal promise.

For them both, the past ceased to exist and the future glistened with everlasting bliss.

"Cheira, come with me to Imla Dun." Siri broke the silence, gripped by a sudden inspiration. "I want to share with you the desert night, to show you why it is like no other place on earth, so you will love it as I do. Will you come?"

"Mmm," she assented sleepily, squirming closer against him, her arm flung possessively across his chest.

"Now. Tonight," he insisted.

She opened her eyes wide twisting around to stare at him. "But it's the middle of the night," she protested.

"And the desert is breathlessly beautiful," he retorted happily, his voice mellowed by a tone she had never heard. "It needs only your presence to make it perfect," he added, kissing her.

"This is perfect," she said, responding to the caress, her body lazily resisting the excitement he felt.

Untangling himself from her arms, he was out of bed in one swift movement, throwing on his clothes before she could protest. He laughed.

"I'll be waiting," he said on his way out the door, "in fifteen minutes." He paused, adding softly, "Wear a gown like the ones you wear at Arx Vetus."

Cheira lay alone in the big bed. Now she was wide awake. She was nonplused by Siri's impromptu action. His frivolous use of power shocked her. *It's something else I never thought about.* She smiled to herself. She was amazed at how serious her life had been, how lacking in the joy of living.

She rolled over, feeling the warmth of the sheets where Siri had lain, reveling in the closeness the warmth recalled. She thought of the rules that limited her life, of the unquestioning acceptance of them that was second nature. *They're not necessary after all,* she concluded. Frowning, she propped herself on her elbows to look at the pillow, still dented from the pressure of Siri's head. She laid her cheek in the depression. Then, she laughed. Jumping out of bed, she donned a simple gown of gold and ran from the apartment, feeling light and carefree, alive to the moment.

The spaciousness and luxury of the sheik's tent surprised her; but the biggest shock was the realization that she could be there with the sound of his voice drifting through the open flap of canvas—ordering his tribes-men—and she could hear it—in the place where he was master—without fear, in fact, with joy swelling her heart in the knowledge that she belonged to him.

She wandered aimlessly, touching the things that were his, feeling an eager willingness to take her place among them, to be forever obedient to his wishes and conversely to let him bear the responsibility for her exis-tence.

Siri came up behind her soundlessly, the thick fur of the rugs muffling his steps. She jumped, startled when he kissed the nape of her neck, blush-ing guiltily at the thoughts she had neglected to conceal.

"If you truly feel like that," he said, turning her around to face him, "then I am content."

In a rush of possessiveness, she threw her arms around his neck, bury-ing her face against his chest. "I know now that I can never live without you," she murmured.

"That's as it should be." He laughed, forcing down the doubt that rose in his mind. He would allow nothing to spoil this moment.

The impatient call of the stallion waiting outside the tent interrupted them. "Skotias grows impatient"—Siri grinned, leading her out under the awning—"to show you the desert as I promised."

The big stallion snorted, sidestepping as Siri lifted Cheira onto the saddle, protesting the unaccustomed double burden and the fluttering of Cheira's gown against his shoulder. Siri spoke to him soothingly, settling the animal, willing him to submit to the unusual situation. Convinced that what-ever his master asked must be accepted, Skotias moved off quietly, skirting the line of tents and heading onto the desolate sand. The landscape rose in undulating waves of light and shadow under the illumination of the moon, which hung like a great white ball just overhead.

Cheira relaxed, enjoying the security of the strong arms, which held her so effortlessly. The voluminous folds of Siri's burnoose made a warm shelter against the cool night. The steady, monotonous movement produced a feeling of euphoria. She couldn't remember when the ride had begun or when Siri had started to speak. Time was suspended; it could have been minutes or hours. She didn't care. Siri's words were blurred in a fog of contentment; only the sound was necessary for her to hear, not the meaning.

"You're not listening," Siri accused gently after a while. "My lecture on the beauty of the desert has been wasted."

In answer, she clung more closely to him, sighing.

They left the dunes and entered a low outcropping of rocks, a jagged, barren stand, the remnants of a prehistoric mountain range worn by centuries of blowing sand, only its roots left as evidence of its once majestic height. Skotias picked his way carefully along the faint path; the sound of his hoofs struck a loose stone now and again, breaking the lifeless silence. Siri steered the stallion unerringly, the stark shadows revealing to his keen eyes the treacherous footing they concealed.

Siri stopped beside a secluded grotto. The musical splashing of water could be heard. A few stately palms stretched above the boulders, their heads stark in the moonlight. He spread the burnoose and set Cheira gently upon it, like a miser displaying his greatest treasure only when he has assured privacy. A thin shaft of moonlight illumined the spot of soft grass in the shelter of smooth rock jutting like walls supporting a starry roof.

"It's beautiful"—Cheira's tone was awed—"and unbelievable in the middle of these barren rocks. How did you ever find it?"

Siri threw himself down beside her, his hands cupped behind his head as he lay on his back. He gazed up at the twinkling constellations like diamonds embedded in velvet. "I stumbled on it one day and have dreamed ever since of having you here. Like this. In the moonlight."

Clearly she heard the note of yearning in his voice. She could recognize now what the long years of separation had caused. She rose, knowing intuitively what he wanted, what she alone could give him. The overt proof of her uniqueness presented to him for his pleasure would be the concrete demonstration of her love and of the sincerity with which she offered herself totally. It was what she could do to erase the lingering doubt, the only flaw left between them.

She stopped at the spot where the minute stream twinkled merrily over the rocks to rest in a quiet pool. The moonlight, highlighting the cascading droplets and shimmering on the surface of the pool, caught her as she moved. The path of its rays, the cold light, shone on the long golden strands of her hair and her golden gown impartially. She raised her arms, inviting the unfeeling beams to caress her skin. She held the tableau.

She turned slowly, her arms lowering with the motion.

Siri, leaning up on his elbow, watched her intently. With a smile on her upturned face, she welcomed the scrutiny of those dark, piercing eyes. Her body began to glow. The light grew brighter and brighter until, obliterating the feeble light from the moon, the grotto burst into the reality of sunlight.

Her movements leisurely, she loosened the delicate chain which was the belt of her gown, letting it slip from her fingers noiselessly to the grass. The same slow motion of her hands unclasped the gown at the shoulders. It slid easily down the length of her body. She stood, her arms hanging at her sides, clothed only in the intense brilliance that emanated from her.

Siri didn't move, but she felt his gaze travel openly down the length of her body. It set up a response in her nerves that pulsed like an electric current, commencing at the base of her throat, bursting at a point low in her pelvis. She saw his eyes narrow. She noted the unnatural emphasis of his cheekbones above the hollowness of his cheeks. An indrawn breath unconsciously held told her he felt it, too.

She glided toward him. A step. A pause. The wedding march.

Each movement increased the intensity of the current to the point of agony. She waited, close now, prolonging the tension, knowing that it must be experienced to the fullest, its identity realized beyond doubt, so they could know the desire for each other as a necessity.

She lay down at the edge of the spread burnoose, just out of reach. Her part was ended in this final act of surrender. He must move now to take the whole of that which was offered, the whole of her being for his own: the woman and the goddess as one without reservation.

He touched her lightly. His fingertips contacting the current within brightened the glow of her body. He trembled with the intensity of his vibrating nerves.

He took her blindly, involuntarily. His body controlled the action, his mind shocked into quiescence at the brute strength of the physical sensations: the sensations an ascending spiral where each pulsation was an ultimate, an ultimate of which no increase could be endured—but was endured and eagerly with an unending craving from the greedy demand of each cell in his body until the top of the spiral was reached, until it burst into a blinding flash that obliterated all sensation.

Cheira's cry split the silence of the night, echoing against the confining walls of the grotto. Siri rolled away from her. He lay on his back, spread-eagled on the rocky ground, unseeing in the darkness.

Awareness returned in disconnected spurts. Primarily, he was only conscious of the all-pervading weakness, which permeated even to the extremities of his limbs, to the numbness of his fingertips. A sharp stone out into his shoulder, but he could summon no strength to move. He felt his inert weight pressing down against the jagged earth; still there was no response from his muscles. Time passed gently, guarding his helplessness.

The moon had sunk unheeded below the horizon, and the black hours before the dawn settled like a shroud over the grotto. His mind timidly began to resume control. His attention was drawn to the dull, steady thud of his heart laboring against the inertia of his torso.

A movement beside him captured his attention.

"I'll wait for you at Pemberly House," Cheira whispered, the sound alien in the darkness.

"Don't go!" he begged, reaching blindly to detain her, not caring that the tone of his voice revealed the penury of his soul.

The next moment, he was deluged with despair. He felt, without seeing, through the vibration of his nerves, that she was gone.

A long while later, he found Skotias by the sound of his munching. The stallion fastidiously picked the tenderest blades of grass at the periphery of the tiny oasis. He nickered softly at Siri's approach. With the reins tied securely to the saddle, Siri set the black horse on a homeward course. He knew the animal could find his way unerringly back to his own paddock, where Hasi would find him in the morning.

It took a supreme act of will to summon the energy to teleport back to Pemberly House.

Siri slipped noiselessly into the bedroom. Cheira's even breathing denoted deep sleep. His own exhaustion cried for the same respite.

But he was to be allowed no restoring rest so easily. The advantage he had hoped to gain had been wrested from him. Nothing, apparently, could dissuade her from her course. That she had returned here even after what they had experienced was certain proof.

Cheira moved close when he lay down. He slid his arms around her. She sighed, but didn't awaken.

His mind, now in full control, annoyingly started over the argument again. *Why does she have to be so damn stubborn?* he wondered helplessly. She was disregarding not only his opinion, but that of every member of the organization. Yesterday, he had decided to cooperate if there was no way to change her decision. He had loved her for so long she was part of his being. Tonight had proven that beyond doubt. *Of what use would pride or life itself be without her?*

He wondered about the limit of her power. That last time at Arx Vetus, how long could he have withstood the strain if Ameur hadn't stopped her? He shifted restlessly. If he decided to defy her, it would be to the death. And for what purpose? To deny himself the happiness of the last few days? To separate himself forever from the bliss of her love? To pretend that what he had felt tonight was less than total commitment? He'd be a fool!

His arms tightened around her. He buried his face in the fragrance of her hair. His fingertips caressed her shoulder.

Now that she was his at last, he'd be insane to give her up because his confounded pride rebelled at being used. *That is probably the true reason for my reluctance,* he accused himself. He had been able to uncover no valid reason to fear for her safety.

Mott's experiments are thorough, he admitted. The young scientist was very intelligent and conscientious. He had built in every safeguard. At any time, the procedure could be terminated.

What then is my objection? Being used in that manner.

To breed on command like one of my prized stallions! Well, he'd never hesitated to use any woman for his own gratification. Since when had he become so sensitive? Had he not sworn to give his life to her? God, how he loved her—loved her.

Dimly aware that his thoughts had begun to ramble, he made no effort to collect them. He drifted into a deep, exhausted sleep.

Siri was awakened by the brightening light which matched the natural dawn outside the windowless apartment. Carefully he extricated himself from Cheira's arms without disturbing her. His muscles felt cramped from maintaining the same position for so long. He went silently into the other room.

His thoughts resumed where they had left off last night, giving him no peace. His power over her was minimal, he conceded, leaning against the mantel of the fireplace. He had no way of assessing her feelings. An uneasy instinct warned him that it might be her head rather than her heart that prompted the abrupt change of attitude. Probably, she didn't know herself.

Therefore, he must admit that any influence he might exert would have little effect. He had already failed to sway her more than once. Neither separation nor the pleasure they knew together changed her decision.

He smiled. He had to admire her determination. She displayed more courage than anyone he had ever known. Sure of his love, then, he'd stay at her side, protective and helpful, truly subverting his opinions.

He frowned. Usually, he spent little time examining motives. The finality of his will was the habit of years, a fact obeyed without question by those around him. *Can I discipline myself to submit to Cheira's demands? Damn, why did she have to do this?* Realizing that his argument had come full circle, he laughed aloud.

"Siri?" Cheira called, her voice floating uncertainly through the half-open door. "Oh, God," she moaned.

Siri rushed to her side, gathering her into his arms.

"I thought you were gone," she whispered, moving her lips against his chest.

"I'll never leave you," he promised, dismissing the twinge of doubt, "unless you send me away."

"No! No! Never!" she protested, clinging desperately to him. "Haven't I proven that to you?"

"You've made me certain that only the desert is the proper setting for you. That we could live there forever and it would be heaven. That existence could hold nothing greater."

"It will be that way soon," she promised.

He winced at the words; yet in conformity with his decision, he kissed her tenderly. She lay quietly, allowing the pleasure of his touch to wash over her, savoring the first sensations of the ecstasy to come.

" 'tention!" he chuckled softly, noting the passion dawning in her half-closed eyes. "It's hardly fitting for the mistress of Pemberly to lie in bed all day making love." Grinning, he headed for the shower.

Cheira lay listening to the sounds of the splashing water, feeling contented and fulfilled. Then she rang for Jennie.

The maid appeared immediately. Her glance surreptitiously studied her mistress, then took in the entire room. She was uneasy when Siri was here. She felt a nagging need to protect Cheira from the cruelty of the desert-dwelling highlander. She had heard all the stories of his life at the Fort, her active imagination painting pictures of outlandish barbarity, fed by the innumerable books she read. She had felt the strength of his personality the few times he had glanced at her. Her heart stopped when those piercing eyes turned in her direction. She understood Cheira's surrender and her fear for her mistress increased. That he might treat her beloved lady like one of the women of his harem haunted her. When they were together in this suite, all she could do was hover helplessly in the hall, waiting to be summoned. She was painfully aware that her thoughts could not penetrate those walls. Before she had been grateful for the protection and privacy it had afforded her mistress. Now the fortress had been violated.

"That's enough, Jennie," Cheira's stern tone terminated her thought. "Would you want his lordship to know what you are thinking?"

Jennie blushed, murmuring a confused apology. Busily, she set about her morning tasks.

*   *   *

Shortly, Cheira joined her husband at breakfast. Jennie departed to inform Sir John that Lady Pemberly would receive him. It was the usual custom at the beginning of each day.

"Your ladyship is well, I trust?" John uttered the regular words of greeting. He had used them since Cheira had become head of Pemberly. Now, his glance meeting Siri's, the words sounded hollow.

Siri lounged, his chair pushed away from the table and rocked back on its legs, the delicate piece of furniture so appropriate for a woman's boudoir, creaking and trembling under his weight. He nodded to John, but didn't change his position. His resolution hadn't included clemency for Pemberly's chief executive. Siri smiled, enjoying the man's discomfiture at being forced to witness the proprietary attitude.

"Yes, thank you," Cheira answered mechanically, with an impatient wave of her hand, ordering him to get on with his business.

"Professor Harmon, whom you will recall is on an archeological expedition to Nepal"—John obeyed with customary directness—"has sent word that he happened upon a group of priests in the mountains who exhibit all the powers of transfiguration. He was sure your ladyship would with to know."

Cheira sat up, focusing her whole attention on what John was saying.

"Perhaps," John continued, "you will wish to send someone out to investigate. Professor Harmon's research has already taken him elsewhere."

"Is that all the information he gave?"

"He only sent a short note with the supply train," John explained.

Cheira sank into deep thought for a few minutes. Excitement was evident in her voice when she spoke. "Of course, this may be the lead we've been hoping for. Anyway, I don't want to miss any chance to learn more about our condition. Notify Ameur to send for Stuart Mervin."

John glanced at her sharply.

Noticing, she laughed. "How can I leave anyone under censure when I am so happy? I've been looking for an excuse for a long time. My heart

212

ached for him when I saw him in New York. Don't you agree he's suffered long enough?"

"We'll be happy to welcome him," John smiled.

"Good!" she answered. "I'll receive him at Arx Vetus. Also, can you get away for a day? Mott has set tomorrow afternoon to start the experiment. Therefore, tonight we must begin."

John nodded. They then fell into a discussion of the stock transfer John had tried to interest her in the day of Siri's return to England.

Siri was silent during the exchange. His knowledge of Cheira had always been personal. Even in the days when he was under censure, he was only vaguely interested in the empire she commanded. Now his admiration for her ability increased as he watched her handle her duties so competently.

John was gathering up the contracts with satisfaction. With Lady Pemberly's signature, he could complete the overdue agreement. He hesitated.

"Anything else?" Cheira noticed the action.

"May we not at least postpone the experiment?" John dared to suggest again, not wanting any opportunity to pass ungrasped.

Cheira looked full at him. For an instant only, he withstood the power of her mind. Then, he slowly knelt, bowing his head and extending his hands, in the traditional attitude of submission.

Siri was surprised at the action. John was not weak; his submission had to be intentional. *His pledge,* Siri remembered. He smiled. It was obvious that Cheira had no fear for herself. If she was protecting him, was that a proof of her love?

That glimpse of the power Cheira held over even the strongest members of the society gave him still another view of the problem. He frowned. She was willing to relinquish that position and place herself at the mercy of the weakest member. Did John, perhaps, realize the foolhardiness of her action even more than he did? Maybe he had better have a talk with John.

"Instruct Ameur," Cheira continued calmly, "to have two candidates ready, a man and a woman. Be at Arx Vetus at eight. You may go." Her voice was imperious, the tone forbidding any objection to her orders.

She turned to Siri when they were alone. Smiling, she came into his arms. "My love, may we have this last day together? There is no way of knowing what tomorrow will bring."

He saw her resolution wavering. So, she had not been as untouched by John's suggestion as she pretended! "And what will my punishment be if I add my protestations to John's?" he asked, lightly smoothing her hair.

"I'll surely cease to exist without your support," she whispered, her head against his chest, taking reassurance from the steady beat of his heart.

"Then I shall not." His arm tightened around her. "Let's go to Lamborn. The gray pines for you and the moor is desolate without your presence."

"No other woman has known so great a love," she innocently exaggerated, lifting her lips for his kiss. Now her eagerness for his touch was a constant yearning. The loneliness of the past, most poignantly realized in these first few days of surrender, demanded payment. All the barren years were a void needing to be filled.

"Come!" he commanded, picking her up and holding her tightly in his arms. "We'll teleport together."

Unresisting, she opened her mind, dimly conscious of surrendering the long-guarded bastions of her power. His eyes locked unblinkingly with hers; she relinquished her will to his direction. The pleasure of union permeated her body. She knew no thought but his; and her body dematerialized at the command of his will.

The light filled her, expanding her being, mingling the atoms of her substance with his. There was no separation or identity, nor any need for there to be. Her will acquiesced, accepted the state. There was only a longing for eternal continuance. She understood, intuitively, that she belonged in this existence, that this was the reality of a love she hadn't been able even to imagine but that she had longed for from the beginning of time.

Simultaneously, they knew that this was more total consummation than their bodies could ever achieve. Waves of ecstasy pulsated through them, the energy of their combined power spiraling to higher and higher peaks, the fusion of their minds producing an eternity of sweet sensation.

There came a time when he willed her body to materialize. She knew a wish to resist, to prolong forever the indescribable sweetness; but she had no power that was not his to command. Again she failed to name the feeling.

He set her down, holding her swaying body.

"Oh, God!" he breathed heavily, his skin white under the tan, all color drained from his lips. "What have I done?"

They were in the library at Lamborn Heath. He barely noticed. Pouring some whiskey, he held the glass to her pale lips. She swallowed meekly, her eyes following his every movement.

"Are you all right?" The concern he felt drew his mouth into a thin line and caused his hand to tremble. He guided her to the sofa.

Smiling languidly, she reached out for him, drawing his head to her breast. The experience, which had so shocked him, was for her familiar; but she couldn't remember. "Surely no two people have ever had such an experience," she comforted, discarding the effort to remember as too strenuous and unnecessary. Together they felt the exhaustion pervading their bodies, the weakness of each separate muscle precluding movement. The strange, unaccustomed quietude, the tranquillity produced a kind of lingering sweetness.

We'll never be able to hide our thoughts from each other.

It was a moment before Siri realized that it was her thought, so clear it seemed to originate in his own head. *I know, my love,* his thought answered hers. *May I always prove worthy of your trust!*

I love you, the thought said. She was confident that those words would always protect them.

They lay contented in each other's arms, unconscious of the passing time, unconscious even of its existence. They floated in the euphony of creation where the essence of being was the only reality, where unity was the only necessity and its continuance the only desire.

It was not until Ahmed knocked on the door that they noticed the evening shadows lengthening outside the windows.

"You ordered the horses for this afternoon, master. Do you still want them?" Ahmed inquired.

Siri glanced at Cheira. Now their physical separation emphasized with stark clarity her thought present in his brain.

"Right now," he told the servant.

Cheira left the room. She hurried to change into the riding clothes she had left there on her previous visit. She was conscious of Siri's presence even when they were apart and could follow his movements as if they were her own.

In minutes, they were riding side by side out into the emptiness of the moors, the only sound the soft thud as the horses' hooves sank into the yielding turf. Alive to the wordless communion, the union of their minds manifested itself by the quiet pulsing of their nerves in harmony. They were one, not only with each other, but with all existence, a part of the Eternal Principle. They could feel exhilaration in the growing heather and hear the music in the movement of the air.

Finally, as the last rays of the sun withdrew below the horizon, she spoke, "I must go to Arx Vetus. Will you come?"

He shook his head. *Tomorrow. I'll wait for you. The desert has relinquished its hold over me. We are united with the universe. Time and space are irrelevant.*

There was no room now for differences of opinion. They had only one will, one duty. There was no question of individual pride or supremacy. Oneness cannot be divided; it cannot be unequal.

She turned the gray, urging him to the smooth long-strided lope of which he was so capable. The animal responded eagerly, having grown impatient with the unusual slowness of the pace.

Siri matched the stride of his own mount with the gray's. He drew close and reaching over, loosened the net which confined her hair. The breeze obligingly flowed through the glossy strands, tumbling down her back. She smiled, shaking back the hair that fell against the face.

In my heart, you shall ride thus forever, his thought filled her mind, *my eternal love.*

Forever, she repeated, and the thought was his own.

She left him at the entrance of the manor house. He stood watching until she disappeared.

Minutes later, Cheira was within the familiar rambling walls of Arx Vetus. Tiana rose to greet her when she entered the audience chamber.

"You are more beautiful than ever." Tiana kissed her cheek. "Love suits you well, my dear."

"How could I have been such a fool to resist so long?" Cheira retorted, embracing the dark woman she considered a cherished friend. "The emptiness and futility of life without love is now impossible to conceive. I hunger for the touch of my beloved and long every second we are apart for the time he'll possess me again."

Tiana smiled, happy now to banish the secret worry that had gnawed at her peace of mind all the time Cheira was absent. Knowing Siri's love for Cheira but acknowledging, too, the life he had led, she feared him incapable of the tenderness Cheira needed before the unemotional suzerain could become the fulfilled, loving woman. The fury of the couple's last meeting at Arx Vetus had increased Tiana's uneasiness. She was relieved to see Cheira's radiance.

"I'm so happy for you."

Cheira thanked her absently. Impatient to return to Siri, her mind was already on the task ahead. It would require all her power of concentration.

"I'll change," she said. "Is John here?"

Tiana nodded affirmatively.

"Are the candidates ready?"

"Yes."

"The woman first then. It will be easier."

Cheira explained, "I'm asking you to accept a tremendous responsibility. You are one of the most powerful members of our society and the one best qualified to take my place. The enormous output of energy required to induce the change can be produced only by a few: Ameur, of course; but he has another role to play in the scheme of the future. He will be responsible for the operation of the organization. So please understand how vital is the necessity for your cooperation. Our relationship has progressed far beyond the point at which I would attempt to force you to undertake so much responsibility for the lives of others."

John knelt before her. "Have I ever refused to serve you in any manner?" The question was his answer.

"Then, rise. You are master here now." She handed him a toga of fine linen as white as her gown. It was to be the symbol of his authority.

"You will need to concentrate all your power," Cheira instructed, "with little time for recuperation as we'll attempt to alter two candidates consecutively. The woman first. They seem to resist less. Probably with hypnosis you can overcome any reluctance on her part. Then, direct your energy into her brain. You must cause the pineal gland to swell at least triple its dormant size. The irritation will bring about the alteration desired in two or three hours."

His glance questioned her.

"No one knows yet exactly how or why. You know Mott is at the point where he can reverse the process; but so far attempts to use mechanical energy to induce it just causes irreparable brain damage. I have refused to allow that kind of research.

"After today, the decision of whom to alter shall be yours alone. Ameur can advise you, but the responsibility will be yours. There is a list of tentative names you may inspect, if you wish. I've developed my own little psychological tests, but the main criterion is that they are intelligent enough to cope with this kind of existence.

"If the rest of the experiment is successful, your task will be simplified. You'll no longer need to consider that, in granting the gift of prolonged life, you are also extracting an immense price. That's been my greatest deterrent. I've been creating a static society."

The bell cord summoned Tiana with the first candidate. John took a deep breath. He was by nature a gentle man. Cheira hadn't needed to emphasize the responsibility involved.

"This is Maria Cortez," Cheira introduced a capable-looking woman in her early forties. "She is a surgeon in Toledo. Tiana has instructed her in the procedure."

"Welcome, Maria," John spoke kindly, taking her hands in his. "We are happy to have you become one of us." He smiled, allowing a pleasurable sensation to emanate from his grasp. He held her gaze. In a moment she had slipped under the spell.

She was aware of nothing but the hypnotic eyes fastened on hers and the tingling rippling along her nerves. She wondered that she was unafraid, that her consciousness submitted so willingly, that there was no desire to resist. Many thoughts flowed through her brain—the long struggle of her life, the triumph of the hard-won medical diploma, the initial disbelief when Ameur explained this state, the final reluctant agreement.

All thought was cut off by a throbbing in her head, just threatening to become pain. "Enough!" She heard Cheira's voice, but now she felt too sleepy to wonder or care. She fought to keep her eyes open, but her lids were too heavy; it took too much effort. Her mind seemed to have stopped working. She sagged limply to the floor.

John stared at the prostrate figure. Amazed. Disbelieving. What he had done became real only with the awareness of the uncontrollable trembling of his body. Weariness engulfed him. Cheira and Tiana led him to a divan.

"Lie down for a while," Cheira directed.

He protested, horrified at the idea of reclining in Cheira's presence. Even in such a deenergized state, the habit of years was strong. Despite a concentrated effort at control, however, he staggered against Tiana. He wiped his hand across his eyes to clear the blurred vision.

"I command you!" The sternness in Cheira's tone was superficial. "The unaccustomed drain on your energy has left you weak. You must rest."

He complied without further protest. Relief flooded through his exhausted muscles freed from the added strain he had tried to impose on them. Tiana held a cup to his lips. The liquor was strong and stimulating, spreading a warm glow. He felt better immediately.

"The woman—Maria?" he worried. "Is she all right?"

"Of course," Cheira reassured him. "Ching Li is taking care of her. You did an excellent job. Rest a while. Then, we'll have dinner; and you can try the other candidate when your energy is revived."

Ameur joined them in the dining room.

"The transfiguration's successful," he reported, laughing at the skepticism in John's face. Ameur's practiced eye had been able to detect changes in skin texture and muscle tone in the still-unconscious woman.

"You're a better man that you thought," he teased.

"Try me!" Jon challenged. "No, don't!" He laughed. The light exchange bolstered his confidence. The new experience was reduced to manageable size.

The hour was late; the four were alone.

"The experiment begins soon, then, mistress?" The laughter faded out of Ameur's face. He looked at Cheira intently.

"Tomorrow afternoon."

"And Siri has agreed?"

"Yes, reluctantly; but yes, he agrees."

"So be it!" he responded, leaning back in his chair in an attitude of finality, discarding any idea of further protest.

"Ameur, you will guard the members?" Cheira fretted. "You know how absorbed they get in their work. Don't let them forget their time at Arx Vetus."

Ameur promised, suppressing a smile at the concern she betrayed. He caught himself wondering again what purpose drove her to such dedication.

"Feeling better?" Cheira turned to John.

"Yes, I'm ready whenever you wish," he answered, rising.

"In about five minutes, then," she said to Ameur.

On the way back to the audience chamber, Cheira told John about the next candidate.

"His name is Ian McDonnell. He'll be the replacement in the guard at Pemberly when Harry Giles leaves for China. He's intelligent and brave, but high tempered. He may be difficult. At the moment, his highest ambition is to serve Lady Pemberly; but he's been objecting vehemently to the black magic—his words—ceremony that goes with it. He refuses to believe that any witch—his word, also—in the desert could have any connection with Lady Pemberly." She laughed. "Ameur's been trying to convince him all week. Even mild punishment hasn't brought him down. So you may have to be severe to make him submit. He'll be very loyal and valuable when he understands, I'm sure."

"How far do you want me to go?" John worried.

"As far as necessary. You can't transfigure him as long as he resists."

Cheira accepted the tenet unquestioningly. Now John did, too.

Ameur brought in a handsome, red-haired man whose strength was evident in the effort Ameur had to exert to control him. He displayed the agility and muscular development of a boxer.

"Welcome, Ian," John's voice was quiet, but dominating. "We are happy to have you join us."

"What is this gibberish?" Ian spit out the words, crouching, ready to defend himself.

"Hasn't Ameur explained to you?"

Cheira stood in the shadows of the ornate dais, unnoticed by the distraught Irishman, but ready to come to John's aid if necessary.

"The man's a lunatic!" Ian rolled his eyes, expressively. "All I want is to get out of here and back to England. I've a good job waiting. I don't want to lose it."

"And you shall not." John maintained his calm attitude, approaching the man casually, locking his gaze.

Without warning, Ian swung, fist clenched. John was ready. Ducking the blow, he delivered a quick slice to the man's neck with the edge of his hand. Ian fell. Before he could rise, John had a hand on his shoulder. The pain shot through his body. Ian cried out as much from surprise as agony.

John increased the pressure, his fingers digging into the man's shoulder, sharpening the pain.

"If you want to serve Lady Pemberly, submit now," John hissed.

Ian gasped. "All right!" acknowledging the advantage of a superior opponent, but not defeat.

John released him. The Irishman writhed on the floor, the spasms of his tortured nerves shaking his body. If he had been in any condition to notice, he would have seen sympathy in the face of the man standing over him. John was seeing himself in the same position. It was many years ago, but the memory was still vivid.

It was ever thus, he thought sadly, *that mankind has been dragged, kicking and protesting, into a better future. Will we ever learn?*

John raised the man gently, quiet now, unresisting; but not broken. With one-pointed concentration, John was able to penetrate the brain. It was easier this time. He could judge when the physical change had taken place, by gauging the dilation of the pupils. Ian's eyes widened; but they were focused into an unseeing stare.

Afterwards, as Ameur took the man away, John smiled, thinking how surprised Ian would be when they met again.

"Well done, John," Cheira congratulated him. "You've come through much better this time. Rest now. You won't have any trouble after this. I'll see you in London tomorrow."

Early the next morning, Cheira summoned Stuart Mervin.

"Look at me!" she ordered when he knelt at the foot of the dais.

Slowly he raised his head. He had left off the disguise of age. He was young again.

"Your appearance has improved considerably since the last time I saw you." She smiled. She saw the pain in his eyes. That had not been removed with the disguise. He had lived with it too long. "I think it's time for us to resolve our differences," she added.

"The fault was entirely mine," Mervin stated earnestly.

"But in view of the trouble in the Near East, your opinion was justified," she protested.

"There can be no justification for disregarding your wishes," he persisted, obstinately refusing the excuse she offered.

"Then you believe I had the right to censure you?"

"Yes, mistress," he answered without hesitation.

"And to continue it, if I wish?" Disbelief grew in her voice.

"Please, mistress." Misery was plain in the tone of his voice. "I'd rather die. I can't bear it any longer."

Her voice softened. "It's possible that I grow wiser with the passing years. I wish to welcome you back and offer you reassignment."

Joy leaped into Mervin's face at the realization of her words. In gratitude, he bowed low to kiss the hem of her gown.

"Don't!" she cried, stopping him. "Why are you grateful? You should be angry. Why have you allowed me to do this?"

Cheira's femininity, blooming at last, brought a new clarity to the arbitrary position she held. *From Wang Lu through a long list of very powerful men,* she thought, *not one has challenged my authority, even when I have caused them years of humiliation. Siri only had deliberately set out to match my power; and even he had not wanted to usurp my position in the organization.*

"Why?" she repeated, confused by the alien thoughts.

Mervin shook his head slowly, puzzled by the sudden change. "You're the source of my life. It's at your disposal. I've never felt otherwise." He spoke as if he were obediently reciting facts they both knew, as if it had never occurred to him to investigate the verity of a dogma.

"Life is always better than death," Mervin attempted to explain, not questioning her right to require the obvious. "Mankind only accepts death because they have no alternative. I have no wish to die. Only your prolonged censure made life too unsatisfactory to make its continuance worthwhile. I

221

have lived almost a century; but I'm still young and vigorous. I owe that to you."

"But you are master of your own power. I do not control it," she protested. "The requirement to return to Arx Vetus is only to give you time to practice and increase it."

"Perhaps"—Mervin looked at her directly—"every man must have a deity, a focal point of existence, a belief he will not challenge even at the expense of his life."

Her eyes widened.

He added, "Haven't you known that it was not fear that makes the members obedient to your wishes?"

"I'm beginning to learn many things." She hesitated, then added softly, "I'm truly sorry for the suffering I have caused you."

Mervin didn't know Cheira well enough to know that this was only the second apology she had ever offered to anyone.

"My only desire is to serve you in any way I can. I deeply regret my defiance. My punishment was just." He bowed his head.

Cheira frowned. For whatever his reasons, Stuart Mervin refused to see her as a flesh-and-blood woman. The able financier whose talent for shrewdness was respected throughout the world had chosen to give her unquestioning loyalty. She sighed. How many others felt as he did? She had no right, then, to waver in her decision. Even the rapport she had with Siri must not be allowed to sway her from her duty to the organization.

"Would you be interested in this?" She handed Mervin the letter from Nepal. "I'd like you to search them out. Study them. And find out if we are like them."

He raised his head and looked at her. The pain was gone from his eyes at last, replaced by a youthful enthusiasm.

"I need to know if I was ever one of them. I've no memory of what I am or where I came from. Wang Lu found me, but he never could find any trace of my past. Will you do this for me?"

"I'll be grateful for the opportunity," Mervin answered promptly.

Both of them were ignorant of Wang Lu's real part in their lives.

Through the years of association, Ameur had become so attuned to Cheira's actions that now he entered even before Mervin left. He came directly to her, knowing it was the time of parting. Although she hid her thoughts from him, he knew her so well he could easily guess the trend of her thinking. Now her eyes told him what she could not, would not say.

My darling Ameur, she felt without actually framing the thought. *My gentle love! Without Siri's fire, the strength of your will is love! Would that I could have surrendered. You have been my salvation. You mended my spirit when the abuse I had suffered at the Fort left it a poor broken thing. You gave me rest and refuge. Your attention and devotion made the loneliness of my life bearable. It was only the fear you could not take away. That was the barrier that kept us apart.*

Tiana came to stand by her husband's side. His gaze broke away from Cheira. He smiled, putting his arm around his wife. Cheira accepted the gesture and was glad. It was Ameur's way of telling her that he loved his wife, that he accepted the separation.

"This is farewell, my friends," Cheira spoke, her voice barely audible. "If the experiment is successful, I shall return in a year or two." She did not voice the alternative. "The organization rests on your shoulders. Once I'm without power, I'll not trust my ability. Work with John. Give him the benefit of your experience with transfiguration. He'll need your advice and support."

She came to them and kissed them, her body touching Ameur for an instant to impress the memory indelibly in her mind. Then she withdrew.

At the doorway, Cheira turned to look at the room that held so many memories. "Farewell!" she said again and disappeared.

CHAPTER XIV

It was noon when Cheira returned to Pemberly House. Siri was waiting in her suite. She ran to him, throwing herself into his arms. He laughed at her eagerness. It hid the emptiness he had felt in her absence.

My love, my love, his thought filled her mind as he covered her face with kisses. *Our bodies as well as our minds must be always together.*

As a test, she raised the barrier in her mind to shut him out. He held her at arm's length, grinning. *Don't waste your energy,* his thought told her. *It won't work for either of us anymore. Didn't you know I was with you every second you were away?* He sobered, speaking aloud, "When you spoke to Mervin, I thought you had changed your mind and would not return. I was glad and sad, at the same time."

"I was tempted. To be with you always the way we are now—what more could I desire? But I owe the society more than my own selfishness. I don't understand their feeling for me; but I know that such loyalty deserves the best I can offer. Leaving Arx Vetus was more difficult than I had imagined. I may never see it again . . . " Her voice caught in her throat.

"Or Ameur?" Siri teased, letting her know he knew that, too.

"Yes," she admitted, blushing faintly as the tears welled up in her eyes, "but for you I could have loved him. You always stood between us."

"It's a good thing"—he grinned, sitting down in a deep chair by the fireplace and gathering her into his lap—"otherwise I would have killed him."

"Don't talk so." She put a finger on his lips. "He is a good friend who helped me through those years when I thought I hated you. Did you know that it was he and Wang Lu who convinced me that transfiguration was right for you? You can be so fierce and uncompromising that I never would have suggested it."

"But you've tamed me." His eyes twinkled. "I'm as gentle as a kitten."

"Pooh!" She laughed, tilting her head to trace the line of his jaw with her lips.

Jennie's discreet knock interrupted their carefree moment.

"It's time to get ready." The little maid waited with bowed head.

"All right," Cheira responded, rising.

Siri held her gaze as she left his arms. He noted the firm core of her decision intertwined with tracings of uncertainty. The power of his mind replaced the wavering with the sweet harmony of unity, supporting her, wrapping her in the protection of his love.

Siri refused to leave Cheira at the clinic. His dark eyes never left her face, yet he seemed to follow every step of preparation. Dr. Mott did not object. In the hour that followed, the physician's admiration for Siri increased a hundredfold. His scientific curiosity was piqued at Siri's reactions. Although the earl was silent during the entire procedure, Mott could have sworn that he was one with Cheira, feeling what she felt, enduring the same pain. Mott vowed to explore the exciting possibility further.

Cheira was heavily sedated. Mott wished to avoid as much discomfiture for his patient as possible. The lead cap of the deenergizer was placed in position, the tubes taped precisely at her temples, forehead, and the nape of her neck.

The procedure was simple enough: two rays crossing directly in the swollen pineal gland would cause it to shrink back to normal dormant size. The necessary intensity of the beam, however, convulsed the body and caused sharp, sudden pain. The only danger lay in the misjudgment of the physician. The crossing must be exact in order to avoid brain damage.

Mott checked every step of the procedure himself before he gave the signal to proceed.

Cheira cried out only once. Siri's reaction was simultaneous. His head jerked back; his jaw tightened. His eyes narrowed, but never wavered from her face. He relaxed immediately, only a lingering pallor around his indrawn lips hinting at any unusual reaction.

"It's done!" Mott announced, more to relieve his own tension than to inform those present. He checked Cheira's condition quickly, his practiced eye scanning the electroencephalograph. He sighed. The machine was tracing a normal pattern of waves across the screen.

"Her ladyship left orders to be returned to Pemberly House, if all went well," Mott told Siri, a question in his tone.

Siri nodded agreement. He lifted the pale, unconscious figure onto the stretcher, walked beside her to the waiting ambulance, and managed to wedge his frame into the confined space.

Mott sat on the other side of Cheira, continuing the monitoring of her condition. There would be no irregularities that could be avoided.

John met them in the Great Hall. A few brief words from Mott assured him. The manor household waited silently. All activity ceased. They kept a vigil which was to last over twelve hours.

The artificial lighting in Cheira's bedroom was imitating the first rays of the sun when she stirred.

"Siri, Siri," she called faintly.

Before she was fully awake, he was holding her in his arms. "I'm here, my love," he whispered.

"I've been asleep forever. I was so tired." She sat up.

Dr. Mott examined her quickly. He was satisfied with the healthy condition of her eyes and skin.

"Okay!" He smiled, the relief in his voice intended as much for Siri as himself. "Just stay in bed for today. I'll see you in the morning."

"I'm awfully hungry," Cheira complained.

"Good!" The doctor laughed. "Jennie will bring you whatever and as much as you wish."

"If there is anything unusual about her behavior or physical appearance, call me instantly," Mott told Siri in the sitting room.

"If she was any different then she appears now, how soon will the change take place?" There was just a trace of fear in Siri's voice.

"Within twenty-four hours," Mott told him, reluctantly. "However, there's no reason to believe there will be any change. Keep her as quiet as possible. I'll be at the clinic. Don't hesitate to call me." Mott tried to sound reassuringly professional.

John came in, having waylaid Jennie in the hall. Siri went back to the bedroom, leaving the explanations to the doctor.

Cheira was eating heartily from a tray across her lap. She smiled when he entered.

I love you, I love you, Siri thought, *more than my life, more than existence.*

Cheira patted the bed, inviting him to sit beside her, and continued eating.

Answer me, my darling. Siri concentrated the full force of his thoughts.

"Sit beside me," Cheira invited. "I'm so lonely when you're not with me."

My God, he thought, *there is no reception. Her mind is dead to telepathic communication.* A heavy depression settled over him, making his shoulders sag helplessly. He remembered what he had read in Mott's summary of the experiment: loss of all powers, complete return to unaltered human state. He hadn't actually believed it could happen. He had nursed a secret hope that Cheira's power would prove too strong to destroy.

"What's the matter?" Cheira asked, seeing the scowl gathering on his brow. Her voice held a note of uncertainty. A little flicker of fear widened her eyes. Her mind searched for an action of hers that might be responsible.

Siri hastened to smile. He leaned over, kissing her shoulder, allowing his power to pass into her body.

She screamed and jumped away, sending the tray and its contents over the bed and onto the floor. She cowered against the pillows, fear full-blown in her eyes.

Siri stared at her, shocked. *Good Lord,* he thought, *she felt pain.*

"Forgive me," he said aloud. "I didn't mean to hurt you."

Jennie rushed to Cheira's side, her eyes wide with defiance.

"It was a mistake," Siri condescended to give her an explanation. "She's all right." He shrugged, turning away. "Get this mess cleaned up and get out."

Jennie obeyed quickly, her love for Cheira vying for supremacy with fear of Siri. Her movement slowed. She lingered, fussing unnecessarily with the covers. She tried desperately to determine what had happened to make Cheira so frightened. When Siri finally turned and glared at her, she fled unceremoniously from the fierceness of his gaze; her courage failed.

Siri stood beside the bed. Cheira cowered under the covers, fear making her body tremble.

"My love, my life," he murmured tenderly, kneeling beside her. "Don't you remember anything?"

"Yes," she whispered. Her thought told him she was remembering the time at the Fort.

He groaned. "The last few days," he prompted. "Yesterday at Lamborn, the other night in the desert."

"It was a dream!"

"No, no. It was real! I love you. Yesterday we were one." He dropped his head beside her, his attitude despairing.

Timidly she put her hand on his hair. "I remember but I couldn't understand, so I thought I must have dreamed it. I feel so alone, heavy, dull. I love you; but I'm afraid. I thought it was only my desire for your love that

227

made me imagine that it happened." She paused. "This is what it's like. Doubt clouds my mind and fear controls my body. All the people in the world are like this." There was wonder in her voice. "I can't concentrate," her voice rose. "My power is gone. Siri, what are you thinking?" She was near hysteria now.

He cradled her in his arms, gently caressing her hair. "Only how much I love you," he whispered soothingly. He was careful to withhold his power.

She clung to him desperately, her body still shaken by spasms of fear. "And I'll never hurt you again." The words were a vow in his mind.

Slowly she calmed down, quieted by the murmured endearments and caresses. Hours later, she fell into a restful, healthy slumber. Siri put her down carefully and went into the outer room.

Siri went to the door. He ordered Jennie to bring coffee.

John paced the hall. He stopped expectantly when the door opened. Siri glanced at him, leaving the door open in tacit invitation. He went to stand by the fireplace. John followed him into the room.

John poured the coffee himself. A kind smile dismissed the still intimidated girl.

"It must be a hobby of yours," he said sarcastically, handing Siri the steaming cup, "to scare the wits out of defenseless women. Poor Jennie is beside herself. What did you do to her this time?"

Siri looked at him, puzzled. For a moment, there was no understanding of what John said. Then he shrugged. Jennie was the least of his problems. Turning his gaze to the fireplace, his attention was caught by the hammered gold shield that hung above it. Cheira's symbol was so familiar he hadn't really noticed it. The odd combination of letters, enclosed in a circle, was carried by every member in the form of a tattoo.

Cheira must have been tattooed as a child. The thought startled him. The symbol was now only a tiny circle on her breast, but it must have been placed over her heart. By whom? Why? Another startling, puzzling thought: the realization that the perfect bliss they had enjoyed was the embodiment of the symbol. Without knowing the cause, he was certain it was so. The answer seemed to hang tantalizingly just beyond his grasp. It engendered an undefined fear. *Were they tampering with an unchallengeable power?*

"John," Siri measured his words to impress the man beside him with his sincerity, "is there no way to end this nonsense? Any use of my power brings pain to her now. My thoughts are completely cut off from her." His knuckles shone white with the strength of his grip on the mantel. "Only yesterday . . . " His voice trailed off.

"I can change her back into what she was." John's voice was low. "By forcing submission through hypnosis. But then, when she regains her power, wouldn't we have it to do all over again? You know she was adamant. She doesn't change her mind easily. You know her well enough to understand that any pain she must endure would be of no consequence nor influence her decision in any way. I would think this is a good time to use that control you are so famous for."

"I can't go on with it," Siri murmured.

John looked at him in surprise. Weakness was a new attitude in Siri. *What had happened yesterday,* he wondered, *that he could be so changed?*

"You must." John spoke firmly, bringing his thoughts back to the issue. "Cheira has entrusted herself to you. You have no choice."

Siri poured another cup of coffee, lacing it liberally from the carafe of brandy on the table.

"Go easy!" John cautioned. "Why don't you get some sleep? Jennie can sit with Cheira. Come back in time to have dinner with her."

Siri downed the scalding brew in one gulp.

"You're probably right," he conceded uncharacteristically. He walked out abruptly.

John stood immobile for a long time. Once he started toward the bedroom, then stopped, his head bowed. He was worried; but another emotion intruded. His heart pounded. He pictured her sleeping just a few steps away, only his own integrity to prevent an intrusion on her privacy. He shook his head sadly. Was he never to conquer the contemptible feeling which made him ashamed to face her? Squaring his shoulders, he swore softly. Jennie was waiting when he opened the door. He motioned for her to go in to her mistress.

The light was fading when Cheira awakened. Jennie slumped in a chair beside the bed dozing. *Poor dear,* Cheira thought, *she must be exhausted.*

Jennie sat up suddenly. The thoughts, which Cheira no longer had the power to conceal, reached the consciousness of the maid clearly.

"I'm here, my lady," Jennie said, coming swiftly to her side. "Shall I call his lordship? He left word to be summoned immediately when you awakened."

"Sit with me a while, Jennie." Cheira shook her head. "I want to talk to you. Do you remember how you were before?"

"Yes, my lady."

"I'm like that now. Is it very awful?"

"Oh, no!" Jennie responded reassuringly. "Only inconvenient some-times. It takes so long to get places. You have to walk or ride always. You never know what anyone else is thinking even if you try really hard. But you get used to that. The worst is you get old so fast." Jennie paused, then in the faintest whisper she added, "But you can have babies."

Even in the dim light, Cheira could detect the deep blush that spread over the girl's face. Laughing, she grasped Jennie's hand. "That's exactly what I intend to do," she confided.

"Oh, my lady!" Jennie knelt beside her, pleasure and enthusiasm spreading over her face. "That will be lovely!" Then her features clouded. "Does his lordship know your intention?"

"Well, yes and no," Cheira answered, smiling ruefully at the memory of the announcement that had been discussed only perfunctorily between them.

"Oh, he'll be angry," Jennie worried. "Men are always upset when women have babies. They're sure the worst will happen; but they don't want anyone to know, so they get angry."

"I certainly hope not," Cheira answered both statements, frowning; but the smile quickly returned. "Go and call him now," she ordered the little maid.

Jennie hesitated. Cheira looked at her questioningly.

"I'm always afraid for you when he's here," Jennie found the courage to say.

"Don't be silly, Jennie," Cheira said sternly, stoically ignoring the jump of her heart. "He loves me. He would never hurt me."

Cheira was curled in a chair by the fireplace when Siri came in.

"Mott said you should stay in bed."

"I will, as soon as dinner is over," she promised, then added, hoping to forestall his ordering her back to bed, "I feel fine. I'm not an invalid." Her tone was defensive, yet pleading. Her mind was clear now. She remembered everything, especially the pleasure she had known so recently. In a muted way, her body still felt the ecstasy of the Lamborn experience. There was a latent humming along her nerves. Absently, she rubbed the small, forgotten circle on her breast.

Siri came to sit at her feet. "I can read your thoughts, you know," he reminded her.

She blushed. "Oh, dear, you have the advantage. I don't know a single one of yours."

"There's only one that's important and I can tell you that: I love you." He laid his cheek against the hand lying in her lap.

"This morning," she began timidly after a moment's silence, ". . . I'm sorry. My head was still fuzzy." When he didn't answer, she continued, "Do you think it will be like that?"

"I don't know," he answered honestly, making no attempt to conceal his own fear. "I never cared enough to find out," he answered her thought. She was thinking about the oda women.

"Oh, how could you be so cruel!"

He laughed. From no other would he tolerate rebuke. The remorse he felt was the measure of his love for Cheira. That love had the intensity to control his actions even when her power was no longer able to do so. *Even if it ever did,* he thought wryly.

"They will live in peace until they die of old age," he promised. "I have no desire to ever visit that part of the Fort again. You are the only woman I can ever want."

Jennie entered and began to lay dinner on the little table reserved for that purpose. Siri rose, going to stand by the fireplace. In the last few days, it had become an accustomed posture. *I'll soon be a fixture here,* he thought wryly, *along with the other furniture.*

Cheira came to his side, linking her arm through his. "Why are you smiling?"

"Because I have secret thoughts," he teased.

She didn't smile. Her head drooped sadly against his shoulder. "One of the unpleasant things," she murmured. He understood the painful awareness of, to her, a new status.

"Don't worry," he continued the bantering tone in an effort to make it easier. "I'll join you soon. Then we can both have secrets."

"Only for a few weeks," she said. "And John can change you back."

Too late to catch the words she meant to be hopeful, she felt him stiffen. His face set in a dark scowl, a flash of defiance in his dark eyes. She didn't need telepathy to know what he was thinking. *Am I to be the principal stud in your stable or only one of many?* he had snapped when the subject had been discussed. It was a futile effort on her part to try to understand his view on the subject.

Jennie interrupted to announce dinner. Siri turned toward the maid, the anger still on his face. *Oh, Lord,* Jennie started to think, then stopped

231

abruptly lest he notice the criticism. With an inward sigh of relief, she saw the shrug with which he threw off the irritation; and the smile returned to his face as he escorted Cheira to the table.

The conversation was sparse but pleasantly general throughout the meal. Siri left soon afterwards in compliance with Mott's suggestion that Cheira would rest better alone. Jennie was present the whole time.

Dr. Mott arrived early the next morning.

"You're in perfect health, my lady," he announced after a brief examination.

"Then I was human before?" There was hesitation in her voice.

"It's very evident that you were," Mott assured her. "There's absolutely no sign of change. Although," he cautioned, "this state must be continued no longer than necessary or normal aging will begin. Also, the dangers of disease or malfunction are now greatly increased."

"I'll be very careful," she promised.

"Resume your normal activity for a few days," Mott instructed. "Then at the clinic, we'll determine if your normalcy includes a regular cycle of fertility."

"Oh, yes." Her eyes shone with eagerness, and her face took on an expression of softness.

Mott's professionalism was pierced for an instant. For the first time, as she lay propped up by the pillows, her hair spread out in heavy masses, he saw her as a beautiful woman. Her new status wiped out the cold haughtiness of demeanor that had previously characterized her. He could understand Siri's attitude. The man who possessed this unique creature could lose his soul in her love and consider it well lost.

"The ultimate object of our experiment!" Cheira mused.

The words wrenched the physician back to his duty.

"Yes, my lady. That is the purpose!" He bowed, leaving hurriedly. Though there was no danger of her discovering his thoughts, he still felt guilty.

Siri met him in the hall.

"Well?"

"Everything is normal. She's a perfectly healthy young woman. In a few days, she can come to the clinic for a gynecological examination. That will determine our course."

"Damn it, Mott, you're not going to do that!" Siri's voice was icy, his head thrown back in defiance.

The doctor was taken aback. *Now what?* he thought. Then he smiled, wondering at Siri's old-fashioned morality. So that was the reason for Siri's insistence on being present whenever he attended Cheira. Well, he could get around that. No need to jeopardize the experiment.

"Of course not! We have a veritable genius on our staff whose specialty that is: Dr. *Irene* Carpenter." He stressed the name. Siri hadn't noticed her at the clinic. David was gratified to see Siri relax. "In fact, I'm hoping John will consider letting her join us. It would be a shame to lose such a brilliant mind in thirty or forty years. In any event, the examination will take place as part of another experiment. There are about twenty women involved. Dr. Carpenter need not even know that one of them is Lady Pemberly."

Siri's mood changed abruptly.

"I'm opposed to this whole thing, David." Siri's voice was low. He had unconsciously used the physician's first name. He liked and had confidence in the young doctor. Mott flushed with pleasure.

"I understand that, sir. I'll do everything I can to make it easier."

"Thank you," Siri rejoined, simply.

"Siri!" Cheira hopped out of bed to rush into his arms when he entered. "I was just going to send Jennie to search for you."

"Get dressed!" he ordered, his voice almost formal. "The good doctor recommends some fresh air. I'm going to take you for a drive. Two days in this place is enough."

His manner was gentle as he put her from him, but there was no hint of the passion she now craved. He had not even offered to kiss her. Ignoring the hurt look in her eyes, he went back into the sitting room to wait. He took a stand by the fireplace.

Cheira was left standing forlornly, her bare toes digging into the carpet, her arms dropping despairingly to her sides. She searched in vain for the reason for such callousness.

Silently she obeyed. There was a determined set to her chin, a firm resolution dawning in her eyes.

Siri didn't see it. He had wrestled with the problem many hours last night. The pain that his kiss had caused Cheira tortured him relentlessly. He had seen the fear leap into her eyes as a result of his thoughtlessness. And he had sworn never to hurt her! At the first test, he had failed. *And I should have known!* his mind castigated. He had uncomfortable visions of the oda woman screaming and writhing in his arms after his transfiguration. He had ceased to find pleasure in them, but had taken them only to satisfy the heightened demands of his body. He had not bothered to withhold his power, using their agony to express his contempt for himself and for them. *Even Lira,* he now remembered, *came to him in fear.* And he had been more gentle, more considerate with her than any other.

The tribesmen, too, had stood in awe of him as his power increased. He had laughed bitterly when he heard rumors that he was possessed. He had shown no mercy for the hapless fellow who crossed him, seizing any excuse as an opportunity to practice his power. And wreaking his fury on the victim at hand, a substitute for his own inadequacy to overpower the woman he wanted. No pleas for mercy had deterred him from his purpose. He wanted power and more power. He intended to surpass her power and force her submission. He hated her. He desired her. The desire would not be quenched; and the hate was fed by every humiliation she inflicted. How many years it took for him to recognize that what he felt was love!

Now the past returned to haunt him; now, when all he wanted was to protect her. *If I forgot myself,* he reasoned, in the heat of the passion she aroused, *what damage could my unleashed power do?* He couldn't trust his ability to control himself when every fiber of his being clamored for total surrender. No, the only safe way was not to touch her, not to pre-cipitate an intimacy that might prove uncontrollable. How long he could maintain his resolution in face of the necessary proximity he refused even to consider.

Just a few days and Mott would remove the problem. He felt his blood rise and his muscles tighten. His whole system protested.

He supposed he should be thankful to Mott's experiments, which had given him this much. The frustration was a small price to pay. *How will it all end?* he wondered. *Will the day ever come when Cheira will be truly mine?* The future he wanted seemed forever beyond his reach. He was being forced to accept a day-to-day existence repulsive to his nature; but his sworn oath and his love had the power to make him adhere to the course she had set.

"I'm ready!" Cheira announced. She stood demurely just within the room. At that moment, he was glad she had lost her power to know what he was thinking. He felt his resolution waver even then as he beheld the fragile figure emphasized by the trim lines of the suit she wore. She had wound her hair into coils that looked like ropes of gold at the nape of her neck. A transparent scarf covered the abundant mass.

Stevens had the Benz waiting for them. Siri took the wheel. The powerful little two-seater shot forward obediently at his touch. He skillfully negotiated the city traffic and in half an hour was speeding along the open road.

Cheira sat silently beside him, taking pleasure in watching his strong fingers manipulate the wheel. Although still puzzled by his attitude, she found an exquisite torture in the thought of his body so close, yet forbidden by his manner to her touch.

Siri glanced at her sternly. She giggled like a child caught in a sinful act, remembering too late that he could read her thoughts.

She hadn't asked him where they were going, presuming that he intended to go to Lamborn; but he turned in the opposite direction, heading toward the sea.

He drove steadily for two hours. The exhilaration of the speed and the wind in the open car brought a flush to Cheira's pale cheeks.

Breaking the silence at last, Siri called her attention to the farms with their quaint clapboard houses shimmering white in the glare of the morning sun and surrounded protectively by the squat stone outbuildings, Invariably, a nondescript mutt or two came tearing down the lane to bark at them as they sped past. He pointed to the fields, still dark brown from the recent plowing, and the pastures lush with the green of spring. They laughed when a herd of sheep crossing the road at a leisurely pace detained them for endless minutes.

"Sorry, sir," the farmer apologized, tipping his hat.

"We have all the time in the world," Siri told the man solemnly, winking at Cheira.

At last the smell of the sea met them, freshening the air with its indescribable odor of turbulent water. A subtle undercurrent carried the smell of teeming sea life intermingled with man-made flotsam. Grinning, Siri told her to breathe deeply.

"Doctor's orders," he said, the twinkle in his eyes belying the sternness of his tone.

Cheira loved his grin. It was the only time that the boy he must have been overshadowed the man he had become. It was hard for her to conceive, when he grinned like that, that she had ever cowered at his feet in moral terror. His swiftly changing moods always caught her unprepared; she thus overreacted many times with a violence for which she was later ashamed. *I'll do nothing today,* she vowed silently, *to destroy this mood.* The thought made her lips tremble and her heart swell with love.

Siri pulled up at a quaint, wharfside cafe in a village called romantically Wells-next-the-sea. An attendant met them. *We're expected,* she thought absently, but the feeling comforted her.

The attendant gave no sign that he might be aware of their identities. Siri gave the man a few instructions, then took Cheira to walk on the promenade where the sea lapped lazily at the pilings just beneath their feet.

They walked slowly, unconsciously measuring their strides to the monotonously colorless boards stretching into the distance, letting their muscles adjust to the movement after the long hours of cramped inactivity.

Siri remained withdrawn. The attitude puzzled her. She had never seen him like this. She wondered if he could understand her feelings, how she felt just being with him. Her new status had done nothing to change that. Or had it? The thought popped up in her mind: *Had it been only her drug-fogged brain that reacted with pain when Siri touched her? It was,* she decided. Her fingers moved caressingly on the rough cloth of his coat, following the contour of the muscles of his arm. The action produced the security she needed so desperately.

She glanced at Siri. He was looking at her sadly. She flushed guiltily and stammered in confusion, "What are you thinking?" The statement was a confession of the weakness she now possessed.

"Only of these last few days," his voice held a note of regret, "when you were mine. Such a short time. And the magnificent, unimaginable unity we achieved was not enough to hold you."

"But that's ridiculous!" she protested, shaking her head to deny the words.

"Is it?" His voice held the same reserved tone. He stopped, looking directly into her eyes. "Is it ridiculous that we are deprived of the perfect consummation we have known? I'm sorry I find it galling to accept the dominance of the sovereign instead of the love of the woman."

She bowed her head. "I love you with my whole being. You know my duty. You know my reasons."

"None of which I can willingly comply with, only submit to." He resumed walking.

She hesitated. He smiled in answer to her thought, the smile however so mirthless as to be more a grimace.

"I am your obedient servitor. For, you see, even without your power, you have left me no alternative. I need you so desperately that I will accept any terms just to be near you. You may demand anything of me and I will obey. The punishment is just."

His voice was so contrite that she hated herself for bringing him to this. The present situation was bad enough without remorse for the past adding to it.

"Oh, I hate it when you act like this," she burst out, irritably moving away from his side.

He looked at her for a moment, then laughed.

"As you command," he said with a mock bow. "I'll be the perfect companion for the rest of the afternoon. What would amuse you most? Would you like to know what an incorrigible youth I was? Perhaps you can discover the origin of the grin which intrigues you so much."

Cheira blushed furiously, but quickly succumbed to the charm Siri could wield so expertly when he chose. And true to his word, he regaled her with stories of his life at sea. During lunch, he related the adventures of his seventeenth year. His mother had died the year before, taking with her the only softening influence his father tolerated. Chafing under the unrelenting iron discipline, Siri had run away from Lamborn Heath and made his way to the sea. He had shipped aboard a sailing vessel as cabin boy and had his first glimpse of the desert from a Moroccan port on the Mediterranean.

He was captivated by the desert; besides, he was tired of the constant abuse of the drunken captain. He jumped ship. He wandered for the better part of a year, hitching rides with caravans crisscrossing the sand. It was only the gnawing sense of duty that had finally made him make his way back to Oran and find a kindly captain who would let a fellow Englishman work his way back home.

He arrived at Lamborn Heath bristling with defiance. He could admit that now, in retrospect. The earl covered his feelings with gruffness. If he felt any joy at the prodigal's return, he didn't show it. It was years later before Siri found out that his father had sought out the abusive captain, making the surprised rogue pay dearly for mistaking the young Lord of Lamborn Heath for a homeless waif.

Cheira was fascinated with this glimpse of Siri's boyhood.

"How wonderful it must be to remember your childhood, to have known your parents, and to have a home to which you belonged." Her eyes shone with eagerness and a strange feeling she had never felt before. Surprised, she decided it was envy.

Siri shrugged. "Most of the time I felt suffocated. I hated the idea of becoming the next Earl of Zetland with all the protocol it entailed. My father never seemed to enjoy it, only to be owned by it. I wanted to be free. At last, when I could stand it no longer, I fled to the desert. I didn't leave again before my father died, however." He grinned sheepishly, reluctantly admitting the love he had borne for the gruff old man.

"He must have been a great man to have inspired such devotion."

Siri frowned. "I've learned that it takes more courage and determination to accept chains than to be free. Now I can realize he felt that way, too. Well, someday," he dismissed the subject, "you can read all about it in the family history."

By the time they started back, the sun was already low in the sky. Cheira settled comfortably into the deep seat. Shortly, the vibration of the car and the soft droning of the big engine lulled her to sleep.

Siri didn't disturb her. He pulled over once to tuck a robe gently around her. The sad expression had returned to his face.

That evening they dined with John and the Duke and Duchess of Yerby in the small dining room off the library. The pleasant room with large windows opening into the garden was filled with flowers, which mingled their aroma with the dewy scents of grass and trees drifting in the open windows.

The conversation was light and festive. The diners enjoyed the relief from the tension that had characterized the last uncertain days. The first step of the experiment was obviously a success.

Cheira was radiant. Her cheeks were rosy and her eyes sparkling from the salt air of the afternoon drive. Her deep blue chiffon dress with its modestly high neckline gave her the air of a healthy child. The tight bodice, by contrast, did nothing to conceal the feminine curve of her figure. The full skirt clung to her slim legs when she walked. Her hair was gathered into a coil on top of her head from the center of which a heavy portion cascaded down her back heightening the effect.

Siri seemed to have recovered his humor and was gallantly responding to Lady Yerby's outrageous flirtation.

Constance Yerby was still young. She reacted naturally to the air of masculine sensuality, which lingered about Siri like an aura. It was the first time since she had known him that she was able to hold his attention. She determined to make the most of it, for her own pleasure and for the retelling.

She would be the envy of everyone in her set.

Even John had relaxed his usually formal demeanor. He related in detail the consternation of Ian McDonnell when he reported for duty with the Pemberly Guard only to find that the maniac of his wild desert adventures was indeed the chief deputy of Lady Pemberly.

"I think it was the first he even admitted the possibility that the whole episode wasn't a nightmare." John laughed. "Now he spends all his spare time studying. He's captivated with teleportation. His captain tells me they are no longer surprised in the barracks if he comes crashing down into the middle of mess. Once he landed on the roof and they had to get a ladder to get him down. He had lost his nerve and couldn't concentrate enough to extricate himself."

"Oh, Baron Cavoren's hunt!" Cheira interjected, her mind making a circuitous connection.

"Lady Pemberly was indisposed." Lord Yerby winked. "Constance and I filled in. John called us at the last minute. We arrived just in time to save Pemberly Enterprises from disgrace."

They had coffee in the library. The dimly lit room with its overstuffed furniture and walls of books standing like silent guards encouraged relaxation, stressing the enjoyment of a leisure moment in life when, in the company of a few chosen friends, the body replete with good food, one's mind can rest from the memories of the past and the cares of the future to savor the perfection of the present.

The conversation became desultory, the four reluctant to break the tranquilizing influence of the silence with the effort of speech. It wasn't long before the duke dozed off, his head sagging onto his chest, causing Cheira to laugh and the duchess to frown.

Constance rose with a sigh, eloquently expressing her disappointment at the abrupt halt to what she had hoped would be a long, long evening. With courageous resignation and murmured apologies, she carted her husband away.

John left shortly after.

Siri sat, silent and unmoving, his long legs stretched out comfortably on the tilted recliner, his eyes closed. Cheira waited, practicing the patience she needed more and more these days.

Finally, galled into action by the continued indifference, Cheira came to stand beside his chair.

"Did you enjoy the adulation of Lady Yerby?"

Siri opened his eyes slowly, his glance traveling over her with cold appraisal. She felt like a piece of merchandise being examined critically by a prospective buyer. Memory sent a little shiver up and down her spine.

"She's very beautiful," he stated, his voice as icy as his glance. "A pleasant companion, I would think."

Cheira exploded. "Oh," she gasped, "you're insufferable!" In a fury of frustration, she jumped on him, landing with her knees in his stomach and grabbing a handful of hair to steady herself. She sank her teeth viciously into the soft flesh of his lip.

Siri's movement was quick. He snapped the chair upright, tumbling her onto the floor. Before she could right herself, he pinned her arm behind her back, lifting her in the same motion. The other hand held her jaw in a vise-like grip. She was helpless as his mouth roughly crushed hers, forcing her lips back from her teeth. A scream of pain died in her throat as waves of sensation began to curl along her nerves, melting her bones. She sagged against him, gasping. He released her.

"I didn't intend to do that," he apologized, cursing the momentary loss of control.

She crumpled, sliding down the length of his body like a rag doll deprived of support. Lying at his feet, she breathed, "You were wrong!"

He picked her up gently. "Cheira, my eternal love," he whispered into her hair.

That night, pleasantly exhausted, she slept in his arms.

Dr. Mott was pleased with the stability of Cheira's condition. The next stage of the experiment could proceed. The doctor was doubly encouraged when he saw the improved relations between his patients.

"We'll begin the next phase tomorrow," he told them with satisfaction.

"It's not so bad, only inconvenient," Cheira mimicked Jennie when the doctor had gone.

"I remember," he reminded her, then was immediately contrite when he saw the hurt expression on her face. "I'm sorry. Well, even though the reversal hasn't provided you with a memory of the past, maybe Stuart Mervin will come back with something."

She smiled, recovering her good humor. "Yes, maybe. Anyway, I guess I shouldn't complain. I haven't turned into a two-headed monster or Medusa or something else horrible."

"I'd probably love you even if you did." He laughed, putting his arm around her.

"You wouldn't! You wouldn't!" She set the mass of her hair swinging in vigorous protest. "You'd love a beautiful woman like Constance."

"Aha!" Siri grinned, his arm tightening, pressing her against his side. "There is a little green monster peeking out from those lovely eyes."

She blushed, hiding her face against his chest. "I don't want you to even look at any other woman."

CHAPTER XV

"I'd strongly advise an anesthetic, sir," Dr. Mott stressed as he adjusted the cap of the deenergizer.

"No!"

"But the pain," the doctor protested. "We haven't had a chance to measure it yet on any human subjects."

"Then what kind of scientist would pass up the opportunity?" Siri laughed.

Dr. Mott pasted a monitor wire to Siri's chest just over his heart.

"You're fussing like an old woman!" Siri frowned. The young man jumped, flushing guiltily. "Never mind," Siri grinned, "In an hour, your machine will have done its work. I won't know your thoughts, then."

"We're ready," Mott said, ignoring the remark.

Siri raised a hand in compliance.

A low hum filled the room. Mott watched his patient closely. He could detect no reaction. Siri absorbed the pain by a relaxation of his muscles. The only indication of what he was enduring was an increased heartbeat. At the peak of the energy drain, his racing heart was recorded only as a fluttering on the monitor.

Mott signaled his assistant. It was done. Siri sat immobile while they freed him from the machine. His heartbeat returned slowly to normal; a rush of color to his skin indicated resumption of normal circulation. He wiped the drops of perspiration from his forehead.

"That all?" he quipped, only the faintest quaver in his voice indicating the exhaustion he felt. "Your machine is gentler than Cheira when she's angry." He stood up, reaching for his shirt. "You're white around the gills, David."

Truly, the physician was pale. "It's unbelievable!" he gasped. "You can tolerate so much. The control you can exert is fantastic."

Siri shrugged. "May I collect my partner in this monstrous experiment?" The irony was plain in his voice. The tone conveyed what words could not.

Mott finished up mechanically, his mind racing. Someday, he promised himself, he would do a series of experiments on Siri. Did the man realize what had just been accomplished? If he did, he certainly didn't show it.

They joined Cheira in Mott's office. The worried expression on her face changed to a smile of relief when Siri entered.

She rushed to him, laying a hand on his cheek. "Are you all right?"

"Of course!" he answered impatiently, absently kissing her palm. "David did a good job. I'm as ordinary as a human being can get." He turned to the scientist.

"Take it easy for the next day or so, sir. Send for me immediately if you have any discomfort. I'll drop in to see you the first thing in the morning. I don't anticipate any difficulties, but that would be a poor excuse to become lax."

Seated in the car, Cheira put her hand shyly into Siri's. "We are the first!" The note of pride was evident in her voice. "The experiment is a total success. Now we can welcome all those young people into the organization. John can go ahead. He doesn't need to wait for me."

Siri looked out the window. She couldn't see the scowl on his face.

"I'm sorry, darling." She put her head on his shoulder. "John will transfigure you as soon as . . . " She felt him tense. "I didn't mean it to sound like that," she ended lamely.

"No need to be polite about it!" The heavy sarcasm in his voice made her recoil. "That won't make what you have in mind less disgusting. I'll do my best to be ready to perform whenever you command."

"Oh," she whispered, hurt. "It's not like that. I love you. I love you."

He laughed bitterly.

"So you keep assuring me," he stated tonelessly. "The repetition grows tedious. It's a pity your actions contradict your words so plainly."

"What you would have me do would be a betrayal of my duty to the organization."

"And your duty to me, Cheira? Where is my place in your scheme if every member of your precious organization is before me?"

She quavered before the onslaught. His attitude had changed again, just when she had relaxed, thinking he was convinced of the soundness of her course, that she had his willing cooperation. *We have become one,* she thought. *The numerous demonstrations of my love must have assuaged his doubts.* But she was wrong.

Somehow, the reversal had changed him.

"But I have given myself only to you because I love you."

"That wasn't even poor logic," he scowled. "It's just wishful thinking. The one is no proof of the other. That you should even try to use such an argument with me, of all people, is foolhardy."

"It's true!" she insisted stubbornly, apprehension growing inside her.

"You're deliberately closing your eyes to the life I lead. Do you think I keep those women at the Fort because I like the way they dance?" He laughed coldly at the expression of shock on her face. "Or is it that you can't be honest with yourself? Doesn't it seem at all suspicious to you that suddenly after years of despising me—and don't try to convince me that I misinterpreted your actions—you conveniently discover that you love me? Handily, too, just at the moment when you need a husband."

Cheira hid her face in her hands, unable to keep back the tears. His cruel words hurt and bewildered her. The reversal had permitted the basest facets of his personality to gain dominance. The horror of it made her shudder. *Oh, God,* she thought, *what have I done?*

"If you would wait just a little longer, perhaps science would discover a way to preclude even that requirement," he continued in the same cutting tone.

"Oh, please, don't!" she whispered, cowering into the farthest corner of the seat. With her mind functioning on the primitive level to which it had been reduced by the reversal, her thoughts were a jumbled mass. Any decision loomed overwhelming. Any problem was unsolvable.

"Show me then," he demanded, "that my conclusions are wrong."

She couldn't answer.

When the car drew up in front of the manor, Siri leaped out. Cheira huddled in the seat unable to move.

Stevens helped her out. He sent a telepathic SOS to John.

"Stevens, please watch over him. He must rest." Her words were halting, distracted. "And, Stevens, remember he has no power. He mustn't leave the house. Be gentle." Tears welled up in her eyes and her lips trembled.

"I understand, my lady," Stevens replied softly while silently cursing Siri for what he personally considered a ridiculous show of defiance.

Cheira walked slowly up the steps, very aware of the reality that the only way she could get to her suite was to put one foot past the other. Her body felt heavy and clumsy, misery adding to the discomfort.

Her thoughts matched her steps. At the clinic, she had been pronounced normal in every respect. That proved the feasibility of reversal, didn't it? What elemental desire now drove her to continue a course so abhorrent to the man she loved? Her primal instinct refused to believe that Siri would not come to feel as she did. The instinct was the fulfillment of their love, wasn't it? She was safe, so it wasn't fear for her health that made him rebel. He doubted her love. That was it! He felt she was using that most sacred function to accomplish impersonal objectives. He felt she was allowing the organization to rule their personal lives. Of course! But the two were identical, weren't they? How could she convince him? How she knew the identification was true and correct she was unable to explain even to herself.

John met her in the hall. "What happened? Has the experiment failed?"

"The procedure is completed and successful," she managed to get the words out with a husky voice. "But . . . " Her control broke and she ran past him, sobbing. There was no need to explain further. She no longer had a barrier to protect her thoughts.

John retraced his steps. At Siri's door, he entered without knocking.

"Get out!" Siri growled from where he stood at the window.

John ignored the order. "You gave your word. Have you no honor?"

"I've not broken it—yet." The threat was obvious in his voice.

"Cheira is crying. Near hysteria, I'd say," John said flatly, controlling with difficulty the anger rising in his throat. The galling knowledge that this man had the power to cause Cheira such unhappiness was hard quelled.

Siri shrugged.

"Don't hurt her!" John's voice rose. "I'm warning you! I'll kill you!"

Siri laughed. "It would be merciful!" His voice was bitter. "I'd welcome it!"

John took a step toward him, his eyes blazing, his love for Cheira and hatred for Siri combining to rob him of his usually rigid self-control.

"But not without the command of your mistress," Siri sneered. John hesitated, "Get out, you coward!"

John retreated. The reminder of his pledge to Cheira was effective.

Stevens was waiting. "Post a guard," John ordered. "Make sure he stays put!"

"His excellency wishes to see you," Jennie announced.

Cheira nodded, raising a tearstained countenance from the pillow. Rising, with an almost imperceptible squaring of the shoulders, she took the time to douse her face with cold water. She brushed her hair. How much she could hide from John, she didn't know.

She entered the outer room. There was no trace of emotion on her face and no evidence of the recent surrender to a fit of crying.

"What did you wish to see me about?" There was only the slightest tremor in her voice.

John bowed low. His heart felt like a concrete knot in his chest. Her efforts at control were pitiful. *Damn, Siri,* he thought.

"My lady, may I renew my pledge of faithful, unswerving service?"

"It's only because of my trust in you that I undertook the experiment," she answered. "I rely on your promise, on your judgement. I have no power now to do anything." She raised her hands in a gesture of helplessness.

"Whatever power I have is yours to command. I will not hesitate to use it on anyone who has hurt you." His voice was low and ominous.

"No! No!" she gasped, her eyes growing wide with fear. Her thoughts were easily known by him.

"I've given my word," he assured her. "But, perhaps, you might wish to release me from it. Siri's actions are unpardonable."

"He has his reasons. You said yourself that he's a proud man."

"He needs to be taught humility in your ladyship's service," John retorted.

Cheira shook her head sadly. "He's my husband." John winced at the words. "Ask him to come to me." Her voice was barely above a whisper, but the stress was unmistakable.

"I've already implied as much, my lady; but he refuses."

"Then tell him I'll be waiting . . . whenever he wishes."

"Don't subject yourself to this, I beg you," John pleaded.

She looked at him, but made no answer. Her thoughts gave him all the explanation necessary. She would not change her mind.

"Then let me transfigure both of you," John suggested. "This has gone dangerously far enough."

She screamed, dashing for the haven of her bedroom. The terror on her face giving him his answer.

Late in the evening, after some long hours of wrestling with the problem, John went to see Siri again. He found him standing at he window in the same place. He wondered irrelevantly if Siri had stood there all the time. A glance at the empty liquor bottles and the stale odor pervading the room told him how heavily Siri had been drinking. John suppressed surprise. Overindulgence was not one of Siri's vices.

Siri turned his head when John entered. His expression was sullen.

Also uncharacteristic, John thought.

"Dr. Mott told you to rest," John said with a grimace of distaste. "I'm sure alcohol wasn't part of the prescription."

"I'll do as I please," Siri muttered, his words thick and slurred. John noticed he was supporting himself by leaning against the window frame.

"You'll do as Cheira pleases." John's voice was heavy with disgust. "The reversal hasn't released you from your allegiance. She wants you now."

"Is that a command?" Siri sneered, his lips tightened into a line of defiance.

"No," John answered quickly. "It's her desire."

"She has lots of that." Siri laughed insinuatingly, deliberately misinterpreting John's meaning, noting with satisfaction the other's clenched fists. "If you killed me"—Siri's eyes gleamed, taunting his rival—"perhaps she would lie trembling in your arms as she has in mine."

John lunged and swung, his knuckles cracking against Siri's mouth. Siri fell back against the window frame. Reflexively, his hand went to his mouth. He stared at the blood, then smiled. *So that's how he plans to handle his pledge to Cheira,* he thought.

"You're a fool!" Siri hissed, throwing his weight against his opponent. They crashed into the table, sending its contents shattering to the floor.

The noise brought Stevens instantly, the guards at his heels. Despite Siri's unusual strength, they were able to subdue him.

"Never mind," John told Stevens. "We both have our orders. Let him go." He stalked out of the room.

"Get me some more," Siri ordered, eyeing the shattered bottles.

Stevens hesitated, then went out. He'd get more liquor; but he'd also summon Dr. Mott, he decided.

The young physician responded instantly.

Stevens apologized for taking the responsibility of calling him, but he felt the matter serious enough to warrant his attention. The servant didn't mention that John hadn't handled it too well; but listening to Stevens's recital, Mott agreed.

When Mott came in, Siri was slouched morosely in a chair, staring into nothingness.

"Has she sent you to nurse me, David?" Siri's tone held a note of infinite weariness.

"Stevens sent for me," Mott answered, examining the cut on Siri's lip. "He's told me what happened. What I can't understand is why."

Siri sighed. "I'm a beast, David, who has the unmitigated gall to stand up on his haunches and demand to be treated like a man."

"Sir?" Mott was more puzzled than ever. As a young man reared in the twentieth century, he failed to understand Siri's antiquated standards of morality; and as a scientist, he would do anything rather than jeopardize the experiment.

"She has every right, you know." Siri spoke so low as to be almost talking to himself.

"Of course," David agreed. "We are all pledged."

"No," Siri contradicted. "It's not that. It's because of what I've made her suffer. But, God, David, I'm a man, not an animal. I can't perform on command."

"It's not like that, sir," the doctor admonished. "Love makes the difference."

Siri laughed bitterly. "Love! My poor, innocent gull! You don't know what you're talking about! Haven't you ever wondered why her love bloomed so conveniently at this particular time—just when it was a necessary part of your experiment? No, of course not. Or why she chose me whom she has every reason to despise? You don't know her as I do. She'll go to any lengths to get what she wants. You've already seen her determination to go ahead in the face of so much opposition."

"I admire her for that," David interjected.

"And to maneuver me into a position where my manhood is hers to command is too sweet a vengeance for such a woman not to grasp. The stupid fool that I was wanted so desperately to believe that she loved me I closed my mind to the consequences, strangled my doubts with self-accusations and lived for the joy of the moment. Well, now when it's too late, I complain at the punishment."

David made a gesture of protest. "You're tired," he said in his best professional tone. "The reversal has sapped all your strength. I've seen how she acts toward you. That can't be pretense."

"So you think she loves me?"

"There's no question about that in my mind," David affirmed.

Siri sighed, resting his arms on his knees. The liquor and the lack of control engendered by the reversal prompted a need for confession.

"Let me tell you a story. And we'll see what your opinion is then."

"You're a great man, my lord." David couldn't keep the admiration out of his voice, remembering what Siri had endured that morning.

"Spare me your plaudits," Siri commented dryly. "No intelligent man

248

makes a decision without all the facts. If you care to listen, I'll give them to you now."

David assented, eager for the confidence of the man he esteemed above all others, sure that nothing Siri could tell him would shake his respect or alter his opinion.

"I had lived in the desert about three years." Siri stretched his long legs, leaning back with his fingers laced behind his head. "I spent my time carefully assembling my tribe. It was a dream I'd conceived many years before when I first roamed the Sahara as a teenager. I lured the men I wanted away from their sheiks by challenge to personal combat. It was the customary way. When I won, which I always did—I had studied the art of combat and kept myself in top physical condition with just such a purpose in mind—it was an easy matter to obtain the loyalty of the vanquished sheik's followers. I became an honored and powerful sheik, respected by my tribe and feared by all others.

"One day in Touggourt where I had gone to order supplies, I happened on a slave auction. Ahmed, the grandfather of the man who is with me now, accompanied me. We stopped to watch out of idle curiosity. When they brought out a lovely young girl, Ahmed dared me to buy her. Until that time, I had never given such a thing a thought. I turned to leave, revolted by Ahmed's suggestion, when, for some reason, the auctioneer struck the girl, sending her sprawling. She cried out in fear and pain; but the onlookers only laughed, shouting such obscenities that the poor girl covered her ears to shut out the horrible words. At the same time, her eyes filled with terror.

"I was furious at the callousness of those men; and before I realized what I was doing, I bought her. Ahmed took her away to the Fort. It was a week before I returned. In the meantime, I had forgotten about the girl; but I soon remembered when she came that evening, instead of Ahmed, to serve my dinner. It was the first opportunity I had to really look at her. Even my inexperienced eye could appreciate her loveliness. She had black hair and black eyes with olive skin that gave the impression of a carefully cultivated tan, but was obviously her natural color.

"Although I had decided to spend my life in the desert, I hadn't embraced all the customs of my adopted people. That evening, however, during my usual walk around the grounds before retiring, I mulled over the possibilities of such a course. I had no rigid moral standards to combat, as my previous indifference to women had precluded the necessity. It was then I noticed an unusual number of tribesmen lingering about. By their furtive grins, it became obvious that they were waiting to see what I was going to do. Apparently, Ahmed had spread the news, embellishing the story with natural native exaggeration. To take a slave woman was to them a normal expression of manhood, even more so as the leader of a tribe. Was this, I wondered, a final test of my decision?

"I returned to my quarters still undecided, but with a quickening heartbeat and an eagerness which surprised me. Lira was waiting in my bed.

"Lira was the daughter of an old sheik and one of his harem women. He was killed during a tribal war. Lira was captured and sold as a slave because her virginity made her too valuable for her captors to keep. During her years in the sheik's harem—and she told me this later when I was puzzled by the scope of her accomplishments; yet even I was not so stupid as to know that no man had possessed her—she had been instructed in the art of love so when the day came for her to be sold—she was told by the other women to expect this—she would know how to please her master. It's the only way these women have of surviving.

"About six months later, one night Lira brought a young girl to my quarters while I was having dinner. She was very young, no more than a child, with tawny hair and skin and big, frightened brown eyes with golden flecks in them. Lira begged me to buy her from the dirty camelteer who was her owner. I was surprised that Lira would suggest such a thing. But she persisted, reciting the child's accomplishments, which she presumed would interest me.

"Naturally, I protested. My relationship with Lira was extremely satisfactory. I had little desire for what such a purchase implied. Lira saw that her arguments were having little effect; so she played her ace. She unclasped the girl's gown, exposing the ugly red welts covering her body.

"That persuaded me in a hurry. I couldn't humanely send the child back to such treatment. Within the month, I found her in my bed one night. She begged me not to send her away for she feared Lira's anger if she did not please me.

"So, Lira became the head of my household. It's a way of life hard for a European to understand, much less condone. But it was a way I accepted. I offer no excuse for my behavior." Siri frowned, eyeing his drafted confessor.

When David said nothing, Siri resumed, leaning forward, his arms on his knees, staring at the carpet.

"From that time on, Lira picked the women carefully, apparently by requisites of her own. I had no complaints with her choices. They were consistently beautiful, young, and virgin when they came to me. My life was altogether pleasant.

"Then one day a few years later, I was in Touggourt, again passing through the same market, by chance, where I had found Lira. This day, however, the girl on the block had drawn a sigh from the usually clamoring spectators. Their unusual behavior drew my attention. I was stunned.

"The girl was white with long golden hair; her features could not have been more perfect had she been sculpted from marble by the most talented hand. I had never seen anyone like her. Neither had the others, apparently, for the bidding was brisk.

"This time I was no nonchalant savior. I wanted that girl as I had never wanted anything in my life. I was determined that none of those slobbering natives should get the chance to touch her. She cost a fortune; but the price was nothing compared to the passion she aroused, driving every other consideration out of my mind. I took her to the Fort immediately, leaving Ahmed to take care of business. And it was sale week in Touggourt!" Siri added, to emphasize how he felt; but the young physician wouldn't understand the full import until later.

"Lira was evasive when I called for my prize, for that was the way I thought of her. 'Don't take her, master,' Lira begged. 'She's not one of us!' Lira's behavior was unusual; she never criticized any of my actions, always remembering her place. Anyway, there was no way I'd listen to her imaginings. My desire for the exquisite creature had me blind with passion.

"When she was brought to me, she was even more beautiful than I remembered; but her actions were startling. She didn't come to me willingly as the others had done and as I had come to expect. She acted as if she didn't know what was required. She cowered away like a cornered animal guided by instinct, a fear in her eyes that the oda women never had. Her beauty and strange manner only inflamed my desire. I wanted to conquer her. When she struggled, I took her by force, any thought of control discarded. My strength left her body a mass of bruises.

"Oh, my God!" Siri interrupted his story. "How could I have been such a brute!" With an effort, he continued, his face heavy with an expression of self-condemnation. He drew a deep breath, which ended with a sigh.

"I found myself impatient for the days to end so I could be with her. I'd swear to myself to be gentle; but when she came, the fear in her eyes and the shudder of revulsion that shook her, drove me to violence again. After the first time, she endured all that I did to her in silence.

"Lira disapproved vociferously. I thought she was jealous, considering the girl a threat to her position. It was the first time I had shown preference among the women. I paid no attention.

"Then one night about a month later, Lira came to me openly distraught. 'She's gone, master,' she announced in tears. I sent my tribesmen to search for her. They had no rest for weeks while I forced them to comb every inch of desert for a hundred miles. Every caravan and every nomad was cross-examined. There was never a trace. Finally, I had to give up. Lira swore she was an huriyah. Five years later, I found her again at the pile of ruins that has come to be called Arx Vetus."

Siri ceased speaking. The silence lengthened.

Finally, David spoke in a low voice. "She has forgiven you, sir."

"A woman cannot forgive such treatment," Siri responded in a tone of hopeless finality.

The young doctor, feeling awkward because of lack of experience in such matters, dared offer no further contradiction. When it appeared that Siri would say no more, Mott left quietly.

Mott paid his regular morning visit to Lady Pemberly, a plan half-formed in his mind. While he examined her perfunctorily, he assured her of Siri's physical well-being. Finally, he decided to risk telling her what he thought should be done for the sake of Siri's psychological health.

"My lady," he began hesitatingly, carefully choosing his words. "I know you are wondering whether or not to order his lordship to come to you. I beg you not to do it. Give him some time, if you love him. The reversal has allowed all the former experiences to surface. And without the control that he usually has, his dynamic personality is swinging like a pendulum from one extreme to another. He doesn't trust himself."

Cheira listened attentively, anxious to discover a solution to the dilemma that had kept her awake most of the night.

Mott continued. "Last night and this morning, he has been considering a return to the desert."

Cheira inhaled sharply; but the doctor forestalled the negation that rose to her lips.

"Will you trust me?" he hurried on, extending his hands supplicatingly. "Let him go and let me go with him, if he'll allow it. In a few weeks, he'll be ready to come back."

Cheira buried her face in her hands. Her whole body seemed to shrink into a point of pain in her heart. There was nothing but emptiness around her. It was dark and frightening, moving with shadowy figures too indistinct to see. She shuddered. At last, she assented.

Mott could barely conceal the triumph he felt. "Will you direct Sir

John to dismiss Stevens and allow us to leave?"

Again she assented. He didn't notice the forlorn expression settled on her face.

Mott hurried away, intent on the next step in his plan. He was certain that all Siri needed was rest and a chance to reorient. The experiment could then safely proceed. The romanticism that made the young doctor so keen in the pursuit of scientific knowledge now bloomed fully with a sense of impending adventure. The story Siri had related, far from disgusting the young scientist, had sparked his admiration for the heroic. That glimpse of Siri's life fired his imagination. He was determined to go with Siri as much for the excitement he was sure would follow as for any idea of being a watchdog.

Besides, he seriously doubted his ability to prevent any adverse decisions Siri might make. He humbly did not maximize the amount of influence he had over his friend.

When David entered, Siri smiled, his liking for the young man very evident.

"Well, Doctor," Siri spoke with mock formality, "have you diagnosed the patient? What's the remedy to be? Shall I continue with large doses of medicinal spirits?"

David knew telepathically the decision to leave had been made.

"That's a good idea!"

Siri looked surprised.

"I mean the trip to the desert, sir!" David corrected hastily.

After a moment, Siri shrugged. "I must remember that my mind holds no secrets from you. You have the advantage, my friend." Siri's tone was subdued.

David protested, "Only to be of service."

"So," Siri surmised, "Cheira has already agreed, I presume."

David nodded, not wishing to emphasize the fact by voicing it. He hurried to say, albeit shyly, "May I go with you, my lord?"

Siri looked at him steadily. "Is that a condition?"

"Oh, no," David flushed. "It's my own idea. I'm entitled to a vacation. And I've always dreamed of seeing the desert more closely. I was only at Arx Vetus once and then only for two days."

"All right," Siri agreed. "Carl, my pilot, can be ready with the plane by two. Can you go then?"

"Yes, sir," David answered eagerly.

"Damn!" Siri said suddenly.

David jumped. Intent with his own plans, he hadn't been paying attention to what Siri was thinking.

Siri grinned. "I'll have to phone Carl. This is bloody inconvenient!"

David left. There were arrangements to be made at the clinic so they could carry on in his absence. He barely noticed that Stevens and the guards had withdrawn. As he was about to teleport out of the manor, he received a summons from John.

"What the devil is going on?" John demanded as soon as David entered his office.

"His lordship needs a short vacation to recover his health," David reported with an exaggerated air of professionalism. "Her ladyship agrees."

"Voluntarily?" John's voice rose angrily. "Or was she coerced?"

"I assure you, sir," David responded innocently, "that her ladyship understands that it will be best for all concerned and be a major factor in the ultimate success of the experiment."

"The way she grovels to him is disgusting!" John spat out the words. "I'd know how to bring him to his knees."

David volunteered no comment.

"All right," John conceded reluctantly. "It's her decision. But make sure you bring him back or you'll answer to me. Understand that!"

David bowed. John assumed that the doctor's silence was assent. David happily left it at that and escaped.

CHAPTER XVI

The young scientist's great adventure began with a breakneck ride to the airport. He held his breath and onto the sides of the seat. He relaxed only when he realized the skill with which Siri guided the powerful Benz. The heavy traffic proved no impediment to speed. But then he worried when he noticed how much Siri was exceeding the speed limit. Finally, Siri noticed his fidgeting.

"There has to be some advantage to being the husband of the richest woman in England." Siri's laugh was mirthless.

Of course, David thought, *the special license plates.*

The sheik's jet was circling to land when they arrived. Siri drove out onto the field to meet it. He went aboard immediately. Carl, after a brief greeting, turned the car over to an attendant with a few terse instructions.

Siri took the controls. The tower cleared them for takeoff promptly, holding a commercial flight on the ground. As the order crackled over the radio, the sheik took a moment to turn around and grin at David ensconced in the navigator's seat.

"One of the advantages," he quipped.

They landed in Paris to refuel. *Evidently, Siri wanted to get out of England as fast as he could,* David thought wryly.

It was dark when they set down in the desert. David had never seen Siri so alive and eager. *This is where he belongs,* he thought, sad that destiny had chosen him for a very different existence.

The old jeep waiting for them under the guidance of a salaaming, grinning tribesman muffled to the ears in the folds of a burnoose, clattered across the sands. The Fort lay sprawled in the moonlight, silent as a slumbering Behemoth.

Suddenly, the air was filled with shouts and gunfire. Tribesmen burst out of the gate, horses at full gallop. It was a welcome to their chief. The sand swirled into clouds as the yelling men circled the jeep, recklessly risking serious injury crossing the path of the speeding vehicle.

Just before they rolled into the courtyard, Siri raised his hand. It was the first indication that he noticed the demonstration. The silence was instantaneous. The riders hauled in their horses to stand motionless as the dust settled slowly around them.

David's eyes bulged with the excitement of the scene. He marveled at the open acknowledgment of these fierce-looking men to Siri's authority. His heart pounded in anticipation of what was to come.

The quarters of the sheik enhanced the strange atmosphere. The huge, rambling structure appeared to lean against the back wall of the compound, its main entrance facing a gate down a quarter mile of dusty pavement.

Inside, the contrast was startlingly unexpected. The decor was sumptuous. Marble alternated with thick carpeting for the flooring. The vaulted ceilings vanished into darkness overhead, implying vast spaces. The furnishings followed the design of the country with rich tapestries and oriental appointments; a concession was made to the comforts of the modern world only in the lavish use of electric lighting.

David's suite was so comfortable that his imagination failed when he tried to compare it unfavorably to the best palaces he had seen at home.

After a shower—another welcome concession to the twentieth century—David donned the desert garb provided by an old servant. He laughed at himself in the baggy pants and tight vest. The high boots felt more comfortable; but the voluminous burnoose made him wonder if he had lost his mind to try to fit into this world so foreign from his own. He joined the sheik in the library for a late supper.

"You'll pass," Siri eyed him critically. "But one doesn't wear one's outer garment indoors."

David flushed. "At Arx Fetus . . . " he stammered.

"That's an exception." Siri's expression sobered.

David quickly changed the subject. Laying the offending cloak on a divan, he went to examine the book-covered walls. Cursory inspection informed him that all the classics were there, as well as some books on desert ecology. Languages, medical and engineering volumes shouldered each other in a patently indiscriminatory manner.

"I've had many years to perfect my collection," Siri answered his query on the comprehensiveness of the knowledge assembled. "But, come on"— Siri smiled—"you didn't come to the desert for that kind of learning."

Later, over drinks, Siri explained that in the morning they would leave for Imla Dun, the oasis that quartered the sheik's main stud. It was here that the famous horses of Siri ben Ange were bred and raised. The annual sale at Touggourt was only a month away. The sale horses had to be selected, trained, and driven to the tiny desert town.

"We'll leave at daybreak." Siri finished. "It's a full day's ride."

David rose. He was tired enough to be grateful for an early bedtime.

"By the way, can you ride?" Siri asked.

"Not very well," David admitted, pausing at the door.

"Maybe you'd better come with the transport trucks, then."

"No!" David was definite. "I'll manage. I didn't come here to be coddled."

"As you wish!"

David was grateful that Siri didn't try to dissuade him, but gave him the respect of allowing him to make his own decision.

David considered himself an early riser, but the old servant had to shake him to get him out of bed the next morning. It was still dark and the clock on the bedside table stood at four-thirty. Even the soft glow of the lamp pained his outraged eyeballs, and the warm blankets clung to his body invitingly. Mumbling incoherently, he forced his sleep-drugged muscles to support his frame in an upright position. The performance of the motions required to dress were an extra effort.

He was led to a little room on the main floor filled with greenery and a table heaped with food.

Siri was already there, stowing away huge quantities of ham and eggs, washing them down with steaming black coffee. The mingled aromas made David's still dormant insides writhe uneasily; but he smiled bravely as he took a seat opposite his host.

"Better eat," Siri advised, noticing David's expression of distaste as he eyed the mounds of food. "We won't stop for about seven hours."

Later David was never quite sure how he survived that first day.

He was just really waking up from the stimulation of a queasy stomach when Siri led him into the courtyard. There a servant handed him the reins of a tall brown horse.

"She's very gentle," Siri assured him, as the tribesman helped David to mount.

David only had time to wonder what the others were like when, no sooner was he in the saddle, than the horse bolted down the road toward the gate, slamming the precariously balanced passenger onto the saddle at every hard-hitting stride. The gate was still closed. The animal stopped suddenly, swerving to miss the barrier in its path. David was catapulted through the air in a graceful arc over the confused animal's head.

When his ears stopped ringing and his shocked lungs started to function again, he was greeted by the derisive laughter of the circle of tribesmen. Livid with anger and embarrassment, he realized they were cheering the horse.

Siri made no attempt to stop the merriment. He rode up to David, asking politely if he were hurt, but not bothering to dismount.

In silent fury that showed only in the red of his face, David rose painfully, surreptitiously checking for broken bones while he dusted himself off.

"Want to wait for the trucks?" Siri asked.

David was sure Siri was laughing. "No!" he answered sullenly.

One of the men brought the mare and helped David to remount.

"Keep your heels out of her and sit up straight," the sheik advised, the corners of his mouth twitching with a repressed smile. "A gentle tug on the reins will slow her up."

David growled in reply. He cursed his imagination for lying to him about the pleasures of the desert. He gritted his teeth. He felt battered from head to foot and deeply humiliated. He, the famous scientist, looked like a fool in front of Siri and his men.

His anger sustained him for the next few hours—until his body was numb from the jolting. The party had started out slowly enough; but as soon as the horses were warmed up, they took up a steady, long-strided lope—a ground-covering gait, which the specially bred animals could maintain almost indefinitely. David stood, sat, and crouched in turn; but could not find a point of comfort.

By the time they stopped for lunch, he was close to unconsciousness and so stiff that one of the men had to haul him off the horse and support him into the small tent. His "kind" helper then unceremoniously dumped him on a pile of cushions.

At a small stand in the corner, Siri was briskly washing away the dust of the morning, happily whistling an accompaniment to the splashing water. David groaned, unreasonably resenting Siri's obvious enjoyment of what had been unceasing torture for him.

Lunch was served on a low table next to where David lay.

"We'll be here for two hours to rest the horses." Siri settled cross-legged onto a cushion opposite his companion.

"Want to wait for the trucks? I'll leave some men here with you."

David sat up abruptly. "No! I'm all right!"

"Just thought it might be easier."

"I'll be ready to ride whenever you are."

Siri gave him an admiring glance. "You're game!" he commented. "Better eat, then. Food will give you strength."

"I'm a doctor, remember?" David retorted peevishly, indulging his bruised nerves with the relief of sarcasm.

Touché! Siri grinned.

After the meal, the sounds of the camp ceased. The tiny oasis was still except for the clicking of the sand beetles as they industriously performed the rites of life. David was grateful for the respite. Too exhausted to sleep, his mind restlessly dragged him over the events of the last two days. *Was I right,* he wondered, *to encourage Siri to return to the desert?* What if he decided to stay? The man obviously loved the life and belonged to it. The experiment would be stopped. All the years of work were being gambled on one man's honor. Abruptly, his mind changed. He didn't care. He'd rather be here with Siri than anywhere else on earth.

He glanced at the sleeping figure, curled up in a burnoose. Even his complaining muscles didn't dim the pleasure he felt.

David was still stiff and sore when it was time to leave.

"Only about three more hours." Siri intended to be kind. David groaned silently. But to his surprise, once they were underway, he felt better than he had in the morning. His aching body was accustomed to the motion. He found that, if he relaxed, the sensation of the loping animal was quite tolerable.

The light was fading when the palms of Imla Dun appeared on the horizon. The early moon sat like an over-inflated balloon on the tops of the feathery trees, defying the last rays of the sun. David was tempted to reach for it in the clear sky, which shrank distances. It looked like a man could hold the softly undulating mass in the hollow of his hand.

Shortly, it was possible to detect a party of horsemen heading out to meet them. As usual, they were moving rapidly, raising a cloud of sand that rolled before them like a triumphant vanguard. The sheik's party spurred their mounts to greater effort, impatient to shorten the time of meeting. Shouts of greeting floated through the dry air as brother tribesmen met each other, embracing clamorously in a melee of excited, plunging horses. From their enthusiasm, David concluded that they had been separated for years.

In reality, it was only a matter of months, Siri explained later. The men rotated every three months because their permanent dwellings and families were at the Fort.

David had a small tent of his own pitched beside the sheik's larger one. After a hot bath—which he was pleasantly surprised to see provided in this remote outpost—he was able to join the sheik in his tent for dinner, feeling relaxed and hungry. Now he could do justice to the meal. And after a drink, David bade his host good night to throw himself on his cot in the soundest sleep he had ever known.

The sun was already blazing high overhead in the cloudless sky when David awakened. He dressed hurriedly and went to stand outside the tent.

A young boy rose quickly from where he had been squatting a short distance away. Obviously, he was waiting for David to appear.

"Good morning, Doctor," he said in perfect English. "My master sends you greetings and bids you welcome to Imla Dun. May I serve breakfast?"

"Yes, of course," David suppressed a smile at the boy's quaint formality. David's affirmation was evidently all the boy needed for motivation. He scampered off, reappearing almost immediately bearing a large tray.

"Would you like to eat here, Doctor?" The lad indicated the front of the tent, sheltered by an awning. When David nodded, the boy skillfully set up a table with folding legs, which had been concealed in the tent's flap. He held the tray balanced precariously in one hand while he unfolded the table with the other. Securing a chair by the same means, he whisked off the spotless linen cover of the tray and stood with it draped over his arm, as poised as a seasoned French waiter.

"Where did you learn that?" David inquired, smothering a laugh at the comic figure, incongruously curling his bare toes in the grass while solicitously uncovering steaming dishes of food.

"My master taught me," the boy answered proudly.

"And the English, also, I suppose?"

"Yes, and many other things besides," the boy boasted, his black eyes flashing.

"And where is your master now?" Leisurely, David tackled the breakfast, thinking how the desert air sharpened the appetite.

"On the other side of the oasis selecting the sale horses." The lad waved his hand knowledgeably. "My master said you should rest now and he will be back for lunch."

"Very considerate of him, I'm sure," David commently, dryly.

"My master is just," the boy corrected him innocently.

"Hm." David refrained from further comments on what was evidently a ticklish subject. He surveyed the area in front of the tent, impressed with the order and neatness of the camp. The tents marched like soldiers in single file away from the sheik's at the hub. There was considerable bustle in the immediate area as tribesmen hurried about their chores. Each seemed to be responsible for some function of the camp's maintenance.

There were horses everywhere: some tethered in front of the tents, saddled and ready for use; some wandering free, apparently so domesticated they could be trusted not to stray too far.

The supply trucks were backed precisely against a cement block building, the only visible permanent structure. The drivers were lounging in the shade of the vehicles haughtily viewing the scene around them. Theirs was an honored position in the tribe, and they were doing their best to keep the others aware of it.

Flocks of brown chickens searched for a meal at random, sometimes coming precariously close to the feet of horses intent on the same search. No mishaps occurred, David noticed with interest, as the animals seemed to have a mutually workable agreement by which they avoided each other. It was only the big, rangy hounds who sent the birds scattering when a luckless one happened too close to the dogs' resting place. Then, the raucous barking and indignant squawking drowned out the other, more peaceful sounds of the camp.

David strolled along the open space in front of the canvas dwellings, absorbing the activities. This was the heart of the desert as few foreigners were allowed to see it. Appreciation flooded over him in a warm glow that did not originate from the sun.

The boy followed closely at his heels. *Assigned by the sheik to look after his awkward guest,* David decided, amused. Covertly, he studied the lad, his interest quickening as he noted the handsome, beardless face with its intelligent dark eyes.

"What's your name?"

"Hasi," the boy replied promptly, strutting in a circle around David.

"And your father is here, also?"

A look of perplexity came into Hasi's face. "I don't know." He stood thoughtfully. Then his expression brightened. "My mother lives in my master's house." He grinned broadly, having thought of an answer to satisfy the visitor.

261

David studied him with renewed interest. The dark eyes, the aquiline profile, the proud bearing were somehow reminiscent of his friend. And the obvious care which had been taken with the boy's education! *My God,* he wondered, *could it possibly be?* He was curious enough to want to ask Siri.

He had not long to wait. The sheik rode in shortly before noon. Siri went directly to his tent. Lunch was already being laid out. He joined David in a few minutes, his hair still damp from a quick shower. The white costume was, as usual, fresh and immaculate.

"I'm never civil till I get the dust off," Siri apologized, smiling at his young guest. "Was your morning comfortable?"

David nodded, inhaling deeply to bolster his nerve. *After all,* he chided himself, *even if what I suspect is true, it is none of my business.* But the streak of curiosity could not be quelled.

"About Hasi," he began.

"The little devil hasn't given good service?" The sheik interrupted him, a scowl settling over his face.

"Oh, yes," David hastened to reassure his host. "It's not that!"

Siri paused momentarily from concentration on his lunch and looked at David questioningly.

"He's remarkably well educated for a simple desert boy," David observed lamely.

Siri shrugged and resumed eating. "It amuses me."

"I asked him about his father," David plunged on. "All he knows is that his mother lives in his master's house at the Fort."

Siri nodded. When David didn't go on, Siri looked at him. Then understanding dawned in his eyes. He threw back his head and laughed. Several tribesmen paused in their duties to watch their master in wonder. He seldom relaxed that stern attitude in their presence.

"I think I'll have to revise my opinion of your scientific astuteness." Siri chuckled. "Have you so soon forgotten the characteristic of transfiguration your experiment is designed to correct? And I haven't had time since the reversal to accomplish that much." He laughed again at the flush of embarrassment that rose in David's face. "Never mind," he continued, rising and clapping David on the shoulder, "in view of that drunken confession, it was a natural mistake. Do you want to go with me this afternoon?"

"Oh, yes," David replied gratefully.

"In two hours, then," Siri said, turning toward the tent.

"I'm sorry," David murmured, silently cursing his stupidity, as his host disappeared. Why when he wanted so much for Siri to like him did he have to act wholly asinine? He was so lost in sophomoric adulation that his brain ceased to function. He shook his head in self-disgust, vowing to maintain a rigid surveillance over his actions in the future.

The camp lapsed into silence as the community rested under the stifling heat of the midday sun. Only the young foreigner remained awake and restless, not foreseeing that in a day or two, he too would be able to fall naturally into the custom and even be grateful for it.

When Siri emerged from the tent, the sun was making its way slowly toward the horizon; the horses ready and waiting. As they rode out, Siri described the layout of the camp.

"It's like a fan," he told his guest. "The tents at the apex, the pastures spread out to the south."

David's gaze followed the sweep of Siri's hand. He could see, now that the tents were behind them, the lush greenness of the fields stretching away into the distance.

"This is all oasis?" David was amazed.

"With a little help from irrigation." Siri was gratified by the other's interest. "We can reclaim nearly ten acres a year. In about four years, the area is productive—perhaps, a little less now with modern methods." Siri warmed to a subject dear to his heart. "Liberal applications of commercial fertilizer with a top-heavy percentage of nitrogen encourages thick rooting of legumes, providing a good topsoil basis when plowed under for a few years. We've got two thousand acres now, which has allowed us to expand our operation. We should have seventy-five head for sale this year."

David noticed that it was the first time he had ever heard the sheik speak in the plural. He was obviously proud of the success of the program and gave his men credit for the fine job they were doing.

They halted before a corral in which three men were already working with a young horse.

"They're all tattooed before they leave," Siri explained. "That way, should the necessity ever arise, they are always identifiable. Precise records are kept, giving not only lineage, but the stage of training at the time of sale, and both physical and personality characteristics."

"I didn't realize horses had personalities," David commented.

"You'll find out if you stay a while," Siri answered, laughing.

A man detached himself from the group and came forward.

"This is Mohammed, David." The note of pride in Siri's voice was clear. "Without his help, none of this would be possible."

Mohammed grinned broadly, preening under his master's praise.

David appreciated the esteem Siri held for his headman. He was the first to be singled out for introduction.

After a brief conference, Mohammed turned back to his work. Siri rode the short distance to a yard holding a number of milling yearlings and two-year-olds. One by one the animals were brought up for his inspection. If the animal was selected for sale, it was ponied to the tattooing corral. The others were turned out to pasture.

As the afternoon waned, the yard emptied slowly. The judging was a tedious process. No horse with the slightest imperfection would be allowed to pass through the sale under the sheik's tag. Every man watched with intense interest because the proud reputation of the tribe was at stake.

Siri not only inspected each animal meticulously for physical imperfections, but listened attentively to the description of the personality recited by the man under whose charge the youngster had been reared.

Each man had four animals as his personal charge. He was expected to know exactly how each one was progressing. The men vied for the honor of having the most animals selected. To have fewer than half of one's charges accepted was a great disgrace. More than likely, the poor fellow was relegated to camp maintenance for the coming year, being considered too poor a horseman to be trusted with the supervision of the valuable animals.

David was fascinated when he finally figured out why some of the men were laughing and talking happily while one or two others slunk away sheepishly, accompanied by the jeers of their fellows. The system was novel, but apparently workable because the number of animals rejected was very small.

It was early evening before the yard was finally emptied. Siri had worked steadily, drinking numberless cups of scalding native coffee provided by the women.

At last, the sheik turned to his guest. "This must be boring for you," Siri apologized.

David protested. "It's exciting! It's the desert—like no other place in the world."

Siri laughed. "Careful, David! Once the desert gets hold of you, it will never let go!"

"I love it!" David insisted. "I want to learn all I can. Do you think I could help? Maybe I could pony the yearlings?"

Siri nodded, pleased with David's interest. "We've still got about ninety head to inspect. You can help tomorrow."

The passing days were filled with hard work. David learned to rise with the sun, work with the horses until noon, take a siesta in the heat of the day, work again through the afternoon, and fall exhausted but satisfied onto his cot as the cool evening breeze swept over the camp.

He slept better and ate heartier than he had ever done in his life. He raved over the simple fare prepared by the women over open fires and in primitive stone ovens.

After a week, he felt as at home on a horse as off. He took the friendly jeering of the tribesmen with good humor; and he learned how to ride as a consequence. The morning Mohammed handed him the reins of a high-headed prancing gelding instead of the quiet mare he usually rode, David knew he had been accepted by the tribe. The pride he felt was equal to that of the day he had received his hard-won diploma from medical school.

He laughed at himself for delighting in the heavy knots of muscle lining his chest and bulging on his legs and arms. He felt confident now to engage in the friendly tussling that periodically broke the tedium of the long, hard days, even though his only victories were over the adolescent boys.

The London clinic and the experiment that had absorbed his whole life seemed very far away. The only use he found for altered consciousness was that it enabled him to learn the tribal dialect quickly and with little effort. That he might have used transfigured strength to gain mastery over the tribesmen never occurred to him.

Most days he saw little of Siri. When they dined together, the talk was centered solely on the activities of the camp. David was enjoying himself so much that he failed to notice the lingering sadness in his friend's eyes. Siri usually retired early or spent the evening preparing the records that needed to be ready to be transferred with each horse sold, the duplicates being stored at the Fort. Then Mohammed worked with the sheik, and David would excuse himself to join the men at the campfire.

It took three days to complete the judging and tattooing. Then the horses were sorted by age, and a group of men were assigned to round off the stage of training for each. The assignment was the occasion for much friendly competition, the men boasting, within earshot of their master, of course, of their many accomplishments. Very rarely did the comments affect the sheik's appointments nor did they expect it to. However, it was part of the game and did not deter them.

David drew a post with the yearlings, accompanied by the derisive groans of the men of that group. David submitted happily to the remarks, proud that Siri felt he was capable of the task.

He was pleased with his developing way with horses. He was beginning to get glances of approval from the men; and the absence of criticism from Siri was like an accolade. He spent hours over books on horse training just to be worthy of Siri's approval.

One day, during a break in his own training group, David was watching the trainers put the four-year-olds through advanced paces. He was fascinated by the expertise shown by the men and gravitated to the training ring whenever he had a free moment.

Siri headed this group personally. David never ceased to marvel at the sheik's limitless patience and gentleness with the young animals. He seemed able to communicate with them in a manner that stimulated their willing cooperation.

Some of the horses in Siri's group were already earmarked for foreign buyers. Their training, then, was highly specialized, the buyers having ordered a horse for a certain purpose.

David's attention was caught by a beautiful chestnut being put through a course of jumps. He imagined the new owner somewhere in Europe or America eagerly awaiting the arrival of this desert-bred charmer.

The noise of the crash jarred him out of the reverie. The trainer had put the inexperienced colt at the fence from an awkward angle. The youngster lost his balance and, unable to recover, had gone down with his rider underneath him.

David was at the man's side by the time the trembling colt scrambled to his feet. A cursory examination of the fallen rider revealed a broken pelvis, along with a compound fracture of the leg. David looked for Siri. The sheik had gone to examine the horse for injury and paid no attention to the rider. David was too busy with the patient to feel more than a passing resentment toward the sheik.

"Leave him alone," Siri spoke at his shoulder. "They will take care of him." He motioned toward the men hurrying across the ring with a stretcher.

"I haven't forgotten my medical training," David stated, anger coloring his tone.

"Neither has Gamiel," Siri answered, stepping back as the young tribesman approached. David reluctantly allowed the man to take over. The criticism he was about to voice died in his throat. The native physician cared for the injured man with consummate skill.

As the man was being carried away, he looked pleadingly at Siri. "Forgive me, master. The horse, is he injured?"

"No," Siri spoke sharply, turning away. The man followed him with his eyes. There were tears in them that were not from pain.

"You could have been more sympathetic," David criticized, still angry at Siri's callousness.

"His carelessness might have damaged a perfect animal," Siri snapped. "The fool should have watched more closely."

"But he might have been killed. And it still remains to be seen if he is injured permanently."

"The colt might have been marked," Siri retorted, "and cannot be easily replaced." He turned back to the animal he had been working with.

David fumed. The implication was obvious. The young doctor flatly disagreed with such an attitude. This was an aspect of desert life he was not prepared to accept. How could Siri? The man he admired so much could not be so indifferent to human life. Or could he?

After supper, Siri, aware of his young guest's disapproval, offered to visit the injured man. It was one of the few concessions the sheik ever made and—had David known it—was the measure of Siri's liking for him. David, prepared for the worst, accompanied Siri.

David was surprised and impressed with the little block infirmary. It was equipped like a miniature modern hospital. He felt even better when he had inspected the injured tribesman. Gamiel had done an excellent job. The skill with which the cast had been molded was apparent. The desert physician even presented X rays of the broken bones for David's inspection.

Siri, leaning lazily against the door, observed David's amazement with a twinkle in his eyes. The corners of his mouth curled upward in a half-smile.

"Gamiel graduated from Stanford," he mentioned, as if the information were of only passing interest. "Even a poor desert man can be taught that the earth is round."

Gamiel smiled understandingly.

"I'm sorry," David apologized. "Out here I seem to have acquired the habit of jumping to the wrong conclusions."

At dawn the next morning, the trucks set out with supplies for the men and horses. The training completed, it was now the task to get the animals to Touggourt in time for the sale.

"Three days to the Fort," Siri told David. "We move slowly. It's a long trek for the young horses; and we want them in perfect condition when they go into the sale ring."

Even with the utmost care, some of the animals would probably have to be withdrawn, the fatigue of the unaccustomed journey knocking them out of condition.

"Two days rest at the Fort," Siri continued, "then another two days to the sale point."

David was reluctant to leave when the time came. He had grown to love this life. It was an existence stripped to the bare essentials. A man had his work and it was hard; but there were also moments of leisure. He remembered fondly the nights around the campfire with Hasi drawing a melancholy tune from the pipe he had fashioned from a reed and the men swapping tales of past adventures or just discussing the problems of the day. Siri was never present at these gatherings; and it was then that David came to know the extent of the loyalty and respect the men had for their leader, mingled liberally with a feeling of awe. They recounted incidents of what they considered superhuman prowess. David smiled.

But soon David was busy with the horses in his charge. The excitement of departure took hold of him. Siri was so pleased by his rapid advancement as a horseman that he had given David three of the valuable animals as his sole responsibility.

The moment of parting with new comrades was sad, and David glanced back many times until even the tall palms of Imla Dun dropped below the horizon.

Now the strain of the task increased. The problem of keeping the frightened youngsters calm and uninjured required all of David's ingenuity. Relieved and exhausted, he brought his charges safely into the Fort on the night of the third day. He was grateful for the comfortable quarters the Fort provided and retired early.

The habit of the last few weeks was deeply implanted. David was awake at the first hint of dawn. He was no longer self-conscious about ordering the servants and had coffee brought to his room. He was informed that the sheik was occupied with business this morning but would join him for lunch.

David took the opportunity to explore the rambling compound. He discovered that the main building was built in an U shape with a lovely garden in the enclosure completed by the back wall. He was surprised that the garden contained a swimming pool.

Investigation revealed that the sheik lived in only one wing. The offices of tribal government were contained in the center. The other housed the serail. It was the only area he was barred from entering. He guiltily put aside the temptation to teleport past the guards. Instead, he retreated toward the dining room.

David wandered slowly across the main hall. He was amazed at the collection of rare vases, ancient native weapons, ivory statuettes, and a tasteful assembly of fine paintings. The displays revealed to him another facet of the character of the man he had come to admire so much.

The other rooms on the ground floor were decorated similarly and with obvious care. This was Siri's home, he realized; and he felt guilty that he was an instrument for depriving his friend of it. *Does Cheira know,* he wondered, *what she is asking Siri to give up; and if so, did she even consider it?* David felt the first stirrings of resentment toward the mistress of Arx Vetus.

David was idling over a cup of coffee when his host came in. He was startled at the black scowl on the sheik's face.

"We've got three days." Siri's voice was flat.

David jumped up, tipping his chair backwards onto the floor. "You mean Cheira has sent for you?"

"John." Siri shrugged. "The official order came by the supply plane this morning."

"I'll go back and get an extension," David offered hastily.

"No!" Siri slammed his fist on the table. "I won't have you begging for me!"

"But the sale!" David protested. "We need at least another week!" Unconsciously, he used the plural pronoun.

Siri glanced at him, his eyes narrowed; but his voice was expressionless. "Mohammed will see to it."

David lapsed into a brooding silence. He righted his chair, flopping onto it morosely. He had come to know Siri well enough to realize the futility of further attempts at persuasion.

"If we start tomorrow"—David's face lit up—"we could at least see the horses safely to Touggourt."

"Yes," Siri agreed. "We could do that, I suppose."

David was gratified to see his friend's expression lighten slightly. He stood up. "Well, then," he enthused, impatient for action, "let's get the trucks started."

Siri smiled at the young man's enthusiasm. He followed him out without protest, glad enough himself for a job to do. Both neglected their lunch.

It was dusk before they saw the last truck loaded and ready to depart at dawn. The two comrades had worked side by side all afternoon. They parted long enough for showers and a change of clothes, meeting again for dinner. This time they did justice to the food.

The hard work has helped, David decided. The black scowl was gone from Siri's face and his mood brightened a little.

Just as they were finishing, Ameur appeared. Siri greeted him warmly.

David was surprised. For some reason, he had never thought of friendship between them. But, why not? Arx Vetus was only a hundred miles away, and they had known each other for more years than David had been alive.

"Dr. David Mott!" Ameur turned to the young scientist, extending his hand. "I heard that you'd come down with Siri. The rumor is that you've abandoned civilization for this barbaric existence."

David had only met Ameur—and then formally—on one short visit to Arx Vetus. He felt shy before the man who headed the whole organization. He blushed.

"It's the greatest!" David stammered, enthusiastically defending the last few weeks, which now that they were almost over seemed to have been the most satisfying of his life.

"You've made a convert!" Ameur laughed, addressing Siri.

"I warned him!" Siri responded in the same light tone.

They passed into the garden where comfortable chairs and drinks awaited them. Torches stuck on long poles challenged the illumination of the rising moon. The dancing shadows lent an air of unreality to the scene. Their grotesque shapes mingling with the graceful waving of the palm branches overhead. David thought of Cheira and wondered.

"No visit to the desert would be complete, David," Siri continued, "without an evening of entertainment."

"Your conversion will be total," Ameur agreed.

The sheik clapped his hands. David was soon lost in the spell of what followed. He saw acrobats and jugglers, a magician and a snake charmer. Entranced, he perched on the edge of his chair.

Ameur and Siri talked quietly.

"After all these years, old friend," Ameur said, "we must speak because you can no longer understand my thoughts."

"Sometimes, it's been a relief," Siri countered, refusing Ameur's sympathy. He shrugged. "The thoughts of others can be an unwelcome burden."

"With the reversal procedure a success, I have wondered why you're here." Ameur's gaze was intent, watching Siri's expression carefully, refusing to be put off by the other's lightness. It was this worry that had brought him to the Fort this night.

The sheik sat silent, slumped in his chair, his chin resting on interlaced fingers. His thoughts gave Ameur his answer.

"How can I do what she wants?" Siri groaned. "And the reversal has made it worse. I'm returned to the way I was before. You know my character was less than admirable then."

Ameur frowned. Siri's revelation threatened to dangerously prolong the unaltered state for both Cheira and himself; yet he could understand the psychological struggle Siri was experiencing.

"Has your love died then?" Ameur questioned.

"Oh, God, no!" Siri responded vehemently, sitting up. "I love her more than I ever thought possible. All these weeks without her have been hell. It's her feeling I doubt. And consequently there is a rage inside me which I can no longer control. I can't believe her declarations of love are anything more than the means to expedite her goal. I'm tortured by the memory of what we have known together—the ultimate state of transfiguration, the heaven that men have always strived for. And it was ours!" Siri's shoulders sagged. "She threw it away without a moment's hesitation!"

"Just suppose," Ameur ventured, "that somehow the two are one."

"Ah!" Siri raised his hand for emphasis. "That's the crux of the problem: her profession of love for me versus what she claims to be her duty to the organization. She refuses to see any incompatibility in the two."

"And must there be?" Ameur challenged.

Siri looked at him. There was no mockery in his glance, only a lifeless acquiescence. "Always loyal, Ameur?"

Ameur bowed his head, silently accepting the accusation.

"Have you ever thought she might be acting out of vengeance?" Siri suggested, raising his hand to stop Ameur's immediate denial. "Hear me out, please. You know very well she has no reason to love me. You, more than anyone, must know what I did to her. You rescued her when she had nowhere to turn. It is you she really loves!"

"God, I'd have willingly given my life for you to be right." Ameur spoke vehemently, earnestly, leaning forward in his chair. "But you're wrong! It was only your abominable behavior that made her fail to recognize that what she felt for you was love. Her emotions were so mixed up with fear."

"They became unmixed very suddenly," Siri replied, dryly.

"I'll admit that you're correct," Ameur conceded, "in believing that it was the experiment that forced her decision at this time. It made her face her feelings honestly."

"Very convenient," Siri remarked.

"Are you unwilling to make any concessions for her?" Ameur's tone was exasperated. "My God, man! What more do you want?"

Siri sighed, admitting that whether his opinion was right or wrong, it did nothing to alter the course of his actions. "The order came this morning. We are to be back in London the day after tomorrow." He looked at Ameur solemnly. "I will hold to my commitment."

"You have no choice, it seems," Ameur stated with finality. Neither man had actually ever questioned the strength of Siri's honor.

David gasped. To his delight, he realized he was about to witness a legendary harem dance. He looked at his companions in embarrassment. They both laughed, deliberately throwing off the gloom of their conversation.

"You're privileged, Dr. Mott," Ameur teased. "The sheik has allowed few men to gaze upon the occupants of his seraglio."

David looked at Siri questioningly, a frown of disapproval coming into his face. He couldn't believe that Siri had lied, that he still had a reason for keeping those women.

"They have nowhere to go," Siri shrugged. "The fate of a cast-off woman in this country is too unpleasant too contemplate. So here they must remain." Siri's pride allowed only a partial explanation.

David shuddered. He had had a taste of the harshness of desert life. He had seen the existence of the women who were the respected wives of the tribesmen. These lovely women, as the discarded concubines of a powerful sheik, would suffer unspeakable horrors. David found himself wishing that his friend hadn't succumbed so easily to this way of life. His puritan upbringing was revolted. It spoiled his enjoyment of the entertainment.

They were on the move at dawn the next morning. The toil was steady. The sand swirled up by the horses' feet, suffocating. Neither Siri nor David spared himself. They seemed driven to exhaust every ounce of strength so that nightfall would claim their weary minds and bodies in dreamless sleep.

Carl was waiting for them in Touggourt. It was the afternoon of the third day by the time the stabling of the horses was accomplished and Mohammed had received final instructions.

The sun had set and the night chill was creeping into the town when David got his last glimpse of the desert he had grown to love.

CHAPTER XVII

John met them at the airport. His worried countenance relaxed only when he saw Siri descending the ramp.

"I see Cheira takes no chances. She's sent her jailer to apprehend me." Siri's tone was sarcastic.

John flushed. "Her ladyship knows nothing about this. I sent the order."

"What?" Siri frowned, the dark gleam coming into his eyes. "Since when have you acquired such authority?"

"She's making herself ill with grief and longing. It's affecting her physically. Dr. Carpenter is worried," John explained. "Her health has deteriorated rapidly since the death of Wang Lu."

"Ameur told me," Siri nodded, his irritation fading.

John continued. "She insisted on attending the funeral. Dr. Carpenter objected, but to no avail. She hasn't left her room since she came back. Jennie tells me she spends her time grieving for Wang Lu and crying for you, although she forbade me to summon you. I've never disobeyed her before. For some reason, she's convinced that you'll come back when you're ready. She feels she must wait for that time."

"You have the power to end this absurdity," Siri reminded him.

"I've considered that. I've begged her to allow it. She's adamant in her refusal. The only alternative would be force; and she would resist me with the last of her already depleted strength. Dr. Carpenter is against it. I haven't dared take the risk." John looked questioningly at David.

"That's probably a wise decision," Dr. Mott agreed. "From what we have learned about transfiguration, we know it's an abnormal strain on the body. Even a submissive subject must be in good health to sustain the change."

"I'm begging you," John turned to Siri, his hands outstretched, the enmity between them thrown aside, "if there is any truth in your love, if you have any honor, go to her now."

Siri bowed his head. "Yes," he said in a low voice.

During the ride to Pemberly House, they were silent. Siri's face was white and set. The situation crashed in on his mind. He had been a fool to desert her. He had selfishly disregarded the weakness caused by the reversal. Because in his arrogance he had doubted her love—his pride rebelling against the terms she had every right to make—he might lose her. *My God,* he thought, *if anything should happen to her* . . . He hadn't even considered what the reversal might be doing to her. His life was hers. There could be no existence for him without her. How many times must he foolishly put his feelings and hers to the test?

He burst out of the car before it was stopped, taking the steps two at a time.

Jennie leaped up with a cry of welcome when the door opened. Siri glanced swiftly around the room.

"She's sleeping," Jennie whispered. "Dr. Carpenter gave her a light sedative."

He walked slowly toward the bedroom.

Cheira was sleeping restlessly, the rumpled covers plainly demonstrating the torment. Siri cursed softly. Even the dim light didn't hide the hollow cheeks and dark circles under her eyes. The long lashes stuck together in clumps, and the golden strands of her hair lay in limp disarray on the pillow.

"God forgive me," Siri muttered, falling onto his knees beside the bed. "My love! My love!"

The sound roused her from the shallow stupor.

"Siri?" Her voice was blurred. She kicked at the covers in a struggle to sit up. When she saw him so close, she fell back sobbing, burying her face in the pillow.

"My darling, I am here," he coaxed. His voice was harsh with emotion as he smoothed her hair. She turned to him, her eyes wide, searching his face. She touched his cheek uncertainly. He took her in his arms, holding her tightly. "I am here."

She nestled against him, sobbing quietly. He held her gently, soothingly, repeatedly murmuring declarations of love. Over her protestations, he cursed the selfishness that had separated them, groveling in self-abnegation, tearing to shreds the pride that controlled him—until she crushed his head to her breast to stifle the words she could not bear; until her own grief was suffocated in sympathy. She was appalled at the vision of her own monumental selfishness that had brought the man she loved to this.

The hours passed and still he cradled her in his arms. He confessed the torture of remorse he still felt at the memory of her days at the Fort. He recalled the years of anger and resentment—denying her avowal that the blame was hers, insisting it was caused by his pride and stupidity.

Driven by self-reproach, he told her of the passion that prompted him to accept her declaration of love, to bury his doubt and ignore the disagreement with the conditions she posed—until she silenced him with kisses.

He dwelt for a long time on the few days of their happiness, the night in the tiny hidden oasis near Imla Dun. He had dreamed that it would always be so. The day they teleported together to Lamborn Heath; and the glimpse of eternity they had experienced—he was sure existence could offer nothing greater.

"We will know it again, my darling," she asserted; but the sadness remained in his eyes.

Finally, they lapsed into silence.

The artificial light brightening signaled the coming dawn. Siri felt cramped, his muscles aching for the relief of movement. He looked down at his burden lovingly. She had fallen into a peaceful sleep, her cheek against his heart, the dark circles under her eyes nearly vanished.

Despite the discomfort, he dreaded the moment she would awaken. Nothing she had said, even in her grief and the joy of his coming, led him to believe that her intention had changed. So, the decision was still to be made. Would he be able to accede to her wishes? Why did his whole being revolt at the idea? He had scarcely ever thought of children and had accepted the sterility as a small price to pay. Now the prospect of fathering her child, not because he loved her, but because she commanded him to do so, repulsed him. Even if he were able to convince himself that he capitulated out of love, could he force his body to obey? He noticed . . .

She stirred, opening her eyes. When he looked down, she was studying his face. "Am I dreaming?" she whispered.

"No, my love." He smiled, kissing her forehead. "I'm here."

She asked hopefully, the humility in her voice wrenching his heart. "Will you stay?"

"Yes. I will stay." He answered gravely, as one taking a vow. He must trust the future for the fruition of that decision.

She sat up then. She said, "Wang Lu is dead." The tears spilled out of her eyes again at the pronunciation of the beloved name.

"I know." He gently wiped the tears from her eyes with a fingertip.

"Without you, now there is no one."

"You exaggerate," he scolded, in a tone one would use to console a child. "John is beside himself with worry. Ameur came to the Fort just to remind me of my duty. And the others, whose adoration you cannot doubt, are arrayed to help in any way they can."

"I don't mean that," she explained, a frown marring her smooth brow and her teeth making ridges in the lip caught between the even rows. "I mean—even if I were a two-headed monster."

He laughed. "Sometimes I think you are, my darling."

"And you'd love me anyway?" she persisted.

"With my whole being," he answered, solemnly.

Finally, he called Jennie. Over breakfast, he told Cheira about the horses he'd readied for this year's sale. His stories of David's acclimation to desert life momentarily buried her grief under laughter.

Later, they walked in the garden. Dignified spruce protected their way along the stone walks; and curious mums peeked at them from their beds, smiling in bright autumn colors.

Siri listened patiently, supporting her with sympathy, while she talked out her grief over Wang Lu. They had been estranged for the last twenty years. He had remained unyielding in his decision not to return to transfigured life. The few times she had seen him, his aging had broken her heart. He was the only parent she had ever known. Then, even worse, he had refused to see her at all. In the last year, he had even refused to communicate with her.

Only once, did he break that rule: the day she had gone with Hardy to the restaurant. Despite her pleadings, he hadn't allowed her to visit him. She'd had to resort to telepathy. And then, they quarreled. He disagreed with her intended participation in the experiment and predicted that it would bring her sorrow.

During the weeks she had waited in vain for Siri to return, Wang Lu's prediction hounded her mercilessly. Her respect for his wisdom made her certain that doom was imminent. It didn't occur to her to doubt what he said or to wonder if her understanding of it were correct.

"But you're here!" She smiled at Siri happily. "Wang Lu was mistaken. Our love will endure forever!"

Siri returned her smile, ignoring the uneasiness that picked at the edges of his mind. Through the previous night, holding her in his arms those long hours, he had surrendered his pride, his self-esteem, all that he was into her keeping. He had discovered once and for all that his love was so boundless he could grant whatever she desired, no matter what the cost to himself.

But now with the morning and their continued intimacy, he became aware that his deepest fear, over which he seemed to have no control, was a certainty and would affect the fulfillment of her plan: It was increasingly apparent that he was impotent.

In the afternoon, Siri kept his appointment at the clinic.

The weeks of camaraderie in the desert had fostered a friendship that didn't fade with the return to civilization. The respect the two men held for each other permitted a candor foreign to the nature of both; this now proved invaluable. Siri related his surmise with a facility he would not have deemed possible. David accepted the information calmly.

"Above all, don't worry about it," David instructed. "It's a common enough problem in the human male, usually due to psychological upsets. You've been resisting the plan from the beginning. A sudden decision to cooperate has been made by your mind. Your body has to have time to catch up. What you're experiencing is the lack of instant control you enjoyed as a transfigured being."

Siri grimaced, finding this condition as confining as a straitjacket and just as uncomfortable.

"Well," David said, putting on his best professional manner, "let's get on with the physical. I'm anxious to see how you fared under the rigors of the last few weeks. To all outward appearances, the reversal seems to have had no ill effects; but we'd better make sure. And we'll want to make certain there's no physical reason for this problem."

"I feel fine," Siri answered, taking off his shirt in compliance with the physician's orders. "There's probably nothing wrong that a good night's sleep won't cure. I haven't felt this tired in a hundred years." They both laughed.

Mott administered a heavy dose of sedation to Siri, which, added to the sleepless night, soon took effect. The young scientist found he needed all his professionalism to subject his friend to the test that had now become necessary. The sedative was intended to mask his betrayal. He felt like a traitor. The friendship, which was the basis of Siri's trust, was being subverted for the next step in the experiment.

Mott placed his patient face down on the narrow table constructed specifically for that purpose, carefully monitoring Siri's mind for the least sign of resistance. All his previous subjects, Mott remembered, had been eager volunteers, mostly young men from the nearby university whose interest in the advancement of science was inducement enough.

Now his power, which he had never before been called upon to use, was the only tool he could summon to his aid. He silently prayed for the skill to use it successfully.

Siri lay quiet, unresisting, his breathing deep and even, indicative of the drug-induced torpor. David placed his hand tentatively on Siri's shoulder and concentrated. He gradually increased the pressure. Siri caught his breath, but made no movement of resistance. In that moment, the young doctor wished he had been more faithful in learning to increase his power. He concentrated with all the intensity he could command.

Siri moaned softly. He stiffened, raising his head to protest; but the reaction of his body had already progressed beyond the point where his weakened will could control it. He sagged onto the table. The test was accomplished, the required specimen obtained.

Mott administered a milder, longer-lasting sedative. He prayed there would be no memory of the experience for his friend. And he would use all the means at his command to that end.

The test had proven not only that Siri was fertile, but that his impotence was purely psychological.

With the help of assistants. David got Siri into an ambulance and back to his own room at Pemberly House without awakening him.

David sat watching his friend. He convinced himself that it was his professional duty to monitor his patient's condition under the heavy sedation.

His mind wandered over the events that had led to this moment. Since high school, the most exciting times of his life had been spent in a laboratory surrounded by test tubes. People had passed through his life only as adjuncts to its central theme. Siri was the first person to have held his interest. He was amazed at his own good fortune in having the opportunity to become the friend of this exceptional man. Siri epitomized his ideals: a man who controlled his environment, shaping a life of freedom to his own personality. Wasn't that really the goal of science?

David frowned. He wished he could understand better the love that consumed his friend now. He had never loved anyone. And he was not sure he wanted to. That emotion was nothing but misery to his friend. It led him of his own volition to sacrifice everything, even his devotion to the desert. David could not understand that. If he never had a chance to revisit the Sahara, it would remain the most treasured memory of his life. *Could love for a woman be greater than that?* David shook his head.

As the hours of the night rolled away, David dozed and dreamed. Desert experiences unreeled before his mind's eye. His subconscious cast him in assorted roles: once he was Mohammed efficiently wielding the tattoo needle on the lip of a young stallion; once he was the man with the injuries begging his master's forgiveness. His leg was aching with a vengeance. He woke up.

Siri was still sleeping peacefully. David's leg was cramped under him where he had wedged it between his body and the cushion. It was the real discomfort that he had incorporated into his dreams.

Stevens appeared silently. *Lady Pemberly is worried,* he telepathized.

He's all right, David returned by the same means. *Look for yourself.*

Stevens nodded and disappeared.

David looked at his watch. It was only just after midnight. Siri would not waken for at least another six hours, he estimated. The strenuous weeks just past and a night without sleep had taxed even his extraordinary strength. Even after the sedative wore off, David was sure Siri would continue to sleep.

David settled down for a long wait. *This is foolish,* he thought. *I should get Stevens to fix me a room. I can't do that,* he decided, feeling guilty again. His conscience accused him of betrayal of a sacred trust. He squirmed uneasily, shifting to a more comfortable position, the movement a symbol of attempted justification.

He dozed again. After a while, he dreamed he was at the Fort. The oda dancers were circling before him as on his last night in the desert. This time he looked at them through Siri's eyes. He was not revolted, but felt excitement as they turned and twisted, bowed, and knelt. Their shadows, cast by the torches, enhanced and enlarged the movements. His subconscious, freed now from the restraint imposed by artificial inhibitions, fully appreciated the suggestiveness of the gestures. He appraised their charms as they came, each in her turn, to prostrate themselves before him. The desire mounting through his body made him hot and uncomfortable. He stirred, but did not waken. The dance went on. He knew he had only to nod and the chosen one would be his for the taking. He deliberately postponed the decision, floating in a delicious limbo between fulfillment and the exquisite torture of anticipation.

A sound startled him, bringing him guiltily wide awake.

Siri was leaning up on his elbow watching him. David blushed, thankful that Siri was no longer telepathic.

"What are you doing here?" Siri was surprised at finding David asleep beside his bed.

"You were exhausted," David hastened with an excuse. "I wanted to be handy if you needed me."

"Why should I need you? I'm perfectly all right. You said so yourself. Or have you found something wrong?"

"No, of course not!"

"Then why is one of the world's most eminent scientists playing night nurse to a perfectly healthy patient?"

"Well," David answered lamely, "it just seemed like the right thing to do."

Sir looked at him suspiciously.

David caught his breath. He waited.

Siri shrugged. "Well, then, nurse, how about some breakfast for your patient?"

Relieved, David called Stevens and gave the order. Even without power, Siri was very perceptive. A moment ago, David had almost answered the question in his friend's mind. He couldn't lie, he decided, but there was no necessity to volunteer information. Only if Siri asked, would he answer.

Siri stowed a hearty breakfast.

The clock at the beside stood at five. The light was just beginning to shorten the shadows. The hush of dawn pervaded the garden. David stood at the open window. Even the breeze of the night had departed, leaving a lingering mist swirling at the bases of the trees and mantling the shrubs like a living tableau of the dawn of time. *In the beginning . . .* David thought.

"How about a ride?" Siri suggested stretching, noticing David's seeming reluctance to leave. "We'll probably have to tack the horses ourselves. The grooms won't be about for an hour or so yet. There are some fine animals in the Pemberly stables. Raised most of them myself." Siri grinned, throwing a pair of breeches at David and donning a pair himself. "The trouble is there's little room to ride; but the fences are excellent. You could stand the practice."

"Agreed," David admitted. "And it seems I'll have the full attention of one of the world's foremost horsemen."

"Touché," Siri laughed, clapping him on the shoulder.

It was eight o'clock when they returned to the house.

David was pleased with Siri's good humor and relieved that he had not questioned him about the proceedings at the clinic.

They parted at Lady Pemberly's suite.

Cheira was reading a voluminous report with absorbed attention.

"From Stuart Mervin. He's in the Himalayas. You won't believe what he's found out."

She accepted Siri's greeting kiss absently, handing him the sheets she had already read. Though the hollowness was still in her cheeks, her eyes were lively with suppressed excitement.

"Easy now." Siri smiled, accepting the disordered pages; but Cheira was too intent on reading the tightly written sentences to respond.

Patna, Pradesh. [Mervin headed the report.] My first stop was Calcutta with the idea of familiarizing myself with the dialects of the back country and also to collect whatever information I could from the historians at the university. I decided to let my intentions be known in the hope of getting a lead on these people. The university faculty was helpful, but seemed ignorant of the particular tribe I was in search of. I returned to my room rather depressed. I decided I'd just have to push off into the mountains and hope for the best.

Imagine the surprise with which I received a caller that very night. He introduced himself as Liem [Lee-em] and offered to be my guide during my stay in India. He was a quiet, humble man in his early fifties, or so he appeared at first appraisal. I was struck by his perfect English; and when I so commented, he asked with a shy smile if that wasn't my native tongue. If not, he offered to converse in any language of my choice. Amazed, I tested his knowledge of the half-dozen languages with which I am conversant. He spoke them all as well as or better than I and suppressed a smile when I confessed the limits of my ability. I'm sure he could have gone on with a dozen or so more. Yet he was obviously a native, although not with any of the markings of a member of the caste system. I was embarrassed that my curiosity was so apparent when he informed me that the group to which he belonged did not believe in the caste order, that social system being a misinterpretation of the religious teachings of the country.

My interest arrested, I wanted to know how he had heard of me so quickly since, as yet, I had only settled in. I had spoken to no one except the faculty at the university. It was then he admitted that he had known for weeks of my visit and had come to meet me. I was astounded, especially when he informed me exactly of the purpose of my mission. Why, then, I demanded, hadn't he contacted us before? It was not their way, was the only explanation he would give.

Although he could not tell me if you, mistress, had come from the area, he offered to lead me to people who had powers similar to our own. Then I could make whatever judgement I wished. Of course, I accepted eagerly.

I traveled north with Liem. I discovered that his power of telepathy was

281

better than mine, even to the point of anticipating my thoughts. No barrier I could raise was powerful enough to interfere with his talent. Although I was sure he knew of my ability to teleport, he did not refer to it. Perhaps he was concerned with my ignorance of the country. Whatever his reasons, we traveled by train to the foothills of the mountains where Liem hired horses for the rest of the journey.

Naturally, I had many questions, which Liem seemed more than willing to answer. He explained the truths of the Didaskes—as he called those of altered consciousness. Death, he said, was not a natural law; but, he thought, a sort of transmutation was a better word to use. Even aging does not take place inevitably. Both should be considered as avoidable accidents. Also, disease can be treated in the same way. Knowledge is the answer; that is, true and correct knowledge. Man's ignorance causes aging, disease, and death. Because man is unaware of the cause, he accepts, as inevitable, the effects. Even most accidents are preventable when attention is directed toward causes. What men think of as the prime of life is attainable by all men, for an unlimited period of time or to the extent of their purpose, if they recognize their identity with the One Principle, if they realize that physical life is only one level of that principle and that it is their right to enjoy it until they attain their own transmutation. That is the natural way, he stated.

Our first stop was a village at the base of the mountains. Its principal structure is a marvelous temple made of the finest grained white marble. It is called the Temple of Silence. Its origins have been forgotten by the inhabitants, but the building looks newly constructed. It's in perfect condition. The astounding fact is that it repairs itself. I chipped off a piece of marble myself while Liem stood by smiling at my labor and disbelief. While I held the chip in my hand, the depression in the stone faded away. I was dumbfounded, to say the least. I examined the spot carefully and had to admit that the piece I had removed was replaced. Then the chip I held faded away.

Liem's explanation was that silence is power. It is the necessary environment for the concentration of the mind into a single point of force, which makes the atoms of the universe obedient. It was only then that I noticed that Liem had not spoken or moved during the entire operation.

We made our way deeper into the mountains, examining temples along the way, visiting with Didaskes whom we met working with the people. They were invariably open and friendly, more than willing to allow me to observe their way of life. They communicate telepathically so that our coming was known to all. Their hospitality always included comfortable quarters and plenty of native fare, prepared in surprising but delicious ways.

Now I was prepared for anything. The wonders seemed unceasing. It is a humbling experience. I was beginning to have a new look at transfiguration;

and I had to admit we have just scratched the surface of it.

At one point, we were welcomed about twenty miles from the village of our destination by a group who teleported out to meet us. Apparently this was Liem's home village, which he had not visited for many years. His relatives and friends were impatient to see him. The conversation was boisterous and joyful. They were like a gang of happy children. Imagine my surprise when they all negotiated the river, which separated us from the village, by walking on the water. Not wishing to risk a dousing, I teleported to the other shore—to the delight of Liem and the others. Good-naturedly, they joshed me for my lack of confidence in my power. They decided with mock seriousness that I was inhibited. They insisted that I had set my own limitations. That sure gave me something to think about.

They explain their power as a method of raising the vibrations of their bodies through concentration. Imagination is the only limit, they say. They teased me that mine was so underdeveloped.

Individuals with these powers are widely scattered through Tibet, China, and India, with the largest concentration in the Himalayas; especially those working on the acquisition of power. Something about the altitude and isolation makes the process easier.

I have spoken to several women who have children. Although there have been hints about the ability to conceive, under certain circumstances, I've been unable, to date, to obtain any concrete information. I'm very careful, as their guest, that I don't overstep the bounds of propriety and ruin the chance of learning more. Also, the complexity of the situation and their way of describing it—in what we would consider a very unscientific manner—confuses the issue.

As far as I can estimate, the biggest difference between our society and theirs is the method of reaching a state of expanded consciousness. Each of them has devoted many long years of study to achieve this state, which they must attain through their own efforts. The Didaskes only provide guidance. From some vague feeling of reluctance, I've refrained from explaining our method. Anyway, no one has thought to ask me.

There are a few who claim to have reached an even higher state where they dwell continuously in the invisible—a sort of prolonged teleportation—where the activity of that world becomes available to the consciousness. I've had no trouble seeing and talking to them; but they say that those of unaltered consciousness cannot. I must devise some sort of test to prove this. A difficulty is that I don't wish to insult them by implying disbelief: I learned my lesson at the Temple of Silence. Also, I want to hear about the wonders they describe as the natural environment of their existence.

Liem took me to a village that contains, in caves hewn into the mountains, the records of the ancient people who first practiced transfiguration. He claims that these tablets hold many valuable aids for anyone wishing to achieve that state. However, they must be studied by the individual himself and are of no help if translated by another person. I examined the tablets. They are in no alphabet known to the modern world. I questioned several of the students; but, although I'm sure they tried their best because their sincerity and desire to help was obvious, I could make no sense of their explanations. We all ended with feelings of frustration and I was humbled by my sense of inadequacy. Liem was too kind to remind me that he had told me so, but instead assured me that the records would remain available for my use at any time and that whenever I made a sincere commitment, a knowledge of the strange language would come to me.

Strange experiences are being thrown at me at such a rate that only altered consciousness enables me to handle it. Understanding is still a far-off goal. Sometimes, the wonder is almost too much to bear.

The other day, for instance, I saw a man raised from the dead. Fantastic as this statement sounds, I'm willing to swear to its verity. I was there when the man died. He was an old man who had not undertaken the accomplishment of the altered state until well into middle age. Although he knew about it, he had kept postponing the years of study for one reason or another. Evidently, he waited too long. His old heart gave out before he reached his goal. Fortunately, a group of Didaskes were in the village at the time. With none of the devices of modern science, using only the power of combined concentration, six Didaskes brought the man back to life. His revived state was accompanied by all the powers of altered consciousness. When we left the village several days later, the man was not only in good health, but had recovered most of the appearances of youth.

And then there is the power of creation. I can't describe my amazement when I first witnessed it! The Didaskes provide themselves with food and money whenever necessary. What would happen to the economy of the world if everyone could do that? On attempting imitation, I have found I cannot do this. Liem assures me that it's only because my mind refuses to accept the possibility. He may be right! All my determination hasn't been able to overcome this limitation—much to Liem's amusement! He calls it another one of my culturally induced inhibitions. I'm learning the value of scrutinizing beliefs and of accepting no idea indiscriminately.

The Didaskes have also developed another use of power that seems curious to me, but probably only because the need for it never arises in our society. They can project their thoughts onto a wall and produce any scenes they wish, complete with audio, by the regulation of the atoms of the air. The combined concentration of several is needed. It is a valuable aid to the more advanced students. In this way, they have visualized for me what they say happened thousands of years ago to the founders of their tenets. They can do some projecting into the future, too; but like all predictions only that future holds verification.

The Didaskes practice healing whenever asked by the villagers. They never offer their services, as they believe it's wrong to encourage others to be dependent on them. They try to foster a desire in those around them to seek transfiguration for themselves; but the long years of study and the strict discipline are a deterrent to most. However, the art of healing is interesting because it's the same ability we use in a different way. For example, a woman was healing a child's broken leg. She knelt beside him. I was standing by as an observer. When the woman moved to rise, I extended my hand to help her as a matter of courtesy. The sensation shooting along my nerves left me absolutely helpless momentarily. Ironically, the woman apologized for her thoughtlessness.

One of the Didaskes explained the meaning of power as a means to control one's environment: weather, fire, water, and even other men. Nevertheless, he cautioned, power must be handled carefully and only for the good humanity; or it will turn upon the possessor and destroy him. He explained that this happens because only the good is positive and projects energy. Obviously, they are in awe of what they can do as they don't understand the physical basis for their ability. To them, it is entirely supernatural and spiritual and as such is treated with deeply ingrained religious connotations. With the power to provide the perfect existence for themselves, they have no reason to seek scientific explanations. Our own efforts along those lines are probably the result of a different heritage.

Only once did I witness the use of power to cause pain. This was the situation: The villagers are sometimes plagued by roving bands of primitives who live by plunder. In this instance, the usual offers of food and trinkets failed to dissuade the marauders. This time the threat was a cooperative effort of several gangs. They sent a messenger into the village with the ultimatum that unless all the animals and grain were surrendered, every person would be annihilated. One of the Didaskes met the fellow and heard his terms. The man's arrogance was too much of an insult to be tolerated; and the Didaske's anger blazed forth. The intensity of the emotion threw the man to the ground, unconscious. I was standing some distance away but the force of the vibrations hit me like a bolt of lightning. My muscles were paralyzed. It was hours before the tension disappeared. Needless to say, the Didaskes made short work of the invasion, sending the superstitious oppressors fleeing for their lives.

Later we discussed this, to me, new facet of diffusing energy without direct contact. Liem explained that the body could be used like a generator, collecting and magnifying energy. It could then be projected outward, by an act of will, with an irresistible force. It can also be used as a protective shield, deflecting even bullets. In fact, whatever the force being used, it can be turned upon the attacker to become the instrument of his own destruction. Resistance magnifies the force, causing retribution to be swift and total. Conversely, lack of resistance, or acceptance, heals the possessor as well as he to whom the energy is directed.

I asked Liem how this function could be acquired, as I didn't think it was an ordinary attribute of altered consciousness. He intimated that it was an additional aspect which required greater control and stricter discipline. He described the method most often used as including breathing exercises, but mainly requiring enormous powers of concentration—relaxed concentration from which every trace of tension has been removed, like catching a piece of down floating in the air or like trying to contain cotton wool. The mind and body must be still so the cosmic force can enter unobstructed. Liem added that the possessor of this power could stay young forever.

Liem has promised to take me to the annual meeting of the *chelas*, or students. This actually includes everyone, as they all consider themselves students, forever seeking the next higher level of consciousness. Liem says that then I'll be able to make my mission known; and if anyone holds the knowledge I seek, he will reveal it. No knowledge is ever withheld from those who seek it, Liem stated with certainty.

Mervin concluded the report with a request for permission to contact Jim Connors to ask him to come out and do a few tests. The Didaskes had indicated their willingness to participate.

Cheira handed the last page to Siri. She watched his expression.

"What do you think?" she asked eagerly, barely waiting for him to finish reading.

"Now, don't get your hopes too high," he chided. "So far all he's found are other people in the world with power similar to ours and who use it in some different ways. That shouldn't come as too much of a surprise. Even scientific discoveries are made by widely separated researchers at the same time without them having knowledge of each other's work. Besides, there are a few statements in the report which don't add up."

Cheira questioned this. In her enthusiasm, she had noticed nothing contradictory. Her heart skipped a beat.

"Those people have excellent communication," Siri explained, "yet Mervin has to attend a meeting to find out what he wants to know. He also said that they have no scientific knowledge of what they're doing; yet many of the explanations he gave sound to me like an astute scientist explaining a very complicated process in layman's terms and tying them to moral restrictions with the very intention of preventing abuses. I think Mervin mistook their nonaggressiveness for religious fanaticism."

Cheira sank back, the excitement dying out of her face. She saw the logic of Siri's argument.

"Don't look so disappointed, my love!" Siri put his arm around her. "Did you think that anyone who has these powers could also be simple?"

"But Mervin said they are open and very friendly!" she objected.

"Of course, they are. Remember, they have received him on their terms. Apparently, they have known about us all along, but haven't made their presence known to us." Siri paused, a new idea flashing into his mind. "But, of course, they have!" He got up to pace the floor. "There have been other anthropological expeditions to that area over the years; but only Mervin has ever contacted these people. Doesn't that make you wonder? It certainly would have been easy enough to stay out of his way, which must be what they did with other explorers. And this fellow—this Liem—has almost overemphasized his willingness to help. He and his friends have a pat explanation for everything that happens. On the other hand, he could be making sure that Mervin only sees what they want him to see."

"But why?" Cheira asked, perplexed, absently rubbing the tiny mark on her breast. The habitual gesture went unregistered by them both.

Siri flopped back onto the couch. "I don't know," he admitted reluctantly, his idea having reached a dead end. He looked at Cheira and saw tears in her eyes. He pulled her to him, cradling her head against his chest.

"Does it mean so much to you?" he asked, his voice tender.

"More now than ever," she whispered. "I counted so much on the reversal to help me remember. But nothing has happened. I can't get beyond the blank wall I seem to have in my brain. Wang Lu always advised me not to worry about it, that I would remember when the time was right. But I've waited so long," she ended plaintively.

"Well, I'll love you anyway." Siri smiled, hugging her.

"But I want to know who I am," she persisted.

Siri laughed. "If it's ancestry you want, I have enough for both of us. My family goes back a thousand years. In fact, since I've never particularly wanted that, you can have it all. I'll gladly give you all those hoary old Vikings."

"It's only because you have so much that you can be so flippant," she accused.

"There's only one that I want and need," Siri returned.

Jennie interrupted with breakfast.

"Sir John is waiting, my lady," she announced.

"Let him wait," Siri snapped with a glance at Jennie that sent her scurrying from the room.

Even though Jennie had spent many private hours arguing with herself that Siri no longer had any power, that even her small power was greater, one direct word still left her quaking, her obedience reflexive.

John was pacing the hall when Jennie came flying out.

"What's the matter?" he demanded, grabbing her arm. He could feel her tremble. His grip relaxed when he read her thoughts. "Isn't it time you stopped letting him frighten you?"

It was perhaps an hour later when Siri stepped into the hall.

"Your mistress awaits." He swept a bow to Jennie. As he straightened, his eyes met John's. They were filled with mocking laughter.

John cursed him, calling him callous and cruel, lacing the words liberally with descriptive adjectives. Siri threw back his head and laughed. He strode away to his room without deigning to answer.

CHAPTER XVIII

Dr. Mott was waiting to see Cheira when John left. After much thought, he had decided that Cheira must be told. It would be her decision to call off the rest of the experiment or wait an indeterminable time before it could be resumed. That course held many inherent dangers because of the prolongation of the reversal. He was sure in his own mind that Siri's condition was only temporary and that Cheira was bound to find out one way or another. Perhaps he could spare his friend further humiliation if she knew before some accidental encounter made it too plain.

"You must understand," he told her earnestly. "He's been under terrific strain. For a proud man, he's been subjected to the most humiliating conditions in the last few weeks. Even his strong will cannot control the rebellion of his body."

Cheira bowed her head. "But there's danger in prolonging this state. I want him to return to transfiguration as soon as possible."

"No more dangerous than for yourself, my lady."

"That's a risk I'm prepared to take—with my own life, for my own reasons—but not with his." She sat thoughtfully for a moment. "How long?"

Mott shook his head. "There is no way of knowing," he admitted. "I'd advise canceling the rest of the experiment. After all, we've accomplished a great deal already. Others can take it from here."

"No. There may be another way."

Before he could stop himself, he found he was following her thoughts. He didn't understand most of what she was thinking, but the part he did understand shocked him.

"Is that a wise course, my lady?" he burst out.

Cheira glared at him. "I must do what is necessary. It will be my responsibility." She rose, the cold, imperious look that he had not seen since the reversal underlining her decision.

"Please be careful," David ventured.

She looked at him, startled. Then realizing that he knew what she had been thinking, she blushed. "I still forget sometimes."

289

"Perhaps you should wait a little while," Mott suggested, taking advantage of the softening of her attitude.

"The longer I wait, the more danger he's exposed to. Nothing must ever happen to him."

David acquiesced, recognizing the expression in her eyes. He had seen Siri look like that when he spoke of his love for Cheira. He had learned not to oppose the strength of that emotion, even if he couldn't understand it.

"Go to Siri now," she ordered. "Tell him I'm resting or whatever excuse seems most plausible. Keep him away until dinner. Have him join me then."

Feeling that further attempts at dissuasion would be futile and having no alternative to offer, David obeyed.

Cheira paced steadily after Mott left. Her thoughts raced over the plan. She fought down the trepidation they evoked. *My love,* she decided, will *see us through.* She called Jennie.

"Go to the tower and summon Tiana," she instructed.

Jennie's eyes grew wide with doubt.

"You can do it," Cheira encouraged, shoving the girl toward the door. "Don't let anyone discover you. And don't let anyone see Tiana when she comes."

Cheira calculated swiftly. It would take Tiana at least an hour to arrive, even if Jennie reached her directly. The thought of the little maid concentrating with all her might tilted the corners of Cheira's mouth in the hint of a smile; but her eyes remained pensive. She paced the floor, her thoughts mulling the plan over and over. She hesitated.

If Siri found out ahead of time, what would his reaction be? Did he know about these things? A tremor shook her. She squared her shoulders and resumed the trek back and forth across the room. *Would he be angry?* Maybe she should follow Mott's suggestion and call off the rest of the experiment.

But it was no longer really the experiment, she reasoned. She didn't care about that; she cared about Siri. So much! She wanted his child more than anything in the world. There was a way! And it wouldn't jeopardize his safety! The time was now. Dr. Carpenter had told her that only yesterday.

She tossed her head impatiently. Since the reversal, she had been timid and vacillating. Never as long as she could remember had she hesitated on a course of action once determined. Well, she'd have to overcome that in spite of her condition.

She threw herself onto the sofa, feeling the pressure on her heart that made it hard to breathe. *Never before,* she admitted, *have I known the meaning of love—a love so intense that it causes a physical reaction assuaged only by the presence of my loved one.*

Restlessly, she went to stand by the fireplace, unconsciously assuming Siri's habit. She relived again the happiness of their first days together, the gentleness of his touch, the sweetness of his arms about her, her realization of what it means to be a woman.

The dull glow of the symbol above the mantel attracted her attention. The letters stood out harshly, threateningly. The experience of that day at Lamborn Heath filled her mind. Had she thrown away that precious existence for all time? Why had it seemed vaguely familiar? Siri had been overwhelmed by it. She hadn't. She tried to recall. Nothing but a faint feeling of danger responded to her effort. Was the symbol warning her? What did it mean—those letters she bore on her breast like the brand of a slave? Did she belong to someone?

She recalled the odd coincidence of the symbol's acquisition. It was on the occasion of the first anniversary of her appearance in Darjeeling. Wang Lu presented it to her. It was like a birthday present. He implied that he had picked it up by chance at the market. She had been pleased and hadn't thought to question him further. Later, the symbol had become so ordinary and familiar that she had forgotten about it.

She laughed nervously, turning away. What sort of illusion was she indulging in? But the feeling persisted and the idea came into her head that the answer was somehow to be found in what she and Siri had experienced. Unconsciously, she touched the tiny mark on her breast. *If I could only remember,* she thought, frowning; but the dark cloud remained firmly anchored over her memory.

A soft knock interrupted her pondering. Tiana rushed in, greeting her with a concerned, perplexed expression.

"Is anything wrong?"

Cheira laughed. "Not really." She hugged Tiana. The incongruity of Tiana's desert costume in Cheira's very European drawing room was a ridiculous picture. "It's just that I don't have much time." Quickly, she confided to her friend what she wanted to do and why. "As Jennie says, sometimes it's very inconvenient to be ordinarily human. So I have to ask you to do my errands for me."

"Are you sure you want to do this?" Tiana frowned. "Siri will be furious if he ever finds out."

"How will he find out?" Cheira asserted with a confidence she didn't feel. "Now go to Lira and tell her what I want. You must be back before dinner."

Siri was unaware of Lira's existence. She had died many years ago—or so he thought.

Through secret methods of her own, Lira had discovered Cheira's whereabouts months before Siri discovered her at Arx Vetus. Cheira secretly accepted Lira into the society. The time Cheira had spent at the Fort had created a common bond between the two women: the love of one and the fear of the other, their emotional responses to the same man. Only the desert way of life could be the basis for such a friendship.

For many years now, Lira had lived and worked among her own people. Her efforts improved their living conditions and introduced them to the value of education.

Only the sorrow of the necessary separation from the master she worshipped blighted her life.

Her love for Cheira had welcomed the announcement of the marriage. She had never doubted Siri's love for the mistress of Arx Vetus. Her own misery was nothing, if only he were happy.

Surreptitiously, Lira satisfied her longing to see him. It was an easy task to enter the Fort with a wandering caravan and, in the guise of a pilgrim seeking rest from the tedium of the journey, be allowed the hospitality of the tribe without anyone's considering it necessary to announce her presence to their leader.

Only once, however, had she been able to watch him freely with little fear of detection. This was the last time at Imla Dun, after the reversal; she had had him before her for weeks from early in the morning until late at night. From the safety of anonymity among the group of women who brought coffee to the trainers, she could watch his movements with impunity.

She loved best the early mornings when, in the coolness of the dawn, he would work, stripped to the waist, Western fashion, wholly absorbed in the animal under his tutelage. It was torture to see the play of his muscles beneath the tanned skin. The sweet agony of remembrance! Her body ached with longing as she watched his hands caressing to calmness the silken hide of a nervous colt.

She fully realized the futility of her actions. She accepted the fact that he would never again belong to her, that she no longer existed in his world. But she did exist, and no amount of self-castigation could still the love in her heart. She envied David Mott for the easy camaraderie he enjoyed with Siri. She raged against the culture that forbade her even his friendship.

She made it a practice to follow as soon as she heard the men leave in the morning. It was only a ten-minute walk to the training corrals. In the bustle of beginning a workday, no one paid her any attention.

One time, she had crept thoughtlessly close to the fence, absorbed in the skill Siri exhibited in putting his young mount through its first lesson on the two-track. She was unprepared when he dismounted abruptly in front of her.

"Bring me some coffee, woman," he commanded.

She gasped involuntarily. "It's not here yet, master," she managed to reply, pulling the veil more concealingly across her face. He had hesitated in his stride, frowning at the sound of her voice as if trying to recall a memory. Then he shrugged. "As soon as it gets here, then."

Her breath was stopped in her throat the whole time. She vowed to be more careful in the future. It was only the absence of his power that had saved her from detection. She hurried back to the tents to speed the loitering women on their way. She herself remained behind, the incident having destroyed her composure for that day.

David found that circumstances contrived to make compliance with Cheira's directive an easy matter. Siri was waiting impatiently for him.

"Well?"

"Her ladyship's recovery is occurring rapidly and satisfactorily," David answered. "Her condition was purely emotional. Now all she needs is rest. She promised to do just that if I would ask you to join her for dinner."

"Good!" Siri laughed, relief in his voice. "Carl just called and those fillies we picked out at the Fort are arriving in Edinburgh this afternoon. I'd like to be there. Ahmed is worried about Customs. They're already giving him a hassle. Quarantine rules are vague, it seems; and anybody's interpretation stands as long as they have enough authority. Want to come along?"

"Sure," David agreed eagerly.

The long, monotonous drive did nothing for Siri's temper. He cursed the roads and the reversal for his lack of power, which made the long drive necessary.

David tried to be appropriately sympathetic, hiding the joy he felt at having the whole day with his friend.

Siri's mood improved when the horses were safely unloaded and the Customs officials had decided that the Earl of Zetland could fulfill the quarantine laws adequately by isolating the animals at Lamborn Heath. There was even time to escort the animals to their new home and personally supervise the stabling, then outline a program of conditioning and training that Siri wanted Ahmed to follow.

Late in the afternoon, they headed back to London.

"You know, David," Siri told him thoughtfully, "the moors do have their attraction. Lamborn is a beautiful place. I guess I'm just beginning to appreciate it. I used to think it was too confining. My father always made such a job of it. Did you notice how well the barns are constructed?" Siri's thoughts slid onto the subject that interested him most. "There's room for thirty horses. I remember when it was full."

David smiled in answer.

"When I was a child," Siri continued, reminiscing, "I spent every spare minute in the stable. Every inch was explored regularly. Every animal a close, respected friend." Siri sighed. "It was a long time ago."

A heavy rain swept over the countryside, hastening the night. The car droned on, fleeing southward. Neither man realized that it headed to a rendezvous with destiny.

David settled back in the seat. He liked the sense of isolation the black night provided. It was like catapulting through space, the headlights making visible only that portion immediately ahead. Idly, he wondered about the feasibility of space travel using teleportation. *One step at a time,* his scientific mind reminded him. Belatedly, he began to worry about the fatigue of the trip for Siri. Rest was one of the important requirements of Connors' regime. His experiment had proved beyond doubt the importance of rest to combat disease and nourish health.

The worry increased when David thought of Cheira. *What is she planning to do?* Modern science had determined that aphrodisiacs were an ineffective superstition. The word she had been thinking about meant nothing to him. He wasn't even sure it was a drug.

"How long?" Siri broke the silence, jarring David back to the present.

"I don't know," David replied honestly.

Siri laughed; but the sound was not happy. "We've reached a stalemate, it seems."

The rain stopped with the drifting away of the heavy clouds. A full moon appeared to cast an eerie glow over the damp landscape. A blinding glare on the wet pavement caused Siri to slow down.

"I guess it won't make much difference if we're late," he said.

While waiting for Tiana's return, Cheira set about to enhance her already perfect beauty.

She lingered in the bath. The silken sensuousness of the water, combining with the audacity of her plan, nudged the recall of her first days at the Fort.

Lira had insisted on a strict routine. To Cheira's horror, she supervised even the most intimate details of grooming. Cheira's initiation into the rituals of the oriental harem shocked her sensibilities. The impressions were permanent. In passing, she wondered if Siri had any idea of what went on. *Probably not,* she decided.

The afternoon hours were reserved for instruction in sexual accomplishments. Lira insisted that everyone be present. Even illness was not considered a good excuse, as Cheira quickly learned. That she could possibly be in a position where the knowledge was useful amazed her.

She had Jennie brush her hair until it gleamed like pure gold, its heavy mass cascading over her shoulders, dipping to her waist.

The gown she chose was of finest moire. Its silken threads appeared to shimmer and flow with the muted colors of autumn leaves, complementing the color of her eyes. The bodice was contrived to cling without visible support; her shoulders were bare. The skirt fell simply in gores, revealing the lines of the body intermittently with its movement.

Cheira's preparations extended to strict instructions to Jennie and the unobtrusive role she was to play in serving dinner.

Tiana was uneasy as she handed Cheira the packet.

"Lira has acceded to your wishes," she said. "But she strongly objects to the use of the plant. She wonders if you're sufficiently knowledgeable of the possible consequences."

"She's forgotten how thorough were my instructions," Cheira retorted with a toss of her head. "She was a very strict teacher. I'm sure none of her pupils has ever forgotten the lessons she taught."

Siri arrived promptly at nine. He kissed Cheira's hand, telling her how beautiful she was, surveying her appreciatively. He was relaxed but subtly distant. His actions convinced Cheira that what Mott had told her was correct. Any other man might act this way, but not Siri. The last trace of indecision was removed. She would go ahead with her plan.

Mott, who had accompanied Siri, stayed just long enough for a drink.

His unyielding attitude informed Cheira of his disapproval.

It's the only way, she thought glaring at him. *Maybe I can't know your thoughts; but you can know mine. So if you have a better idea, say so.*

He said nothing.

She was glad to see him leave.

Siri's mood remained unchanged during dinner, the formality of his manner forestalling any gesture of intimacy. Cheira imitated his attitude, cooperating with the impersonal conversation, biding her time.

Siri gave her a detailed account of the successful sale in Touggourt. He praised Mohammed for the excellent job he had done.

"The average price is 20 per cent higher than last year," he said, acting as if the information were the most important happening in his life.

Cheira put on her most interested smile.

"Altair was the highest," Siri continued. "He was bought by the Bursley Stud in Melbourne. He'll be the leading sire. They've big plans for upgrading the stock out there."

"And the others?" Cheira encouraged, lest he notice that it was she who kept his glass filled, Jennie being, she feared, conspicuously absent.

Siri launched into a lengthy account. At any other time Cheira would have been truly interested. Instead, her heart pounded. She was distracted by the loud thumping and prayed for the signs to appear.

"And . . . " Siri yawned, then smiled in embarrassment. "I guess that long drive to Lamborn took more out of me than I thought. Do you mind if I lie down for a while?" He got up, going to the couch. "I forget how limited . . . " His voice trailed off.

Cheira brought a pillow to sit on the floor beside him. Relaxed, he smiled dreamily, stroking her hair. "So beautiful . . . "

She noted the soft slurring of the words with satisfaction.

Timidly, at first, she kissed him. Then she let her mouth creep along the line of his jaw, her lips caressing, lingering, moving down the skin of his throat. Her fingers unbuttoned his shirt. Her tongue skillfully tortured the sensitive areas of his chest, revealing a knowledge known only to a few. Her hand deftly opened the buckle of his belt. Lira had, indeed, taught her well. His body responded. She smiled, continuing to follow the pattern, growing more and more aggressive.

She was unprepared when Siri suddenly tensed. Grabbing a fistful of her hair, he jerked her head back.

"Where did you learn that?" he demanded, the lethargy gone from his eyes, but the slurring still evident in his low, angry voice. She gasped as the pain of his hold deluged her skull. The words stuck in her throat. "You put caru in my wine," he accused. "Where did you get it?" His voice was a low growl.

"Please, don't!" was all she could whisper.

"Where?" She closed her eyes, but could not avert her head as his hand crashed across her mouth.

"Lira!" she managed to cry through the taste of blood trickling down her throat.

"You lie!" He twisted her arm behind her back, bending her head backward with a vicious jerk of the hand that gripped her hair. "Lira is dead!"

"No! She's transfigured!"

"She agreed to this? I don't believe it!"

"Yes! Yes!" The words were barely audible. The position in which he held her choked off speech. A dizzying swirl floated before her eyes; her body sagged, held upright only by his grip on her hair. She tried to scream, but no sound came.

"So you know," the low slurred word were almost inaudible. "You think I need help to be a man. Bitch!" He hissed. She felt his fingers grasp the bodice of her dress. A single yank parted the fragile threads. "So you have chosen this time." His voice held a hard, cruel edge as his eyes scanned her trembling, naked body. "What a fool I've been to blame myself all these years! You deserved no better treatment!"

Loosing his hold, he let her drop to the floor. He threw himself down on top of her, not bothering to spare her the full burden of his weight. "I believed no atonement I could ever make would make me worthy of you," he snarled. "Whore!"

She screamed with the pain that shot up from her loins, churning in the pit of her stomach. "Please, Siri, please," she gasped. "Oh, God, I'm sorry."

"God!" he mocked bitterly, anger increasing his passion. "God damn you!" His mouth closed over hers, forcing her lips apart, causing a fresh flow of blood from the clotting cut. The pressure of his body on her ribs was suffocating her.

She felt a drop of blood travel along her cheek, pass under her ear, and come to rest in her hair. It took forever. The sensation was revolting, the final agony. She wrenched her head away, gasping for breath.

297

Digging her nails into his back in a futile effort to free herself, she felt the shudder of agonized pleasure pass through his body. For a moment, he lay still.

"Lira forgot to tell you that caru dissolves all of a man's inhibitions," he snapped, glaring at her; the words were so slurred she could barely understand. He stood over her, a look of hatred in his eyes. Stepping over her, he left.

She curled up instinctively, drawing her knees tight to her chest. The position eased the stabbing pains she still felt in her abdomen.

Jennie rushed in when she saw Siri thunder out. He slammed the door with such uncontrolled strength that even the thick walls trembled. A look of horror crossed her face when she saw Cheira crumpled on the floor. She sent a telepathic summons to Dr. Mott.

John intercepted her message.

Cheira lay where Siri had left her, covered only by a rug Jennie had hastily thrown over her. She was sobbing, the sound muted by the blood-stained fingers she held tightly clamped over her mouth.

John clenched his fists, surveying the scene. His mouth twisted into an ugly snarl. He stared at the torn remnants of Cheira's gown. The sorry shreds fanned his anger. Nothing now could stop him from taking revenge on the man he despised.

Mott arrived in minutes.

One look gave him all the information he needed. "A brilliant plan!" he said sarcastically.

"Doctor!" Jennie was shocked.

"You're right!" David conceded. He picked Cheira up and carried her into the bedroom. There was little gentleness in his quick examination. "Except for a few bruises, you're all right," he said, unsympathetically.

"Find him," Cheira begged, fighting down involuntary sobs. "Save him from John!"

"Good Lord!" David burst out. He'd forgotten Siri in the disgust of the whole situation. "John was here?" he questioned Jennie. She nodded. He knew Siri could expect no mercy from the man whose loyalty was a religion. "Siri can't defend himself!" David rushed into the hall.

He paused, directing his mind to scan the manor, floor by floor. If John forgot, in anger, to mask his thoughts, David might just pick up their location. Luck was with him. *I can't believe it,* he thought. The vibrations he contacted came from the deserted dungeons three floors below. Only the vermin had remembered their existence for the last two hundred years.

The tableau David beheld was reminiscent of the darkest days of the Inquisition. He was shocked into silence, his stomach turning over, threatening rebellion.

Siri was suspended by his hands, tied to an old rusty ring high in the wall. The seepage wet the few remnants of clothing stuck to his body. A guard had striped his back with a knotted whip until the flesh hung in shreds. The open wounds exposed the raw muscles underneath. The blood was already beginning to clot in rivulets. His head lolled sideways. He was unconscious.

The guard was dousing the limp figure with water in an attempt to revive him. John cursed the man, impatient to resume the punishment.

"Stop!" David shouted, his voice echoing down the empty corridors. He swallowed hard, the revulsion rising up in his throat. "Your mistress commands!"

John turned, the expression of hate contorting his features. "I haven't used my power on him or he'd be dead already," John spat out defensively. He was bent forward at an ugly angle, his neck bulging above his collar. *Like a vulture,* David thought. And he saw what the vile emotion could do to even one of altered consciousness when it gained mastery. No matter that love and loyalty had spawned it, the results were the same.

David took a step forward, prepared for battle. He concentrated all the energy he could muster. "Cheira sent me for him." His voice was icy, leaving no room for doubt. "Cut him down!" He held his breath for the endless time that John glared at him.

John dropped his gaze, motioning to the guard to obey.

David exhaled sharply. "Take him to his room!" he shouted at the guard, then turned threateningly to John. "Just stay out of this!"

John sagged against the wall. David's use of Cheira's name had jolted him back from the insanity of vengeance. David's will had been able to overcome his own stronger one weakened by the intensity of the negative emotion. His arms hung limply by his side.

"Is she all right?" John's voice was barely audible.

David answered tersely, affirmatively, and swung away to tend his patient. He thought with wonder at the age that had birthed these men. They had bred into them a violence and code of behavior that had no equivalent in the modern world. With a grimace, he admitted that the men of the twentieth century were pale by comparison. Hurrying to minister to his friend, he put the thought out of his mind, passing no judgment on the observation.

Siri lay on his stomach; the thick bandages artfully held together the torn skin of his back. When he regained consciousness, David was waiting beside the bed.

"Get me a drink!" Siri eyed the young doctor distastefully.

David obediently brought him a double Scotch.

"I assume you stopped him from killing me." Siri downed the liquor in one gulp. He groaned as the movement sent searing flashes crisscrossing his back. "I don't thank you."

"Cheira forbade it," David answered truthfully.

Siri handed David the glass with a grimace. "Damn her!"

David refilled the glass and handed it back to the prone figure. He let the curse hang in the air, deliberately smothering the sympathy he felt. He said harshly, "Her first thought was for your safety. Any other man would jump at the chance to take your place."

"I'd kill him!" Siri admitted. "And her, too!"

David hid a smile of relief. It was the answer he had hoped to illicit. He wished he knew more psychology; then, in the same thought, he wondered how it could help him deal with a man whose ideas had been formed before the discipline existed.

"Or have I already done that? John must have had a good reason." Siri painfully heaved himself off the bed and made his way to the liquor table.

"She's all right!"

"I can't remember." Siri stared at Mott. He brushed a hand across his eyes. "Only a few lucid moments that I shudder to think of. The rest . . ." He let the words hang in the air. Tipping his head, he downed the glass of fiery liquid.

"It might be helpful if you'd tell me what you do remember," David suggested.

Siri thoughtfully leaned against the table.

"Are you familiar with caru?"

David shook his head. "Never heard of it."

"It's an extract from a moss that grows in oases only after one of the infrequent rains. It must be gathered immediately. In twenty-four hours, it has dried up without leaving a trace. The desert people prize it highly for its ability to suppress inhibitions and increase passion—with indiscriminate use—to the point of frenzy. Tribesmen use it before important battles. It enables them to face death fearlessly. Harem women use it to arouse the flagging urges of their masters, thereby saving their place in the master's esteem. After all, he is the means of their existence."

300

"That's what Cheira gave you last night?" David was incredulous. "But where did she get it?"

"I don't know," Siri shrugged, then winced at the pain the movement caused. "I'm having trouble believing her explanation. She might have told me anything at that point. I'm not even sure I heard her correctly." Siri smiled ruefully. "I was stupid not to have known sooner. By the time I discovered what she was doing, I had already lost control. I can never forgive myself for that. It took all the strength I could muster to get myself out of there. Though not before the damage was done, I guess."

Siri poured another drink. David didn't try to stop him. He sympathized with Siri's desire for oblivion. He was feeling guilty himself.

"You needn't take all the blame to yourself," David confessed. "I told her about your condition hoping to forestall her finding out in a way that would be humiliating for you. And I knew she was planning something when she ordered me to keep you away all day. I should have warned you."

Siri looked at the young doctor searchingly.

"You're sure I didn't hurt her?"

"Positive," David asserted, wondering what Siri had in mind and hoping that his quick examination of Cheira was correct. "Why?"

Siri threw back his head and laughed. The bitter laughter rolled up from deep in his throat. Then he gasped with the pain it caused. He poured another half-glass and downed it.

David stood up in alarm. Siri was rapidly reaching the danger point.

Siri laughed again and staggered back to the bed.

"Don't ever underestimate the deviousness of a woman determined to get her way. She thought she could control the situation. Well, it backfired!" Siri slumped over, still chuckling. He was asleep.

David was sure that the groan he heard was not from the pain of the wounds.

David left instructions with Stevens that Siri was not to be disturbed. No one was to be admitted to the room. He stressed *no one.*

He met Dr. Carpenter in the hall. She reported, "Besides a few bruises, her ladyship is unharmed."

"Thank God!" David said, hurrying into Cheira's suite.

Cheira was ensconced in mounds of pillows. *Looking quite bright and cheery,* David thought.

She sat up expectantly, a worried expression coming into her face.

"I sent Dr. Carpenter for news. Did she find you? Is Siri very angry?"

David was amazed at her calm after the ordeal she had just gone through. *Or had it been an ordeal? Could the gleam in her eyes possibly be contentment? Should I tell her what John had done? That would wipe that look off her face. Siri, it seemed, had appraised her correctly. Of all the possible reactions, I would never have thought of this one. It would serve her right if Siri left her. Still, it is not my place to bear stories. I've probably done enough damage already by doing that. I'm a scientist. Remember that,* he reminded himself sternly.

"No, he's not angry," David answered, wondering if his estimate of the situation were correct. How would Siri feel when he sobered up? "He blames himself for not knowing sooner. He told me a little about the drug. May I ask your ladyship about it?"

Cheira blushed, looking away. A vision of Lira swearing her to silence forever flashed through her mind. Her irritation at the memory of that silly promise, which forged a bond of sisterhood among the desert women, made her turn defensively on the physician. Ignoring the question, she countered with one of her own. "When can I see him?"

David, smarting under the rebuff, already blaming her for the torture his friend had endured, retorted, "Whenever you wish. You have but to command." He made no effort to mask the belligerence in his tone. His hand itched to slap her face.

Cheira was at first surprised. Then, accepting the challenge he had thrown at her, she glared at him.

"Get out!" Her voice was low and venomous, more thought than actual sound. The bruise on her lip was emphasized by a white circle.

"Whatever your ladyship desires," David answered in the same tone. He bowed, the attitude of his body making a mockery of the action.

David's scientific mind stood coolly aside, observing with interest the body to which it was attached, like a collector watching the final squirming of a bug under his microscope. He seethed with anger—the emotion so strong, it made his face red and his muscles tremble, the more so because of his inability to vent it. He cursed the code that forbade him to challenge Cheira outright. He clenched his firsts, his sympathy vacillating between John and Siri. *Both men are victims,* he decided. He cursed his own part in making the situation possible.

He got as far as the hall when the realization of how far he had already gone hit him. He felt too weak to hold himself upright. His lungs collapsed with an outrush of breath. *Instead of helping Siri, you've probably made it worse,* he castigated. *If she sends for Siri before his wounds heal, she'll know what John has done, too.* What his own punishment would be interested him less, except for the certainty that Cheira would not spare him. He sighed. At that moment, he was too tired to care.

She'll probably banish me to some fishing village up the coast, he thought wryly. His imagination promptly obliged with the picture of a cluttered, musty office through which paraded an endless line of fishwives with rheumatism. The imagery was not conducive to softening his feeling of resentment.

One thing was certain, his actions had done nothing to help his friend. How Siri would handle the inevitable meeting with Cheira, David couldn't even guess. If Siri continued blaming himself even after he sobered up, Cheira had won again. David had a feeling it would be that way, always.

Well, he thought resignedly, discarding the impulse to go back and apologize, *no point in making matters worse. With your usual finesse, you've really botched it! Go back to the clinic where you belong.*

He straightened up, about to obey his own advice.

CHAPTER XIX

John and Stevens came rushing down the corridor. John was flushed and angry. Stevens bewildered.

"Where did you take him?" John accused.

"But I tell you, sir, he didn't leave," Stevens insisted.

John stopped before David. "This time you'll not get away with it."

"What are you talking about?" David frowned, the irritation flooding back to the surface. He was too tired to tackle John again. He turned on Stevens as the handiest victim. "I told you to stay with him!"

David eyed John suspiciously, trying to detect a trick. Without conscious consent, his mind began scanning the building.

"Forget it!" John snapped. "We've already done that! He's not here, I tell you."

"So, then, where is he?" David retorted. "Can't you even keep your eyes on an ordinary human?"

"I swear he never left the suite," Stevens protested. "I was there all the time."

"He must still be there, then," David said sarcastically. "Unless he climbed out the window."

"He's gone!" Stevens insisted, his voice perplexed as if he couldn't believe his own words. "I went in to see how he was when his excellency inquired. He wasn't there!"

"Impossible!" David still felt that John might have something to do with this, but he could detect no concealing barrier to John's thoughts. *I will have to believe them,* he thought tiredly.

"We both checked. Thoroughly!" John interjected. "And I didn't do anything to him!"

"Okay!" David gave in. "Find him then!" David turned on his heel. He wanted nothing so much at the moment than to forget the whole mess for a while. He was a scientist, a dealer in facts. Understanding the motives that drove his fellowmen was not in his line. When he tried, he just muddled it worse. *From now on,* he promised himself, *I will tend strictly to my own busi-*

304

ness. He needed sleep desperately. He summoned the effort to teleport back to the clinic.

"Wait!" he heard John call, but he ignored the command.

There was a small room off his office in the clinic outfitted with bed and shower, and a few comfortable chairs. It was a private sanctuary when he needed a few hours of solitude. Dr. Carpenter had hung a Do Not Disturb sign on the door. David smiled, his hand on the knob. The big black letters stood out in the dim light. The lady had a sense of humor. He liked that. He'd have to get better acquainted with her. *When I'm not so tired,* he added.

"I'm afraid you can't rest yet." The low, familiar voice came from one of the chairs as David entered the darkened room.

David snapped on the light. "My God! Siri!" David exploded. "How did you get here?"

It seems my power is returning.

David started to answer before he realized Siri hadn't spoken.

I thought your scientific curiosity might be aroused. Siri sent the thought clearly, smiling at David's disbelief.

"How did you discover it?" David was so astonished, he reverted to speech.

"After you left, I was thinking how I needed to get out of there for a while. That damn Scotch didn't work for more than half an hour. I considered having another round; but my stomach knotted up and turned over at the thought. So I thought of Lamborn Heath. I needed some open air to clear my head. I thought of calling Carl. The picture of the moors in my imagination was so inviting. I wanted nothing more than to be able to ride out, to smell the heather. I wanted to forget everything—that nightmare. I came out of that reverie, if you can call it that; but instead of sitting on the bed in my room at the manor, I was sitting on the couch in the library at Lamborn."

"How did you know that wasn't still your imagination?"

"I called Ahmed to get the horses ready and we went riding." Siri stated flatly. "I thought you'd want to know; but if you don't . . . " Siri disappeared.

"Come back!" David shouted. "I believe you!"

Siri reappeared, laughing.

David flicked the intercom. He felt better. This was the kind of situation with which he had been trained to cope. "Send Dr. Carpenter to my office," he ordered.

Siri looked at him, an eyebrow raised.

"Dr. Carpenter has become one of us. Compliments of his excellency, Sir John," David explained with a wry smile. "With the approval of our mistress, of course!"

"David, remember she has first claim on your loyalty," Siri admonished, gently.

Dr. Carpenter was waiting for them in the examination room. Siri patiently submitted to tests and X rays.

"Get these damn bandages off me!" was his only comment. "The itching is driving my crazy!" The lacerations were nearly healed. It was another proof of Siri's return to transfiguration.

Later, over coffee, they settled down to evaluate the unexpected event. Dr. Carpenter set up the X rays and put the results of the tests on the desk for David to study. She brought out the bulky file containing Siri's records for comparison. There was little doubt that physically Siri had recovered the transfigured state.

"This is entirely opposite of what we had expected," David mused. "If return is possible spontaneously, it could prove disastrous to the experiment."

"Cheira!" Siri burst out.

"Yes!" David agreed, a worried expression coming into his eyes. "Her ladyship must be examined immediately. If there is any change . . . I don't know." David extended his hands helplessly.

"It's almost certain conception has occurred." Dr. Carpenter answered Siri's questioning expression.

"Of course, we won't be certain for several weeks, at least." David tempered the statement.

Dr. Carpenter smiled, but didn't contradict her employer.

"And besides," David continued, ignoring her, "your condition may be an exception. After all, she has shown no signs of it."

Siri dropped his head into his hands with a groan.

"Dr. Carpenter has kept close tabs on her and would have spotted any indications." David encouraged.

"Mervin said something in his report . . . " Siri looked up thoughtfully, trying to remember, but the reference escaped him. He shook his head. Glancing at the clock on the wall, he saw it was morning.

He rose, sighing. "I'll go to her now."

David had heard that tone before: the quality soft and gentle. After Siri disappeared, he sat thoughtfully for a long time, staring at the vacated chair.

Siri materialized in front of the door leading to Lady Pemberly's suite—to the dismay of the two guards posted there. Siri noted them with amusement. So, if Sir John couldn't keep him confined, he was at least going to keep him away from Cheira. *Always loyal and faithful, John,* Siri sent a thought to the absent enemy. *We'll see!*

The guards saluted respectfully, but stepped in front of the door, barring his way. "You may not enter, my lord," one stated.

Siri smiled; a dangerous glint came into his eyes. "On whose orders?"

The guard shifted uneasily. "Sir John."

"So I thought. And Lady Pemberly?"

The guard was uncertain.

"Then you will step aside!" Siri walked calmly between them. A force they had never encountered before held them immobile.

"Good God!" the guard gasped when he had recovered. "He's got his power back—and more than before. Even Sir John couldn't stand against that!"

"We'd better notify his excellency," his partner frowned, making off down the hall at a run.

Siri closed the door quietly, pausing just inside. The quick return of power surprised him. *Now this!* He had thought only to push past the guards using his transfigured strength and a skill he knew was greater than theirs. The energy that had obeyed his thought seemed to come out of the air. What was happening?

He shook his head. Whatever it was would have to wait for later analysis. Cheira had to be warned. And the first moments of facing her had to be gotten over. Mott had assured him she was calm; but it was probably only an act. He was sure her reaction would be less than loving.

He strode toward the door of the bedroom. A picture flashed into his mind, stopping him in midstride. He saw the coming meeting. He saw Cheira, even noting the discolored bruises he had inflicted. *Imagination,* he thought and shrugged.

Jennie was sitting on a low stool, humming softly. When she saw him, she jumped up, wide-eyed, her hands flying to her mouth. He silenced her with a look. She rushed out and he didn't bother to stop her.

He stood for a moment, gazing at the slim figure almost lost in the expanse of the big bed. She lay still, her face buried in the pillow, the golden hair in disarray, catching here and there the reflection from the dim light in the room. His breath caught at the sight. He was reminded that he had seen her exactly like this in his imagination minutes before. Puzzled, he also saw the next few moments.

"Cheira!" He moved to the bed, his voice soft.

She sat up. The blood rushed to her face, staining the fair skin and leaving white circles around the discolored bruises.

"I'm so sorry," she whispered, clutching the sheet to hide the black marks on her arms and throat. "I'm so ashamed."

Siri stared, the words echoing familiarly in his head.

"I wouldn't have blamed you if you never came back. Now you'll never believe that I love you." She covered her face with her hands.

Siri sat down beside her, gently but firmly removing the sheet from her grasp, examining the damage he had done.

"Did it mean this much to you? Didn't you realize the danger? If I had hurt you . . . " His voice trailed off hoarsely.

The self-condemnation conveyed by the halting statement drove her into his arms. She stopped the words with a kiss, unmindful of the aching bruises. "I knew the danger. And, yes, it does mean that much. There was very little time. I don't know why, but I felt it."

He drew away to study her. Her words were like a recording. He felt like an actor who had the script well memorized. *My God,* he thought, *what's happening?*

And I have accomplished my purpose, my darling, Cheira was thinking, a smile playing at the corners of her mouth.

He stiffened, fear coming into his heart. "How do you know?" *No,* the vision told him, *it's not what you think.*

"My darling," Cheira said softly, "I have something to tell you." Her thoughts raced ahead of the words. *Would I not know the instant your child began his life in my body, my love? Would I not feel it?* Her face beamed with the happiness of the thought.

"You might have waited." Siri chuckled helplessly. "Do you think it proper for a child to be conceived in such a way?"

She looked at him, puzzled. How could he have known her thoughts? She had just been going to tell him. She had been worrying how to bring about his transfiguration. John was furious. He wouldn't do it. Transfiguration!

Wonder dawned in her eyes. "Your power! It's come back!"

Siri shrugged. "First things, first. You still have some explaining to do. I vaguely remember that you said Lira gave you the drug."

"Yes."

"Well, you could be a little more explicit," Siri prompted. "I have believed Lira to be dead for a long time."

"When I got away from the Fort," Cheira said, reluctantly, "you gave up looking for me after a few weeks. But Lira had her own methods. She told you what I was; but you wouldn't pay any attention because you thought the native expression was only superstition. Lira had second sight. She slipped away and came to Arx Vetus. The rest you know."

"And Lira taught you what I never dreamed you knew?"

"She held classes." Cheira giggled, lowering her eyes. "Please forgive me for knowing."

Siri sighed, taking her into his arms, a twinkle in his eyes. "I may even come to enjoy it." He bent down, brushing his lips along her neck and shoulders.

The sweet tingling sensation coursed along her nerves until her whole body seemed to explode with pleasure. She gasped, a low moan escaping her lips.

Siri stood up abruptly.

Cheira opened her eyes, a film of pleasure still veiling them.

The scowl on his face deepened as he watched her.

"I'm so glad your power has returned, my darling," she whispered. Suddenly she sat bolt upright. "My God! Did it come back spontaneously?"

He nodded. He realized there had been no conscious release of power just now. His mind reeled, trying to understand.

"Have you told Mott?"

"Yes."

"He may be stupid in other matters; but he knows about the reversal. What does he think?"

"He doesn't know. It's unexpected; the last thing they thought would happen."

"What if that happens to me?" her voice was breathless.

"David wants you to come to the clinic the first thing in the morning."

"Oh, Siri," Cheira whimpered. "It can't come back. I don't want it. Not now!" Her voice rose hysterically.

"Don't jump to conclusions," he scolded, taking her face in his hands. "Promise me! Give Mott a chance to do some tests." He straightened. "Now, we are about to be interrupted."

A timid knock on the door made her exclaim, "You knew it before it happened!

"Come in, Jennie," Cheira snapped, distracted. Too many things were happening at once.

The girl crept in, opening the door as little as possible. Her expression was rigid. She felt trapped. With Siri in the room in front of her and Sir John in the salon, more angry than she had ever seen him, Jennie felt that her will would never be strong enough to move her paralyzed body.

"His excellency demands to see you, my lady," she announced with a final effort, her voice low and labored, her eyes on the floor immediately in front of her.

"Demands?" Siri repeated the word derisively.

A tremor she could not control was the only indication Jennie gave that she heard. There was no way she could speak. Her voice was stuck somewhere deep in her throat.

Cheira looked at Siri. He shrugged. The unwanted vision already pictured the meeting for him. A faint glimmer of understanding was beginning to dawn in his mind.

"We'll see him in the other room," Cheira said. "Ask him to wait."

Jennie slipped quickly out.

Siri laughed; but the flash in the dark eyes betrayed an emotion clear to Cheira.

"Please don't be angry," she pleaded. "John has a right to know. He's concerned for my welfare."

"He loves you," Siri retorted scornfully. "He's madly jealous. He'd do anything to keep us apart."

"Oh, no," Cheira objected. "It's only loyalty."

Siri shrugged. So she didn't know about the other episode. Well, there was no need to upset her further.

Cheira hopped out of bed, donning a heavily brocaded dressing gown. She smiled. *There's admiration in Siri's eyes,* she thought with satisfaction. She wound her hair into a knot at the nape of her neck. The long-sleeved, high-collared robe concealed the bruises. *Will he notice?* she wondered. By pulling up the fur collar, she could even hide the swelling around her mouth. *Yes,* she decided, *he knows.* She saw Siri's eyes narrow and his jaw tighten at her efforts. *He knows what I'm thinking.* She inhaled sharply. *I will only think how much I love you.* Her mind held the words for Siri, but his expression did not change.

John acted swiftly when Siri stepped through the door.

"Take him!" he ordered the two guards.

The men lunged forward, but their momentum was stopped short a few feet from the target. One man was dropped right there. The other bounced back, his hands flying to his face. He had hit the shield head on. It had the impact of a stone wall.

"What the hell!" John exclaimed. "What was that?"

Siri smiled. "Will you agree that I have the right to defend myself? Call off your men; and we will meet as two equal, honorable men should. Cheira will release you from your pledge."

The electric effect of Cheira's name turned John's attention to her. She was looking at Siri in amazement. It was apparent that what had happened was a mystery to her also.

"Are you all right?" John stepped toward Cheira. Worry coming back into his eyes, he ignored Siri's challenge.

"She's my wife." Siri's voice hadn't changed as he answered for her. "And my concern."

John stood his ground. "And at the moment, helpless to defend herself. Your actions give me no reason to believe that your habit of abusing women exempts your wife."

"For that I'm prepared to atone," Siri answered, his voice strangely lifeless. "If you are to be the executioner, I'll accept that."

"Oh, stop it!" Cheira cried. "I'm all right! There's more than that to be discussed here. That other was my fault; Siri was not to blame." She drew herself up in a facsimile of the old imperviousness. "I order you both to forget this silly enmity. Siri's power has returned, stronger than before. We must deal with that."

Siri nodded slightly. John looked away, his attitude softening.

Cheira turned to Siri. "Please tell John what has happened."

"Of course, you're right," Siri conceded. "John?"

"Of course," John repeated. He eyed Siri suspiciously, but indicated a willingness to listen.

"I was in my room," Siri began. *After you beat the hell out of me,* he sent the thought to John. "Trying to find oblivion in a bottle of Scotch." *And trying to remember just what had happened.* "But the liquor wore off in an hour or so." *I really would have been grateful if you had killed me.* "I wanted to get away for a while." *Cheira doesn't know so watch what you say.* "I thought of Lamborn Heath and there I was."

John's expression was one of growing amazement.

311

"So I decided to try for the clinic. David had to know. And I had to make sure it wasn't just delirium." *If transfiguration can return spontaneously, there may be a great danger to Cheira,* Siri telepathized. *Dr. Carpenter is almost certain that she has conceived. Cheira believes it, too.*

"My God!" John worried.

Siri glanced at Cheira. *Careful,* he warned John.

"So David spent most of the night testing. It's confirmed. Then when I came to see Cheira this morning, I found your guards posted outside the door."

Guiltily, John's glance shifted to Cheira; but she was intent on what Siri was saying.

"I thought to push past them. The energy which answered the thought stopped them in their tracks."

"We know that self-induced transfiguration is possible from Mervin's report," Cheira interrupted. "And he described an incident of the use of force without physical contact."

"Yes," Siri answered. "I'm going to spend some time on this myself. I'm not sure what I've gotten hold of. This is something Mott's experiments don't cover."

"You'll work with Mott?" John's voice held a note of excitement. "This might prove to be the greatest advancement in the society since its inception."

"If I do, it won't be for the good of the society," Siri retorted dryly, "but for my own satisfaction. I'll leave the altruism to you."

John stared. *Of course,* he thought, *why didn't I think of it before? This is the basis of our enmity, even more than rivalry over love for the same woman.*

Siri shrugged, amused at John's thought.

This is the reason I can't trust Cheira to your care.

You're wrong there. Siri's thought had no trouble overcoming the barrier in John's mind. *That's why she is safer with me than anyone else. And she knows it.*

John's eyebrows shot up. *So,* he thought, *your power can now bridge any barrier. Is there no defense against you?*

Do you need any?

"Very well," John ignored the challenge. "However you do it, the results will be the same." *But if you step out of line once more . . .* he thought.

John turned to Cheira. "Your ladyship will forgive the unwarranted intrusion?"

Cheira waved her hand, dismissing the question.

"With your permission, then, I shall withdraw." John bowed.

David could scarcely control his excitement. He had spent the hours since Siri's appearance revising the experiment. He brushed a hand across weary eyes.

"Yes, I will." Siri smiled when they were alone.

Dr. Carpenter had taken Cheira for the examination.

"But only after you've had some sleep."

David grinned sheepishly; but the grin faded into a look of astonishment. "How did you now what I was going to ask?"

It was Siri's turn to grin. "I can anticipate the future," he said, lightly; but his eyes were serious.

David grabbed a pencil to make a hurried notation. "What do you mean by that?"

"I can see anything by merely turning my attention to it," Siri explained. "Anything that will happen in a few hours is especially clear. Anything in the past, too. Now I can see all the moments of your past. Your motives stand out clearly in your actions." Siri frowned. He was staring at a spot above David's head. "I can see the actions of your ancestors that eventually led to your conception."

"Incredible!" David exclaimed. Then a thought jumped into his mind. "Then that means all my actions are predestined."

"I don't think so," Siri answered thoughtfully. "The future becomes very fuzzy after a while. However, the intellect does act on previous experience. It seems to me that predestiny would mean that something or someone outside yourself has determined your course. That's not so. Your actions are limited only by the world in which you live."

"Have you discovered all this since your power returned?"

"Only the ability to picture the past and the near future. I believed the other before. Now I'm more certain it's right."

David observed an indefinable change in Siri's expression.

"There is no malevolent God who toys with men's lives for his own amusement. There is, however, a single consciousness to which all men belong. Progress toward that realization is the purpose of life. Transfiguration is the first step."

David wasn't sure he understood. He shook his head doubtfully.

"Then you already know the results of Cheira's examination?" David left the subject and returned to a more familiar, more comfortable area.

"Yes," Siri answered, his attention only slightly on what David asked. "She's in no danger."

"Then there isn't anything you don't know." David threw down the pencil and pushed away from the desk.

Siri smiled. "I don't know how the process operates. I want to go out to Mervin and see how transfiguration works in some of those people. From what he said there are some very advanced individuals. More than any of us. None of this is going anywhere without knowledge of the process."

As a scientist, David agreed. He took the thought a step further. "You said you could tell everything about me. Then, do you know Cheira's past?"

"Yes." Siri hesitated. "But I can hardly believe what I see. I certainly won't tell her until I've checked. This ability is new to me. I could be wrong. I'd like to prove some of it before I rely on it too strongly."

David threw up his hands, laughing. "What else can you do?"

"That's what we're going to find out together," Siri told him, dryly.

Cheira returned with Dr. Carpenter.

David quickly scanned the results of the tests. "Good!" He glanced at Siri. "No change."

Cheira eyed the young doctor coldly.

"I'd like to set up a small lab at Pemberly House, if I may," David requested. "Your ladyship's condition must be monitored frequently. It would be most convenient."

"Stevens can arrange whatever you need." Cheira's tone was one of icy condescension.

"That attitude toward David is unworthy of you," Siri chided when they were in the car.

"I won't tolerate his insolence." Cheira frowned, tossing her head impatiently.

"The man's a scientist," Siri reminded her. "Not a courtier."

Cheira's expression didn't change. She bit her lip.

Siri laughed. "My darling, it's your guilty conscience."

Cheira's eyes widened in disbelief.

"Yes, I know he asked you about the drug. And no, he didn't tell me."

Cheira inhaled sharply.

"And he's probably the only man in the society impervious to your charms," he added, raising her hand to his lips. "An attitude which I can't understand, but have had reason to envy him for."

"Oh!" Cheira snatched her hand away peevishly. "If he didn't tell you, how did you know?"

Siri was pleased by the gesture. It emphasized the change in Cheira. The coldness of her previous manner was lacking entirely. He knew now that it was an important part of her experience. He had a fleeting image of that manner magnified to exaggeration, but it was unclear and he misinterpreted it.

"I just know. I'm going to work with Mott to explore this new phase of power." Siri avoided a direct answer. "There's a lot to be understood. But I know this much, it's tied up with our experience that day at Lamborn." He slid his arm around her shoulders. "I'm waiting for the day you will join me."

"Oh, yes," Cheira responded, nestling against him. Absently, she rubbed at her blouse. It was the first time Siri noticed the gesture. He remembered the symbol.

"Why did you do that?" he questioned.

"It's nothing." Her mind was back on her dislike of Mott.

Again the image flashed into Siri's mind, but passed so swiftly he failed to notice.

"I think Mott should be replaced." Cheira sat up, shrugging off his arm. "I'm going to order Vendier to London."

Siri grasped her shoulders, turning her to face him. "You'll do no such thing." His face was stern. "This is David's show and he must be allowed to direct it. Call Vendier—if it will make you feel better—but as an assistant, not as a replacement. Cheira, promise me!"

She saw the hard look in his eyes, the displeasure she couldn't withstand. *He means it,* she thought.

"Oh, all right!" She gave in grudgingly. "I promise. But I won't promise to like him."

"I wouldn't dream of asking you to do that." Siri laughed. "Instead, I'll ask you to go to Lamborn with me. I want to check on the horses that came in from Imla Dun. And since you're so ordinary, we'll drive."

"I won't be always," she vowed, her face bright with happiness. "Just for a little while."

315

CHAPTER XX

After a long strenuous day at Lamborn, Cheira willingly retired early.

Siri was glad for the chance to examine the enhanced ability now at his command in preparation for his session with David. He slouched in the chair by the fireplace, only the dying embers of the evening's fire casting a warm glow into the room. This time he watched attentively the images that appeared when he thought of Mott. The circumstances of the tests he was planning to perform slid through Siri's brain.

He sat up. *That's it,* he thought. *Precognition! That's what I'm doing.* "One down," he muttered aloud, sinking back into the chair.

He eyes were drawn to the shield above the mantel. It glinted dully, the letters standing out like a new brand. He waited. He noticed a slight tingling deep inside his head, but there were no images this time. He tried harder. *There's a connection,* he thought. *I know it.*

The tightly written pages of Mervin's report appeared. Mentally he scanned the pages, looking for something, not really sure what it was. He stopped at Mervin's remarks about the Didaskes' ability to create. He held out his hand and drew up the image of a silver coin. "Good Lord!" he said aloud and hastily wiped the image from his mind. The coin had begun to materialize in his palm. His shoulders tensed. It was clear that now he would have to control his every thought.

Well—he let out the breath held unconsciously—*it will remain to be seen whether this is an average or disadvantage.*

"Let's test one attribute at a time," Mott suggested the next day when he and Siri sat in his office.

Siri nodded. "This may surprise you, David; but I'm wondering if I can handle it."

"There's only one way to find out. I've set up a few simple tests to start with," David explained. "That stunt you pulled with the guards, for instance. John was really shook up; and the two men had to be sent to Arx Vetus for a rest. Ameur is demanding to know what the hell is going on."

Siri smiled; but his eyes were serious. "That was only a small part of the force I can control."

"Let's start with that, then." David stood up. "There must be an electric basis and we can measure that."

Siri was hesitant; but he followed David.

In the lab, Mott pasted electrodes to Siri's chest and temples. "We'll start with the lowest voltage and work up from there."

"Shall I resist?"

"No. But let me know the minute you feel any discomfort."

Siri lay back, relaxing. As the voltage increased slowly, his body began to radiate energy in a visible aura. This time his heartbeat remained normal. He smiled at David. The electromyograph indicator shot upward. The monitor of galvanic skin response showed no reading. Skin resistance was lowered in direct proportion to the skin's rise in temperature.

David worried. There was no longer any measure. The machines had reached their limit. "We'd better stop."

"No," Siri said without moving.

There was a point where Siri's skin had to begin to burn. By then, the internal damage would have already been done. David's worry became real fear. He flicked the switch to cut the voltage. He could stand the suspense no longer.

"Why'd you do that? We're not done." Despite the ordinary words, the tone of Siri's voice was like a bell. David watched and listened fascinated. The energy field around Siri faded.

"You'd have burnt yourself up in another minute."

Siri shrugged.

"I've seen how much pain you can tolerate," David accused, the perspiration beading on his forehead.

"There was no pain," Siri told him. "Nothing."

"What do you mean by that? There had to be."

"I tell you I felt no discomfort at all. In fact, it was rather pleasant."

"Incredible!" David made a few notations. He wrote down exactly what had happened. He wondered if he'd ever be able to evaluate it.

"Shall we go on?" Siri asked, laughing.

David hesitated.

"You want to know, don't you? You're a scientist, remember?"

David grinned, embarrassed at the reminder—his habit of jumping to conclusions again. In every instance, Siri had known better than he.

"All right. Let's see what happens if you resist."

317

Siri hesitated. "I'll blow that machine, David," he warned.

"You can't. It's insulated. The most it can do is short-circuit."

"Turn it up, then. We might as well really prove what I can do."

"That's too dangerous," David objected. "I don't want anything to happen to you."

"Do it!" Siri commanded. "And head for cover."

David obeyed. It was a habit he had acquired in the desert. That tone in Siri's voice was not to be countermanded.

Siri sat up, frowning.

The voltage flowing through the machine was stopped and a greater force reversed it. The generator exploded.

"Good Lord, you turned it back on itself!" David screamed over the noise of alarms going off all over the building.

"Any more bright ideas?" Siri grinned.

In the ensuing days, they checked every facet of Siri's power they could think to devise a test for. Siri could absorb or emit more energy than they had a machine to measure. He felt no pain, and any injury healed almost before it was inflicted.

It was Siri who dreamed up the most outrageous tests. David agreed, reluctantly and worried.

"So you are indifferent to pain. What about pleasure, then?" David wondered.

"Do you want to practice on me again, David?" Siri laughed.

The young physician turned a livid red. "You know?" he blurted out.

"Of course! I know everything, remember. And you're blaming Cheira for what she did. My wife and my friend have made me a pawn." Siri assumed a pathetic expression.

"I'm sorry," David choked. "Please forgive me." He was too mortified to notice Siri's amused glance.

Siri clapped him on the shoulder, laughing. "My ego has survived, although a bit bruised and battered." He sobered. "And we have learned much as a consequence."

David raised his eyes, sheepishly.

"Forget it!" Siri said.

"Cheira, dearest," Siri sighed, "David and I have gone as far as we can go. You must trust me. I have to go. Mervin can't find what you're looking for. At least not for some time. I can. And I'm the only one who can at this point. It's a state reached only by a few. And I can reach it. I know most of it already; but I have to make sure. The time has come for us to know."

Cheira clung to him desperately, shaking her head. "I don't care. I don't want to know if it means you must leave. I don't need anyone but you." The minute mark on her breast was burning again. The pain of it had intensified over the last few days. It scorched her skin like a new brand. She clutched at it, groaning softly.

Taking her hand away, Siri gently kissed the spot. The pain was replaced at once by the sensation of pleasure.

"That's only a warning," he told her decisively. "If we continue to ignore it, it will grow worse."

"Are you asking me to believe the gods are angry?" Cheira retorted sharply.

"If you want to call that which is the essence of your being that, yes. Isn't what you've been searching for locked in your memory under a cloud you refuse to lift? Hasn't the mark you carry been bothering you only since you've become aware of it? Your subconscious knows the connection and is trying to force you to acknowledge it."

"It's only a tattoo. It means nothing," she insisted stubbornly. "Lots of people in the Orient have many more than this. I only used it for the organization because it was convenient, an inconspicuous mark of unity. Dr. Carpenter thinks it's bothering me because of a rapid change in hormonal balance. She says it will stop when my body has adjusted. Oh, please, don't leave me again. My heart hurts so much when we're apart," she ended, plaintively. Large tears stood on her lashes, proclaiming her helplessness.

"Is there no way to make you understand?" Siri spoke earnestly. "That's not right. Dr. Carpenter is well intentioned; but she can't know. That symbol is our future. I want you with me forever. So I must go now."

"What do you know? What won't you tell me?" Cheira demanded. Her eyes widened in disbelief at the idea that came into her mind.

"I know where you came from and . . . "

"I don't want to hear that?" Cheira interrupted, her voice rising. "It's just an excuse to get away from me."

"I swear to you, I'll return." Siri looked at her, solemnly. "It's not other than our love. It's the measure of it. Believe me!"

Cheira wailed despairingly. "What will I do without you?"

"Have you forgotten the child so soon?" Siri smiled. "That's why you must wait, why you cannot go with me."

"I'm afraid," she whimpered in answer. "I feel you'll be gone such a long time. You'll never really come back to me. It will claim you. Forever." She grabbed at the tattoo as if she wanted to tear it away.

"There's only one way I could stay." Siri frowned, watching her intently. "Look into your mind. Tell us what we must know."

She stared at him, hope dawning in her eyes, then fading to despair and terror. She shook her head, lunging into his arms as if for protection.

"I can't!" she whispered.

Siri appeared in Patna before the end of the congregation of the *chelas*. The knowledge of his arrival was in every mind simultaneously. A hush fell over the white-robed multitude.

Siri stood uncertainly on the edge of the throng, uncomfortably aware that his presence had interrupted the ceremonies. He had come with the intention of locating Mervin and his friend, Liem, hoping they could help him in his search. He hesitated, feeling the impact of a thousand eyes. The knowledge was certain that no barrier he could raise would be strong enough to shield his thoughts from any of them. Perversely, it was a relief. It gave him peace. It was as he wanted it to be. The time of games was over. They posed no threat to his well being. In fact, they promoted it. They were brothers—in the highest universal meaning of the term. Intuitively, he knew it. He knew that whatever support they could give was his.

A young man stepped out of the crowd. Siri caught his breath. The golden hair and delicate features were instantly recognizable. The masculine characteristics enhanced rather than detracted from the perfection of his person. He stood smiling, guilelessly submitting to Siri's scrutiny, waiting for the shock to pass. Siri wiped his hand across his eyes, an involuntary shudder passing through his body.

But I knew it, he protested silently. *Then why is it so hard to believe? It's obviously the only plausible explanation.*

The young man came to him, the green eyes, highlighted by gold and brown flecks, intent on Siri's face.

"Greetings, Siri ben Ange." The young man's voice displayed the musical qualities of a highly trained singer. "You are most welcome. There is only one other whom we await more eagerly." The young man's smile shone with an indefinable radiance. Siri could think only of the words "guiltless innocence" to describe it.

"My name is Delfaum."

"Who are you?" Siri was surprised at how harsh his voice sounded.

"But you know it, my brother," the young man replied. "Why do you doubt?"

"It's too easy," Siri objected. The thoughts in his mind shone forth clearly, impressed indelibly on his consciousness. "I've done nothing to deserve this. In fact . . ."

"Have the centuries of waiting been as nothing, then? Has the restlessness been the joy you were seeking?" Delfaum smiled.

Siri felt humble, like a small child on the first day in school already drawing the reprobation of the teacher. He shook his head. He tried desperately to resolve the revelation presented to him in the figure of this golden man.

Stuart Mervin and another man appeared beside Delfaum.

"We've been waiting for you." Mervin smiled without greeting. Siri was shocked at the change in him. With his enhanced power, he could easily see the aura surrounding Mervin. It was more startling to see it in someone he had known well for many years.

"Siri, this is Liem," Mervin indicated his companion. Liem bowed.

The physical reaction set in unexpectedly. Siri felt as if he were in a whirlwind. He fought frantically to slow the dizzy spinning.

"We have waited a long time." Liem enforced Mervin's remark. "The barrier was not erected by us."

Siri accepted the rebuke humbly. "I know that now," he confessed with effort. *We've been playing at transfiguration,* he thought, *like stupid children. Deliberately closing our minds to reality. The barriers we raised to protect ourselves from each other were just a poor imitation of what we were actually doing.*

Away in the background, he heard the muffled chanting of the *chelas* resume. It was the punctuation of his thought, the final dismissal of his past as it had been, the reaching out—more than halfway—to an acceptance of all that he was or had been. His mind filled with fear. He stood still, only vaguely aware of what the others were saying.

"My mission here is completed," Mervin said.

"Stay with us," Liem and Delfaum invited. "You only have a little way to go."

"No! Not yet! I must return to the others. They'll need me. The time will be short." Mervin turned to Siri. "I have made my choice. You must make yours."

Siri heard him as if from a great distance. Like watching a movie, he saw Mervin raise his hand in farewell.

"Wait!" Siri shouted, fear forcing out the words. "Wait!" Even as he spoke, Mervin disappeared. In panic, Siri wondered if Mervin had heard, if he had only thought he had spoken, if . . . But Mervin would not heed his plea; he knew it. Mervin was a protection against what was about to happen. He was a lifeline to that old familiar world.

Desolation, he thought. *Decision. I can't save myself. Decision. Make it! You know you must! Do it!*

He fought against it; but the desire grew stronger. He was being torn apart. The watching faces were sympathetic; but they could not help him. He was alone, enmeshed in a grid of conflicting desires, desires of his own making—and fear, a fear that he could recognize only from the memory of a small boy who quavered, terrified before the Earl of Zetland—his father, yes, but so stern and unapproachable, so huge that he had to tilt his head way back in order to see his face.

A horse nickered close at hand. Siri turned to the dear, familiar sound. The beautiful animal trotted to him. The black was free without saddle or bridle. He came, prompted only from love of his master. The sun highlighted the sleek coat when the muscles bunched as he moved. He stopped before Siri, nudging him with a velvety muzzle, his big, dark eyes pools of limpid trust; his ears flicked questioningly.

"Skotias?" Siri murmured, struggling to see through blurred vision.

The stallion raised his head, his ears still for the moment, picking up the strange sound. He swished his tail impatiently, chagrined at his mistake. This man was not the master he sought. His not the name that the strange voice uttered. He snorted, trotting away.

Desolation flooded the rejected man, but now he understood. He felt cold. The heat of the sun could not penetrate the dark void which descended around him. It was the iciness of death. His heart seemed to have stopped beating; his blood cooled in his veins. He gasped for air, but there was none.

The multitude of white-robed figures floated before his eyes, like ghosts in a vague nightmare. Their presence repelled him.

Resist. Obstinately, he held on to the impulse. He struggled against the malfunction of his lungs. He fought to clear his vision. *Resist.* Scenes of his beloved desert drifted before his eyes like mirages. The old Fort beckoned. The big tent at Imla Dun was too dear to abandon. The horses. His men formed into a tribe. He had done it all. He closed his eyes, the longing bringing drops of cold perspiration to his forehead. His stomach churned.

The sound of the chanting throng rose, the crescendo pulling him back, demanding his attention. *This is your goal,* the thought pounded in his head. *Men united in a universal consciousness, not by the slavishness of mutual dependence, but by the majesty of complementary independence where total knowledge is the common norm instead of varying degrees of ignorance.*

He could waver no longer. His strength was failing under the unrelenting onslaught. The compassion in Delfaum's eyes was too much to bear. He willed air to enter his belabored lungs and with the exhalation thrust forth the heavy weight pressing on his heart. He surrendered.

A gentle sigh like the ephemeral passing of a summer breeze on a sunny day was drawn from the expectant crowd.

He felt a flood of joy permeating his body; his well-being restored. He had lost nothing. He had gained everything.

Now the oneness with them that he had become was a natural mode of existence, the other state an incongruously ugly way of life, an insult to the magnificence which was a man.

He knew now how to proceed. He had put all doubt behind him forever. Never again need he suffer the agonies of indecision. It was a part of his being that no longer existed. Any future choices would be made in the joy of full knowledge.

He saw the bright glow of the *chelas* expanding to engulf him. The radiant figure of Delfaum was the link. He welcomed it, embracing the energy for the restoration of his depleted strength. It was his portion of the fathomless reservoir to which he now had a right. He matched the salute in Delfaum's eyes with his own.

His body felt as if it were expanding, filled with an intense light that submitted each of its atoms to the control of his will. His will now had omniscience at its disposal; whatever judgments it should make would be infallible, no longer subject to the errors resulting from faulty information or enslaved to the whim of defective emotions. He experienced the intense sweetness of fulfillment. The vibration of the eternally sounding vowels of creation was attuned to the rhythm of his being. The symbol they all bore without knowing the meaning, without seeing the perversion; the mark Cheira had received at birth, the enduring reminder of her origin, the promise of eventual return; the beginning and the end, the sound which was the basis of the universe, the goal toward which mankind blindly struggles—he knew it all. It was his. There was no more nor need there ever be.

The final decision must still be made. Delfaum's body glowed brighter. Siri felt he should be surprised; but he was not. Their minds were one.

323

What decision? Siri thought.

Epχουχαι ide [erchouchi-ìdê]; *Come and see.* The glow which was Delfaum's body moved off. The thousand faces in the gathered crowd looked upward. The chant of the eternal vowel burst forth from their lips. It sounded harsh and discordant—a poor imitation of the real thing. Siri wanted to get away from it. He followed Delfaum. He noted objectively the glow of his own body as it rose in the air. He was conscious of no movement. His being was there behind him as well as with Delfaum on a mountaintop in the vastness of the Himalayas. It was natural for others to be there, as it was natural for him. He knew them all.

He knew the man and woman who stood before him. He waited, though, for the introduction to come.

This is Petraum, our father—Delfaum's thought was in his mind—*and Aletha, our mother.*

Welcome, Siri ben Ange, they greeted him.

Why then is your daughter not here? He wanted the answer to originate in their minds. He wanted the proof that what he knew was true.

You know it, the thought came.

I want it confirmed, he thought stubbornly.

Petraum smiled. *Many years ago our daughter, Cheira, came to the moment of decision. All this was already hers; but of her own will she had to accept it eternally. The others—humanity—called. She saw their suffering and their blind groping for the transfiguration their clouded minds only dimly glimpsed. She decided to go among them, with no knowledge of her past, with only the undeveloped power to return to us through her own efforts. It was her decision. We can only wait for her return.*

You think her effort futile then?

No, Aletha's thought came to him, *amazingly successful. It is only the suffering and the separation she has had to endure. We cannot reach her. We must wait.* The glow of Aletha's body dimmed slightly.

Could there be suffering even here? Siri wondered.

But Petraum moved to Aletha and the glow brightened as if in answer to Siri's question.

There is no unhappiness here, Delfaum revealed, *because the end of any trial is already known.* He smiled. *It is only our mother's love which makes her impatient. Even we must abide the time of humanity.*

Siri bowed his head. *If I had known,* he thought, *how much of her suffering was caused by me.*

And how much of her happiness, they added.

324

And now her salvation? Siri questioned.

As an individual, each must seek his own salvation, Petraum thought. *You have no obligations.*

But my love, Siri countered. *Even this is not enough without her.*

It is your decision, they reiterated. *We can only wait.*

Was the sweetness of harmony pervading his being heightened? Was the sounding of the eternal vowels seeping more deeply into the atoms of his body expanding his essence into the fabric of the universe? Was this delaying his decision? Was a still unseen presence calling him to remain forever?

There was nothing but the conflict in his mind. There was no struggle with raging desires. There was no passion to contend with. Yet there was love. Was his love for Cheira as great as this? He knew the future; he knew his decision. Yet he lingered. The hesitation was part of it, necessary to the full realization of the existence he was postponing by his own choice.

Cheira, my love, he thought, *you who are part of my being, even this I cannot accept without your presence.* The thought pervaded his mind; his body drew into itself; the sweetness faded. The silence beat against his eardrums like the pressure felt by a surfacing deep-sea diver. His body was unbelievably heavy; his muscles fought against the pull of gravity, his bones bending under their own weight.

He forced himself to stand erect, squaring his shoulders like a soldier brought to attention. With an effort that made him grimace at how ridiculous it was, he raised his arm to push open the door to Cheira's suite, habit instigating the action. He smiled, thinking of Vendier's dismay when he learned that his impenetrable substance, his unmatched invention which was Cheira's inviolable protection, was only a level of consciousness; that the stable atoms which lined the walls were only a deterrent to a certain grade of being.

As soon as he entered, he knew Cheira was not there. The salon was the same as when he had left. It seemed so long ago. Memories flew at him from every inch of the room: the sofa where he had lain the night Cheira slipped caru into his drink, the cushions on the hearth where their love had been reciprocated, the door to the bedroom where John had first encountered his magnified power, the mantel where he had stood so often in the agony of indecision. His eyes stopped on the circle of gold above the fireplace. Now the letters were familiar, as the known and experienced is familiar. It was the promise of the future.

Jennie was about to open the bedroom door. Siri waited.

The girl gasped when she saw him, her eyes growing wide with surprise and reflexive fear.

Siri smiled, voicing a question whose answer he already knew. "Where is your mistress, Jennie?"

His voice was kind, his expression gentle. All trace of the former arrogance had disappeared along with the fierce glint in his eyes. He was not conscious of the change. The startled maid was aware of nothing else.

"She's in the garden, my lord." Jennie curtsied. The expression on her face, just relaxing from the surprise of his presence, changed to astonishment at his next words.

"Yes, you may notify John. But please allow me a few minutes with my wife."

Siri left Jennie dumbfounded. She was dazzled by the brilliance of his smile. In the absence of the haughtiness of pride in his attitude, he was even more handsome than she remembered. The fierceness in his eyes, which always left her numb with fear, had been replaced by a look of such serenity that Jennie shook her head in disbelief.

The man she had just seen was not the same man who had left seven months ago, leaving her beloved mistress in despair; but this was the person that man was always meant to be. She could wait as he asked. She need no longer fear for the safety of her mistress.

Cheira had grown to enjoy the solitary walks in the garden. She forbade Jennie to accompany her. She welcomed the loneliness.

Wrapped in a warm cloak, she listened to the slow, steady click of her heels on the stone walks. The clicks echoed hollowly ahead on the curving stones, marking the passage of time. It was a time of waiting. She had learned patience at last.

The leafless hedges, the empty flower beds, the sharp crispness of the winter days waited with her; and like her, they bore a hidden new life within.

She sat for a while on the stone bench at the far end of the enclosure. The sounds of bustling traffic muted and concealed by the tall evergreen wall emphasized the isolation. She let it sink into her consciousness and identified with it.

Leaves rustled faintly in the dry fountain, moved by a random breath of air; and in the distance the house rose, somber and quiet, but like a beckoning refuge.

She remained until the cold of the stone seeped through the wool of her cloak. She even removed her gloves and pressed her bare palms against the frigid bench in order to make the contrast more poignant.

Then she hurried back to the warmth which awaited—cheeks flushed, eyes bright, back to stand just inside the glass doors of the library—and let the heat rush to meet her, to feel it at first repulsed by and then triumphant over the chill she had brought to challenge it. She stood, unmoving, to feel more sharply the movement of the infant in her womb, already asserting his right to independent action.

She smiled. Even if Siri were forever beyond her reach as Stuart Mervin had intimated, she would always have him in the person of his child. If that were all the future would grant her, she would be satisfied with that. With a determined toss of her head, she ignored the pain that squeezed her heart, making breath difficult. She had learned to live with that reminder of separation. It was the price she must pay.

Automatically, she threw off the heavy cloak, uncomfortable in the warm room. She paused in front of the recliner reliving the night Siri had lounged lazily in it, the feeling of security she had known for such a little while. The image of his face in repose came to her. The eyes were closed, the lids hiding the fierce dark eyes, giving his features an unusual serenity, his body in relaxation revealing a latent strength made more vivid by the inactivity of the moment. She sighed, turning away.

"Cheira, only the despondent must be satisfied with memories." The low beloved voice seemed to float in the air. Then Siri appeared before her.

Her vision blotted out everything but the sight of him. It was not surprise she felt, but the permeating quietness of a dove returned to rest in its own cote after a long and strenuous flight. She wondered at the smile on his face, which turned to concern as he reached to support her swaying body. It was so natural that she surrender to his control. *Why does he look so worried?* She had waited through all the days and nights of his absence for this moment. It had not been even conscious waiting, but only a knowledge buried deep within that she would recognize as the cessation of pain in her chest. Her mind only had to frame the words: *Yes, my love. I am here. I am yours. No further effort would be necessary, ever.*

"Cheira, no!" Siri's voice was firm. He shook her gently. "What you are seeking cannot be had by the surrender of one's will to any other. That's not love, but bondage."

She realized her eyes were closed. She opened them. What had he said? Was he rejecting her? Even that could be borne if only he were near, if only the pain stayed away from her heart. She felt the child kick. It brought a secret smile to her face.

Siri chuckled helplessly, gathering her into his arms. "You didn't even hear me," he accused.

The words of her answer drifted on a slowly exhaled breath. "I hear your voice. I feel your arms around me. What more is there?"

"There's more; but let it go until later," he said softly, more to himself than to her. It was his own impatience to sweep her into the existence he knew, the existence which was her real home, but which must be submitted to the passage of time. The hours and days must grind their inexorable path into the future before she was ready.

He thought of the others: Delfaum, her brother, unbelievably more beautiful than she in the innocence of that ethereal existence, yet denying himself the eternal joy of full commitment so that his sister might have a link with that other world to which she must someday return; Petraum and Aletha lingering on the edge of eternity waiting to welcome back the daughter who had chosen a tortuous sojourn into the world. His own sacrifice in the name of love was puny by comparison. The strength of will Cheira displayed was even more amazing now in the light of full understanding. There were no words to describe the courage she had shown in choosing such a course. With a shock, he realized she had known what the future held. She had foreseen this moment, she would voluntarily, commit her existence to the control of another. The future as she saw it would be subject to the inflexible laws of nature which did include unforeseeable accidents and the oftentimes fickle actions of humanity. No wonder the others waited. But he had to realize it himself. They would not influence his decision.

His arms tightened about her. She sagged against him. He raised her face with a finger under her chin. "My darling, I love you," he whispered. "If I could only tell you how much." He caressed her lips with his own. She lay against his arm, yielding to the remembered sweetness of his touch, so much more intense now, as it coursed along her nerves. Her arms stole around his neck, clutching him with spontaneous possessiveness, storing each second in her memory as a hedge against the unknown, against the possibility of a time when he might leave her again.

"I'll never leave you," he murmured, knowing her thought.

She heard the certainty in his voice with the same perception that she felt the warmth of his breath against the skin of her throat. She accepted the statement, without question, as she would now accept anything he chose to say or do. There was no faculty in her to offer resistance. Only the short-sightedness of her human subconsciousness retained the shadow of doubt. She was not aware of it.

He led her to the sofa, pulling her down beside him. She leaned against him, letting the awareness of his arm around her seep into her body. She closed her eyes, sharpening the sensation of the warmth of his skin reaching her cheek through the thin silk of his shirt. From deep in her imagination, she saw herself alone, the endless days marching like phantoms across her field of vision. A sob rose in her throat as utter desolation settled into the marrow of her bones. She wanted to cry until the last breath was wrenched from her exhausted lungs. She wept; but there was no one in the whole world to hear her.

"My darling, please don't," Siri pleaded, the identity with her suffering prominent in his voice. "Your long journey is almost over; and now I will be with you the rest of the way. There will be no more separation—forever. I swear it!"

She tilted her head to look at him. Her eyes were dry. There were no tears, only acceptance.

"Cheira, let me tell you," Siri propositioned hopefully. "It's like nothing you can imagine." He paused, grinning. "I should say—remember. It's like that day at Lamborn, only so much more. And those who are there . . . " She put her fingers over his lips, stopping the words, her eyes misted with pain. He saw the image in her mind—the desolate landscape engulfing her.

"All right!" He sighed. "The time is not yet. I must remember." He grinned. "Now it is patience I must learn."

Siri straightened, releasing himself from her embrace. "John is coming. I must speak to him. I owe it. Go up and wait for me. It won't be more than a few hours."

The fear flared in her eyes. "Please don't send me away." The words were choked by the indrawn breath of a sob. The tone wrenched his heart; but the passing of the next few hours was beyond his control.

"I swear to you, I will come." Siri kissed her hands. The fear in her eyes died away to be replaced by a look of resignation. "My God, Cheira, don't!" Siri begged. "If I can't explain, what can I do?" He groaned, helplessly. *It was your choice,* the words resounded in his brain, mercilessly.

Oblivious to the suffering she was causing, Cheira rose obediently, picking up her cloak and making her way slowly to the door. She accepted his statement that John was coming. By what power he knew, she couldn't even guess. She ceased thinking about it. It didn't interest her. She knew

329

only that she must obey him no matter what her own inclination. She expected John to open the door.

John bowed, stepping back to let her pass. She walked by him without acknowledgement, with the remoteness he had grown accustomed to in the last few months. Her actions were so normal that he wondered if Jennie had been hallucinating, sending him to meet a figment of her imagination.

Siri's prolonged absence was a burden he was more than eager to relinquish. Although his feelings hadn't changed, he had to admit that the desert man was the only one who could help Cheira. Her attitude worried him, the more so because all his effort had failed to alleviate it. He had enlisted Ameur's help; but the visit had only upset her more. He couldn't think of anything else to do, nor could Mott.

Cheira made her way across the great hall toward the staircase, her spine forced slightly back from the vertical to compensate for the weight of her abdomen. She didn't notice the change in her posture. Her attention was focused in her heart. This constant awareness of her body had become second nature. The contrast was unrealized. Calmly, she felt the familiar, aching throb. She had anticipated it; it was why she had pleaded with Siri not to send her away. She knew it would begin the moment John closed the door. She didn't try to fight it. She didn't even hesitate in her stride. She accepted it, welcomed it for its very intensity would mean a greater relief when Siri came. *If he comes,* her subconscious pricked. It didn't bother her. If necessary, she could bear that, too.

"Hello, John!" Siri smiled as John came into the room.

"So you did come back!" John ignored the greeting with his usual brusque manner.

"Still doubting, John?" Siri's smile deepened. He turned away to pour a couple of drinks from the bottle in the well-stocked cabinet. He handed a glass to John, then settled comfortably in the recliner.

"Mervin said you'd be a fool to come back!"

"And what is he calling himself?" Siri grinned.

John stood, refusing Siri's invitation to be seated. He openly studied the man before him, the long-nurtured antagonism plain in his face.

"Mervin said you'd be changed, if you did come back," John challenged.

"That you must judge for yourself," Siri countered, his voice low and calm.

330

John searched for a sign of arrogance, for the self-conceit that brooked no interference, for the monumental pride that denied the importance of any other living being. All he saw now was the quiet dignity of a man who knew himself thoroughly, and an acknowledgement, apparent in the eyes, of the existence of others that enhances rather than threatens his own.

Siri submitted patiently to the scrutiny, raising no barrier to John's probe of his thoughts.

"My God!" John breathed as the full realization of the change swamped him. He sank onto the sofa, shielding his eyes with his hand.

"It's there for anyone who wants it," Siri said softly.

John sat unmoving. He needed time to recapture his self-control, to try to grasp the implications of what he had just learned.

Siri waited.

John squared his shoulders, taking a long gulp of the drink he held forgotten until now. He looked at Siri, still disbelieving the serenity of the glance that met his; gone were the traces of the fierce hauteur characteristic of those dark eyes. John felt the hate he had borne against this man collapse.

"You gave it up for love of Cheira?" John struggled to understand.

"I've given up nothing," Siri corrected. "You see, I'm still the most selfish man you've ever known. My return is only the acknowledgement that Cheira is necessary to the fullness of my eternal existence. You may call that love, if you wish."

"Then her total submission to your control pleases you."

"No!" Siri sat up, for the first time the vehemence unmistakable in his voice. "This you must understand. That's not the way. I must help her to find herself again. The struggle has been too long; but now I have the strength to show her the way back."

"Dr. Carpenter says her health is excellent. You'll not endanger the child she carries." The old threat came back into John's voice.

Siri smiled. "It's my child, too. Why do you still find it so difficult to trust me with Cheira's welfare? It's for that that I've allowed you to see so much."

"You've given me sufficient reason in the past," John reminded him.

"The greatest flaw, John, in all of us is limited knowledge. It's the basis of every misunderstanding. Ignorance has created all the suffering in the world."

"And now you are master of all knowledge!" John couldn't suppress the sneer, involuntarily curling his lip.

"Not all," Siri answered simply, smiling at the other's insinuation. "But more than any other man in our world."

John stared at him, but could detect no attitude of boasting. Siri had stated the truth. That was all.

John tried another tack. "What do you intend to do?"

"Stay with Cheira—until such time as she is ready to resume the existence of her origin."

"You know that?"

"Yes. I have been there."

"Will you tell her?"

"When she is ready to hear it. Right now all we can do is wait." Siri rose. "I want to see Mott for a few minutes. And I don't want to stay away from Cheira any longer than necessary."

"Wait!" John raised his hand. "I know you're not interested in the welfare of the society, but will you come to Arx Vetus? I'll summon only the oldest members. They've a right to know. Mervin stated that the realization of that state would rest on your decision. He said that, if you came back, you would possess the means."

"I'll not leave Cheira." Siri's eyes hardened.

"Here, then," John persisted.

"All right! Tomorrow evening."

In David's office, the desk was piled high with papers. He pored over them. With the success of the initial experiment, enthusiastic requests had come in from all corners of the globe. Every woman in the society wanted to chuck her career to have a baby, it seemed. *Is this all the progress that transfiguration afforded?* he wondered. After all the centuries devoted to the search for a means to control reproduction, the instinct was still flourishing healthily. He shook his head, frowning and smiling together.

Another part of his work was the evaluation of the tests he had conducted with Siri. He had tried to duplicate Siri's feats in order to measure the amount of energy needed to perform them. Hultz from Warsaw and Vendier from Paris, two of the oldest and very powerful members in the society, as well as brilliant scientists, had come to help him. An instrument for measurement was defying the best efforts of the three of them. They had enlisted Ameur's help several times. As the oldest member of the society, it was assumed he had the most power and control. But Ameur was only erratically successful. They decided that his constant worry over Cheira and the responsibilities of the society made his full attention to their tests impossible.

David frowned. *Cheira.* She was living like a cloistered nun, refusing to see anyone. Jennie and Dr. Carpenter, infrequently John, were the only ones allowed into her apartment. Once, when he had determined to examine her himself, she had become hysterical when she saw him. He was forced to rely solely on Dr. Carpenter's reports. Again, he was grateful for her competence. He realized how heavily, now, the success of the experiment rested on her shoulders.

Personally, he didn't give a damn. His relationship, if you could call it that—he smiled ruefully—with Cheira had deteriorated rapidly since that day they argued over the drug. He had only to wait until he was dismissed anyway. He wondered what stayed her hand. It was his loyalty to Siri, however, that demanded he give his best for her welfare.

Shrugging impatiently, David reached for the report from Jim Connors on the examination of the Didaskes. While the notes fired his imagination, he was overwhelmed with the enormity of what Connors had observed. *We're a thousand years behind,* he thought.

"More than that, David." Siri laughed. He appeared standing before David's desk. The young physician jumped up, the frown on his face transformed into one of pleasure.

"Siri!" he shouted, rushing around the desk to embrace his friend. "I never thought to see you again. Mervin was doubtful you'd come back. He said you went with them—whoever they are—and that very few ever return." In his excitement, the words tumbled out until he was breathless; his face flushed with happiness. He looked at Siri, his hand still on Siri's shoulder, as if reassuring himself that his friend was really there.

"Mervin seems to have reported to everyone." Siri smiled.

"Naturally! We all wanted to know what happened. He's been holding seminars, lecturing on what he found over there. He says it'll be easier when the time comes. But he doesn't seem to know exactly for what. And I have a report from Jim Connors. You won't believe how far advanced some of those people are . . . " David stopped, withdrawing his hand from Siri's shoulder, embarrassed and confused. "I don't have to tell you this. You know, don't you?" His voice was low and awed.

"Yes, I know," Siri answered, his tone matching David's.

David studied him closely. "You've changed." His voice was almost accusatory.

"Very much," Siri admitted, his dark eyes shining. Then he shrugged, grinning at David's solemn countenance. "I can shorten your thousand years to a few days, David. I can tell you everything you want to know."

"Wow!" David gasped. "When do we start?"

Siri laughed. Then his expression became serious. "There's no hurry. It looks like we have plenty of time." He sat down with a sigh. David failed to understand, but sensing the change of mood, he also quietly returned to his chair. "I came here to find out about Cheira. I can't make any sense of her thoughts. The past seven months seem to be a blank in her mind. John, too, seems to have only the vaguest notion of her condition."

"She brought you back," David burst out, the animosity ill-concealed in his voice.

"David," Siri remonstrated, the sadness showing in his expression. "The day will come when you will know what she had jeopardized for all of us. Then, you will curse me, instead, for my recalcitrance."

David pressed his lips into a thin line, repressing the words he wanted to say.

"I know, also—but it is for you to confirm—" Siri continued, "that your feelings have not interfered with your duty."

"Of course not!" David bridled. "But it hasn't been easy. She's living like a hermit. I've insisted that Dr. Carpenter keep detailed reports. That way I can keep close track of her condition. But she's adamant in her refusal to allow any examination by me. I'm one of her least favorite people."

"But you can tell me what I want to know," Siri prompted quietly.

David nodded, taking a deep breath.

"Dr. Carpenter's been in constant attendance. I've relieved her of all other duties. She gives me a daily report. We're especially concerned about spontaneous transfiguration. However, there's been no sign. If anything, it's been just the reverse. Oh, no danger!" David answered Siri's movement of concern. "She's perfectly healthy. Her pregnancy is advancing normally and there are no complications. She's chosen to experience it without help of anesthetic. Dr. Carpenter has given her exercises which will help facilitate that decision. She's following the regimen exactly. In fact, it absorbs most of her time."

David paused. Siri was paying close attention to every word.

"As far as her mental attitude," David resumed, a note of uncertainty in his voice, "she's withdrawn into herself. She's turned everything over to John. Any attempts to interest her in the workings of Pemberly Enterprises or the society have failed. Everyone's been wracking their brains trying to find something to hold her attention even for a little while. Ameur has begged her repeatedly to see him, if only for a few minutes. She's refused flatly. No explanations offered. According to Jennie, she hasn't mentioned your name since you left, which is certainly odd. She seems to be waiting only for the birth of the child. Her mind is fixed on that one goal. It's eerie! More so because there's nothing wrong. Only it's such a change from the way we've known her."

David sat back. There was nothing else he could tell his friend. He wished he could have reported something cheerful, especially when he saw Siri's expression sadden.

"Thank you," Siri said quietly, rising. His course was clear now, but no shorter.

"Will you stay?" David jumped up, wanting to detain his friend as long as possible and surrendering to the question that had pricked at him since Siri first appeared.

"Until Cheira is ready to go with me," Siri replied.

"Oh!" David raised his hand; but Siri was already gone. *Now what did he mean by that?* he wondered.

Siri materialized in Cheira's suite. The room was bathed in the half-light of early evening. The furnishings seemed to float on their own shadows. Only the gold disk above the mantel gleamed brightly as if proclaiming itself the only reality. Melancholy music drifted into the room from hidden speakers. The somber tones contributed to the heaviness of the air.

Cheira was sitting cross-legged on the floor in front of the fireplace. Her position and the long, golden hair falling over her face as she studied some pictures spread out fanwise made her look like an innocent child were it not for the obviously advanced state of her condition. She rocked slowly, back and forth, unconscious of the instinct that prompted the movement, unaware even of the movement itself. Her mind was filled with memories of the man in the pictures: only old snapshots wrested from Ahmed; fuzzy prints taken with a camera Siri had picked up in Paris years ago. When Ahmed had become intrigued with the appliance, his master had laughingly presented it to him and had obligingly posed for the neophyte photographer.

Cheira passed hours examining the beloved mannerisms which the shutter had captured: the way he held his head, thrown back when he laughed; the proud posture exuding the arrogance of absolute authority; the gentle skill of his hands on the reins of a plunging horse; a lock of hair that shadowed the fierceness of his gaze—all imprisoned forever on the little squares of paper. She impressed every detail into her memory.

Siri stood in the deepening shadows of the foyer. He frowned, surveying the scene. Neither Cheira nor Jennie noticed him. *Is my view of the future in error?* he wondered. A feeling of doubt flooded over him. Perhaps, he had only dreamed the last months. Had his actions reduced her to this? Cheira's love had become a fixation that threatened to immerse her personality. It and the child she carried had become the sole purpose of her existence. He felt an involuntary tightening of his skin as if he stood in a sudden cold draft. He confronted the only monster with the power to defeat him: instinct—blind, reasonless, purely animal instinct. The state that no power of mind could reach. Indeed, a state in which the mind was enslaved, beaten into base submission to the emotions, expressions of ancient primal urges.

Oh, my beloved, he thought, a pressure on his heart making respiration a labor. *Is it worth this? Is your commitment so total that all of yourself must be sacrificed? Is this the price of compassion?*

His body remembered the fragility of hers, the fineness of her bones under the soft flesh. Then he remembered the cold determination in her eyes demonstrating the strength of her will. It was his answer.

The depressing notes issuing from the speakers flooded back into his consciousness. The energy he controlled sought out the mechanism and rechanneled it. He forced the object to amplify what was in his mind. There was only an instant's silence; the sound of a multitude of voices with the sweetness of a celestial choir filled the room with the vibrations of the song of the spheres; the disk above the mantel seemed to quiver in harmony.

Cheira looked up, the radiance of recognition shining in her face. Siri stepped forward, smiling. But before he could speak, Cheira clamped her hands over her ears.

"Shut it off! Shut it off!" she screamed at Jennie.

Jennie was wide-eyed with wonder; but she hastened to obey.

"Cheira, don't do this." Siri's voice was low in the ensuing silence.

"Keep it away!" she screamed at him. "It's taken you and it will take my baby." She collapsed around the bulge of her stomach, folding her arms protectively, shielding the burden with her body, rocking to and fro, moaning with despair.

Siri swore, the words no more than the exhalation of his breath.

"Cheira, Cheira, my love." He raised her into his arms. "Where did you get such a preposterous idea?"

"Have you ever stayed with me?" she whimpered, her words muffled in the folds of his shirt. "I don't know what you found this last time, but I feel it's worse than the pride or the anger which separated us before. It will be as Wang Lu predicted."

"My God!" Siri burst out in exasperation. "Is that the way your brain is working? You've not only lost your power with the reversal, but your common sense as well. Listen to me!" He held her at arm's length, forcing her to look at his face. "Want Lu tried to save you from this. From what you are doing to yourself now. He saw how it would lengthen the time of your stay immeasurably and—he thought—unnecessarily."

She eyed him suspiciously. "It's true then. Wang Lu never really returned to the human state. He never really grew old and died." Her voice rose, a sob catching at the words. "That's why he wouldn't let me see him! He left me. You know it, don't you?" The accusation brought affirmation to his eyes. She turned away, shielding her face so he couldn't see the hopelessness in her expression. "He left me for that other existence," she reiterated resignedly. "Just as you did and you will again."

"His job ended when it was certain that I would assume the responsibility," Siri admitted. "I've seen him. He's still very concerned for you."

"But he left," Cheira persisted. "And so will you."

"What can I do to convince you? A practical demonstration, then?" he suggested. "I promise I will never leave you again even for an instant. Turn on the lights, Jennie, and bring us some supper. We must prove to your mistress the error of her thinking."

Siri grinned, leading Cheira to a chair. With an exaggerated bow, he handed her a glass filled from the decanter of sherry on the table.

Jennie smiled happily, dropping Siri a curtsy of approval. She didn't share Cheira's fear at the change in him. She saw instead a man in the maturity of being, strong yet gentle, like the heroes in the sagas of her homeland. She felt pride now for the man who was the living demonstration of what mankind could become. Jennie couldn't explain how she knew this; she was certain only that a nameless longing for the sight of a man who matched her ideal had been fulfilled at last.

David came with Irene Carpenter after dinner hoping for a chance to talk to Siri while Cheira had her nightly checkup. His enthusiasm had overcome the reticence he felt. But Siri had given no indication in the afternoon as to when he'd be free to continue their discussion. David had paced his office the rest of the day in a fever of excitement. Dr. Carpenter's regular visit was the only excuse he could find. Still, he was embarrassed and unsure of how this audacity would be treated.

Cheira glared coldly at him, but passed into the bedroom without a word.

"You don't need any pretense to see me," Siri admonished, showing his guest to a chair by the fire. "Our positions are reversed since the days at Imla Dun, huh, David? In fact, I can not only tell you what you're thinking now, but what turmoil you've been in all day. I'm sorry, but I couldn't stay this afternoon."

David blushed, stammering an incoherent reply.

"The question that's been bothering you so much is quite simple, depending on your point of view," Siri said seriously, handing David a Scotch. Taking a long swallow from his own glass, he settled comfortably in the chair opposite the young inquisitor.

"Have you examined the subsequent change in the anterior pituitary, David, after transfiguration? Its influence on the rest of the bodily functions is well known; but I needn't tell you that. Now, for a moment, consider the circumstances of transfiguration as we practice it. Remember that total submission of the will is required. Such a condition causes a suspension of the body's instincts for self-preservation. The intellect has accepted a situation outside its range of experiences. In that case, for example, the subject would even destroy himself if he were so instructed by the one to whom he has surrendered. You must realize how encompassing is the commitment. If you think about that, you will better understand the circumstances which prevail in the members' dealings with Cheira, how they seem to have a blind spot which even the most brilliant will not challenge.

"Now, turn your attention to the physical change that is occurring at the same time. The pineal gland, which has been inactive since early childhood, has begun to secrete its hormones, forced suddenly back into activity by an extraordinary input of energy. By the same act, the pituitary is suppressed. They've opposite polarity. It's no longer the master gland, but submits the control of its functions to the all-powerful pineal. The ancients called the pineal the eye of the soul, remember? It seems they knew what they were talking about. From this point onward, this gland will control the physical responses of the body; but it, in turn, will be subject to the will and need to depend on the intellect for knowledge.

"Here, the two meet, physical and mental. The pineal carries out the commands of the will, which by the act of submission has accepted the condition of transfiguration. The subject is informed, for example, that he will possess eternal youth. The mind accepts the declaration. He can see the

338

proof in the others. He is more than happy to receive that state which the other members enjoy. He never questions it. The pineal obeys. That's easy, just a slight rearrangement of the pattern. It already contains the capability of reprogramming the cells, as in altering the growth potential with which you are acquainted. A tiny amount of hormone acts as the catalyst.

"On the other hand, however, the pineal is unschooled. It must be conditioned to execute some of the more difficult feats; telepathy, teleportation, and others. That's why practice and concentration are necessary for their accomplishment. Concentration—to impress on the gland that result which is desired; a sort of bridge-building process between the physical and the mental. Practice—because the pineal learns by trial and error just how much response is required to accomplish the task at hand, like an athlete conditioning his muscles to reflexive reaction.

"The answer to your question, then, is obvious. Why is the price of transfiguration sterility? Of course, there is a price. Hasn't our culture instilled that into all of us? Isn't that one of the basic premises every good parent teaches his child? That idea has prevailed for so long it's almost born into us. And what, then, would be an appropriate price for such a great gift as immortality? We have finally discovered the fountain of youth and it is ours.

"The logical answer is mankind's previous means to immortality—reproduction. That ability which has, up to this time, enabled a man to stake a claim to the future, to know that through his children his identity will be perpetuated, that no matter what his failures he will have another chance through his progeny. Yes, the ability to reproduce himself is man's greatest treasure.

"Sterility, therefore, solves the problem to everyone's satisfaction. The pineal, whose job is to supervise the physical conditions of transfiguration, not pass moral judgements, obeys with the suppression of that function of the pituitary that controls the sex hormones. In its turn, the pituitary fails to initiate what we have come to consider normal fertility.

"And we've always had an example of our folly before our eyes: Ching Li." Siri paused, laughing. "None of us ever noticed that she was born after Wang Lu's supposed transfiguration.

"The whole process, then," Siri continued, "is a complicated result of our own ignorance."

"Like autosuggestion," David interjected, by this time sitting on the edge of his chair.

"If you accept the premise that the will governs the body; but it, in turn, can only act within the range of knowledge possessed by the intellect. Only man has or can have this kind of power."

David exhaled slowly. He hadn't realized that he'd been holding his breath. Slumping back in the chair, he was silently thoughtful.

"You said, 'transfiguration as we practice it.' There is another way, then. You and Mervin have seen it in India?"

"Yes," Siri answered. "But in many respects, it's much more difficult— the process by which an individual transfigures himself. Through many years of rigorous discipline, with only a knowledge of his goal as a prerequisite, it's possible for a person to bring about the desired changes within himself."

"And in a different culture, he wouldn't need to pay for it?" David was leaning forward, his eyes glittering with excitement.

Siri laughed. "You don't always jump to the wrong conclusions, Dr. Mott."

David shrugged at the implication, too involved in the trend of thought to be sidetracked. "And a child of such a union would be born transfigured?"

"Would be spared the dormancy of the pineal," Siri corrected. "The development of power would still take place in the usual way."

"Cheira?"

"Yes."

"Then, why? What is she doing here?"

"It was her own choice," Siri answered quietly. He rose to stand, leaning against the mantel, his eyes fixed longingly on the golden disk.

David suppressed the desire to ask more. Siri's attitude expressed a remoteness that David could not penetrate, nor did he feel that he had such a right. No more information would be forthcoming now. It was his place to wait.

The two men turned to the door when Jennie opened it to John's knock. At the same time, Cheira entered with Dr. Carpenter. The men bowed. With a shy smile of greeting to John, Cheira took the chair Siri had vacated. She looked at Siri, deliberately blotting out everything else from her sight, impatient of the irrelevance of all others to her existence.

Siri frowned slightly, then looked at the newcomer with a smile. "Come in, John. I see you couldn't rest until you had verified your impressions from this afternoon."

"You're right," John admitted, dropping any pretense at concealing his motives. "Can you blame me? I wanted to make sure before I summoned the others to such an unprecedented meeting."

"And risk making a fool of yourself?" This time it was David who uttered the cutting jibe, jumping to Siri's defense. Siri and John both recognized the familiar tone of the reaction.

"And yet another," Siri said sadly, speaking to his rival of many years. Humbly, he let John see the atonement he was making for all the consequences of his ruthless arrogance.

"If you wish!" John's answer was appropriate to the attitude of both men. They would each understand it from opposite points of view. Since the revelations of the afternoon, he felt only sympathy for the long journey of development ahead of David; and in the light of Siri's present value to the progress of the society, only gratitude to his one-time enemy.

David, of course, had no way of detecting this change of attitude.

"You've allayed any doubts I may have had," John told Siri. "I'll proceed with the call. Tomorrow evening at eight, if that's satisfactory?"

Siri nodded.

"Good night, then." John withdrew after a deep bow to Cheira.

"You'll be making your way infinitely more difficult if you continue in that manner, David." Siri's voice held equal notes of reprimand, kindness, and regret. "And you'll not make my burden of guilt less heavy." The added comment was not to enlist pity, but to be persuasion to influence the young man.

"What about the injustices caused to you?" David protested stubbornly, his imagination vividly recalling the image of his friend's unconscious, bloody figure suspended against a dank, slimy wall. Revulsion swelled up in his throat.

"Each of us, David," Siri remonstrated kindly, "must bear the consequences of his own actions. You are mistaken in thinking you can inflict repentance on others."

"I can't help the way I feel," David retorted defensively, "or erase the memories."

"But you can accept the past as unalterable. You've no right to deliberately darken the future from some personal need of your own to exact justice. True justice follows logically the consequences of our own actions."

David shook his head, unconvinced, rejecting Siri's statements because love for his friend blinded his reason. Someone must champion Siri as it was plainly apparent that he had changed so much that he would no longer protect himself. David didn't trust John's attitude. Any adverse incident, real or imagined, would be enough to revive the hate that had rankled so long. He couldn't dismiss the memory of the expression on John's face that day in the dungeon. *If Siri won't defend himself,* David decided, *I'll do it for him.*

Siri frowned. "If your friendship for me means so much to you"—he looked steadily at David—"you will think again. You'll find that the flaw in your argument will preclude the effect you desire."

Siri glanced at Cheira. She hadn't moved since she entered the room. She sat straight in a chair designed to cradle the body in relaxation. Her eyes were attentively fastened on Siri's face in the manner of a soldier waiting patiently for orders from his commander. Siri noticed her shoulders drooping with the fatigue she bravely attempted to conceal.

David followed Siri's glance, his look lacking the tenderness of the other, but the trained eye observing the same condition. "We'll talk again later," he offered.

"Thank you, my friend," Siri answered softly.

"Are you really here?" Cheira whispered in wonder when Siri stretched out beside her in the big bed. "I've been trying to convince myself all day that I'm not dreaming." Tracing the features of his face with her fingertips, she employed the sense of touch in the same way she used her sight with the snapshots. In acknowledging herself powerless to hold him, she strove to keep him in the only sure way she could, by imprinting his image indelibly on her senses. Her eyes closed. She placed her lips against his, memorizing the shape of his mouth, the feel of resistance his teeth made against the yielding softness of her skin. She laid her head on his chest, her hand tracing the length of his body. She listened to the beat of his heart.

"My darling, I love you." Siri smoothed the strands of hair falling across her face as she leaned over him. "In a manner you must learn to understand and accept, we'll never again be parted except by your decision." He paused, groping to judge the expedience of what he intended to say. "Cheira, you are keeping us apart. I know what you've been searching for. I know where you came from. I know, too, how very much you are loved."

The words brought her up straight.

"No! No!" she fairly screamed, turning away. "I don't want to know now!"

"Why, Cheira?" His voice remained low and calm.

"You don't understand!" she wailed. "You don't understand."

He sighed. He recalled the men who fought transfiguration with the

342

last ounce of their strength. He understood. He knew the pull of physical life. He'd experienced it on a barren plain in India: the illusion that kept mankind chained to the acceptance of mortality, preferring death to the abandonment of it. His own final struggle was still fresh in his mind; and that from a much higher state. Yes, he understood. Too well! The way ahead darkened. Could he make the way easier? Or must he stand helplessly by and wait as the others were doing? Did they realize more than he the futility of his mission? The time of waiting loomed immeasurably long, the contest unfair, his opponent her artificially acquired humanity. Again, doubt of his ability to see the future acutely assailed him.

"I want you now. Like this," Cheira whispered, growing calmer. "In the only real way I know, the only way I want to know."

He pulled her into his arms, his lips bestowing the pleasure she demanded, while the icy fingers of foreboding clutched at his heart. His mouth, caressing her breasts, discovered the feverish swelling.

"Good Lord, Cheira, what have you done?"

"I had Dr. Carpenter take it off. I want no symbol of an unknown master." She put her arms around his neck. "I love only you." Her voice lost the vehement tone, becoming barely audible. "It's not important anyway." She kissed him, hoping to divert his attention.

"Nothing is more important," he remonstrated sternly. "You know how important. Remember that day at Lamborn." Siri held her face, forcing her to look at him. The fierceness of his gaze bored into her skull. She closed her eyes defensively.

"I won't!" Her tone betrayed an unreasoning stubbornness.

Siri let her go. *You're a fool,* an inner voice mocked, *to try to combat that.*

Cheira interpreted the action as acquiescence. Triumphantly, she resumed the argument. Her eyes became misty with a sensuousness accenting her words. "You are my owner; and I have the proof here." She took his hand, placing it on the bulge of her stomach.

"But there's no need to forego that other existence for this!"

Her eyes grew wide in disbelief.

"So, even you've never questioned that stupid injunction we've placed on ourselves."

"You're trying to trick me," she accused suspiciously.

"My God, Cheira, I love you." Siri was rapidly reaching a point of exasperation. "I want us to have that future I know; but you must know it, too."

343

"I won't take the chance." She clamped her lips tight. "I won't jeopardize my baby."

"It will be all right," he cajoled, kissing away the stubborn set of her mouth. "The inability to conceive and carry a child is only an artificial restraint that we and all the members of the society have willed on ourselves. There's no scientific reason for it." *How many times and in how many ways must I explain this?* he thought wryly.

"I'll wait," she said, not believing him.

"The child doesn't change anything," he scolded.

The harsh look of defiance came back into her face. "You don't want it!" she accused. "You've never wanted it. But I'll not give up my baby even for you."

He felt the primitive maternal instinct surrounding her, an impenetrable barrier shutting him out. He groaned, a pain wrenched from the depths of his heart. He saw clearly the consequences of Cheira's choice. The reversal, plunging her into a level of human existence she had never experienced, was so thorough that it left her at the mercy of untutored instincts, reactions which in others had been suppressed by centuries of civilization. Her love for him was waging its own battle against the image of the dominant male destroying the life of his own offspring lest the infant survive to challenge his supremacy. The unfortunate circumstances of the child's conception lingered in her mind to strengthen the idea.

What could I do to help her? he wondered. *Must she struggle through eons of evolution before she is once again ready for the existence that awaits? Is my own punishment to consist of the agony of waiting with her?*

"When the baby is born," she was saying, "I intend to take it to Arx Vetus. We'll be safe there. And . . ."

He stopped the words with his mouth over hers, his hands on her body imparting a sensation which trickled along her nerves. She stiffened.

"You're mine, my love," he whispered, "by your own admission. Why do you resist?"

A moment longer she strained against his power, but the physical ascendancy of her body trampled over the weakness of her will. She surrendered. When he possessed her, the child kicked violently, protesting the contraction of muscles that caused his mother to moan with pleasure.

But the next morning, despite Siri's objections, Cheira had the symbol removed from its place above the mantel.

CHAPTER XXI

John had about fifty members assembled in the Great Hall promptly at eight. The air was electric with the excitement of anticipation. Men and women who had years since ceased to anticipate unexpected revelations found their interest scintillated by the prospect of learning what Stuart Mervin had only hinted at. They had attended Mervin's meetings and had been amazed at what he had to tell. They had gone over Connor's experiments. But when they wanted to know what it all added up to, Mervin had mysteriously advised that they'd have to wait for Siri to reveal the rest. He could insist only that there was much more. Now Siri was here.

Ameur paced restlessly up and down the large room, charged with barely suppressed impatience. Siri's possible revelations were only part of his interest. He worried about Cheira. Her prolonged absence, after the years of close association, left a void in his life that nothing could fill. And he had tried repeatedly to see her. He was hurt and bewildered that she shut him out of her life so completely. He told himself over and over again that he had accepted her decision; that she knew it. He could find no reason for her behavior. He had questioned the others: John was vague and busy; Mott was indifferent, shoving the medical reports at him, leaving him to draw his own conclusions while he was totally absorbed in those damn tests. Now the prospect of seeing Cheira again accounted more for the eagerness with which he had answered John's summons than any curiosity he might entertain concerning Siri's discoveries.

"Why don't you sit down, man? You're making us all nervous," Tony Hammond remarked as Ameur passed in front of him. The Englishman had always viewed Ameur's deep feelings for Cheira in the most flippant manner, mocking his own emotions, which had once compelled him to retrace the trail of his superior into the camp of a hostile sheik and over miles of burning sand to a deserted ruin. Trooper Hammond hadn't believed the story of Ameur's demise that the Legion entered in its records. He knew the American too well after five years under his command. Although it had taken him nearly a year, he had proven his surmise the day he spotted the "dead" legionnaire haggling with a merchant at a halted caravan on the outskirts of Touggourt. He had instantly recognized the familiar stance, although Ameur was disguised as an Arab. By skillful tracking, he had followed his former commander to Arx Vetus without being discovered. Once there, of course, nothing could induce him to leave. After Cheira transfigured him, he had indulged an insatiable appetite for adventure by prospecting for gold in America, an undertaking which, once he had succeeded, made the restoration and maintenance of the ancient ruins immeasurably easier.

Ameur paused, glaring at the man whose impudent grin implied that only the foolish held anything or anyone sacred.

"Tony's right, dear." Tiana agreed with the man sitting beside her. Ameur's expression softened as it came to rest on her face. Tiana's composure supported him now as it had so many times in the past. She was ever the helpmate who smoothed the crises of his life. It was only with her that he found respite from the longing which would always be part of his being. He knew it now as he had known it the first day he had seen her in her father's house.

He had gone to the farm near Portgruaro on the Adriatic plain of Italy to buy fruit trees for the garden at Arx Vetus. The exiled Greek owner, famous for his horticultural successes, had been overjoyed with the discovery that a customer who spoke his native tongue was also a dedicated gardener. Ameur, of course, was delighted with the man's willingness to share his knowledge. At his insistence, Ameur had stayed for dinner and subsequently lost his heart to the beautiful daughter of the orchardman. The feeling was mutual. When Ameur returned to Arx Vetus, Tiana went with him.

Now he threw himself into a chair next to her, taking her hand and raising it to his lips. "I'm sorry," he said. "I didn't realize I was being so obvious."

Across the room, Simbar Abu was deep in conversation with Stuart Mervin. For the past six months, Abu had been embroiled in a dispute over the boundaries of two Aftican nations. He had come directly from the negotiating table to answer John's summons. Mervin explained the purpose of the unusual meeting, since the black man had been too busy to attend the seminars.

Simbar Abu was the third person to join Cheira's infant society. He had stumbled into Arx Vetus with the last of his failing strength after a flight of more than thirty miles across trackless desert, without food or water, with only an indomitable determination to support him, preferring death to the life of a slave. Before reaching Arx Vetus that day, he had spent fifteen years in slavery, escaping from six masters, yet unable even after all the years of abuse to give up the desire to return to the tribe of which he was chief. Since that time he had expended his energy unstintingly in the service of the people he loved, doing more than any other person to aid the primitive cultures in their struggle to become citizens of the modern world.

"So this is the point to which destiny has been leading us." Ed Peterson spoke to Sam Hackett and John Westing while they waited for Siri to appear. "Remember that day Cheira walked into the press room of the *Atlantan?* Good Lord, she was beautiful! And the most dedicated abolitionist we'd ever met. We never could figure out what she did to Charley Bennett, but that straitlaced Confederate editor reversed the policy of the paper—to the dismay of all the slave owners in the country. Sam and I took to following her around like a couple of puppy dogs, although we justified our actions by calling ourselves her bodyguard. She sure stirred up a hornet's nest!"

"And when she left, we followed her halfway around the world!" Sam laughed. "These young fellows who fight transfiguration . . . I can't understand that. We begged for it. But I guess by the time we found out, we would have followed her through hell, if necessary."

Hultz and Vendier, with David in tow, joined the group. John frowned. The young physician was present by Siri's invitation. It was an exception of which John disapproved. The other two scientists were the results of Cheira's efforts to gather into her organization men of superior ability whose innate intelligence would be magnified thousands of times by transfiguration. These two men, more than any of the others, had proved her right. Their accomplishments had precipitated the world into the prosperity of the industrial age a hundred years before ordinary men could have achieved it.

"I wanted to ask you about this fellow, Liem, mentioned in your report." Vendier turned to Jim Connors. "How could you determine he's probably about four hundred years old?"

Jim grimaced. "We had a problem with that one for a while. Physically, of course, he's a man about fifty. Only one thing would have remained unchanged through the years: the dye used in the symbolic tattoo. They use it, too. We were able to make a fairly accurate estimate after analysis of a sample. Judgment was based on the amount of deterioration of the chemical structures involved."

Vendier shook his head skeptically. "That's pretty shaky scientifically, when you have no way of knowing the original chemical composition."

"Oh, but we do," Jim corrected, "or are very nearly certain. It's the same dye Wang Lu used. We took a sample of it from Ameur and used that as the standard. It's the oldest known sample available."

"Wait a minute," David interrupted. "There's another sample, if you want it. Dr. Carpenter just removed Cheira's tattoo. It's at the lab."

The eyes that turned to the young doctor were set into blanched, shocked faces. David blushed, embarrassed for he knew not what. The heavy silence added to the perplexity. "She ordered it done yesterday," David added defensively. "You've all read the reports. You know how she's changed."

They knew; but until this moment when the words were actually spoken, the comprehension of the unwelcome facts could be evaded. None of them had seen her since the reversal. Cheira was a never-changing spot of beauty in their lives, a focal point which gave purpose to existence. The written reports had made only a tenuous connection in their minds with the reality. The most scientifically oriented among them had not really identified blood pressure charts and psychological data with the idealized being they knew. In this case, recorded facts had not represented an individual personality.

David failed to understand the impact of what he had said. He stared at the others, bewildered. "Well, in a few minutes, you'll see for yourselves."

Jim Connors fled, shaken by emotion he couldn't hide. He had a wild urge to teleport out of the room, away from the unacceptable horror: Cheira, ordinary; her body grotesque with child; her mind degenerated to a subhuman level. Every word of the reports hammered in his brain for attention. The realization that others held casually a knowledge of her person was like a knife twisting in his chest. He hadn't ever thought that she carried a tattoo; but that it had been removed was the greatest sacrilege he could conceive.

The sound of Stevens' footsteps on the marble stairs echoed in the silence. The reverberation tinkled through the unresisting crystal globules of the massive chandeliers before being absorbed by the wooden beams overhead. There was a soft rustle of movement as those who had been seated rose expectantly.

"Lady Pemberly and the Earl of Zetland," Stevens announced, only after he had descended to the foot of the stairs. The formal tone of his voice crisply sailed its uninterrupted course ceilingward to disappear like the sound of his footsteps in the huge arched trusses.

A feeling of dismay swept the still figures. For Cheira to come to them as Lady Pemberly was like a renunciation. They felt cast adrift. The focus of their allegiance, always considered permanent and unquestioned, was crumbling, threatening dissolution. The permanent future they had all believed in yawned as an empty void. They shifted uneasily; all eyes watched the head of the stairs.

"Oh, my God!" Ameur gasped when Cheira appeared at the head of the stairs. She supported herself on Siri's arm. It was not that she had lost her beauty, but the accustomed radiance, which enhanced the perfect features, had been replaced by a common dullness. There was a strained look in the hollowness of her cheeks and the shadows that circled her eyes. The loose gown she wore, despite the designer's cleverness, did little to conceal her misshapen figure.

Siri had suggested that she forego this meeting, unsure whether he wanted to spare her or the others from the ordeal he foresaw; but she had insisted on remaining at his side, the thin rein controlling her emotions threatening to break at the slightest hint of a moment's separation, the veil of resignation which wrenched his heart descending over her as the only defense she had against her weakness. He relented.

The assemblage bowed. Ching Li began to cry. Lira drew her into a recessed window, soothing her with words appropriate to the consolation of all present. Most experienced with the devastating effects of emotional shock, she endeavored to project the calming cliches to all. She was only partially successful.

Cheira smiled; but she had no special greeting for anyone. She walked with Siri to a seat at the center of a semicircle of chairs arranged for the meeting. Without telepathic power, the others' shock did not reach her.

"Lady Pemberly extends greetings to all present," Siri began, his voice echoing around the room. "She asks that you excuse the absence of personal welcome, but under the circumstances . . . " The words droned on in an acceptable manner. They were what he wanted Cheira to hear. The message he conveyed to the others came to them through telepathy. Yet the whole introduction was intended to cushion the shock. Startlingly clear thoughts came to them. They noticed this, as well as the change in the sender, also. It was that as much as what he conveyed that made them believe him. Mervin's report was at once comprehensible. *Cheira is in no danger,* Siri ended. *This ordeal will pass.*

"It's my understanding that all of you have talked to Stuart Mervin or at least read his report. Therefore, we'll skip reiteration of those points.

349

That's not why you're here. For all present, it's time to consider the next level."

Siri slid into vocalization smoothly. Now his thought matched his words, lending an extra force of energy, which demanded their attention, holding in abeyance the emotional shock of the previous moments. "This state of expanded consciousness, which we enjoy, is only the first step. It's possible for man to attain a condition that is wholly consciousness, to become an entity no longer subject to the laws of nature as we understand them. Total knowledge becomes available to the mind without the tedium of learning and research because the intellect has joined the eternal principle from which it sprang. With the acquisition of omniscience—notice the specific construction of that word—no errors of judgment are possible. Naturally then, there is total accord not only with the universal consciousness but with all other beings. The result is harmony on a level inconceivable to ordinary men. Yet it is that which we spend our entire lives trying to achieve. Call it happiness, if you wish."

The room was devoid of sound, except for Siri's voice. They had forgotten Cheira. They had forgotten the shock of her appearance. They saw a new and brighter beacon ahead.

"This total awareness makes available a knowledge of the past, individually and collectively. And from that an understanding of the future. Therefore, this state transcends time. It becomes an existence where all events are present because all knowledge is present in a very real sense, an existence of transcendent happiness because misery is caused by ignorance—the errors of judgement based on lack of all the facts, which leads to faulty actions.

"This eternal condition is within the grasp of all men. Only deliberate rejection keeps us from it. Deliberate rejection is not too strong a term if you consider the time we spend wallowing in wishful yearnings, mindlessly hoping for the concretion of those wishes, closing our eyes to the flashes of intuitive revelation that come to us in the stillness of our minds. From the first man who said, 'It's impossible!' and believed it to the man who excuses the excesses of his life with the phrase, 'I'm only human,' from all the generations who have rejected the exercise of intellect, preferring to follow blind emotions or something they call 'instinct,' to the men whose total lives are devoted to the acquisition of someone else's inventions: Deliberate rejection is too weak a term.

"This is the only state which will satisfy the whole of the complex structure that is a man, that will give him the timeless existence for which he longs and which he is able to attain without the necessity of sacrificing his body. Those few atoms will gladly serve for as long as man has need of them. On the other hand, it's in the nature of man to cling to the physical part of himself. His body is his individual identity, his vehicle of expression in the world. It's this misunderstanding that has made man choose to exist wholly in the physical. Through the compounding of faulty choices, he has acquired the stultifying fear of loss. In his twisted mind, he has learned to accept death as the inevitable end of himself and to hope blindly for some miracle to give him eternal existence thereafter.

"We here present have taken the first step. But we are still chained to the ways of those around us. We have accelerated the acquisition of knowledge; but only that. We still learn in the same old way. Without conscious intention, we have set limits on our power and have accepted those limitations without question. Don't we all accept the possibility of destruction by accident where our wills are restrained from acting? Haven't we all conceded that food, shelter, and sleep are still requirements of transfigured bodies, that use leads to diminution of power that only rest can replenish? Aren't we all living 90 percent of our lives just like the rest of humanity? We use our power intermittently as an adjunct to our daily lives, as a convenience.

"That power which is the goal toward which we are all struggling is, through our ignorance, used as an easy means of transportation or swift communication. Do you see what we've been doing? Vulgarizing that power to fit within the framework of existence as we want it. All we have really done is prolong very ordinary lives. Where have we buried our imaginations or even the great intellects of which we are so proud?

"And know, if you wish to take any blame to yourself, that I reserve the greatest part of it. I am the only one of you who has devoted his life entirely to the development of power. And you are all aware of the baseness of my motive." Siri paused, looking first at Ameur then at John.

"Know, also," he continued, "that atonement for one's transgressions need not be sought. It is inherent in the acts themselves. I am bound to this existence, which I despise, through a bond that I am powerless to sever."

Siri's voice had sunk almost to a whisper. Every eye followed his turn to Cheira. He raised her hand to kiss the tips of her fingers. She smiled. It lighted her features with a hint of their former radiance. Easily he locked her gaze, for her eyes seldom left his face.

"Sleep, my love," he whispered, "only for a little while. And you'll wake refreshed."

Without protest, Cheira sank back against the chair; her eyes closed.

Ameur leaped forward, grabbing Siri's arm, his voice tense. "What are you doing?"

"Trust me, *mon cher ami,*" Siri replied quietly. "Where we are going, she cannot follow. This way, she'll be unaware of the waiting."

Ameur's shoulders sagged. "I can't bear to see her like this." His voice was harsh, choked.

"I'd like to say that what you're about to experience will make it easier; but when you are living what she gave up to come to us, I'm afraid the knowledge will be even harder to bear." Siri looked at Ameur, the glance full of compassion. "All I can ask is that you remember that she foresaw this time and accepted it. It was her own free choice."

Jim Connors sat at the far end of the room, his head in his hands, experiencing in silence what Ameur had voiced.

"There's nothing any of you can do," Siri continued, turning to include the others, forcing their attention to his words. "Cheira made a choice long ago, with the full knowledge of what the future held, with the full realization that the slowing of vibration would rob her of her memory, with the full acceptance that only her own efforts would bring her back to that state."

Siri shrugged. "We are powerless to change it. There is no way to alter one hour of another's destiny. And remember, if you reject what is offered, you make her sacrifice meaningless. The way has been made known by her efforts. Yet, each man must choose for himself. Ladies and gentlemen, you must now make yours."

Siri straightened, his voice deepened into a tone of command. He intoned the words, *"Ερχουχαι ide."*

The power of his mind washed over them, drawing them on to follow the glowing spectre that was his body. The strength of his will permeated them. It was irresistible. The glow expanded, pulsated; and with the intensifying vibration came the sound. The familiar symbol come alive; its meaning instantaneously known; unity experienced, possible to those who are omniscient; the ecstasy of harmony with the everlasting principle. Yet, each enjoyed an independence incomprehensible to ordinary men. Will, no longer subject to circumstances or environment, no longer linked to the necessity of action within the boundaries of a limited place in time; will, entirely unfettered, at last, free. As they knew themselves, so they knew each other and every other being who dwelt in this state.

They felt the atoms of their bodies vibrating in accord with universal matter, providing total awareness. The sweet sensation more vivid than any intimacy they had ever known, more satisfying than the most sensual acts of humanity; the unity achieved revealing the true meaning of brotherhood: totally independent; yet wholly equal, a conscious state of completeness of both mind and body; man made whole with every desire fulfilled, every need satisfied, forever.

Their bodies were light, brilliant and shimmering. An ordinary man immersed in the ignorance of superstition would call it ethereal. David stared, aghast. Nothing that had been said prepared him for this.

The light died suddenly. The young scientist stood for moments dazed by the change. The electric lights seemed dim, barely illuminating the room. The elation he felt dropped into restless depression. He satisfied the urge to do something by walking around turning out all the lights but one. With a start, he recognized that the way he felt was normal.

Three people stayed behind with Cheira: David, Jim Connors, who still sat morosely in the corner, and Lira, who turned away from eternal happiness because its acceptance would separate her from the one person necessary for her existence. Consciously, she told herself that her work was not finished, that her people needed her. Neither man noticed when she disappeared from the room.

Jim looked up at David when he spoke. *What had he said?* he wondered, his attention caught by the end of the sound. *Who was he? Oh, yes—* his brain collected itself—*the young man who headed the experiments at Pemberly Institute, the man responsible for the reversal procedure.* He scowled.

"Are you all right?" David repeated, failing in the effort to penetrate the other's mind, but increasingly alarmed at his posture and the fact that he'd not gone with the rest.

"Yes." Jim's voice was barely audible. He stood up, fatigue making the action torture. "I'm sorry; but I didn't hear what you said."

"I said, 'Please go, you've earned it.'"

Jim looked toward Cheira, his eyes expressing the emotion he couldn't voice. He shook his head.

"Didn't you hear what Siri said?" David felt exasperated. *Is there no end to men who love Cheira to the point of idiocy?* he thought, frowning. The look in Jim Connors's eyes was too familiar to be mistaken.

"She's all right," David heard himself saying for what seemed to be the millionth time. "And Siri told us it was her choice. There's no need for you to stay." David felt he was talking to an inanimate object, which only by accident resembled the human form. His words bounded off the man with no

353

effect. Irritated, David shrugged, going back to his chair to wait for Siri's return.

Cheira, Cheira. Jim Connors allowed his heart to savor the name as his gaze captured the sleeping figure. *What do I care for eternity without you? If you're not there, I can't be either. What does it matter if I can never have you? Just to be near is enough. You must not send me away again. This time I'll refuse to go. I'll do anything else you wish; but I won't leave you, not this time, not ever again.*

Connors stood rigid; every muscle taut, his mouth drawn into a tight line. His thoughts floated unreceived in the empty room, the sleeping figure at whom they were directed unable to know them. His eyes focused unblinkingly on Cheira. She lay back in the chair, a hand under her cheek, her head sunk against the knobby upholstery. A loose wisp of hair strayed across her face, adding its shadow to those of the long lashes fringing the closed eyelids. One arm relaxed along her body, the fingers bent unconsciously around her ankle, tucked under the sacklike dress covering her in a shapeless mound of material.

Objectively, in the detached manner of a scientist, the man gauged his feelings by the constriction of the muscles of his throat. His breath came in short gasps like an exhausted runner. His diaphragm labored to pull the air into his lungs past the pressure on his larynx. The suppressed emotions freed at last after years of subjugation washed over him in unhindered waves, swirling through the long lines of the slender body with the violence of an erupting volcano. He surrendered to the devastation of its course.

"Stop it, Jim!" Siri's voice was harsh, commanding, as he clamped his hand sternly on Jim's shoulder. "An orgy of self-pity won't alter the facts."

"Get away from me!" Connors snarled, wrenching away from Siri's grasp. "You should have been destroyed years ago. Look what you've done to her!"

Siri smiled sadly. "You can blame me no less than I blame myself; nor can you have devised a more fitting punishment than that which I must endure. But the guilt is not yours. Don't take it on yourself. Go with the others."

"And leave her at your mercy, I suppose?" Jim accused, his eyes blazing with hatred. "You can keep your heaven. I want no part of it. Nothing can make me leave her again. Not you! Not anyone!"

"I explained it all. There's nothing to be done," Siri reiterated patiently. "Time is the only remedy; time, which has the power to enslave us all."

"Time to subject her to more of your barbarity," Jim snapped, glaring at

Siri. "What subtle tortures has your savage imagination invented that you want us all out of the way? Well, I won't go!"

Siri sighed. The burden of atonement, lightened as it had been for the last hours by the fulfillment he had been instrumental in bringing to the others, settled heavily into his heart. "Very well," he answered in a low voice.

Striding swiftly across the room, he bent over his wife's slumbering form. "Cheira, wake up! The meeting is over."

She responded instantly to the sound of his voice, sitting up with a smile, her eyes wide. "Oh," she whispered, glancing around the empty room, "how could I have fallen asleep in front of everyone?"

"They understand. They're gone." Siri reassured her. He called David, bringing the young man to his feet from the depths of the chair where he, too, had been dozing. "We must turn our hands to running the organization temporarily." Siri grinned at the irony of his making such a statement. "John is the only one who'll return. At last, I can appreciate the altruism which motivates him, and even be thankful for it. But until he does, we'd better attempt some semblance of order. Go and see Bob Hardy. Fill him in on what's happened and get him to concoct some sort of public announcement. The disappearance of a dozen prominent men is going to need to be explained somehow. The ones who were known only within the organization will be an easier matter. Then contact Hans Werner and see if he and his wife can wind up their affairs and take over at Arx Vetus for Ameur and Tiana. In the meantime, you can fill in there. Indulge your love of the desert." Siri laughed.

Sobering, he went on. "Jim Connors will stay here. He can make up his own excuses for the move. And the people in the society here can help me cover for you and John."

"They're really not coming back?" David asked in wonder.

"You won't want to either when your turn comes." Siri smiled. "But from now on, we need a rule against unexplained disappearance. This is something the society hasn't had to deal with before. But, I guess, we can safely let that wait for John's return. There's no one with sufficient power to sustain that state at the moment, although the ones who have gone will prove an incentive for the others."

"Wow!" David grinned stupidly, the meaning of the last hours finally sinking into his consciousness.

"That's a ridiculous expletive for a man in your position." Siri grinned back. "Now get going. You must see Hardy tonight so he's ready to act in the morning."

Cheira listened quietly to Siri's instructions. She understood what he was doing and that it was her job to take control if John were absent, but she had no desire to make the effort. The months since the reversal had decreased the interest she had in the society. It became progressively less important as time went on. She felt herself withdrawing from it, without understanding why, without even the desire to understand. She barely noticed the waning activity of her mind as her attention became more and more absorbed in the changes taking place in her body. It seemed natural for the scope of her horizon to narrow, shutting out everything but her love for her husband and child.

David's presence irritated her now. She was pleased when she heard Siri send him away. She'd have done it herself had Siri not forbidden it. *Now, he'll be gone,* she thought. *How could Siri like him so much?* But, of course, he didn't know how Mott treated her. He didn't know the brash manners and the impudent questions. He'd as much as told her it was her own fault for what happened. Intelligent as he was—and she admitted that—he hadn't come up with any solutions. If she'd had power that day, she'd have shown him.

Her gaze wandered around the room, impatient now for Siri to finish and David to be gone. The shadows cast by the single lighted chandelier high overhead blurred the furniture into an indistinguishable mass. She sat up straighter, her attention caught by the man standing on the other side of the room. Recognition of the intimately known figure was instantaneous.

"Jim!" she cried, leaping up and running to meet him.

Connors hadn't moved since Siri left him. The emotions raging through his body held him paralyzed. No action had been possible. He was heedless of the surroundings and the awkward position his tense muscles had assumed. Only motivation from another could move him now: It was the sound of Cheira's voice. The sight of her approach, a smile of greeting on her face, galvanized him to action. Meeting her halfway, he dropped to his knees, clasping her hands to his lips.

"Why haven't you gone with the others?" she spoke softly, reluctant to hear the answer.

"What do I want with any existence if you're not part of it?" His lips, crushed against her palm, blurred the words.

"But I don't love you," she protested, drawing away.

"I know that. It doesn't matter. Only I must be near you. After tonight, my work will be meaningless. I won't even have that to delude myself that I'm serving you. Life will be impossible."

356

"Oh, Jim, please don't wait for me! Look at me! I'm not the same anymore. I don't think I'll ever be again. Don't wait! Don't wait!" Her voice trailed off, ending with a choking sob. Then she turned and ran up the stairs.

Siri watched the scene, not interfering. Now he smiled, approaching the still-kneeling man. "You've done it, Jim!" Siri's voice held a tone of enthusiasm. Jim's shoulders sagged; his head bowed in despair. "You've gotten more positive response out of her in five minutes than anyone else has been able to do in as many months."

Connors pulled himself together, rising slowly.

"What do you mean? I wouldn't call that positive response. I've been rejected in no uncertain terms. All I've done is make an ass of myself." He was tired, only a core of grim determination lay like a stone in his heart.

"Jim, my only concern is Cheira. I'm trying to tell you. I think your presence would help her, if you still intend to stay."

"You heard what I said. I meant it. Whether she wants me or not. Ridiculous as it may have sounded." He eyed Siri suspiciously. "But why would you of all people agree that I stay?"

Siri laughed. "Must we measure whose love is greater? Do you really suppose that I'd keep her at the price of her happiness? At least I've changed that much."

"You'd try to keep her at any cost. Why else have you returned when the others stayed?" Jim glared at Siri defiantly.

"Your accusation is logical and valid," Siri admitted calmly, "but only from your point of view. The choice you have made is the cause of the limitation."

Jim watched Siri intently, shocked that his thoughts were open. He could detect no barrier. He had to believe what Siri said.

"You heard me tonight," Siri explained patiently, "even though you reject it for now. I want that for Cheira. It's where she belongs, where she came from. Before the reversal, she was never like the rest of us. She was born transfigured. Now it seems she's sunk to the most primitive of human levels. You've read the reports. Nothing but the child and a fixation she calls love for me evokes any response from her. She'll not even trust my regard for the child. As for returning to the state of altered consciousness, she won't even hear of it. She's convinced it will terminate her pregnancy. If I force her, it will do just that. So I can do nothing. Just now is the first time she's voluntarily responded to anyone. Now do you understand?"

"I'll do anything I can to get her away from you," Jim warned.

"Oh, good Lord, Jim," Siri burst out in exasperation. "That's beside the point. So and wind up your affairs. You owe that much to your people. And Hardy is going to have his hands full without trying to explain your disappearance, too. When you come back, we'll talk. You can't help her or yourself unless you understand fully."

Cheira was already in bed when Siri entered her room. She made no movement at the sound of the closing door; her eyes were shut and her breathing even.

Siri stood beside the bed, looking down at her. He laughed aloud. "You're going to have to do better than that!"

Her eyes snapped open, the pretense gone. "Did he go?" Her voice was muffled in the blankets.

"Who?" Siri sat on the edge of the bed. "David?"

"Of course not!" The irritation was unmistakable in her voice. "Jim!"

Siri noted the response with satisfaction. Deliberately, he fanned the spark of annoyance. "No, he's moving into David's place. He wants to be near to take care of you. He's gone only long enough to wind up his affairs in the States. Then he'll be back."

"You didn't send him away?" Cheira sat up, dismayed. "But why not?"

"With David gone, you'll need someone to take care of you. Besides, it's for you to do that if you wish." Siri spoke matter-of-factly, as if it were the most logical solution in the world. But he no longer smiled. His eyes were intent on her face, the primitive state of her mind making it difficult even for him to follow her thoughts. He was afraid to go too far.

"But you don't want him here? You won't allow him to stay?" she gasped, misgiving and alarm in her expression. "You're going to leave me. You're going away with the others. So you don't care if he's here."

She threw herself down, turning away from him, the stillness of resignation exhibited in the inert posture.

Siri frowned. "If you continue to act like this, you may force me to it." Intentionally, he spoke with harshness.

"Oh, no!" She turned back, clasping him possessively.

It was the denial he wanted.

"What can I do?" she cried in a low, broken voice. "I love you; but I've no power to hold you. I'm only a burden you can get rid of anytime you wish. If you let Jim stay . . . " The words trailed off, the dread of voicing the implication checking her.

A burden I can get rid of. The words hammered in his brain. He looked down at the cherished countenance. *Cheira, my love,* his mind cried to her, *if you only understood.* Aloud he said, "You have the power to hold me. You always will." There was no emotion in the words. They were said coldly like the recitation of a fact. She couldn't doubt that he meant what he said.

Taking her arms from around his waist, he went into the dressing room. She lay as he left her, listening to the sound of the running water from the shower. His action seemed inconsistent. What had he said at the meeting about clinging to human ways? Understanding came in a flash, like the sudden rending of a veil. He wouldn't leave her; but he could withdraw, knowing the loss she felt with separation. As he now knew everything. It was a pressure he could exert, underlining the change he wouldn't tolerate. Now he had left her with a cold statement hanging in the air, when he knew she wanted a declaration of love. His action was a threat. It made her feel hopeless; and she wanted to please him.

Frowning, she tried to remember how she had been before. In those days, she had never experienced such comprehensive incapacity, a feeling that went beyond despair to a condition where only mute resignation would make survival possible. And there was the dread that stemmed from deep in her heart, which she barely admitted even to herself: the horror of spontaneous transfiguration. What might it do to her child? She didn't know; nor did anyone else. It was the reason she had submitted to the reversal in the first place. She caught her breath: *Siri knew.* Did she dare to ask him? Would he tell her the truth? The old fear returned, clutching at her heart. She believed that he never wanted the child. He'd told her so himself.

But he's changed, she argued.

How can you be sure? an inner voice countered.

I can feel it. I can tell.

But has he ever actually said so? He said the child didn't change anything. And he wants you. Maybe that other state makes passion even stronger, have you thought of that?

Oh, I don't care! I love him! I'll do anything he wants. Her thoughts stopped, daunted.

And your child? You love him more than that? The voice came relentlessly out of the emptiness within her. The child kicked strongly. It was the emphasis to the thought.

"When will you accept the fact that there is no need to make a choice?" Siri spoke quietly. She hadn't heard him come in. She looked at him, startled. "Cheira," he continued, lying down at her side. "It would be a temptation to say that none of this was necessary. That the timing was bad. If we had just waited a little longer, fate would have solved our problems. It's why the Didaskes made their move when they did. Even they try to shortcut

359

destiny sometimes. But it can't be done. Not as long as we are beings of limited knowledge and our wills, although free to act in any way we choose, are also fettered. I deeply regret, no, more than that, my soul writhes in an agony of remorse at the suffering I've caused." He silenced her movement of protest.

"Your not wanting to hear it won't change it. But that doesn't keep me from seeing the logic of it. Every act I performed from the time I was old enough to know what I was doing led up to this moment, the same way as the choice you made, even with the full knowledge of the future. And, my darling"—he folded her into his arms—"if you hadn't made that choice, you would never have been mine. Without you, my life would have ended in the misery of a void I couldn't name. My destiny is fulfilled. I will love the child of your body as completely as I love you. There can be no distinction as far as I'm concerned. So you see, it's the same now as it was in the beginning. Only you have the power to change the future."

"I want to believe you." She begged, "Make me believe you. Take away the doubt and the fear that's driving me crazy. Make me believe that you want the child, that you'll never leave me, that you're not allowing Jim to stay because you want to be rid of me. Now that I'm like this, how can I believe that?"

"Cheira, I can only give you the knowledge you need. To force your mind would be to defeat us both." He stroked her hair, trying by touch to impart the confidence she needed.

"Tell me, then," she persisted, "what the future will be."

"I can only tell you that it depends entirely on you."

"But you know it. With the power you have, you know it! Why won't you tell me? Oh," she moaned, "something terrible is going to happen. Wang Lu . . . "

"No, it's not that! But your idea of my knowledge of the future . . . " he explained, trying to calm her. He slid his arm under her shoulders, drawing her close. "I can see the scenes of the near future. But they become more indistinct as the distance increases. And even in the near future, I must interpret what I see. There's plenty of room for error. The probabilities multiply. So you're wishing for the impossible."

"I don't understand. You said I knew the future before. You said you knew everything. So you must know what I'll do."

He smiled, knowing what she was leading up to.

"You came from that state and descended into this one. I believe that it was a very exalted state, with longer vision and much more accuracy of interpretation than I can hope to master for quite a while."

"Oh," she said, propping her elbow on the mound of her stomach.

"I know the future," he repeated. "What I can see, and also what I've been told. But the decision is still yours."

"Then, I know the future, too," she asserted.

Siri laughed. The way was no shorter, but at least she had spoken about it—considered it. He clung to that scrap of encouragement.

CHAPTER XXII

The next weeks were busy for Siri. From early in the morning until late at night, the procession of visitors continued. The "death" of those who would not return had been skillfully simulated by Hardy with the news of a crash of a transcontinental jet in a remote part of the Andes. Search parties would spend months looking for the survivors before giving up all as lost. But the truth reached the members of the society with the speed of telepathy. Only the strict injunction that normal appearances must be maintained kept the meetings manageable.

Stuart Mervin continued the seminars at Arx Vetus; but it fell to Siri to speak personally with the senior members. It was he, also, who had to act as liaison between Cheira and Lord Yerby who had taken over the lead at Pemberly Enterprises for the duration of John's vacation.

There was only one for whom Siri waited who did not appear.

"What are you thinking about?" Cheira asked one night when they were finally alone.

Siri smiled. He was pleased with the progress she had made in the last month. His constant presence had lent the support she needed. She accepted the future, although she refused the immediate change; her reaction to his mention of it was no longer violent. "Wait until after the baby is born," she would say calmly.

She was uncomplaining of the time he spent down the hall in John's office, insisting only that he take the time to walk in the garden. The withdrawal of the months of his absence seemingly forgotten, she spent the hours preparing for the advent of the child.

Cheira repeated the question.

Siri chuckled. "I've many weighty matters on my mind, inquisitive one, now that you and John have deserted your posts."

"Pooh!" she said, unsympathetically. "You weren't thinking of me or the society. I can tell by the look in your eyes."

He left the place where he had been standing, leaning against the mantel, his back turned to the life-sized portrait which now hung above it. Cheira had insisted that Carl bring it from the Fort. It existed only because of the skill of the artist—a Frenchman whom Siri had once given refuge when his caravan had been attacked by bandits. It had hung in the gallery until Lira had spirited it away to the seraglio. Siri had never thought of it again; but Cheira remembered its existence. She spent hours gazing at the Arab chieftain on a rearing black stallion; but for Siri it was like blaring headlines of each of his sins.

He came to sit at her feet. "And what would you say if I told you I was thinking of another woman?"

"There's only one other whom you'd think of. Were you?"

"Ah," Siri laughed. "Your intuition hasn't failed, has it?" His expression changed to a frown. "She left the night of the meeting and hasn't returned."

"Do you love her still?" Cheira's tone was only the whisper of an indrawn breath.

Siri laid his head against her knees, his hand absently caressing her ankle. The smile returned to his face. "Not as I love you, but as a pleasant memory to be cherished. And now as an obligation to be fulfilled." He looked toward the portrait with a grimace that Cheira didn't see.

"You want to go to her, don't you?"

"Only if you'll understand."

"Call her here, then. I won't mind that."

"Jealous?" He laughed.

"Of course not!" But her blush belied her words.

Lira obediently, though reluctantly, answered the summons.

"Lira!" Siri smiled when she appeared, the ring of pleasure in his tone patently genuine. "I've the feeling you've been avoiding me," he accused gently, lifting her to her feet when she knelt before him.

"I've no wish to intrude," she murmured, her head bowed.

"Lira, believe me! I'm happy that you're transfigured." He put a finger under her chin, lifting her head so she had to look at him. "Although I must admit, I didn't learn of it under the most pleasant circumstances."

Lira remained silent, the natural dignity so inherent forbidding her to beg for forgiveness or even try to dissemble the awareness of the possible consequences of her act. She had made the decision to comply with Cheira's request when she'd given Tiana the drug. It would stand. Her face took on the expression he knew so well, her eyes meeting his without wavering, allowing him to see her submission to whatever he might choose as atonement.

Dropping his hand, he turned away. The attitude, which only months ago would have been a satisfaction to his ego, now only added to the burden of expiation. He felt the light he carried within, the promise of that state he longed for, shrink farther beyond his grasp. Reflexively, he clenched his fists—an outward sign of the mental effort to hold that spark from being extinguished, from slipping into a void. When he turned back, his face was pale from the exertion.

Lira hadn't moved. She stood expectantly, but patiently, for the command, blissfully ignorant of the suffering her love caused. Siri owned her life now, as he had at the Fort. That could never change.

"I want you to come with me and see," he said in a low voice.

"My people need me," she answered, making no effort to mask the lie of the words; but it was the strongest plea she could make.

"You're mistaken!" He spoke earnestly. "To deny yourself that state, which you have in your power to achieve, in the name of love is to brand your loved one as the cause of a lesser state, thereby denying to him also that realization. Is that what you want? Is it love you feel for me; or is it vengeance you desire? Have you thought carefully of that emotion you're calling love? And know this, your refusal will bring about that realization."

Lira gasped. Her eyes hadn't left his face. She saw clearly the change. The arrogant set of the mouth, the proud fierceness of the eyes had been replaced by fine lines of suffering and a look of patient endurance. The whole expression, nonetheless, was one of such total serenity as she had never seen on a human countenance. *He looks older,* she thought; *but not in the manner of physical aging, rather in some indefinable manifestation of the maturity of inner being.*

"You must choose now." Siri's words were flat and unemotional.

With a shock, she detected a tone she never expected to hear from him. She was as certain he hadn't intended her to notice, but she knew him too well. The quality she heard was the pleading of a man contemplating an unbearable loss. Her stupidity had reduced him to that.

"It is love I feel for you," she emphasized, unwanted tears popping into her eyes. "I've never intended to interfere in any way with your happiness. Not ever! But this life is all I can share with you. Just to be in the same world is enough. I can be satisfied with that." She wanted to be silent, but the words rushed out involuntarily like a ruptured dam.

"I used to pretend I was a traveler seeking a place to rest so I could see you at the Fort. I was one of the women who served coffee at Imla Dun. I was there when you came with Dr. Mott. Oh, how I envied him for the time he spent with you. When you'd look at him and smile, my heart stopped. I'd pretend you were looking at me. And I'd remember . . . " She broke off with a sob; the words stopped in her throat.

"I'm sorry, Lira," Siri said, compassion in his eyes.

"That's what you want me to give up," she choked. "Just that little is all I ask."

"You can enjoy a greater existence, where there is no suffering or unhappiness, where this barrenness will be only a memory. You deserve more than that."

"Is it what you want me to do?" She held out her hands, supplicatingly.

"We'll share that existence, Lira. In a manner greater than anything you can imagine. Come and see." He grasped the outstretched hands and drew her close. The smile on his face made her eagerly willing to follow him. She looked deeply into his eyes.

"Ερχουχαι ide!" he said in a low voice.

The return was even harder this time. It was the most difficult action he had ever performed. The effort left him trembling, the enervation of his body unresponsive to the command of his will. The pull of gravity was a dull throb in his bones; his flesh sagged under the heaviness of its substance.

"Siri, what is it?" Cheira rushed to his side as he slumped weakly into a chair. He reached for her as a drowning victim clings to a life preserver. He buried his face against her breast, his breath coming in gasps of uncontrolled reflex.

She knew that he needed strength from her this time. Her arms tightened, her hands stroked his hair. Crooning softly, she rocked instinctively. The unknown she dreaded loomed ominously close, forcing a reluctant recognition. The black cloud threatened to evaporate. She shook her head in protest, fighting to hold it in place.

"You took Lira over, didn't you?" she accused, her lips against his hair. "And you almost didn't come back. Oh, my love, they'll take you away from me. I know it."

"When you're ready to go with me," he pleaded. "And let it be soon."

She backed away, the refusal cold in her eyes. "We'll talk about it after the baby is born," she stated flatly, determination severing the consolation she had just offered.

The curtain descended between them. For Siri, the last month had made the feeling familiar.

365

He lay back in the chair, sighing. Her ruse was transparent. Should he tell her that? And that shortly she'd have to relinquish it? The imminence of the event and the concern she had shown for his welfare prompted him to pursue the subject.

"Cheira, let me tell you about it now."

She shook her head vehemently. "No! No!" she whispered. Her next breath was a scream. The shock of pain from the unexpected contraction gripped her, driving all thought from her mind as the age-old ritual of her body took possession of her faculties.

The sound brought Jennie flying into the room. One glance was enough to send the wise country girl into the hall with a telepathic summons for Dr. Carpenter.

Cheira stooped slightly forward, her expression blank. The strange, unknown pain paralyzed her. She listened to, rather than felt, the slow ebb of agony as the contraction relaxed. She was afraid to move, bracing herself for the next spasm that instinct warned would come unheralded, but with as much severity as its predecessor.

Siri leaped up, the fatigue of a moment ago deliberately cast aside, ignoring the strain he was placing on himself in his concern for Cheira. He cursed the experience that separated them, that prevented him from sharing her suffering. His arms around her, he used his power to soothe her, to relieve the tense muscles, which only aggravated the pain, intensifying it unnecessarily.

She jerked away violently from the embrace; her eyes focused on his coldly. Surprised, he dropped his arms and looked toward the fireplace, seeking the spot above the mantel for wisdom, for the right way to proceed. But only the portrait of himself returned his gaze. The oil figure jeered at him—a full return. His shoulders sagged.

"My darling," he said, desperately, reaching out for her. "I can allay the pain. I can help."

The look on her face stopped him. He saw reasonless instinct in her eyes, more effectively shutting him out than the substance that lined the walls of the room had ever done to intruders.

"But there's no need for this," he protested.

"Don't touch me," she hissed, crouching away.

The portrait loomed monstrously behind her, claiming her for its own. *Oh, my God!* Siri thought. He could endure no more.

When Jennie and Dr. Carpenter rushed into the room, he stood by silently, allowing them to take charge. Cheira went willingly with them, watching him warily all the time until the door shut him from her sight.

Jim Connors threw the door open, in his hurry not bothering to knock. A force greater than anything he had ever experienced immobilized him, interrupting the headlong rush.

"Are you crazy?" he turned to Siri as the force lessened. "I've no thought but to help. With this foolish insistence on natural childbirth, there's only one way to alleviate the pain."

"I know that," Siri's voice was toneless.

"Well, then! What twisted, fiendish motive have you for preventing the help she needs? Neither Jennie nor Dr. Carpenter has sufficient power."

"Sit down," Siri directed, the weariness again plain in his voice. "I'll tell you my motive. Then judge for yourself. If you still think you can help, I'll not prevent it. Remember the state she was in the night of the meeting? You did more than anyone to snap her out of it. And she's been progressing all this time. Or so we thought.—I think I've just understood this now—We only caused the pendulum to pause in its downward swing. Now this very natural event has caused it to move again. All the primitive instinct has risen to the surface. We can't fight that."

Jim sank into a chair. Siri had raised no barrier to his thoughts. The truth of the words was undeniable. "All right," Jim conceded. "What do you suggest?"

"Let her have her way." Siri shrugged. "You know the pregnancy is normal. There's little likelihood of complications. Once the child is born, perhaps she'll be willing to return to transfiguration."

"Suppose this isn't the limit of that downward swing of the pendulum you mentioned. Then . . . "

"It is," Siri interrupted, "It must be. It must be."

His voice was so patently weary that Jim's attention was drawn to the man. His training swiftly calculated the only plausible reason for the exhaustion Siri couldn't conceal. "You've been over there again," Jim accused, using the phrase they had adopted to signify that other level of consciousness.

"You'd better let me have a look at you." Jim rose, fetching the bag he'd dropped on the floor. "I've been doing some extrapolating with this procedure. The society's going to need more knowledge about it as we go along. It seems the tension increases proportionately with the higher vibration and coming back or the reduction of vibration is like halting a hundred-mile-an-hour express train. My advice is: Don't go again unless you mean to stay."

"I know it," Siri conceded, in agreement with the conclusions, but sur-

367

prised at Jim's concern. "I doubt my will is strong enough to bring me back for any reason—or to prolong my stay here indefinitely."

Jim straightened, a look of determination on his face. "Then we must see that Cheira is ready to go with you soon."

Taken aback, Siri stared at Jim, speechless.

"I know! I know!" Jim grinned sheepishly. "It's hard to believe, especially in view of what I said when I came in; but you know I don't make sense where Cheira is concerned." Jim raised his hands in apology. "Nevertheless, in other areas I can act logically. And at rock bottom, I guess, I'm really a scientist. Anyway, I've been watching you this last month; and I'm convinced of the change. I've watched Cheira, too, and know now that it's right for you to be together. I would even go so far as to say there's a chemical affinity. I can't find words to describe it: a sort of complementary polarity." Jim paused searching for the right words.

Siri was impressed at Jim's astuteness, but said nothing.

Jim continued, taking a deep breath of relief as if a heavy weight had lifted from his shoulders. "The honest desire for her happiness is the best proof of my love I can offer. I've thought about it a lot and finally realized that I'm now free to find my own fulfillment."

"You understand, then?"

"Yes. Thanks to you. I've at last got a broader picture of myself and the situation existing in the society. I can see what many of us have done: reacting to Cheira, not in the light of reality, but under the cloud of some grand illusion created by our imaginations."

Siri suppressed a smile.

"We separated her from the logic we apply to the rest of our lives, creating a religion we refused to question. If I'd been able to see her as she actually was, I may have won her." Jim paused, sighing. "Instead, I envisioned a deity. The concept overshadowed the woman she is, always. She was subconsciously seeking the answer. Fortunately, circumstances provided the way."

Siri grinned openly. "Circumstances had a little help from those who truly love her."

Now it was Jim's turn to question.

Siri laughed, protesting. "I'm not thinking of myself. I was the blindest of all. But have you realized that your imagination was deliberately manipulated by Wang Lu? It was he who set up the ritual and mystery around Cheira. Even she never realized it. He's a very clever psychologist. And there are others also who strive to protect her. Such fantastic entities, they'll really boggle your imagination."

Jim was amazed as the truth dawned. It was an angle he hadn't considered, but once suggested the fact fitted easily into place.

Siri's eyes darkened with pain. "I was only the extremely uncooperative means. My stupidity has made the way more difficult. I've created an unnecessary detour. Much of her suffering has been caused by me."

"You mean it could have been different?"

"No. Only that we're the cause of what will be, or rather how it will be; and the suffering generated is certain. No one can evade it."

"But one can eliminate the cause," Jim protested.

"Yes, if one can see what effects it will produce." Siri's voice was sad. "Unfortunately, men usually don't think before they act—maybe I should say react. We become so immersed in a situation that we fail to consider the circumstances surrounding it. Our knowledge is so limited and our field of vision so narrow that it's almost certain that our action will be in error."

Jim sat down. "I've been guilty of that more than anyone in my less rational, more emotional moments." He grimaced. "I'm sorry for having made an already difficult situation more painful. I promise that in the future you'll have my full support."

"You're ready to go over then," Siri asked eagerly, rising from the chair in one movement.

"Slow down!" Jim laughed, raising his hands in protest. "I didn't say that. Have you forgotten so soon that we decided you can't take that journey again? That would be some promise of support if I took advantage like that. And besides, I mean to stay as long as Cheira is here, or at least until John gets back. You know you've nearly destroyed the organization. All the key members are gone. There's a lot of work to be done now."

Siri grinned. "Your vanquished emotions have turned you into an altruist."

"Call it what you wish. The fact remains . . . "

A piercing shriek stopped the conversation.

"It's over," Siri breathed; but the words dropping into the silence did nothing to alleviate the tension crackling in the air.

An eternity passed before Jennie opened the door. She hid a smile at the sight of the pallid faces staring at her.

"You have a son, my lord," she announced. "And his mother is well."

The men looked at each other and burst out laughing. Their joy and

369

relief hid the embarrassment they felt at the unguarded emotions that had shown on their faces.

Siri clapped Jim on the shoulder. "How about a drink?"

Siri wished there was some way for Cheira to see his thoughts. How else could she know without doubt the joy he felt at the birth of his son? He was himself astonished that so ordinary a human occurrence could give him so much pleasure. He smiled, contentedly watching the infant asleep in his mother's arms.

Cheira lay relaxed in the big bed, the look of exhaustion on her face defeated by the light of accomplishment gleaming in her eyes.

"You're almost as beautiful as your mother," Siri grinned at the tiny wizened face muffled in blankets.

"Will you really love him?" Cheira asked timidly, her eyes searching Siri's face, seeking reassurance against the misgivings lingering at the edge of her mind. She felt empty now, and, in a way, even more helpless. She had witnessed the immensity of Siri's power. Without the security of love, that energy turned against the child would destroy it. And now, he didn't even have the protection of her body. Her imagination presented a horrible picture of the tiny body being wrenched from her grasp. She fought that fear desperately, trying to decipher the sincerity of Siri's expression. The old fear was intensified by the change in Siri.

Is his concern just a mask to allay her fears? Will he watch for an unguarded moment, and . . . The confused thoughts goaded her. Her mind vacillated. She had experienced both his brutality and his love. In this event, she couldn't decide which would dominate. She'd have to be vigilant, ready to throw herself between Siri's power and the body of her child.

Her thoughts more than her words brought him to his knees beside the bed.

"My love, what would you have me do?" The words were wrung from him through desperation. "What would persuade you? You must go back to the state of altered consciousness now. Can't you understand that all your doubts are caused by the slow vibration of your mind? Its primitive condition is incapable of the comprehension you're trying to force from it."

He rushed on, trying to overcome the doubt he saw in her eyes. "You've no reason to fear transfiguration any longer. Let me do it now!"

"No!" Her eyes widened with dread; her arms clutched the precious bundle at her side. "Please, don't!" she pleaded from the inefficacy of her position.

370

Siri rose. The scowl she dreaded settled over his face. "Cheira, I can force you. You know that!"

She buried her face against the warm body of the sleeping infant, shaking her head in helpless protest. Fear paralyzed her brain into resigned stillness.

"You must give me a better reason than that!" Siri's voice was cold and stern. Cheira whimpered into the blankets, muffled unintelligible sounds. "You're not an animal to be governed by blind instinct," Siri continued in the same tone. "Cheira, answer me!" he commanded.

She raised her head. He looked enormous standing there. *You can't fight him now anymore than you could then,* her memory declared. She felt Ahmed's hand between her shoulder blades, pushing her into the dimly lit room. The door shut with a soft click of the lock. She backed against it. The ornate carving cut into her ribs. There was no escape. Then she saw him. Only the tittering insinuations of the other women had given her a hint of what to expect He came swiftly across the room. His figure grew until it blotted out even the dim light. There was only blackness. She cried in terror; nothing in her experience told her what to expect. He tore off her cloak. She heard the clasp go sailing across the room to land with a dull thud against the base of a lamp. Then she felt the pain in her arms. His fingers squeezed her flesh. She expected to hear the crack of her bones. She struggled. His face was so close she could see his eyes like arrows, devouring, cruel. She renewed the struggle, terror giving her strength. He chuckled low, crushing her against him, his mouth smothering the cry in her throat. She felt dizzy. Now the memory turned fuzzy for she had been only semiconscious of his flesh on hers, of the bruises his hands left on her body.

The vivid picture helped crystallize her determination. She must try to stand against him. She had more to protect now than ever before. There was danger, instinct warned. She mustn't surrender; her present condition was the only protection she had for her child. Transfiguration would bring her under Siri's control, she was certain. How, she didn't know. Her mind attempted to jog her memory, but the dark cloud settled more heavily into place.

"Oh, please," she begged. "Give me some time. Take me to Arx Vetus. I'll do it then."

The strength of the memory had made it painfully clear to Siri.

"All right," he conceded, guilt demanding the concession. "But I'll not wait long," he warned. "I grow impatient for this time to end. We'll go to the desert as soon as you're fit to travel."

Cheira lay back, exhaustion flooding over the tension. She relaxed, too tired to answer. But she had won what she needed most—time. Siri insisted there need be no choice; but how she couldn't understand. Going with him meant leaving her son behind. What was the solution? She knew only that she must evade transfiguration until she could find it. Once done, how could she resist the attraction of that other state? Ameur and Tiana had not returned. Neither had any of the others. If they chose that existence in preference to the one they had known . . . but she did know. A dim light began to glow in her brain. She recoiled before it, half-wanting to see but afraid she might. And John—Siri had been certain he would return—but where was he?

She fell asleep, surrendering at last to the demands of her devitalized body.

Siri endured an agony Cheira could not know. He was helpless, following the twisted trend of her thoughts. *Was it never to end,* he wondered, sorry now that he had promised to take her to Arx Vetus. The temptation came. *Why wait? Force her. No,* he knew as soon as the thought passed through his mind. *He would defeat his own purpose.* That she was here at all was ample proof of the strength of will she could summon when she chose. And he knew without doubt what it would do to break that will. There was no other way then. He must wait for the time when she'd willingly accept the change. He slumped into the chair beside the bed.

Cheira's breath came softly and evenly, her face open and trusting in sleep. But her arms still clutched the child.

Siri let his mind wander into the future. He focused the power at his command as a drowning man concentrates on grabbing the lifeline. *I'll look closely,* he thought. *And trust that what I see is correct. The answer is there.*

He saw the time ahead at Arx Vetus and the circumstances that would prevail; but he found irritatingly that he could not see the path Cheira would select. *So,* he thought ruefully, *there's a limit after all.*

But you've set it, a part of his mind accused. *You turned back when the others went on. Where are they now? Far into the room to which you only opened the door and stood within, a reluctant visitor.*

He leaned forward, restlessly running his fingers through his hair, staring unseeingly at the carpet.

You felt it, remember? And what are you waiting for anyway? The willing slave of a distorted emotion. You've been thinking that Jim Connors is such a fool! What about yourself? Why don't you change your mind? It's not too late! You can see the future well enough to know she'll eventually find her way.

Delfaum assured you she would, even if you don't trust your own power to see it. What's stopping you? Go now!

The baby began to kick and whimper. The sound jarred him back to the present. Cheira was instantly awake, calling to Jennie. In the first awareness of waking, her eyes met his across the now vehement protestations of their child.

"I love you," she murmured. And he knew he had his answer.

CHAPTER XXIII

Within a minute of John's return, every member of the household was conscious of his presence. It was apparent at once that he intended to waste no time getting the society moving again. The tempo increased immediately, the impetus emanating from the bustle in John's office. Orders were issued for a meeting of the board of Pemberly, an assembly of the present senior members of the decimated society, a press conference, and a call for the archbishop to set a date for the baptism of the Pemberly heir.

During a brief lull, Siri swung open the door.

"What sort of idiot would return to this?" he grinned, lounging against the frame.

John rose, smiling. "I was hoping you had the answer for both of us. Come in and sit down." John resumed his seat, leaning back in the chair. He threw the pencil he held onto the desk and looked at Siri expectantly.

Siri accepted the invitation. "As you well know, there's only one emotion strong enough to dissuade men from their better interests."

"Odd, isn't it?" John acknowledged. "The motive which started us all on the path we're now taking." His expression sobered. "My profanations of love and loyalty make me ashamed. I'm cognizant of the mockery in the face of the real thing. My own puny emotions suffer by the comparison."

"Don't blame yourself for ignorance," Siri remonstrated.

"I won't, any more than you do," John answered, irony in the tone of his voice, but laced liberally with understanding.

Siri grimaced, "I suffer from a lingering morbidity masquerading under the name of honor."

"And our newly discovered state of brotherhood makes me a party to it." John laughed. "I fail to see the change."

"Only now all the moves are known and the line of advancement parallel," Siri reminded him.

"That it was not so before," John answered seriously, "is the ignorance which is my portion and for which I must atone."

"I'll do all I can to facilitate your task," Siri said, his manner matching

374

John's, "to make the time you must stay as short as possible. From now on, the agony of longing will be your constant companion also. Each day will be harder to endure than the last, and each hour of that day will be an eternity without end. Your will shall struggle to maintain the dwindling light each contact with others will draw from you, while you stand helpless to prevent it, knowing clearly the justice of it and that you must endure despite the numbness insidiously creeping into your soul."

John listened carefully to each word, accepting the full meaning of Siri's confession, taking the anguish of his former rival to himself. He tensed, braced to withstand the punishment Siri's next words would inflict.

"You can't know," Siri continued—and John groaned silently—"how she is part of my being, a complement to my essence, a vital completion of myself. So here I stay. Torn in two; the pull each way equally strong." Siri sank into thoughtful reverie. His longing had prompted him to draw on the other's strength.

"How is she?" John broke the silence, forcing the words into sound.

"Waiting to see you." Siri's voice held lingering pain.

"I know that; but what progress has she made? I find it almost impossible to make any sense out of what humans think."

Siri smiled. "A state I know very well." He grimaced, sitting forward. "She wants to go to Arx Vetus. I've promised to take her. There doesn't seem to be any other way." With an effort, he threw off the alien mood that had made him enlist John's sympathy. In a moment of weakness, he had let the other assume part of the burden that was his alone. *John's role is hard enough without that,* he decided, cursing the thoughtless lapse.

John frowned. "I anticipated that. I've already begun to devise a plan that will satisfy the public for her permanent absence."

"I'll leave that to you." Siri shrugged in relief.

"My job and my pleasure," John retorted. "By the way, thank you for filling in while I was gone. You've managed to keep the lid on a very explosive situation." John added, a smile playing at the corners of his mouth, "Even though it's against your inclinations."

Siri countered, laughing. "Thank you for coming back." He stood up abruptly. The laughter faded out of his face, wiped away by the happy sound engendering a growing guilt. It underlined how much he was enjoying John's presence. How badly he wanted to prolong the conversation, using it as an aid to reinforce the memory of that other existence. It was more vivid in the company of a brother who had experienced it as he had. It underlined, too, the recognition of a desire to postpone the coming minutes. Retarding the passage of time, he knew, was a contradiction, the desire futile as well as impossible. He shook his head helplessly.

John rose, his eyes on Siri's face, acknowledging compliance with his thoughts. In silence, their eyes met and held. Like a handshake, the gesture sealed the course of their future relationship.

Words were unnecessary to explain the understanding between them. The more than a century of rivalry and hatred had been erased by the knowledge they now possessed. Finally, there was no possibility that those emotions could ever recur. With a clarity denied to ordinary men, they understood the purpose of their existence. They could accurately gauge the level of their development and what it entailed. They saw their divergent paths to the same goal; the way of one enhancing rather than detracting from the ultimate happiness of the other, mutually complementing each other's progress.

They understood that love was, truly, the motivation of all levels of existence; an intense, all-pervading love in the acknowledgement of one's own worth, which encompassed all others as necessary adjuncts; in the realization that the loss of any creates an intolerable void in the whole. It was this that had brought them both back from a state of being no man should ever have to forego once it is within his grasp. Voluntarily, they had returned because they knew the importance of the sacrifice. The hope that the time would be short gave them the strength they needed.

"It's going to happen anyway," Siri said with an air of resignation, identifying with John's hesitancy. "You'll soon get used to the knowledge you have of the future. It'll get easier."

John squared his shoulders, wishing in that moment that Siri didn't know or see what he was about to endure; yet realizing that this was only a small part of the reparation he owed this man. His lack of understanding at the time did not alter the consequences of his actions.

"If I could change it, I would," Siri spoke softly as John strode past and down the hall to Cheira's suite.

"Oh, my dear, John!" Cheira flew to his side the moment he entered, grasping his hand in both of hers, interrupting the formal bow he had intended. "Thank you for coming back. I've been lost without you."

Even previous knowledge hadn't prepared him for what he would feel when he saw her again. It took a supreme effort of will to pull the muscles of his face into a smile of greeting. "My lady is well, I trust?" he managed to say, the sound of his voice discordant with the echo in his brain.

"Yes, now—you're here—I'm very well. Come," she pulled him toward the bedroom, her face sparkling with happiness. "You must see the baby."

"Have Jennie bring him here." John attempted to pull his hand from her grasp.

"He's sleeping, silly," she insisted, laughing. "He may not wake up for hours. I want you to see him now."

John closed his eyes for an imperceptible second. "You'll get used to it," Siri had said. John prayed he was right. He allowed Cheira to lead him into the room he had never entered.

Aware only of her pride and love for her son, Cheira brought him to stand beside the cradle of the sleeping infant. Obediently, he bent over to let his eyes confirm what he already knew. The resemblance to Siri was unmistakable; only the wisp of golden hair identified Cheira as his mother.

"He's very beautiful," John murmured, postponing the moment when he would straighten up. His eyes were drawn involuntarily to the big bed, which dominated the room. There was no way now to shield himself from the visions his imagination conjured up, the experiences that time had withdrawn from his grasp. The ashes of a dead desire remained as knowledge in his brain, to be relived like the replaying of an old recording. He waited for the episode to end, surprised at the pain knowledge could convey, devoid though it was of emotional trappings. He was grateful to Siri for remaining in the salon. He knew it had been done intentionally, a trust which underscored their new status. Only Siri's physical absence gave him the composure to gather the last shreds of self-control. With deliberate concentration on the mechanics of movement, he followed Cheira back into the other room. Relieved, he saw that she had noticed nothing.

Cheira closed the door carefully, noiselessly, so that no sound would disturb the child's slumber. Then she turned to John with the rest of her news. "Siri has promised to take us to Arx Vetus!" She laughed, skipping lightly across the room to stand beside her husband.

John looked from Siri to the portrait above the mantel. There was only painful understanding in the glance.

"I'll need a few weeks to make your departure appear routine," John said, masking the strain required to make his voice sound normal. "There's your resignation from the Pemberly organization—to devote your entire time to family life, of course. And I don't see how we can avoid a formal baptism." As he talked he grew calmer, slipping back into the old familiar role, behind which he could bury the painful memories.

Cheira dragged herself through the following month, caught between irritation and impatience. After much coaxing, John had extracted a promise of cooperation and Siri held her to it.

She begrudged any time spent away from her son and managed to get through the formalities of resignation from Pemberly Enterprises only with the unswerving support of Siri and John.

John insisted on a public ceremony of baptism with all the pomp suitable to the heir of Pemberly as necessary protocol. Strict adherence to the ceremonies surrounding it left her cold with indifference, mentally and physically exhausted.

The nights were as difficult, her rest disturbed by dreams of being separated from her child. The vividness of the dreams would finally awaken her, driving her to the baby's crib to make sure he was there. And she was alone, only Jennie on the cot near the cradle to share the midnight vigils. Dr. Carpenter had advised the separation for a few weeks to facilitate her recuperation. She hadn't protested. Neither had Siri.

The whole time was an interminable nightmare from which her only desire was to awaken. When at last the day of departure arrived, an almost forgotten vitality surged through her. She felt like leaping joyously. Whatever the uncertainty of the future, it had to be better than this. The longing for Arx Vetus subconsciously suppressed rushed with welcome into awareness. As Siri's plane rose into the air, she settled into the seat with a feeling of total well-being. Her world was complete with her son in her lap and her husband by her side.

The ensuing days fulfilled the promise of happiness. The joy of homecoming was dimmed only by her sensitivity to Siri's constant surveillance. She knew his unflagging consideration masked a continuous monitoring of her thoughts. Although he carefully avoided betraying himself by word or action, she realized he was waiting impatiently for some sign from her. She was almost relieved when he announced his intention to go with David to the Fort.

The old ruin with all its people and animals was to pass into David's care.

At the same time that she was relieved by Siri's absence, she felt the inevitable march of circumstances forcing her to the time of decision. If Siri would give up the Fort . . .

That the quandary was no nearer solution became more evident as time passed. As nature decreed, her love for the child increased daily until the thought of separation was unendurable. And the manner in which she could do both constantly eluded her. Sometimes the cloud over her memory threatened to evaporate, to reveal that part of her past that she had pursued relentlessly and that she now recognized was hidden in her own mind. She felt its pull, tempting her to run to Siri, to beg for the state which would show her the existence she had rejected so long ago. But that same feeling sent her fleeing to her son's cradle, to clasp the tiny figure in her arms, to spend hours rocking with primitive abandon, to the instinct of mother love which from primordial times had ensured the continuity of the race.

She failed to notice the exasperation, which finally drove Siri out of Arx Vetus. He chose to make the journey strenuously on horseback, hoping to release the pent-up energy of overlong suppression in the exhaustion of physical exercise.

David responded with eager enthusiasm to Siri's proposal. He, too, had been chafing at the inactivity imposed by his duties at Arx Vetus. Although he knew Siri's intention would separate him from his friend for an unknown length of time, his youthful vivacity refused to be dampened by a shadowy future when the prospect of adventure was close at hand.

Siri set a killing pace, but this time it only brought a feeling of exhilaration to David. He smiled wryly, remembering his first experiences. Now, instead of a gentle mare, he was mounted on one of Siri ben Ange's magnificent stallions. The sight of the muscles rippling beneath the gleaming coat as the animal made short work of the miles of monotonous sand made him burst out with laughter for pride in his accomplishment. His companion glanced at him questioningly, only to smile at the revelation of the thought.

Siri caught the infectious mood of his young friend and, with a shout threw off the black humor he had been indulging in. He spurred Skotias, urging him to greater effort, but instead causing a surprise that broke the stride. Skotias's temper bubbled to the surface. Resentfully, he plunged and reared at the unwarranted incentive. Siri's laughter rang out. The tussle supplied the release he sought. He let the stallion have his way. Then, after a few minutes, got down to the business of quieting the animal.

David watched with admiration shining in his eyes. There was no doubt in his mind that much less misbehavior would have sent him flying. Siri hadn't even budged. He sat as easily as if Skotias had been standing still.

When Skotias's ruffled feelings had been soothed, Siri settled him into a restful jog. "After we finish at the Fort, David, let's go to Imla Dun. We can make a tentative selection of the sale horses for this fall."

David's heart sank. The words revealed that his friend intended to be gone soon. He was swamped by the realization of what this man meant to him, more even than his love for the desert. How could he ever take Siri's place? How could he ever be master of Imla Dun?

"The years will pass swiftly," Siri answered his thought, "and you still have work to do here. Besides, your power must be greatly increased before you're ready."

"What work? We already know everything," David shot back.

"Still belligerent, David?" Siri cocked an eyebrow at the young man. "When Cheira is ready, you know that neither Jim nor I will stay. John will be here only long enough to implement a new routine for the organization. Someone must head it and also be able to accept new members. Hans and Margo can't do it all alone. Does that answer your question?"

"But I don't have that kind of power," David objected.

"You'll have it before John leaves. Have you been too preoccupied to notice the increase over just the last year? Just in the last few months you've performed some remarkable feats of teleportation, for example. To New York to see Hardy, to Santiago to summon Hans, to London, to Arx Vetus. Could you have done that a year ago?"

David laughed with embarrassment. "I hadn't thought about it. It was just a job that had to be done."

"And now there's an even bigger job that will require the constant exercise of power."

"Do you think I can do it?" David asked doubtfully.

Siri answered, his expression solemn. "In the future, David, I can see an orderly world of transfigured beings. A world of peace whose inhabitants accomplish as a matter of everyday living feats that even today would be considered miraculous. A world without violence where parents can be certain that the children of their love will be happy. Where the end of life on earth is not the decay of the grave, but eternal fulfillment. Where the reason for the sojourn is known and the aim of the individual is to earn his right to that eternity. If that future ever becomes a reality, David, it will be due to you."

David slouched on his horse, indifferent now to the accomplishment of which he was so proud, indifferent, too, to the desert he loved so much. His mind labored to extract the essence of the years ahead, to discover their meaning for himself. For a long time, he was unaware that Siri had stopped speaking. The people he would come to know marched like spectres across his imagination. He felt the weight of his decisions, which would determine the outcome of their lives. One shadow persisted, becoming clearer as it caught his attention. He was not surprised when he recognized the image. He knew it was right that he should see her, not as Dr. Carpenter in a white coat with a stethoscope in her hand, but as Irene dressed in the manner of Arx Vetus carrying a bouquet of lilies from the garden, the drops of dew still glistening on the petals. She was smiling. It gave him comfort and courage.

When he looked up, the eyes which met Siri's had lost the wonder and uncertainty of youth. Instead, there was a look of maturity in the eyes of a man who saw the task with the full knowledge of his ability to handle it. He saw the acknowledgement of his thoughts in the answering look of his friend. It was a salute to his capacity to accomplish the work, an advance payment, the sum of it to be earned in the future.

Irene Carpenter became a doctor because, at a very early age, she realized she was the possessor of an exceptionally brilliant mind. Frankly, she liked the praise of her parents and teachers for faultless performance. And the envy of her fellow students enhanced the singular position.

These reasons were only added attractions, however, to the basic fact that she liked to learn. The acquisition of knowledge was the unchallengeable joy in her life. By the time she went to medical school, she was a dedicated scholar headed for a career in research.

One day, while attending a lecture for a course in endocrinology, the guest speaker was Dr. David Mott of Pemberly Institute. That day, another goal was added to Irene's already well-defined aim. Enlisting the aid of her influential parents and the faculty of the school, she obtained, upon graduation, a place on the staff of Pemberly. The institute was a leader in its field. No one ever questioned her motives.

She was not long at Pemberly before her outstanding talents were recognized. It was a simple matter to be appointed to Dr. Mott's personal staff. It was then that she resorted to a most uncharacteristic maneuver; she prayed every night that he would notice her.

Astutely, she recognized the strangeness of the experiments he was conducting. By the time David explained transfiguration to her, she had figured out most of it. Scientifically, she wasn't surprised. Her eagerness to accept that state was mostly a sign that she wanted to share his life. She secretly hoped he felt the same way.

But his attitude didn't change. He remained distant and professional. She resorted to the old method. Now, with altered consciousness, she was able to fortify her prayers with energy. She carefully envisioned the picture she wanted him to see. It doubled as a barrier behind which to hide the audacity of her thoughts. She fretted endlessly when he left for the desert, swinging between yearning for his return and fear that he never would. She couldn't know that he had subconsciously taken the picture with him.

CHAPTER XXIV

After Siri was gone, Cheira wandered restlessly through the rooms of her quarters. The undefined depression dimmed for the moment her joy in being at Arx Vetus. It usually gave her a feeling of security. But now, the walls seemed to close in, making a prison of her haven. She had to get out.

The sun was dipping toward the horizon, sending waves of heat dancing over the sand with the last of its waning strength as Cheira led a horse from under the stone arches of the stable. The heat hit her like a blanket of fire. She welcomed the discomfort. Mounted, she rode out to embrace the inferno. It matched the turmoil of her thoughts. The cool serenity of the old ruin was a comfort she had not earned.

The horse stepped out onto the burning sand reluctantly, picking his way distastefully, his head cocked defensively against the glare of the low-hanging sun. Cheira encouraged him, singing softly a ballad to set a rhythm to his stride. The task was absorbing. She accepted it gratefully.

Several miles out, she stumbled across a circle of crumbling stones of what had once been a well. She recognized the place, but had not sought it consciously.

The last time she was here, the spot had looked entirely different. In those days, it was a tiny oasis. There were three palm trees, a small plot of grass, and a carefully tended well. Now the shimmering waves of heat created a mirage from the memory. She saw it clearly as it used to be.

It was just after her return from America. The war was over, and she was proud of the small part she had played to hasten the victory. She came home to rest, enjoying the isolation and the peace of the solitary rides to the tiny oasis. She liked to sit under one of the palms and watch the sun go down. Riding home in the coolness of the evening was a pleasant contrast to the discomfort of the earlier ride out.

One particular day the shade of the palms enticed her to stay longer than usual. She leaned against the trunk of the largest, listening contentedly to the click of the beetles. She fell asleep.

An eerie feeling that she was no longer alone finally seeped into her consciousness, awakening her. She opened her eyes to see a heavily burnoosed Arab bent over her. It was by the piercing black eyes that she recognized him. She screamed.

For the moment, she was paralyzed. He said softly, "I've found you, my beautiful one." He reached out to touch her cheek. The movement inspired such terror that she leaped up and onto her horse in one motion, taking the man and his followers by surprise. She was headed full tilt for Arx Vetus before they could get to their horses.

She was running blindly across the hall when Ameur caught her in his arms. She collapsed against him, sobs rasping in her dry throat, terror racking her body with uncontrollable intensity.

"He's here!" she managed to gasp before she fainted.

With Cheira safely in the care of Wang Lu, Ameur stopped Siri in the courtyard. The two men eyed each other coldly. Siri's eyes narrowed. The pieces of the puzzle clicked into place. The obvious reason for Ameur's presence became apparent. He laughed, grudgingly saluting the American's audacity.

"So," the sheik drawled. The tone could be mistaken for indifference by one unfamiliar with his reputation.

Ameur knew better than to commit that error. He held his ground, alert but passive.

"So," Siri repeated in the same tone, like a person stating an already completed thought. "The massacred American lieutenant! How clever of you! Right here, under our noses!" The eyebrows settled into a heavy scowl. The black eyes sharpened behind the narrowed lids. The lips thinned into the outline of a sneer.

"You fool!" Siri hissed. "That woman is mine."

Ameur didn't answer, nor did he move.

The sheik's men crowded closer, waiting only for their master's signal to charge.

"According to custom, you must die," Siri added, his mouth widening into a cruel smile.

"I challenge you then," Ameur spoke calmly. "I believe it's my right."

The sheik threw off his burnoose. It was a gesture of acceptance. The smile was still on his face when he lunged for his opponent's throat. Ameur dodged, catching him off guard with a blow to the diaphragm. Siri staggered, surprised at the speed of the movement, gasping to catch his breath.

The black eyes appraised the American more carefully. He lunged again. Ameur's movement was a swift blur, but the fist connecting with Siri's jaw was as solid as a sledgehammer. The sheik fell back, prevented from falling by the bodies of his men standing so close behind him.

He shook his head. When he regained his balance, the expression contorted his face with rage. Never had anyone been able to stand up to the invincible leader of the Fort; never had anyone bested him in combat. That the American was able to do so calmly and expertly was an incomprehensible occurrence. Siri summoned all his skill and strength. He attempted to catch the American off balance and land a fatal blow to the head. The telling blow came, but not from the sheik. Ameur hit him full in the face. Siri dropped to his knees, blood rushing from his mouth and nose.

A gasp of disbelief was drawn from the watching men. They gaped at their fallen leader. "Aye-ah!" Ahmed shouted and drew his pistol; but his forward leap was stopped by amazement.

An aged Oriental appeared from nowhere. He materialized beside Ameur.

"Violence is never a solution," the old man remonstrated quietly.

Ameur stepped back obediently. Siri rose stiffly, unmindful of his injuries in the shock of the old man's appearance. "Do not seek her, master. She's an *huriyah*!" Lira's words sounded in his head above the ringing in his ears. He ran his fingers through matted hair in an effort to clear his head.

"A wise man knows when to retreat."

It took Siri the passage of several seconds to realize that the Oriental had spoken again.

He forced himself erect. He looked squarely at the American. Then, at the old man.

"I will not!" he said with a tone of finality.

The ensuing silence closed heavily around the motionless tableau. Once the snorting of an impatient horse ruptured the unnatural quiet.

Finally, the old man spoke.

"Wait, then!" It was a command. His voice was kind, but underlying the tone was the air of one accustomed to being obeyed. Turning to Ameur, he nodded. Both men faded from sight.

Siri stopped his men's headlong flight with a rough order to make camp. Only the habit instilled by years of unquestioning obedience forced their compliance.

Cheira spent hours sobbing hysterically in abject terror, defying the combined efforts of Wang Lu and Ameur to calm her. Wang Lu finally resorted to a sedative. She fell asleep, her breath still catching with a dry, choking sound.

"The man responsible for that doesn't deserve to live," Ameur blazed at the Oriental.

"It's not for you to judge," Wang Lu reminded him.

"How can you watch her suffer so calmly?" Ameur shot back.

"And is your anger alleviating it?" Wang Lu retorted.

Ameur exhaled heavily; anger deflated into helplessness.

"What can we do, then?"

Wang Lu surveyed the young man with wise, patient eyes. "I think we should wait for tomorrow."

Dawn saw the situation unchanged. Siri's camp occupied the central courtyard. The tall figure could be plainly seen, pacing its perimeter. There was every indication that he had paced thus throughout the night.

Inside, Ameur had measured his enemy stride for stride. He had kept the vigil at his own insistence, as a hedge against any covert attempt to invade the building.

Cheira rose with the first sign of dawn, exhausted from a restless night. But control returned enough to subdue the hysterical sobbing. And the terror was reduced to a deep-seated dread.

Wang Lu called a conference in the dining room. He insisted that Ameur and Cheira eat before he stated his case.

"Our choice," he began, his long delicate fingers encircling a steaming cup of tea, his gaze moving slowly from Cheira to Ameur, "is to seek a solution to this problem either emotionally or logically. We do not have the choice of evading it. It is also better that we choose the solution, rather than let it be wrested from us by another." He paused. "Do you agree?"

"Agreed," Ameur stated after a moment's hesitation.

Cheira was unable to control the shudder that passed through her body with the inhalation of breath. She kept her eyes focused unseeingly on her plate. Wang Lu reached over to clasp his hand over hers. She raised her eyes to him, gratefully.

"Do either of you think there's a chance to dissuade the sheik from his purpose?" Wang Lu continued.

Ameur and Cheira both shook their heads.

"You're right!" Wang Lu concurred. "I spent most of the night monitoring his thinking." Cheira gasped. Wang Lu's wrinkled old face creaked into a smile. "How could a body rest with this young man here snorting back and forth like an angry bull?"

When there was no response at his attempt to lighten the atmosphere, Wang Lu continued. "I could detect no wavering of his purpose. In fact, it grew firmer as the night progressed."

The old man's hand disappeared into the folds of his robe. He withdrew it holding an antiquated, cumbersome timepiece. Studying its face, he said, "It's his intention to attempt forcible entry in exactly one hour."

Cheira's eyes widened, the pupils dilated with fear. "Oh no!"

Wang Lu continued calmly; his fingers tightened over her hand.

"We've not yet considered the possible solutions to the problem," he reminded them. "First, Ameur has the power to kill him."

Ameur jumped up. He was eager to come to Cheira's defense; and it would be a pleasure to take revenge for the wrong done her. He leaned over the table toward her. She looked at him a moment, then dropped her gaze.

"You have chosen rightly, my daughter," Wang Lu said softly.

Ameur sank back into his chair.

Wang Lu looked at him severely. "You have the power; but not the right."

Ameur looked away, lending reluctant agreement.

"Second," the Oriental resumed, "we can abandon Arx Vetus; teleport away from here; establish our headquarters where Siri ben Ange can never find us."

"Isn't there any other way?" Cheira interrupted, even fear of Siri not great enough to make her want to abandon her home.

"There might be." Wang Lu spoke slowly, watching Cheira's expression carefully. "Make him one of us."

Cheira started to protest with a violent motion of her head; then she stopped. She looked at Wang Lu a long time, slowly shifting her gaze to Ameur.

"Yes," she said, her voice steady.

Ameur materialized in front of Siri, blocking his path. The sheik smothered a gasp; but he stood his ground, waiting for the enemy to make the first move. Through the night, he had accepted and rejected several times the idea of magic. He preferred to think it was some sort of trick; but what the explanation for it was, he couldn't figure out. He questioned the men to verify that it hadn't been illusion caused by the heat of the sun. He thought of some form of hypnosis; but he was almost certain his ability to fight hadn't been hampered and his men had witnessed the materializations. And beside all that, he burned with humiliation. He decided to bide his time.

"I've been sent to offer a solution to this stalemate," Ameur volunteered.

"Why don't you kill me?" Siri challenged. "You proved it wouldn't be too difficult a task. Or has your new life turned you away from what you did easily in the old days?"

"I've no right now," Ameur admitted. "I live by a different code."

"Well, then?" Mockery glinted in the dark eyes.

"If you'll come with me, I'll explain."

Siri laughed. "I've nothing to lose and everything to gain." He was unaware of the prophecy of the words.

Cheira was brought back to the present by the insistent ache between her shoulder blades. She had slumped forward in the saddle; the awkward position strained the muscles of her back. She straightened, brushing the hair from her forehead where it clung damply.

The sun had slipped unnoticed below the horizon. The horse was halted, quietly dozing, only his tail flicking automatically from side to side, chasing from his flanks the last of the day's lingering insects.

Picking up the reins, Cheira turned the animal back toward Arx Vetus, the ancient ruins now rapidly receding into a clump of shadows in the fading light. Impatient now to leave the few fallen stones that were the only visible remains of the tiny oasis, she wondered why the recall of those agonized hours was so vivid.

She shrugged. But the memory was still strong in her mind. Soon the monotonous rhythm of the horse's walk and the undeviating sameness of the unending sand indistinguishable now in the dark hour after sunset again turned her thoughts inward. She saw herself clinging to Wang Lu's arm, her only protection, as she timidly approached the kneeling man whom she dreaded and hated. She stopped, wanting to flee, regretting now the morning's decision; but Wang Lu gently forced her on.

Ameur stood beside the sheik, alert, ready to intercept any unwarranted movement. What trust he had for the tribal chieftain was because he knew his word was his honor. Previous to this moment, Siri had listened attentively to the explanation of the state of altered consciousness. The possibility intrigued him; and Ameur's demonstrations convinced him of its feasibility. The strongest motive, however, remained: to see the woman he loved. He'd gamble that the future would restore her to him. And despite yesterday's encounter, he trusted and liked the American.

Cheira's hands trembled when she placed them over his temples. She fought down the terror rising in her throat like a scream. Wang Lu put his arm around her. "Concentrate," he whispered. She obeyed, summoning the energy for the task she had agreed to.

Siri's only movement was to raise his eyes to hers.

"Cheira," he said, his voice low and husky. It was the first time he had pronounced her name.

The picture in her memory blurred.

"Oh, God!" she cried aloud, startling herself and making the horse shy. She righted herself and settled the animal automatically, her mind occupied by what the memory had revealed. Now she knew why she was afraid to have Siri transfigure her, why the submission to his will had been so easy that day they teleported together to Lamborn; and conversely, why it was so right that she love only him.

Darkness overtook the travelers about halfway to the Fort. Siri halted at a point where the jagged boulders thrust their heads out of the sand. He selected a depression where the formation circumscribed a large oval. The area was conveniently clear of drifting sand, the course of its flow stopped by the unyielding rock, piling it up on the windward side of the solid protrusions.

The ancient stillness was ruptured by the activity of the intruders. Ahmed, who had brought the horses from the Fort two days earlier, took over the direction of setting up camp for the night. The men's high spirits escalated the necessary clamor. They were the honored few who now knew first hand of the mysterious place called Arx Vetus; and most happy reason of all, they were escorting their master home. They hurried to set up the tents and prepare the evening meal, to lengthen as long as possible the time around the campfire. The songs they sang manifested the joy they felt.

David lent a hand building the fire. He performed the task meticulously, taking pride in the exhibition of knowledge acquired on his visit to Imla Dun. He even took time to curry the pack animals after they were unloaded, as well as scrupulous attention to his own mount. His work was rewarded when he drew friendly jibes from several of the men, including Ahmed.

Siri paced restlessly the perimeter of the oval. The men interpreted the behavior as a sign of impatience to reach the Fort. They could conceive of nothing more important. It was the focal point of their lives, their refuge. That their master might feel differently was beyond their comprehension. There was no way for them to know that another existence might draw him more strongly.

The stillness of the night stimulated the longing which during the day could be smothered beneath the conscious demands of activity. Now the long hours stretched ahead offering no such respite. To remove himself from Arx Vetus, at least for a little while, seemed to Siri the only way to control the constant temptation to force Cheira to a decision. Nevertheless, he was certain that it would be the worst possible action at the moment. She must accept transfiguration through an act of her own volition. There could be no excuse of ignorance for her as for others to whom even conception of that state was unimaginable. And if, through the use of force, he accomplished his purpose and she damned him for it, he would be defeated for all eternity.

The pain of separation hit him with renewed force. His heart contracted. The sensation was uncomfortable. He recalled the look of resignation returned to her eyes when he left, yet with her will stubbornly held against him. She preferred to submit to the pain of separation rather than to brave the barrier erected in her mind.

If he could only devise a way to make her believe him, to show her that no need for a choice existed between that life and the child. If she would only face the knowledge she carried in her mind, she'd know. But instinctive fear of the unknown chained her. She was trapped in ignorance like the majority of humanity. Perversely, she fought to keep it so.

His steps subconsciously took him to the edge of the dying fire. An hour or so after the meal, the men had curled into burnooses, quickly embracing the sleep which restored the energy needed in their active lives. David, succumbing to the routine of tribesmen he had come to regard as brothers, followed their custom. Siri was left alone to struggle with a problem beyond their understanding.

He stood, pensively; the dying embers were reflected in his dark eyes. He raised his head, peering in the direction of Arx Vetus as if he could force his vision to penetrate the distance separating him from Cheira. In the solitude, with no witnesses but the stars glittering close overhead in the cloudless sky, he allowed the torture of emotions usually suppressed free play in the expression of his face. What he felt was most apparent in the rigid set of his mouth, the lips indrawn to a fine line with downward curves at the corners.

He shrugged impatiently. Self-pity was not one of his vices. If this were the atonement required of him, then he'd bear it without complaint. Even as this exile was of his own making, he had the power to interrupt it. His body faded away from the place at the fire. He stood at the door of Cheira's apartment, his hand on the knob even before the materialization was complete.

Jennie's voice crooning a high country lullaby drifted to him from the nursery as he opened the door. He walked toward the sound, the thick carpeting muffling his footsteps. Jennie looked up, smiling a greeting; forgotten was the fear that used to paralyze her in his presence. Now she felt only the glow of pride in what he was and in the knowledge that he was her countryman.

"Good evening, my lord," she welcomed, breaking off the song in the middle of a phrase.

Siri smiled, pulling up a chair to watch the ministrations. Jennie was feeding the infant cradled in her arms. The baby interrupted the sucking to follow the movement with big, staring eyes.

"He gained another seven ounces today," Jennie continued, launching into a recital of the baby's progress, pleased to have Siri's attention to a subject so dear to her heart.

My son, he thought, giving only part of his attention to Jennie. He savored the words, feeling a welling of love beyond the realm of choice, beyond the conscious necessity of knowledge, to the recognition of a living being who was the symbol of the bond between Cheira and himself. The love for his son he identified as a constant, an equilibrium, which would hold unaltered and unalterable through all the grades of existence he had known or would ever come to know. It was clear now why Petraum and Aletha waited. This was the feeling of which Cheira doubted him capable. But how could she know when he was surprised by it himself? He thought of Delfaum; and the vision of his radiant countenance rose in his mind. That was the only life his son would know. The child would develop in a realm of continuous harmony. No discord of disease or ignorance, nor the horrible waste of death would ever mar his progress. *I can give him that,* he thought. For even in the distant future, when the child must make his choice, should he decide for some unforeseeable reason to return to this life, he would find a world of transfigured beings a smooth path to whatever goal he chose.

He rose impatiently.

". . . and this afternoon, he sat up for a second all by himself." Jennie stopped, catching the darkening gleam of pain in Siri's eyes.

"She's sleeping now," Jennie volunteered, in answer to the question he didn't ask. "She's worn herself out wrestling with the problem. The indecision will make her ill, I'm sure. And she doesn't seem to get any closer to a solution." Jennie paused. "Is there a solution, my lord?"

"Of course!" Siri peered at the girl intently, a sudden hope dawning in his eyes. "This so-called problem is a fabrication of her mind. It's an illusion which has no reality. If she'd only listen. Will she listen to you, Jennie? Has the relationship between you fostered a trust in your judgment?"

The girl lowered her eyes. But in the first motion of shaking her head, she hesitated. "What can I tell her? I don't know anything that would help."

"Perhaps, you could convince her of my love. You could make her believe that my joy in the child is equal to hers, that her own human frailty is all that keeps us apart."

"I will try, my lord," Jennie whispered, her tender heart going out to him. The actions of her mistress had brought him to this. She felt a flash of anger against Cheira. The sensation was so startling that she shuddered involuntarily.

When she looked up, Siri was gone.

CHAPTER XXV

After an almost sleepless night, Cheira rose determined on a course of action. She felt physically stronger every day; and the mood of resignation which had sheltered her during the months of pregnancy no longer came to her aid. With physical well-being came mental health. She felt more and more like she used to be; and now the ache of separation which throbbed dully in her chest brought only a sense of irritation.

She dressed quickly and silently, not wishing to disturb the sleeping baby or Jennie. She combed her hair, tying it in a knot at the nape of her neck, grimacing at the reflection in the mirror. The dark circles under her eyes betrayed the anxiety of the night, the flesh slightly swollen over her cheekbones. Although her color was healthy enough, her skin lacked the glow of transfiguration.

With an impatient shrug, she turned away.

Whatever the dissatisfaction of her relationship with Siri, it could not dim the pleasure and comfort she derived from being at Arx Vetus. As she walked down the hall, she paused again and again: to let her fingers glide over the warm glossy surface of a hand-carved door, relieving the time years ago when Ameur had worked round the clock restoring the long-neglected wood in order to surprise her when she returned. The best craftsmen, imported from France, had taken nearly six months to complete the difficult job. Ameur's pride in the accomplishment needed only the reinforcement of her approval to bask in the satisfaction of a job well done.

The paintings arrested her attention. She gazed long at the individual masterpieces, appreciating not only the superb skill of the artists, but remembering the unflagging enthusiasm with which Ameur had collected them; the acquisition of each a triumph of negotiation.

Tony Hammond's laughter echoed in her memory when she stopped before a modern abstract which was a particular source of satisfaction to Ameur, who had spent years trying to acquire it from a very rich, very possessive owner. She'd made an effort that day to match Ameur's enthusiasm; but Tony felt no compunction to kindness. It had taken a direct command to quell the ridicule and to prevent Ameur from removing the priceless masterpiece.

She hesitated a long time outside the apartment where Ameur and Tiana lived. Never having entered their private quarters, she was reluctant to do so now. Yet the emptiness she felt was too strong to resist. She opened the door and walked in. It was an unexpected surprise to see the modern decor. The central room looked much like the living room of a town house in any European city in the last quarter century, even to the trim lines of the bar in the corner and the expensive synthetic leather on the sofa and love seats.

She picked up a book from the low coffee table in front of the massive sofa. It was a volume on gardening; and the scribbled notes in the margins in the familiar hurried scrawl brought tears to her eyes. The tears of loneliness flowed freely by the time she held a well-used pipe in her hands. The lingering aroma of Ameur's favorite apple-scented tobacco stimulated a fresh outburst. Were they really waiting over there as Siri promised? The cloud in her mind started to dissipate. She could see the light shining behind it. In panic, she fled the room.

Jim welcomed her into the laboratory with a smile.

"Cheira," he beamed, "this is an unexpected pleasure."

"What keeps you so occupied?" she asked, ignoring the question in his eyes.

He led her to a large table, strewn with drawings of intricate machinery.

"Just lending David a hand," he explained. "We're trying to work up a machine to monitor the increase of an individual's energy output and the potential for control. That's going to be an important consideration from now on and not something to be left to chance." He picked up a large chart and handed it to her. "This is a scale made up from David's experiments with Siri. We intended to use it as a basis against which to measure others."

"Is everyone really that anxious to go over?" She laid down the chart with distaste.

"Of course!" The brevity of the answer underlined the words he didn't say.

"Jim, why haven't I returned spontaneously to transfiguration as Siri did?" She forced out the words, which could no longer be avoided, the question that had hammered at her through fits of wakefulness last night.

The scientist's love had not faded; only its quality had changed. Desire had metamorphosed into a protective tenderness. He cursed his inability to aid her now.

"Have you wanted to?" he replied with a question of his own, forcing her in as kind a manner as he could to acknowledge the responsibility for the condition, knowing that she realized the prerequisite whether she admitted it or not.

She moved restlessly about the room, absently picking up some instrument close at hand, examining it with unseeing eyes, then replacing it with exaggerated care. She made no reply.

During the last month, such a question would have provoked vehement denials. Jim felt encouraged.

"As soon as you truly desire transfiguration, you shall have it." Jim pressed the advantage. "Let me call Siri now."

"No!" She swung to face him; the test tube in her hand crashing to the floor unheeded. "I won't submit to him. You know what he'll make me do." Her voice rose to a frenzy. "He won't give me a chance once my mind is altered. I know it. I won't have the will to resist. He'll take me away from my baby. That's what he wants. He'll never love him as I do." Cheira let the words burst forth—the fear of what she had discovered a burden too heavy to carry alone; yet too incomprehensible to reveal entirely.

Jim frowned. Her words had given him a hint for the basis of her fear; but he couldn't identify it precisely from the jumble of her thoughts. He took a shot in the dark, keeping his voice low and calm. "Siri will never force you to do anything. That's why he's waiting now. Besides, your will shall be stronger afterwards, you know that. Where did you get such an idea?"

"It won't!" she snapped, her voice trailing off to a whisper. "It won't be stronger than his."

"What do you mean?" Jim was shocked.

She shook her head; her body drooping against the table.

"Cheira, tell me," Jim insisted sympathetically. "What's bothering you? Perhaps, I can help."

She raised her head, looking at him with a faint hope. In a whisper, she asked, "Jim, do you still love me?"

He returned the look, holding it for a long moment before he answered. His voice was quiet, but straightforward. The question was so unexpected that he failed to sense the position she was maneuvering him into. "Yes, Cheira, I do."

"Then transfigure me." Grasping the advantage, she put her arms around his neck. "I can show you how."

His arms moved involuntarily to embrace her; but he stopped. Gently, he removed her arms and stepped back. "Even if I could," he struggled for control of the emotions the encounter had triggered, "I've no right."

"You mean you won't!" she shot back, her voice had a nasty ring. "You're a coward. You're afraid of Siri."

"No, that's not it," he protested.

"Your love is a lie!" she accused, before he could say more.

"That's not so!" The pain of the accusation made his voice a low moan. "Please let me explain." He tried to regain control of the situation, quelling the frustration of another lost encounter.

"You want to go over, too," she flung at him. "Well, go ahead. I told you not to wait for me." She saw that her words were hitting him like blows; but she didn't care. She enjoyed his suffering; and its very intensity assuaged her own. She searched for the words which would hurt him most. "Do you think I ever wanted your love? Well, I didn't! You make me sick."

He sagged against the table, his head bowed, only the whiteness of his knuckles where they gripped the hard edge betraying what the spiteful remarks were doing to him.

"Get out of my sight!" she screamed, helpless now to reverse the course she had chosen. "I never want to see you again. I hate you! Do you hear me? I hate you!"

Leaving the venomous sounds hanging in the air, she ran out of the room. Now the precipitous flight down the hall blanked out the surroundings. She threw open her own door, in the blind rush, knocking a chair into the pedestal beside it, sending a tall porcelain vase crashing to the floor.

The noise brought Jennie flying into the room. Behind her, in the nursery, the baby, startled out of a sound sleep, voiced his protestations at the top of his lungs.

"Summon John," Cheira commanded the astonished girl without offering an explanation.

"But he's in London," Jennie objected. "And very busy."

"I don't care if he's on the moon," Cheira retorted, heading for the nursery. "Get him!"

She picked up the screaming infant, coaxing him back into his usual good humor. The baby's happy gurgling smothered her misery in the joy of his existence. The tiny squirming body had the power to deaden the pain in her heart, but not to wholly obliterate it. The tenderness she lavished on the child caused her to regret the scene with Jim.

If only he'd helped me, she rationalized, rocking the precious bundle, *I never would have said those terrible things.* She nuzzled her face into the soft creases of the child's neck making him wriggle from the odd sensation. *I hope his telepathic power discovered the lies,* she consoled herself. *I hope he knows that I only said that because I'm so miserable and confused. I do love you,* she framed the words clearly, attempting to send them down the hall and into the lab. *That's what gave me the courage to ask your help. Why did you refuse? Why?*

Now that she was calming down, she thought more clearly. In the last month, Jim had been constantly sympathetic, caring for her and the baby; but she hadn't seen him that often. Many times he visited the baby when she was in the garden or some other part of the building. He never came unless Siri was present. She hadn't noticed. He'd never repeated the avowals made that night at Pemberly. In fact, he remained in the background. Intentionally? What she had feared from his presence hadn't happened. Why did he change? And then why did he remain? The way he had looked at her had convinced her that he still loved her. Why?

Her thoughts fell into hopeless confusion. She couldn't understand any of it. Clutching her son tightly, she sought refuge in the dark cloud which veiled her mind.

Jennie hurried to the laboratory. With Siri and Dr. Mott away, she turned to Dr. Connors for guidance. It was he who reluctantly obeyed the command to summon John.

"What the devil's going on here?" John lost no time in idle greeting. He appeared in the entry hall, his voice booming off the ancient rafters. He met Connors halfway across the length of the room. "I've got a lot of work to do before I can get away. You hauled me out of a very important board meeting."

Only when Connors came up to him did he notice the gray pallor of his face.

"Cheira commanded Jennie to summon you," Connors apologized.

"My God!" John exhaled with a sharp sound. Connors's power was no match for his own. He brushed aside easily the barrier the scientist attempted to raise to conceal the circumstances responsible for the action. Jim gave in, allowing John to see what was the cause of his torment.

"She must be very upset," John consoled. "It's not normal for her to act like that."

"I know," Connors replied. "I'm not blaming her." It didn't make the bearing any easier, however, John saw. He put his hand on the other's shoulder, a gesture of understanding Connors could accept.

"Where's Siri?"

"Gone with David to the Fort. To settle things there. And to do something. This waiting was driving him crazy."

"I see," John immediately grasped the significance of Siri's ploy. "Well," he sighed, acknowledging Cheira's right to his time. "Perhaps I can help."

Jennie let him into the apartment and announced his arrival to Cheira, who was still in the nursery.

"Tell him to wait," she commanded. Whether from a wish to remind him of the loyalty he still owed or to delay the admission she was going to make, she didn't know or care. She continued rocking the child until he was sleeping peacefully. Reluctantly, she laid him in the crib, mustering all her will to deaden the feeling that she might be putting him down for the last time. She stood looking down at her son, her empty arms already beginning to ache with longing.

John was pacing the floor when she came in. He quickly dismissed the irritation at the sight. Anguish was clearly stamped on her features; but the muddle of her thoughts defied his probing. He proceeded carefully.

"My lady," he greeted her with a deep bow, "is well, I trust?" The old phrase was uttered from years of habit. It hung now like a mockery in the air.

"Oh, I'm not," Cheira cried, grasping comfort from the old relationship conveyed by the words. "John, please help me."

Her tone wrenched his heart; and the suffering in the beloved green eyes was hard to bear.

"I'll help in any way I can. You know that!" It was an effort to keep the huskiness out of his voice. "What is it you wish me to do?"

"Transfigure me." There was effort in the tone of her voice; and she searched his face for the reaction to the words. She hurried on, fear rising in her throat when he didn't move or answer. "Jim says I don't want it; but I do. He refuses to help me. I don't know why. You're the only one I can turn to. You have the power; more now than ever."

He turned away, not wanting her to see what her words forced to the surface. Silently, he cried out to her.

All she saw was the imminent refusal. His reason escaped her. She drew herself up, squaring her shoulders. The hard glint coming into her eyes reinforced the authority of her voice.

"John, I command you!" Her words were clear and precise, very like the old imperviousness.

John knew, through the precognition he now possessed, that this was the most she could ever demand of him. He had no more to give. He knew, too, in the same instant, that no power, no loyalty, no love was great enough to force his obedience. He was committed to his course years ago when the cause was initiated. He was helpless now to avoid the effects, to usurp the rights of the man to whom she belonged. No amount of wishing on his part could change the reality. That Cheira was unaware of what she asked was obvious. The responsibility was solely his. He must accept it without evasion. That other existence weighed heavily in the balance against the temptation. He summoned the memory now for the support he needed.

"I can't!" And his voice was the strangled measure of the torment, a feeble plea against the agony of the next few minutes.

"You can't or you won't?" She spat out the words with the same inflection he had heard in his mind as he spoke. He paled, the strain taxing his strength. "You must," she wailed, shifting back to the pleading tone. "I've tried to do it; but nothing happens."

He looked at her, allowing her suffering to sink into his being. To be part of it, to share it was all he could offer. Conversely, to withhold the help she begged for was the dimension of the great love he felt. But she couldn't know it.

Cheira was instinctively compelled to try one more time. She grabbed his hands, raising them to her temples. "Do it!" she commanded, looking into his eyes.

She gasped. Dropping his hands, she stepped back. Her eyes widened, staring. What she saw was a shock. John stood before her in agony. She was convinced that whatever the cost she had to know the reason for the refusal. Only her knowing would make it bearable.

She recognized the look. She had seen it before—the day she and Siri teleported together to Lamborn Heath. And she understood what John had in his power to do, what he was forfeiting by the refusal, what danger he was protecting her from. "I'm sorry," she said, sinking onto the sofa.

But the words hung in an empty room. He was gone.

A long while later, Jennie came in to turn on the lamps. The artificial lighting had followed the sun into darkness; only a faint glow lingered along the walls attending the final descent into night.

Cheira sat on, oblivious to the surroundings, lost in the parade of incidents marching across her memory. She had known of Ameur's love, Jim's too; and sometimes her attention had discovered a stray word or two that betrayed the feelings of some of the others. But she had always counted John as a good friend and reliable business associate. What she knew now was a shock. How could she have been so wrong and Siri so right? He'd told her the reason for John's enmity long ago. She hadn't believed him.

Then, the explanation became clear. She was different than anyone else. No amount of evasion could change that. So, it was the longing for the attainment of the best in themselves that they saw in her. Through the years of association, the yearning crystallized into love as the highest expression of their feelings. What had Siri said that night of the meeting about prostituting our power? She knew now she was guiltiest of all.

Oh, God, she thought, *there is truly no one left to help me but Siri. But I'm not ready! I'm not ready!*

After watching her mistress pick at her dinner, Jennie could stay silent no longer.

"You must call Lord Siri back, mistress," Jennie burst out, hurrying the words before she lost her nerve. "You can't go on without him. Admit it. Besides, he was here last night to see the baby. He wants me to tell you that all he asks is for you to listen. Please, let me tell him you will."

Cheira sighed; the struggle was too hard and the guilt descending on her shoulders was too heavy to carry alone. She assented.

A leisurely bath revived her spirits. She floated just beneath the surface of the swirling, almost hot water. Her head rested on a pillow, holding it comfortably above the spray, yet filling her nostrils with the scent of evaporating oil. The oil imparted to the water a feeling of silk. *This life is good,* she thought, surrendering to the caress of the water. The sunken tub was just large enough that the sides were beyond the reach of extended arms and legs, promoting the sensuousness of suspension: the whirlpool stimulated the skin to a sensitive responsiveness, turning the thoughts hungrily to that ultimate physical sensation of which the body was so capable. *Why isn't this enough?* she wondered. *What motives drove Siri into a persistent disregard for the beauty of this life?*

A great hope bloomed. She'd try to persuade him once more. She knew the attraction of her singular beauty. She could try again and triumph. She had never actually tested the hold she had, by his own admission, over him. She'd do it now.

She selected the golden gown. It was at once the symbol of her position as head of the society; and, since the night in the little oasis at Imla Dun, a demonstration of the passion she could arouse in him. She smiled, gaining confidence from the memory. That night, her will had dominated. Her beauty had reduced him to a helpless supplicant, panting for the pleasure she could impart.

She chose to ignore the change in herself. Pulling a lamp to the center of the room, she studied the effect. With satisfaction, she noted the gleam of the loose mass of hair cascading down her back, making a pretense of purity while subtly conveying the opposite.

The gown enhanced the picture. Its simplicity and classic lines emphasized the uniqueness of the material. Hultz had given it to her the year he'd discovered how to transform solar power directly into electricity. It was the celebration of the achievement, he'd said. The metal was synthesized to silk fibers. He had never used the process again or told anyone how it was done. She turned from side to side, admiring the gleam of the fabric as it caught the light.

Absorbed in the thought, she failed to hear Siri enter the room. He came up silently behind her, the width of his shoulders blotting out the aura the lamplight had obligingly provided.

"Yes," he said, confirming her thought, "you are very beautiful." His hands on her arms, he stooped to trace the line of her throat and shoulder with his lips. She leaned against him, her head thrown back, lips parted, eyes closed, the scheming forgotten in the pleasure of his touch.

He turned her to face him. When she opened her eyes, she saw by the stern look that he knew her plan; and that this time he would not cooperate. That easily he could take the reins of control from her.

"Do you know everything?" she flung at him, pulling away, her voice heavy with defensive sarcasm. "Oh . . . " She searched for a weakness that would crack that galling self-control. Was there no way she could win?

"I know what you did to John and Jim Connors today," he answered. "I suppose I have even less right to expect mercy."

She stood still, half-turned away from him, her breath held indrawn as she waited for him to continue.

"You know what you can do to me." His voice was expressionless. "What you can make me suffer. I admit it. Are you pleased by the admission? Do you want me to say that I love you and want you so much that I'll do anything to have you?"

She exhaled sharply, sensing a spark of triumph.

It died in the next moment.

"But don't you realize that it will not negate the necessity for your decision? That it's not my will you must conquer, but your own. That day at Lamborn only happened with your consent; and realize that's what you're rejecting and more. This, my love, is the future you asked me to reveal to you; but even now the time ahead awaits your choice."

"Oh, all right!" The insistence of his tone trapped her. There was no extension to be granted this time, she was certain. "Do it! Transfigure me!"

He didn't move. The minutes passed. The big clock in the salon solemnly struck the hour; its melodious chimes reverberated through the silent rooms.

"What are you waiting for?" she asked finally, a note of dread creeping into her voice.

"You've come this far," he urged. "Go all the way, my darling."

"I don't know what you mean." she retorted, fighting down the panic rising in her throat.

"I think you do." he countered.

She felt dizzy. She struggled to keep the room from receding, to turn her attention from the dark cloud in her mind that she had nourished for so long.

"Look!" Siri's voice commanded from far away.

"Help me!" she whimpered. She had no consciousness of her body sinking slowly to the floor. Her whole attention was arrested by the dissipating fog in her brain. The light shone through clearer and brighter, growing unbearably yet desirably more intense. The sound unforgotten and unforgettable swelled, pervading her with its sweetness. Now there was no thought of restraint. She embraced the light, welcoming it, eagerly allowing it to seep into her body, to expand the atoms of her being with its energy.

The hands that lifted her were indescribably gentle. She opened her eyes. It was an unnecessary reflex. The young man who held her was a mirror of herself, so familiar, so loved that there was no memory of separation.

"Delfaum," she breathed.

"Dearest sister." His smile was pure radiance. "Welcome home. The ordeal is ended."

Siri, she called; but it was not a sound, only an omnipresent thought, the natural completion and identification of herself.

And he was beside her, holding their child in his arms. Their bodies glowed.

The glow brightened, encompassing her, fulfilling and completing her being.

The objects of the room stood out luminously, rejoicing with the realization of their essence. The walls shimmered, the atoms of stone awakening to the vibrations after centuries of quiescence.

The glow that was Delfaum's body moved off; the material enclosure offered no hindrance to his passage. They followed: Siri, Cheira, and the child.

The light faded. Silent emptiness reigned supreme. The room settled into the fullness of heavy objectivity, the light of the lamp in the middle of the room casting a brittle luminosity against the vacant mirror.